Philippe van Rjndt is the author of *The Tetramachus Collection*, *Blueprint* and *The Trial of Adolf Hitler*. Born in Montreal of Ukranian-Russian parents, he was raised and educated in France and now lives in Canada and the USA.

He says: "My interest in history and international affairs has remained with me throughout the years. What fascinates me are the powers behind the throne which guide the movements of nations. All my work is based on either past secrets or current mysteries."

D0415682

Also by Philippe van Rjndt

PHILIPPE VAN RJNDT

Futura
Macdonald & Co
London & Sydney

A Futura Book

First published in Great Britain in 1983
by Macdonald & Co (Publishers) Ltd
London & Sydney

First Futura edition 1984
Reprinted 1984

ISBN 0 7088 2509 5

Reproduced, printed and bound in Great Britain by
Hazell Watson & Viney Limited,
Member of the BPCC Group,
Aylesbury, Bucks

Futura Publications
A Division of
Macdonald & Co (Publishers) Ltd
Maxwell House
74 Worship Street
London EC2A 2EN
A BPCC plc Company

For Tad Jaworski, who gave me the idea
and
Jean Mackenzie McConnell, without whose help
this book could not have been written

ACKNOWLEDGMENTS

The author wishes to thank Drs. Michael Weingert and Susan Wollanski of Toronto and Dr. Diana Bell of New York City for specific medical information.

Any deviation from strict medical facts or procedures, is, of course, the author's responsibility.

*Thou art Peter, and upon this rock
I will build my church; and the gates
of hell shall not prevail against it.*

Matthew 16:18

PART
ONE

1

For the city of Warsaw the year was ending as it had begun, with a massive snowstorm born on the western side of the Tatry Mountains. Snow had fallen without pause for the last two weeks, piling up in drifts along the major avenues, reducing the smaller streets and lanes to footpaths. The ice of the River Vistula was altogether invisible under the blanket of fresh snow.

Christmas Eve was only hours away, and the young Polish surveillance officer felt immeasurably sad. With a cigarette held precariously in his lips he leaned forward and wiped the moisture from the inside of the windshield. Orange lamps stood on high posts along Gdanskie Wybrzeze, following the meandering river, and bathed the car's interior in a soft glow. He raised his eyes and gazed out upon the massive stone structure of St. John Cathedral, rebuilt after the war from the original fourteenth-century design. As a boy he had attended Christmas mass there every year. As an officer of Polish internal state security he had not set foot through the massive doors for more than five years.

He drew on the cigarette, inhaling deeply and blowing the smoke out the side of his mouth toward the crack in the rolled-up window. Beside him his partner, the senior man, grunted in his sleep as he shifted against the car door.

In the beginning he had thought himself very fortunate to have been accepted into the security *apparat*. The job paid well. He had been given preferential housing and access to party stores denied the ordinary citizen. There was also the authority, and the respect, that came with it. At the beginning he had been overjoyed. So much so that he disregarded his family's objections. Nor had he listened to the pleas of his fiancée to find other work. Within a few months his own family had come to fear him while the girl quietly and firmly turned away. He had thought he could hide in his police work for a while and most of the time managed to convince himself he had succeeded, but not at Christmas, when memories of a happier time so easily crowded the mind. Nor when his superiors had him posted directly in front of the cathedral of his childhood, to lie in wait for the man who embodied Catholicism in Poland, Karol Cardinal Stanislawski. He slipped the cigarette out the slit of the side window, watching as the wind snatched it away, sparks flying.

What if I'm told to arrest him?

His gaze shifted to the cathedral. Rumor among Polish security personnel had the cardinal preparing a secret address to be delivered during the midnight mass. What would the pastoral message contain? Further attacks on the government's muzzling of trade unions, renewed appeals to Poles not to cooperate with Moscow, and with Russian armed forces units that had been staging maneuvers in the outlying countryside, or perhaps demands for the release of "prisoners of conscience" from the ancient Lavra fortress. And of course the Jews. Karol Cardinal Stanislawski would not overlook the final subject on his list of demands: freedom of emigration. Impossibilities, all of them.

The young man sighed and fished out another cigarette from the battered pack, the tobacco crumbling between his fingers. He struck the match with his thumbnail, rolling down the window with the other hand. His partner shifted as the wind sliced through the warmth of the Volga's interior.

Could I arrest him? the agent thought miserably.

That would be madness, he knew. There would be blood in the streets again. The people, already sullen and resentful, would have their martyr. In his mind's eye he saw strikers once again flooding the boulevards, their factories and machines idle. The inevitable wave of cars would emerge from the underground garage of Place Inwalidow, beneath the Ministry of State Security, en route to their posts. Were the Russians mad?

If only I don't have to take him.

The chances were that he wouldn't. This was his fourth night on surveillance. The rotation would not come into effect until the twenty-eighth. If the rumors were true, his team would act as one of the back-up cars for the primary squads covering the cathedral.

Ash fell down the front of his overcoat, his eyes blinked rapidly against the spiraling smoke. If Cardinal Stanislawski was taken, his own family would hold him responsible, no matter what denials he offered, no matter how true they were.

The light over the radiotelephone glowed red, followed almost simultaneously by the insistent buzzer. He snatched up the handset.

"Surveillance Four."

Beside him, his partner's gray head sunk into his chest, the breathing thick, rasping.

"Yes, I understand," he said. "Message acknowledged."

He replaced the receiver, and the light went off.

"What is it, Ivar?" the older man asked, pushing himself up, one hand rubbing his forehead with thumb and forefinger.

"They're going to pick him up if he shows up for mass. The arrest group is on its way. Ten minutes at most." He did not look at his partner.

"Bring us into the position," the senior man said, "not that we'll be called. But you never know who'll be watching."

"They said they would bring an ambulance in case it's needed."

"That means they will have an executioner with them," the older man said, the voice flat, matter-of-fact. "If they take Stanislawski, he will be dead five minutes after they get him into the vehicle. They won't bother taking him to Lavra prison. He will go straight to the hospital morgue." He looked across at the younger man. "Ivar, move us into position."

The young Pole froze. He was twenty-seven. He had never been called upon to kill anyone. He had never even been in the proximity of death. He slammed the column shift into low and eased the car gently over the packed snow, making a slow U-turn along the corniche.

"Not too close," the old man cautioned. A feeling for the youngster made him wonder if he should have speculated about killing the cardinal. Perhaps Cardinal Stanislawski would not even show himself. The senior man unbuttoned his coat and made sure nothing obstructed his revolver. His deputy would stay in the car. Did they really think they could arrest Stanislawski amid the thousands who would be attending mass? Butchery, he thought. If they try to seize him, there will be butchery.

The ambulance, a white panel truck, turned the corner of Konwiklowska Street.

"That's them," the senior agent murmured. "They'll take him inside, inject a sedative, something to slow him down so they can get him into the truck. The fucking Russians—"

The younger man was out of the car before his partner had finished. He ignored the pleas streaming after him.

"*I need some air!*" he shouted back as he cleared the snowbank at the edge of the sidewalk and started up the wide, shallow steps of the cathedral, the heels of his boots digging into the salt, his breath a fog before him. Even at this hour celebrants were making their way toward the cathedral. Many were already inside, their faces illuminated by the sea of flickering candles as they prayed and waited patiently for their turn in the confessional. By midnight those tiny flames would form a solid wall of light. He suddenly prayed too—prayed that his family would not see him outside St. John Cathedral waiting to capture their revered Cardinal Stanislawski as they walked to mass in an hour's time.

The crowds who braved the swirling white winds paid no attention to the old woman who was moving slowly along the treacherous sidewalk toward the cathedral, one hand set upon a cane on which she carefully leaned. Dressed in a black greatcoat, a kerchief upon her head, and a scarf wrapped around her throat and mouth to stay the frigid air, she was only another babushka, her face a baked apple, gaunt and withered. Her lips moved constantly, the dentures clicking softly to punctuate some private conversation carried on in defiance of the wind. She was like the others: aged, infirm, one of the forgotten hobbling to the last sanctuary, refugees from a brave new world, seeking only a few moments of warmth, the touch of another human being.

This is not how I want to remember it, she thought, looking around at the shuttered square and the bare trees laden with snow. The cafés and taverns should be full, the workers lined up against the bar. I remember students jostling for chairs, snatching seats from the bureaucrats while seeking to strike up conversations with the shopgirls, and over everything the music of the violin and accordion. But all that was long gone from Warsaw.

Katrina Jaworska mounted the steps to the Cathedral of St. John, her cane searching out the safe footholds. Just before she reached for the great iron rings she glanced back at the square. As a young girl she had been happy in this city of her birth, the city she had lived in all her life, except for seventeen months between 1943 and 1945. Those had been months spent in hell, in a place not 55 kilometers away, whose name was Oswięcim, but which the world knew only as Auschwitz. It was because of Auschwitz and the cardinal that Katrina Jaworska had left her bed this day and made her way from the outskirts into Warsaw, to this church which had seen her confirmation, her marriage, and the baptism of her two children, neither of whom had survived to be at her side in this time of need. Brushing the snow from her face, she turned to enter the cathedral.

The priest lit the candle in the red glass cup, moved toward the altar, genuflected and surveyed his handiwork. On either side of the altar three tiers of candles, fifty to a tier, shimmered and swam before his eyes, the flames casting long, thin shadows along the soaring walls, warming them. The podium was covered in fresh, embroidered cloth, the heavy, embossed Bible open at the Book of Luke, from which the last sermon of the year would be read. Twin crucifixes were set on either side of the Bible, the light from the candles glancing off the precious stones set in the stems, bathing the sacristy in soft arcs of red, green, yellow, and mauve. Along the sacristy wall the inlaid icons glowed, and the faces of the saints and the Holy Family shimmered as though they were alive.

Father Smilga crossed himself and backed away from the altar. He turned around and surveyed his flock—a hundred elderly people, most of whom had come in as soon as the doors had opened, though mass would not be said until midnight. As he walked by the pews he smiled at each of them, letting his hand rest for a second upon their heads or shoulders.

"Father . . ."

The priest gazed down upon the old woman. She must have just come in, for he could still feel the cold radiating from her clothing. She was quaking beneath his touch.

"Yes, daughter?"

Katrina Jaworska gazed up at him with watery eyes. He seemed so healthy to her. She wiped her eyes with the back of her glove and looked up at him again. Yes, he was youthful . . . thirty, thirty-five—it was difficult to judge—with soft blond hair and eyes as blue as cornflowers. His smile was kind, and there was strength in the jaw.

"I am looking for Father Gregory Rowitz."

"Unfortunately he is not here," the priest answered. "I am Father Smilga. I am here to help you in any way I can."

Can you help me? Katrina Jaworska thought. Is it possible for one so young to understand the things I must speak of? You are younger than my last born. What can you understand?

Then the spots appeared before her eyes, black floating spots that obscured her vision and made her faint. She gripped the priest's hand, her forehead touching her knuckles.

"You must let me help you," she heard him say. She was rocking from side to side.

It will pass, Katrina Jaworska told herself. It will pass and not come again for a little while. Now the tiredness will come upon me, she thought dully. My body will feel so heavy I will want nothing but sleep.

In a voice she did not quite recognize as her own Katrina Jaworska said: "Father, I have come to confess, but only Father

Rowitz may hear my confession. It concerns the cardinal and is most important, father."

"Of course, my daughter, but Father Rowitz is at the clinic tonight, at Holy Trinity."

"Then you must direct me to him. I must confess to Father Rowitz if I am to save myself and the cardinal. You must help me to reach Gregory Rowitz," she said, and then she fainted.

The Cathedral of St. John. The Russian had last seen it many years ago, during the liberation of the city. Sergei Bibnikov exhaled, blowing cigarette smoke toward the crack in the car window. Behind the wheel Aleksandr Roy shifted his feet up against the dashboard, at the same time tugging back his coat sleeve to consult his watch.

"The procession will be arriving any minute."

As if to confirm his statement, floodlights surrounding the cathedral suddenly came to life, their pink-yellow beams streaking through the rushing snow. The cathedral, ablaze with light, looked beautiful. Aleksandr Roy glared at the silent radio.

"This Stanislawski should have been picked up by now," he said in an annoyed voice, glancing at Bibnikov.

Sergei Bibnikov pinched the glowing end of his cigarette between thumb and forefinger, a habit left over from leaner times.

He was fifty-two years old, tall, and heavy, with a leonine head, bifocals, and a goatee. In the half-light of the car his pockmarked complexion was severe with the crisscross scars of frostbite suffered during the Stalingrad offensive. His life was the department he ruled—Special Investigations, a branch of Soviet intelligence completely independent from the civilian KGB and military GRU. It was designated to root out traitors within the security organs of the Soviet Union and her satellites. This mandate made Bibnikov and his staff pariahs among their colleagues, feared and mistrusted by them, intimidated by those who outranked them and yet had no authority over them. Bibnikov watched the watchers, accountable only to Presidium Chairman Komarov.

Sergei Bibnikov reached out and depressed a button on the

radio. The voice of the operations controller at Place Inwalidow filtered through the speakers, the interference crumbling the words. The order to arrest Stanislawski had not yet been transmitted from Moscow. The situation remained static.

"Stanislawski must have left his home by now," Aleksandr Roy said. His tone was underlined by his characteristic impatience with incompetence. Bibnikov looked at his assistant.

His was a strong, handsome face, though somewhat hard: the cheekbones sharp, the lips a little thin. It was as though God hadn't taken as much time as He would have liked in creating him. But the eyes shone like a cat's. The lithe movements, even when he was walking down the street with a girl, spoke of the predator. Sasha would be thirty-nine in a few weeks.

An orphan, he had learned to look out for himself early on. The youngest graduate of the Frunze Academy, he had performed two years' military service on the Sino-Soviet border before being recruited into the GRU to run couriers in Vienna and Berlin. For three years he had administered a very profitable West German network. Then, without warning, five of his people were lost to a traitor, who turned out to be his immediate superior. Even though the investigation cleared Aleksandr Roy of any complicity, the Mitko affair had tainted him. It had taken every particle of influence Bibnikov had to haul Aleksandr Roy out of the dregs and give him a new start. The effort had been worthwhile. Roy was one of the finest counterintelligence men the directorate had.

"Here they come," Roy whispered; he rolled down the window, the snow on the outside of the glass crumbling onto his thigh. The wind swirled the cigarette ashes in the tray.

The procession was still too far away for Bibnikov to discern individual marchers, but the lamps they were carrying—pinpoints of green, blue, orange, and red—gave him an indication of their number. Hundreds of lanterns covered the breadth of Gdanskie Wybrzeze, a six-lane boulevard along the River Vistula. For every person bearing a light three, four, possibly five others would be walking beside him. Bibnikov wished he had a higher vantage point so that he could see farther down the boulevard.

Roy had been right. The chance to take Stanislawski had passed. Bibnikov took the radiotelephone from its cradle and offered his professional condolences to the Russian and Polish surveillance units, all two dozen of them, strung out between Cardinal Stanislawski's modest two-story house six blocks away and the cathedral. Each third squad was composed of KGB personnel, flown in yesterday in an unmarked transport. All had been in position since nightfall. The plan was simple: if Cardinal Stanislawski defied the order of the Polish authorities not to celebrate Christmas mass, these units would move in to arrest him before Stanislawski could make good his public promise to deliver another denunciation of renewed Soviet interference in Poland. Furthermore, Stanislawski had obliquely threatened to expose what he termed a new and radically horrible program to maintain order within the Eastern bloc. Suddenly in Moscow the alarm bells had sounded.

Bibnikov dearly would have loved to know what it was that had made the Kremlin tremble. Its reaction had been swift: the Surveillance Directorate had been screened for bilingual officers and a quarantine imposed upon those selected for dispatch to the Polish capital. That Chairman Komarov had, from his sickbed at Rudin Hospital, personally ordered him, the chief of Special Investigations, to Warsaw was the ultimate imprimatur. It meant Moscow no longer trusted either the Warsaw police, the state militia, or even Polish internal security, to carry out Stanislawski's arrest.

"There's something wrong," Roy said, his voice laced with irritation. "The operation was to proceed on Chairman Komarov's personal command. Surely the chairman knew that once Stanislawski left his home for the cathedral, the arrest had to be made before Stanislawski reached his supporters."

Bibnikov said nothing. He was watching the progress of the colored lanterns, steady even in the face of the vicious wind. There were three times as many lights as before snaking along the river as the column of marchers stretched out toward St. John's. The head of the wide column was much closer to the cathedral . . . about a hundred meters to go, and still no sign of the car that would be transporting the cardinal.

"You are quite right," Bibnikov said to his aide. "Komarov knows the point beyond which Stanislawski could not be taken. Since there is no communications problem with operations control, I can only assume the chairman has elected *not* to have Stanislawski arrested."

Using his coat sleeve, Roy wiped away the condensation on the side window. "Then why haven't our units been ordered to withdraw?"

The worshipers were marching fifty abreast down Gdanskie Wybrzeze, shoulders hunched forward, heads bowed into the wind. The tails of their coats snapped violently; boots crunched packed snow worn so smooth it was almost ice. Christmas carols and hymns filled the boulevard. Arms linked, they sang as they marched. Teachers, students, doctors, laborers, farmers, government clerks, the elderly pressed between helping hands, the very young swaddled in layers of clothing.

The wind was swirling about the car, but when Bibnikov rolled down his window, he could clearly hear their anthem. The radio crackled and the voice of the operations controller filled the car. Moscow's silence had ended. Cardinal Stanislawski was to be arrested before he reached the cathedral. The order was repeated for confirmation.

"Madness!" Roy snapped as he rolled his window down and thrust his face into the frozen darkness. The head of the procession was turning toward the small plaza in front of the cathedral steps. As the marchers spread out across the base of the steps, two high-intensity car headlights shone from the center of the procession.

"There are hundreds of people around that car," Roy said. "Our surveillance group can't pluck Stanislawski out of the middle of that mob. Fifty men against a thousand! They'll be torn apart."

On the radio Bibnikov heard this warning repeated by the unit commanders. They were all talking at once, some demanding clarification, others asking for support from Polish internal security or the state militia. They were desperately trying to maintain discipline, caught between disobedience and orders that reflected complete indifference to their circumstances.

Bibnikov opened the priority frequency and spoke rapidly in Polish. Although he was not formally attached to the arrest detail, he outranked even the commander of Operations Control. He would countermand the order on his own authority.

"It's too late." Roy shook his head as he stared at the scene before him.

The sedan in which the cardinal-archbishop of Warsaw was riding crawled forward at the center of the procession, surrounded on all sides by a mass of people. As the marchers spread out across the cathedral steps the driver slowly turned the car to flank the cathedral, so that Cardinal Stanislawski might emerge directly onto the steps and into the phalanx of worshipers who would escort him up to the cathedral doors. There was only a moment between the time the crowds parted to allow the car to turn and when they moved once again to surround it.

The unit commander closest to the cathedral must have foreseen such an eventuality. His four-wheel-drive Orbis scout car edged into the crowd just as it parted to allow the sedan to turn. The Christmas hymn had given way to the old Solidarity anthem.

On his left Roy could hear Bibnikov speaking rapidly to the controller, his voice calm, clipped. He kept his eyes on the scout car as it skidded into the crowd. There was not enough time for the controller to get a message to the scout car, nor could Bibnikov give it a direct command.

"It's finished," Roy said.

Still holding the receiver, Bibnikov leaned past him to look. "Shit," he cursed as he watched the doors of the Polish scout car flung open. Three surveillance agents jumped into the snow, leaving the driver inside. Their arms working like windmills, they regained their balance and began half-running, half-sliding toward the cardinal's sedan.

The wind flung the last notes of the chorus into the night. At first the crowd drew back, an ungainly animal rearing up in surprise. One of the agents actually managed to reach the sedan and wrench at the rear door. Bibnikov heard something—perhaps a scream—as the marchers closed ranks, first on the agents struggling with the car door, then on the Orbis scout vehicle. The surveillance team vanished from sight as the crowd converged on them.

"Order the others to station!" Bibnikov was shouting into the radio. "Order them back." But the support units that had been waiting behind the cathedral were already charging into the square. Three other vehicles were rumbling down Gdanskie Wybrzeze, using the broad sidewalks to get around the edges of the procession.

"There's nothing Control can do now," Roy said.

The Polish surveillance agents were following orders. Besides, they would never abandon their comrades to the marchers. From different directions their cars slammed into the human mass. For an instant the Orbises were stalled. The pedestrians were screaming with rage and terror. Blood spattered the hoods and windshields. But the armored cars plowed on against the shrieking mob, even as the marchers hammered the bodies of the vehicles with their bare hands.

Of the three cars coming along the rim of the Gdanskie Wybrzeze, the windshield of the lead vehicle exploded in brilliant orange as a Molotov cocktail exploded across the hood. The second Orbis crashed into the first. For an instant the blazing vehicle hung on the railing on the edge of the embankment. The marchers fell upon both cars. They pushed the first car into the river, then turned on the second. The wheels of the third spun helplessly as it tried to back out of a snowbank.

In the center of the crowd, in front of the steps of the cathedral, a giant fireball exploded, illuminating the night. The scout car was a gutted, burning skeleton. The crowd made for the remaining cars embedded in their midst, stampeding over their own dead to get at them. Armored glass was shattered. Doors were ripped away by frozen fingers while the screams of the dying and injured washed over the fury of their vengeance. A body was heaved into the air, arms and legs flailing helplessly. It came down, disappeared, then was thrown up again. This time there was no struggle as it fluttered up like a limp rag, then fell.

"Where are the Polish reinforcements?" Roy asked. "The militia?"

"Get us out of here," Bibnikov said curtly. "Don't turn on the headlights until we're well away. I hope the rest of our people have the sense to do the same."

Roy slipped the car into gear.

"Where now?"

"Operations Control. We will pick up a military escort and go for the secondary targets."

"Stanislawski . . . ?"

"His car was next to the Orbis that blew up." Bibnikov looked back over his shoulder at the carnage. "We'll find his Eminence in the morning, along with the rest."

Holy Trinity was designated as a full-fledged hospital by the city's Medical Bureau. In reality it was no more than a modest clinic, with ten beds, nominal support facilities, and a staff composed exclusively of nuns, none of whom was a certified medical practitioner, though all had had nurses' training. The state provided physicians on a rotating basis, but tonight the second-year resident had failed to report, not an uncommon occurrence.

The young nun at the admitting desk shivered when the door was slammed back by the wind. Dressed in a black greatcoat, a kerchief upon her head and a scarf wrapped around her throat and mouth to keep out the frigid air, Katrina Jaworska appeared to be just another member of that race of ubiquitous old women as familiar to the twisted streets of East Berlin as the grand avenues of Moscow. As the snow began to fall away from her face and clothing the nun saw the blood frozen to the skin.

"Dear God."

The nun stepped around her desk and ran to the door, forcing it shut against the fury of the winter night. She put her arm around the old woman and led her to the benches by the admitting desk and quickly began to unwrap the gray woolen scarf from around the woman's throat and mouth. Her skin was ashen, her lips blue. Her breathing was fast and shallow, and she was trembling in the ancient greatcoat. The nun peeled away the wet kerchief and tore open the buttons so the woman could breathe more freely. Gently she tilted her head against the wall and backed away to her desk, her fingers searching for the buzzer. She managed to press and hold it down for two seconds before Katrina Jaworska began to slide to one side, her sodden hair streaking the wall. Her head struck the top of the bench, and she slid facedown onto the stone floor. In moments the sisters had come to her aid. The old woman was carried to the infirmary, and Father Rowitz summoned.

In spite of his sixty-five years Father Gregory Rowitz remained a strong man, the muscles in his arms and legs corded from a lifetime of labor. But the ravages of his life, which had failed to break him physically, were painfully visible in his ruined face, an ancient cracked canvas of scars and slashes, the nose broken in three places, the long fingers deformed, two splayed, one foreshortened to the last knuckle. Only the eyes had escaped punishment, gentle eyes that bespoke compassion.

"What can be done for her?" he asked, his voice echoing in the bare, low ward. In the corner three radiators sputtered, giving off warmth. Beside him, wrapped tightly in layers of blankets, was Katrina Jaworska.

The matron removed the thermometer from between Jaworska's lips and shook her head. The fever was raging.

"Warmth, some crushed aspirin . . . and I don't know if she will be able to hold down even that," the matron said. "Her breathing is still too fast. We haven't any respirators or oxygen tanks."

The matron was a small, birdlike woman whose energy and compassion never failed to astound Rowitz. She maintained the small clinic on sheer willpower, ministering to the needs of the poor and elderly in spite of constant shortages of supplies, relying on whatever contributions of bedding and clothes the faithful provided her.

She turned to the priest. "Father, you must not leave . . . You can't be seen in the streets, not after what happened to His Eminence . . ." Her words trailed off, and she turned away abruptly so he would not see her fear.

Father Rowitz covered her hand with his own to calm her. Everyone at Holy Trinity was aware of the carnage on Gdanskie

Wybrzeze. Rumors of Cardinal Stanislawski's fate had spread through the city. One thing alone was for certain: if they had dared to arrest Stanislawski, then they were also coming for his friends and closest supporters. Father Gregory Rowitz had no doubts that his name headed the list, nor that the Russian intelligence service would have difficulty finding him. He made his rounds at Holy Trinity and five other clinics at regular intervals.

"There's little we can do for her," the matron said. "Even if I were to call for an ambulance, it wouldn't come in time. Not with the weather, with what happened on Gdanskie Wybrzeze."

Father Rowitz looked down at the sepulchral mask that was Katrina Jaworska's face. Even with his minimal amount of medical training, it was obvious to him that the old woman was hemorrhaging internally, the blood drowning her internal organs, dribbling over her lips.

"She kept calling for me," the priest intoned, his confusion obvious. "But I don't recognize her. I don't think I've ever seen her . . . yet I can't be sure."

His fingers curled around the old woman's cold hand. The matron held a worn green card before him.

"Katrina Jaworska," Father Rowitz read. "Living in Twarda Street."

He knew the address. Even proud Warsaw had its blemishes—industrial slums sprawling west of the city, and so much worse now since the crushing of the labor movement.

"She was repeating your name over and over again," the matron said. "Her feet are frostbitten. To have come all this way she needed more than strength. She was coming to you."

"Leave me alone with her."

The matron rose and quickly made her way to the door, where the freckle-faced nun from the admissions desk was standing.

"Go back to your work, sister," the matron said sharply. "Lock all the doors and keep a watch out for anyone driving up."

Gently Father Rowitz cupped the flesh of the old woman's cheek and turned her head toward him.

"Katrina."

Father Rowitz leaned forward, wiping her face with a cloth. Katrina Jaworska's eyes fluttered open, closed for an instant, then opened again. Her throat worked convulsively as she tried to speak.

"Father . . ."

"I am here. I am Father Gregory Rowitz. You were calling for me."

The grip that seized his hand stunned the priest. From somewhere inside that emaciated body the woman was summoning a desperate strength.

"I will not leave you, Katrina Jaworska," he said, and began his prayer. "In the name of the Father, the Son, and the Holy Ghost . . ."

The grip on his hand slackened.

"Stanislawski . . ." Katrina Jaworska whispered.

"What are you saying?" the priest asked. "What of Stanislawski? Did you see him tonight?"

The old woman pressed her cheek against the rough linen pillowcase.

"Listen to me, father. I beg of you. Listen to me."

He saw the tears flow from her eyes and understood that she was dying and that he could not leave her, even to save himself.

The call from the agent at Holy Trinity to Polish internal security was logged in at ten thirty-five. The duty officer placed his report in a dispatch envelope stamped with his station number. In a covering note he identified the agent and the subject of his surveillance, noted the exact time, and initialed the upper left-hand corner. He fitted the envelope into a pneumatic capsule and locked the brass gate. Compressed air drove the capsule up to the third floor, the Soviet liaison bureau.

Aleksandr Roy was given the note by the night duty officer and passed it to Bibnikov, who was speaking to a Polish army officer. Bibnikov, still wearing his overcoat, shook his head. He glanced at the captain of the First Rifle Guards, the elite army unit garrisoned within the city after having completed "maneuvers" in conjunction with Russian uniformed forces.

"Do you know the area?"

The captain looked at the street name. He and his men could make their way across Warsaw in pitch darkness if need be.

"Twenty minutes from here."

"Take a squad, not more," Bibnikov ordered.

"We may encounter resistance from the militia or a mutinous army unit," the officer protested.

Bibnikov stared at him. "A squad, captain," he said quietly. "God help everyone if we need more than that to take a single hospital."

2

Katrina Jaworska gazed up at the priest through her watery eyes. Black, floating spots obscured her vision and made her light-headed. "You must let me help you," she heard him say. The spell will pass, Katrina Jaworska told herself. It will pass and not come again, for a little while . . . just for a little while.

Blood rose in her throat, threatening to choke her. She swallowed hard. When she saw the helplessness and concern in his eyes, she cursed her weakness and forced the words from her mouth.

"Forgive me, father . . . I am an old woman, and soon I shall pass from this life. I have sought salvation in the Lord, and I have been comforted by His presence. I have buried a husband and two children, but I did not lose my faith. I believe in the Lord with all my heart and soul, but not once in all those times that I knelt before Him did I speak the whole truth. Not once did I dare mention the thing that was eating away at me."

Suddenly her hands were clawing at her chest. She squeezed her eyes shut against the pain, the fever raging under her skin, threatening to consume her. Father Rowitz leaned forward, holding her by the shoulders. In his mind were the words of absolution. He could feel death approaching her, but the old woman refused to surrender.

"Forty years ago, father, I was at Auschwitz, like you. You mustn't think I beat anyone or starved people. I was a prisoner myself. A young girl of twenty-three, made to work in the

Polish barracks. Not in the women's section. Not that. I belonged to the general administration of the camp. I did not kill, not Jews, not anyone. I . . . I was made a tattooist. I tattooed numbers on their forearms as they came into camp. I tattooed numbers," she repeated. "This was not wrong. It was not right. It was a hideous way to survive, but I killed no one. Yet neither did I save anyone. Not until a man named Telemann came to me and showed me how I could help some of the children. He showed me how I could change the numbers on those who had been chosen for medical experiments or for special adoption, or those who were to be killed. He showed me I could do more than just survive."

Katrina Jaworska stared fiercely at the face that was slowly dissolving before her.

"Can you imagine, father—do more than survive? What more was there, when all those around you are dying, than to live to the next day, to be decently fed, to be able to sleep without the groans of the dying infecting your dreams? More than survive? No, I thought, there could be nothing more. But he shamed me. He knew I was weak. That I would not report him. So he came back, time after time. The man plagued me with his eyes. Telemann was his name. He would stare at me and look into my very soul. In the end I did as he bid me to. He would bring me a child, and I would change the number. The number 1 became a 7, a 6 an 8. He would tell me what to change, and I would do it. He never told me how he knew which numbers had to be changed, nor how many out of the thousands upon thousands had been spared because of my stylus. Even after I was certain the administrators knew what was going on, he kept coming back. And I could not refuse him." Katrina Jaworska paused to catch her breath, and then went on.

"I changed people's lives, father. With a few scratches of my stylus I gave them a new identity. To this day I have never learned what happened to any of them—if they even discovered the change I brought upon them. Stanislawski does not know, I am certain of that."

Father Rowitz felt his heart racing. "Go on."

"I was told the guards had caught him stealing from the kitchen garbage. As punishment, the barrack commandant had him whipped. He should have died then and there. Somehow he survived the night and was finally brought to me by Telemann. He said the beating had left the boy senseless. I changed the numbers on his arm. . . ."

Tears welled up in her eyes. Her mind was consumed by fever and fantasies, terrors that even after forty years were all too fresh.

"And this boy, Katrina . . . was he Karol Stanislawski? Is that what he called himself?" Rowitz asked.

"He was like all the rest," she said. "He was brought to me. And I saved him."

Rowitz looked down at her. He could almost see the physical separation of the soul from its abused body. Her breath was coming in gasps, lips drained of color, the face ashen. Yet for all the pain reflected in her eyes, her voice was strangely composed.

"He is in Amsterdam, and his name is Telemann. He has the ledger."

"What ledger, Katrina?"

"Names," she said lightly, in the laughing tone of delirium. "Many, many names."

"But Stanislawski—"

"Now you know, father," Katrina Jaworska continued in a singsong voice. "You and no one else. I have carried the secret for too long. You must take it from me now. Only you." Her look pleaded with him. "Tell me I am absolved, father!"

Father Rowitz made the sign of the cross over her. "I absolve you in the name of the Father, and of the Son, and of the Holy Ghost."

"Stanislawski is not who he is. Do you understand? Please say you understand!"

But before Father Rowitz had a chance to utter a single word, Katrina Jaworska ripped her hand from his grasp, clutching at her chest. She stared up like one possessed, then darkness exploded in her mind, closing over everything like ink falling upon the brilliance of crystal.

Father Rowitz stepped back from the inert form of Katrina

Jaworska. Without taking his eyes off her face, he lifted her arm. Just above the wrist he saw the five digits tattooed into her flesh, a pale blue brand. Slowly the priest reached out and with his thumbs closed Jaworska's eyelids and drew the sheet over her.

The late arrival of his unit wouldn't have mattered if the faster, smaller squad dispatched earlier to Holy Trinity Hospital had made the drive as scheduled. However, their driver had been too brash. Three blocks from headquarters he had run the car into a snowbank. This should not have delayed their progress, not with the tractional power of the FWD Orbis scout car, except that its momentum had carried the car well into the mass of snow, pushing it right through into the grille, clogging the radiator and the fanbelt. Many precious minutes ticked by before the slower second vehicle roared past the helpless Orbis, arriving at Holy Trinity Hospital eight minutes later than planned.

"You can't expect me to go in there!" Father Smilga whispered frantically to the captain as they stopped in front of the clinic. "It's a convent hospital. I'm wearing my cassock."

The captain knew he would see his career unravel before his eyes unless he found the old woman and the priest she had gone to meet. He pushed Smilga ahead of him. "You think your superiors haven't come to certain, inescapable conclusions about you?"

The captain positioned himself by the door, his ears straining for the signal over the radio transceiver which would tell him his men were in place, that no exit had been left uncovered. When he received the confirmation, he signaled to his sergeant, who splintered the front door of the hospital.

The unit's training had been thorough, and no shots were fired when the sister behind the front desk began to scream. Led by the captain, the eight men fanned out through the interior of the clinic, moving quickly into preassigned positions to seal off the area, then immediately started their search. Secure first, then search, was the procedure.

The radio operator stepped up to the captain and informed

him that no one had gotten out through the back gardens nor was anyone on the roof. The grounds and building had been cordoned off.

"Round up the staff and get them in here. Check the basements, closets, kitchen—everything—then report back."

"There is no one else here, captain," the matronly nun announced.

She came up to the officer, disregarding the machine-gun barrel that followed her progress across the room.

"This is our only ward," she said. "We have only had one patient so far tonight. But I doubt she is the one you seek, captain. You see, she is dead."

The captain's eyes flickered over the inert form in the bed to his right. Without taking his eyes off it, he approached the bed and, with a single sweep of his arm, ripped the sheet away, the gun barrel pointing straight at the dead woman's throat. He looked back at the nun.

"No one else?" he asked quietly.

"No one, captain. Please, tell your men not to harm the sisters. There is nothing we can do to oppose you, nor do we wish to."

But as she said it she wondered if among these men some remembered the faith of their fathers and might be susceptible to her authority. Five nuns were led into the ward, huddled together, their arms locked. They arranged themselves behind the matron, their horror silent, uncomprehending.

"You have violated—"

The captain choked off her words with a glance.

"This is not a church," he said slowly, "but a medical facility, responsible to the Medical Bureau. The authorization for this search originates with the Bureau. I would not advise you to take issue, sister."

He looked over her shoulder at his sergeant, who shrugged. There was no one else in Holy Trinity was what the gesture communicated.

"*Smilga!*" the captain called out.

From the shadows by the front door the informer stepped forward.

Father Smilga. Until tonight, the popular young priest's loyalties had been suspect, at least in certain quarters. When Smilga was first transferred from the parish of St. Stephen to Warsaw, the bishop received word that Smilga might be serving two masters. Innuendoes had enveloped his career; there had always been idle speculation about the curious way he questioned other priests about themselves and their parishioners. The diocese in Warsaw had examined his records, looking for the one indiscretion which would enable them to dismiss him. But the man's dossier was virtually spotless, either by design or because it reflected nothing more sinister than Father Smilga's gossipy nature. Now the truth was known.

And how many others like him do we harbor? the matron thought. We know our ranks are riddled with spies. Boys who are not yet men are planted in our schools, our seminaries. They take priestly vows but never forget their original pledge to destroy us. And we are helpless against them, for what priest, bishop, or even cardinal can say that a novice is lying when he takes his vows, or that a false priest is betraying the sanctity of the confessional? The secret police have thoroughly infiltrated the church, and so easily, so completely, leaving us vulnerable. The traitors are among us, human listening devices free to move from confessional to confessional, from house to house, listening, noting, reporting. Such perfection in simplicity. She looked directly at the young cleric.

This was the end for him. The resignation on Smilga's face was obvious. He had been ordained seven years earlier; he had begun his career with state security two years before that, at the seminary in Warsaw. Just as he had risen steadily through the depleted ranks of the church, his ascent within Department Twelve, Counterintelligence/Internal Subversion, had been similarly unobstructed. He had had three commendations. His passbook at the Narodny Bank held many entries after all these years. As he walked between the ranks of soldiers toward the ward, he wondered whether he would ever see that money after tonight.

How they look at me, Smilga marveled, as he passed the group of nuns. They stare at my cross and my collar. They look at each other and wonder if they have seen me before. One or two have. I remember their faces. To them I have been unmasked as the Devil himself. Every gentle lecture they have been given on the presence of impostors within church ranks is suddenly flooding their minds. They cannot believe anyone could betray his vows to their God.

Smilga smiled to himself and shook his head. You are such lucky fools, he thought, such utterly helpless virgins. *What is it I'm afraid of?*

"Who is that?" the captain demanded.

Smilga looked down at the elderly woman, laid out so respectfully on the simple iron-frame bed, her face devoid of any expression.

"She's the woman who was looking for Father Rowitz. And babbling about Stanislawski's childhood," Smilga said tonelessly, then turned on his heel and walked from the ward.

"Who else was here tonight?" the captain asked, his elbow resting in the sling of his machine pistol.

"There was no one," the nun said calmly.

There wasn't the slightest intimation of what the officer was after. With a casual motion his finger moved the firing selector from automatic to single shot, then slid down to the trigger as he raised the weapon. There was a muted snap—nothing more than a crack—followed by the cry of the novice standing beside the matron, staring at herself in total disbelief.

"An accident," the captain observed, his eyes still on the matron. "Fortunately the bullet passed through her shoulder. Only the muscle is damaged. Not much more than a graze, really. Accidents, matron, they can happen so easily when loyal soldiers are hard-pressed." The novice lost consciousness momentarily as one of the sisters tore back her sleeve, exposing the wound.

"Who else was here?" the captain went on in an unaffected tone.

Father Rowitz absolved me, the matron thought. He said they would be coming for him, that I should not resist to gain time for him. She was to tell them he had been there. Still, she could not speak the name for fear that he was not yet safe but abroad somewhere in the night, a vulnerable black figure against the field of fresh snow.

"Father Gregory Rowitz," she said very slowly and, it seemed, proudly.

"Yes. And why was he here?"

"He had come to give absolution to the dead woman. Katrina Jaworska."

"Was she conscious when he arrived?"

"Yes . . . but not entirely lucid."

"And did Father Gregory console her?"

"He did."

"He heard her confession and administered the last rites?"

"Yes," she said, nodding as she added up the seconds since she had divulged Father Gregory's identity. Almost a minute elapsed. Was that another fifty yards for him? A hundred if he was running?

Her response spared her and her charges further interrogation, for the captain knew that no one else was permitted to be present when the penitent made his peace with God. Given the description of the old woman's physical state by the agent Smilga and her trek through the storm, Katrina Jaworska could well have been totally incoherent. But whatever she might have said, she had said it to Gregory Rowitz and no one else. The priest would not have allowed anyone—not even another priest or nun—to be privy to her confession, no matter what its import. So the matron was telling the truth, for the most part.

"When did Father Gregory leave?"

"I'm not sure of the time." The gun barrel weaved, and the matron stepped directly into its path. "What is the time *now*?" she cried.

He glanced at his chronometer. "Twenty minutes after one o'clock."

"Less than forty minutes ago . . . between thirty and thirty —forty minutes. I can't say exactly."

That seemed about right, the captain thought. We missed him by minutes. No more than five, perhaps less than three. But I missed him.

"Sister Theresa . . . will you let me help her?"

"What is it?" he snapped impatiently.

"The wound, captain. It must be tended to."

"Ah, you're making too much of nothing," he chided her. "She'll lose a little blood. That's not so serious at her age. Besides, you'll be able to give her your undivided attention as soon as you've helped us here. I mean, sister, that I am not satisfied that this Katrina Jaworska carried nothing with her. Papers, an envelope perhaps, information of some kind she might have passed on to you before the good father arrived. Nor have I asked you if she entrusted anything like that to the priest, who in turn may have left it with you for safekeeping. So to satisfy my curiosity, you will now show my men where you keep your records, you will take them through every nook and cranny in this hospital. And when they have reported to me that *they're* satisfied you've held nothing back, then your poor nun can receive medical attention. *But until then, matron, she will stand there and bleed!*"

The captain reached inside his tunic pocket and brought out a metal tin of cigarettes.

"I suggest you hurry along. Even a small wound invites infection."

In minutes the Hospital of the Holy Trinity was a shambles. Files littered the matron's office as cabinets and desks were wrenched open, their contents hastily examined and tossed aside. The infirmary was ransacked, the floor slick with medicine and pills scattered across the scrubbed tiles; dispensary cabinets were rifled, towels and blankets and bandages shaken out. In the ward every mattress was gutted, including the one on which Katrina Jaworska was laid out; the iron bed frames were overturned, the hollow tubes examined. Throughout the entire search two of the captain's men took pictures, especially of the nuns actively helping them—evidence of the church's willing cooperation. All this time the wounded nun stood not ten feet from the captain, who calmly smoked and listened to the clatter of the searchers.

The search revealed nothing. The patrol deployed around Rowitz's church reported by radio that there was no sign of him there either.

"We will take Madame Jaworska with us," the captain informed the matron. "Again, I advise you to make no mention of this incident. Your sisters have cooperated with the security forces."

"Captain," the matron said, looking at him in genuine puzzlement. "Everything you've done here tonight—this senseless destruction, making a helpless girl suffer, defiling the body of an old woman—was all this worthwhile to you? Did it achieve what you wanted?"

"Madam." The captain shook his head. "How can you ask me such a question. Even your church never questions the means—only the end."

With the grace of a well-bred son, the captain moved the matron to one side so that one of his men could hoist the body over his shoulder and carry it out. Within the hour the corpse of Katrina Jaworska would be gutted by a pathologist, the mouth, esophagus, stomach, and intestines examined for anything she might have taken with her into death.

Father Rowitz was no more than a long block from the square when he heard the sound of engines approaching Westerplatte and, glancing back, saw the tentative probes of the pale yellow headlights. The wind had died down, but the snow was falling more thickly than ever. The snow was all he had to help him.

Father Rowitz looked desperately down either side of the street. The shops were completely darkened; there were lights in the windows of the two apartment blocks, and he could make out the sound of a piano coming from one of them.

He had to get off the street.

A few yards more and he saw it—the museum. He plunged into the snowbank, falling across the all-but-impassable sidewalk, and scrambled along the edge of the hedgerow that marked the boundary of St. Florian's. He lifted his knees high, trying to clear the drifts, and made for the door. He fell heavily against the doorjamb, then pulled himself up, his fingers feeling the ice on the pane. He clenched his fist and punched at the glass, the cold anesthetizing the onrush of pain. Father Gregory fumbled with the latch and pushed on the frame with all his weight. There was a sharp report as the ice along the edges snapped and fell away, and he was inside.

For a few seconds Father Gregory stood motionless, straining to catch his breath. His mind swirled with images of the old woman whose eyes he had closed, and of heavily armed men who would soon be pursuing him.

"Out of here," he whispered to himself through clenched teeth, trying to ward off panic. "You've got to get away from here."

He knew he had a few minutes' grace. St. Florian's was a small museum devoted exclusively to religious art and the technique of icon painting. It had been closed for a month now and much-needed renovations begun. All its treasures had been moved, the caretaker given other duties. He would be alone for a time.

But they would be coming. They would go to the hospital, and they would quickly realize that he had barely eluded them, incentive enough to spur on the hunt. He had to move on, but not in his cassock.

Using the faint light filtering in through the high, leaded windows, Father Rowitz went from the back storeroom into the central exhibit halls. He could see the scaffolding lined up against the walls, the electrical wires hanging limp. Bags of plaster and cement were piled up in one corner, the workmen's tools thrown together in the wheelbarrow. Over everything lay the cold, musty odor emanating from the ancient walls.

Father Gregory walked to the wheelbarrow.

"Tools," he muttered.

He found two plastic bags by the barrow, ripped one open, and plunged his hand inside. Overalls. Workman's overalls, stiff with plaster and the cold. They would be looking for a priest. A man in overalls and a coat might get by. At the very least he had to try.

Father Gregory unbuttoned his coat and the cold shot through his hard body. He ripped off the cassock and shrugged into the baggy overalls, then put his coat on again. His entire body shaking, he walked across the central hall toward the front doors, which opened out onto the park along Marika Street.

If I can get across the park, he thought, just as far as the Opera House . . . His fingers fumbled for the bolt securing the front door, and he tugged at it with all his strength. If he could get across the park, then Marika Street, there was a house where he might be safe.

He pulled up the second bolt, and the doors began to rattle. He opened one a crack and looked into the shimmering darkness. Nothing. Nothing but the lamps along the walkways of the park. At that instant he felt himself poised on the edge of an abyss. There was no going back, not to his church, to his congregation, nor the life he had known for forty years. Finished, just like that.

The cherry red fires of Auschwitz slipped into his mind. Could it be happening again?

He had come upon the boy—Karol Stanislawski—by chance. Truly an act of grace. The youngster had been placed in a line for the extermination rooms, the last consignment of the night. A transport had arrived bearing special prisoners—men and women, members of various Christian organizations who had played major roles in the resistance throughout Europe. They were people respected in the free world, whose reputations abroad had protected them for a time. It was obvious there was to be no delay in executing them. From the loading platforms they were herded into a rough column and rushed, at the trot, along the trail winding through the demonic maze at whose center were the ovens. The trail led over several ditches and gullies, covered with planks and scavenged wood.

Much later that night, while returning to the priests' barracks with a ration of delousing powder, Rowitz heard a groan from under the planks of one such ditch. There he discovered him, almost dead, his body broken as though upon the rack. Somehow in the melee the boy had slipped and fallen into the trench and rolled out of sight beneath the planks.

Instinctively Rowitz plunged into the filth and pulled him out. He hefted him on his shoulders and, dragging the bag of delousing powder, he made for the barracks. That he was not challenged made him believe the Lord had meant their lives to be spared, and for the first time Rowitz thought he might actually survive the living hell in which he ministered to the doomed. And he and the boy had. They lived.

By the time he was twenty-eight, the name Karol Stanislawski was known to scholars throughout Europe. The whole of the Polish Church debated his writings, and Bishop Wyzinski himself had asked his advice on several occasions. But his research into Polish political conditions also brought him into conflict with governmental authorities. Stanislawski was not a man who could tolerate the humiliation of injustice. His pride had been forged on the edge of death, and his passion for freedom raged because of the memories he bore. He had survived the worst man could devise; the attempts of the Gomulka government to silence him were picayune and laughable when set against that. So he spoke out tirelessly against the regime's deadening bureaucracy, its terror and oppression. His writings became a beacon.

Stanislawski . . . What had she known about him? What had she known?

Father Gregory stepped outside and closed the door behind him. His flight had begun. Somewhere in the catacombs of the dissident underground he would find Karol Stanislawski if he was alive.

"This is the list of those who had any contact with the operation from its inception," the liaison officer said smartly, standing in front of Bibnikov, feet set precisely six inches apart, hands crossed at the small of his back.

Bibnikov regarded him thoughtfully and said nothing. His eyes zigzagged down the list, noting names, official positions, the point at which each had been involved with the operation, how long, and to what extent, and, last, where each of them was now.

"What about the woman, Jaworska, and the autopsy?"

"The pathologist found nothing ingested or hidden."

"Rowitz?"

"Units searching the neighborhood came across his cassock

in the St. Florian's Museum. It's been closed for the last three weeks, for renovations. He must have found some clothing and gotten out past the cordon."

"They're sure this was Rowitz."

"Fingerprints on the small Bible found in the discarded coat proved to be his."

Bibnikov looked up. "How did they match them?"

"An icon blessed last Easter by Rowitz."

"No end to our ingenuity," the chief of Special Investigations muttered. "I take it the wise priest has wisely disappeared."

"That is correct, and the Poles haven't any notion of which hole he went into. Even our own sources in the city have given us nothing."

"Your analysis, lieutenant?"

"It is my opinion that Gregory Rowitz and Cardinal Stanislawski, if they're not together now, will be shortly. If we find one, we find the other."

"Sometimes it's easier to look for two than for one," Bibnikov agreed. He'd keep an eye on this officer. He might be worth cultivating. "Give me two minutes, then bring Smilga in. And, Lieutenant . . . you've done well. Look me up when you're rotated to Moscow."

The young man smiled. "Thank you, Comrade Bibnikov." He turned smartly and wheeled out of the room. When the door was locked behind him, Bibnikov drew out a cigarette and lit it. The door opened to admit the false priest.

He's about ready, Bibnikov thought as Smilga entered. Tired, disoriented as much from fatigue as from fear. Yes, he was ready to make an arrangement.

"Sit down," Bibnikov said pleasantly. "My name is Sergei Bibnikov."

"Yes. I know, comrade."

The words are too sharp. He's been scalded, badly.

"I know what happened." Bibnikov rose from his chair. "No one is to blame. Events often fail to cooperate with us. I want you to remember that."

Jan Smilga nodded listlessly while his eyes darted.

"I don't want to go over what's happened," Bibnikov continued. "Instead, tell me about this priest, Rowitz." He held up his hand. "I know. The file is thick. What is lacking is the personal sense of the man—not the details. Tell me what he is like, his relationship with Stanislawski."

Smilga seemed to stare blankly. Bibnikov leaned against the wall.

"Would you have a cigarette?" Smilga asked, running a hand through his hair. "I've smoked all mine."

Bibnikov handed him a tin and his lighter and watched; the tremor in his hands was pronounced. Smilga took two deep drags on the cigarette, and that seemed to calm him.

"An informal evaluation?" he asked.

"That's all," Bibnikov assured him.

Smilga nodded and began to speak. "To understand Rowitz you have to accept that he sees his life only in terms of Cardinal Stanislawski. Theirs is a unique relationship. Gregory Rowitz was a priest at age twenty, interned at Auschwitz between 1943 and '45. It was he who hid Stanislawski, then a boy of ten, in the priests' barracks. This was almost a year before the camp was liberated. He took the boy with him, nursed him, placed him in a Catholic school.

"Over the years Rowitz played many roles: teacher, mentor, advisor, confidant, friend. Stanislawski, who rose very quickly in the Church hierarchy, never forgot his debt. He continually met with him, asking his advice, using Rowitz to test his ideas safely. But our intelligence people believed there was more. They speculated that Father Rowitz was a conduit between the resistance network and Stanislawski." Smilga paused. "I assume you know all about that."

Bibnikov nodded. The Network had been a cause for concern for the two years since the crackdown on the trade union movement and the curtailment of certain religious activities. Unlike other dissident factions, and the old Solidarity organization which had been penetrated and broken, it had retained its integrity. Its exact size remained unknown, and no key member had been uncovered. It remained an elusive shadow, strong and well organized. Its primary objective was to protect the most powerful voices of Polish dissent—writers and academicians, scientists, and especially trade union leaders who refused to curb their zeal even when their organizations had been compromised and crushed, their memberships cowed into silence. In the last two years no fewer than thirty-two Polish dissidents had vanished just days before arrests were to be made.

Smilga rubbed his hands together.

"Counterintelligence was convinced that the Network was in contact with Cardinal Stanislawski. Father Rowitz was briefing the cardinal on what positions to adopt on various social and political issues as he continued to speak out on behalf of anyone who challenged the government and the party."

Even Chairman Komarov feared him, Bibnikov remembered. There was a certain authority about him which made the presidium members uneasy. Minister Gorodin wanted the man silenced, but Stanislawski couldn't be intimidated.

"The consensus was that we had to get a man close to Rowitz," Smilga said, looking embarrassed. "I was chosen. I succeeded in obtaining a transfer to his parish."

"Did Rowitz have any reservations about you?" Bibnikov asked.

"Without a doubt. He had survived the war . . . Auschwitz. None of his instincts had deserted him. Yes, Rowitz had reservations. He checked my record in Warsaw—thoroughly. He undoubtedly went back over my entire history. And though he found nothing, he still held back."

"Is that why you failed to produce evidence of a link between Rowitz and the Network group?"

"That's what my report will conclude," he said somberly.

"Why do you think Katrina Jaworska wanted to speak with Father Rowitz?"

"Because of his intimate connection with the cardinal. She had information about Stanislawski, information she was reluctant to divulge to anyone else, including myself."

"So you believe Jaworska herself had no connection with the reactionary Network, that her only objective in trying to see Rowitz was to tell him something that concerned Stanislawski's past life. And she trusted Rowitz because she knew—as the whole country does, I suppose—of the relationship between the two men."

Bibnikov reached across and gently took back the cigarette tin. He removed another cigarette and sat down.

"You were the one who spoke with Jaworska," he said. "The only one who saw her face to face while she was alive. Whatever it was, she felt she had to say it to Rowitz, and in all likelihood she did. In your opinion, was it something of real importance?" Bibnikov squinted against the smoke.

"The woman was old," Smilga answered slowly. "She was very afraid. She knew she was dying. She knew this would be her final chance to make her peace. Her terror lay both in the information she possessed and the fact that she might die without divesting herself of its onus."

"You believe that whatever she had to say about Stanislawski was actually true," Bibnikov said gently.

"Yes, to a certain extent. Though it could have been simple forgiveness that she sought . . . for some past transgression against the cardinal." He shrugged. "Who can say?"

"Have you any idea where Rowitz might have gone?" Bibnikov asked. "He was not prepared to disappear that night. The fact that he's not been found would indicate he had a very fine contingency plan."

"No, the address of a house is the sum total of what Rowitz had. That is the solitary link with the Network," Smilga said.

I believe him, Bibnikov thought, staring at the cigarette butts at Smilga's feet.

"Cardinal Stanislawski," Bibnikov said softly, "why has he disappeared?"

Smilga looked up fearfully. He had no choice but to answer. Bibnikov could harm him far more than his immediate superior.

"Two weeks ago, during my usual Monday debriefing, I was told to mention to Rowitz that Stanislawski would be a target for a special action, that he was proving to be an embarrassment and a dangerous link between the unions and the Church, that the government was willing to risk a major incident. The purpose of having Rowitz know was to prompt him to make quick and careless contact with the dissident Network. If he took my word—and really he had no choice but to believe me—then he would *have* to go to the underground. They were the only ones who could have Stanislawski. Surveillance was to be so total that *in no way* could we miss the contact."

"But you did."

Smilga looked at the ceiling. "Father Rowitz never went anywhere near the Network." He shrugged. "They got to Cardinal Stanislawski first. Now we're turning the area upside down trying to find them. We won't. Not Stanislawski, and not Rowitz. They're gone for good."

"No one ever goes for good unless they're dead," said Bibnikov. He rose and walked over to the imposter priest. "I want you in Moscow, with me."

Smilga stared back at Bibnikov, trying to read the full meaning of his words. He licked his lips, tugged nervously at his chin.

"I'll do anything to help," he said. "There's nothing left for me here."

"That," said Bibnikov, "is the only thing we know for certain."

PART TWO

3

She was a commanding vision in the cold, gray light of Christmas morning, her anti-collision strobes piercing the ice-laden mist a hundred yards off the Statue of Liberty.

The *Robert F. Kennedy* was the last in the line of *Nimitz*-class vessels. Displacing a fraction over one hundred thousand tons, she carried one hundred twenty attack aircraft and thirty helicopters, as well as an arsenal of surface-to-surface and surface-to-air missiles capable of defending a small country. The Pentagon defense budget for 1987 had her listed as a three-billion-dollar investment. The real price was ten times that, for she never sailed alone. Her planes and attendant ships—three *Aegis* cruisers, three *Spruance*-class destroyers, the nuclear submarines *Omaha* and *Defiant*, supply ships, and a medical vessel —stayed at sea as long as she did. She was home for sixty-five hundred men, ranging from galley personnel to a battalion-strength complement of Marine assault troops, complete with their own amphibious vehicles. On this Christmas day, when she was scheduled to depart for her first station in the Indian Ocean, the *Kennedy* was carrying one extra passenger, a former Navy man: Jonathan Telford, President of the United States.

"That's your seventh cup."

One deck below the bridge, in the admiral's conference room, the President retrieved his cup and, without taking his eyes off the video screen, sipped the coffee. The running tape was a direct feed from the National Security Agency in Fort Meade, Maryland. Somewhere in its reinforced bunkers a computer was monitoring transmissions from a series of Paladin satellites swinging over Poland in a rough parabola. Even at two miles up, with a thick cloud layer between its lenses and the ground, Paladin was sending back shots of frightening clarity.

The spires of St. John Cathedral were swathed in black smoke. In front of the church, in the square, rested the steaming wrecks of vehicles. Paladin could focus so closely that the last three digits of the sedan's license plate were clearly discernible.

"Stanislawski's car?" the President murmured.

Laine Compton, the Secretary of State, snapped her lighter shut. "Yes." Her answer came out on a stream of smoke.

The square was cordoned off by military vehicles and personnel.

"Polish troops," Laine Compton remarked, anticipating the question.

Firetrucks were still hosing down the wrecks. Off to one corner, by the cathedral steps, were morgue bags lined up in a row that extended beyond the range of the camera's angle.

"One hundred seventeen dead," Laine Compton said. "Men, some women, two children. Most of them killed when the cars slammed into the crowds. Others trampled to death. Two KGB Surveillance Directorate personnel murdered, thirty to forty Polish security officers literally torn apart when they tried to get to Cardinal Stanislawski."

"What happened to Stanislawski?"

"No one knows."

"Say again?"

"Polish internal security doesn't have him. Nor do the Soviets. He wasn't among the casualties."

"You're certain?"

"The agency tells me the Russians are frantic. Radio and telephone intercepts indicate a massive hunt for Stanislawski. The operation is too big to be a disinformation ruse."

Jonathan Telford watched as three military ambulances penetrated the restricted area, backing up toward the row of corpses. The loading of bodies continued.

"So who has him?"

"My guess is the resistance network."

"You're saying he's alive?"

"Unless someone is holding on to a corpse."

Telford shook his head. "Every Western embassy is surrounded by militia to protect them against 'acts of terrorism.' " The irritation faded from his voice. "God, I feel for him. What could he have had on the Kremlin that it was willing to risk a massacre to get at him?"

"He must have known something," Laine Compton said. "And Solidarity must have felt it had to get him out of there."

"The Russians are in the process of airlifting an *entire* brigade into the city. Warsaw is being turned upside down. I *know* Solidarity remnants and the Network have underground routes to the West, but there is no way, believe me, that they'll be able to move Stanislawski out of the country."

The President sat back in the oversize chair.

"Turn it off, Laine. I've seen enough."

When the indirect lights came on, the Secretary of State saw that the President had closed his eyes.

Jonathan Telford was not a tall man, a shade over five ten with a chunky build his tailor despaired of and a shock of brown-gray hair that was the bane of his barber's existence. He felt most comfortable in loafers, cords, sweatshirt, or—if pressed to don formal dress—a cream broadcloth shirt beneath a dark camelhair pullover. This unaffected simplicity was mirrored in his face as well, in the full cheeks which drooped when he was tired, the gray eyes looking out over dark half-moon ridges, and brows that were forever being pressed down by the horizontal grooves across his forehead.

Laine Compton remembered the men's faces in the central mess as they all sang "Silent Night" together. They were all, Telford included, lonely men, far from home and loved ones on Christmas night. In the case of Jonathan Telford, such camaraderie was all he had. His wife and two sons had perished in a plane crash four years ago. Perhaps the men of the *Kennedy* had remembered his loss and that had accounted for the way they received him—as one of their own.

The Telex began to clatter. Laine Compton read as the paper was pushed out by the machine. This was the continuation of the crisis that had disrupted their Christmas. Not the turn of events in Warsaw, which was a tragic adjunct, but something that had far more serious ramifications.

"What's the update?" Telford asked her, getting to his feet.

"National Security has just confirmed the initial Langley report. Komarov's sick—bad. Calls between Rudin Hospital and the Kremlin leave nothing to the imagination. The Premier of the Soviet Union has an aneurysm in his brain that's going to burst any time now."

"Perhaps that's what they'd be wanting us to think," the President mused.

"Possible," Laine Compton replied. "Though who knows why they would *want* to mislead us about Komarov's condition. In any case, I know how you feel about intercepts, but the Israelis have given us access to their VIPER reports, the cream of their Russian stuff." Laine Compton stabbed her cigarette out. "Copies of the last four tapes VIPER's managed to get out will be waiting for you when we get back to Washington. According to Mordecai Sadfie in Jerusalem, this information comes straight from Komarov's chief physician, Dr. Razminsky. He confirms the intercepts. Chairman Komarov is dying, I'm afraid."

"Can we trust the tapes?"

"We have Dr. Razminsky's voiceprints to confirm his identity. The Israelis owe us some favors and they're making good. We *know* for sure they're in no position to toy with us."

"Then there's not a lot of time for us to act. Your turn to play sounding board," the President said. He pulled out one of her cigarettes, lit it, and began pacing.

"Six months ago Komarov, Semyon Arkadyevich, Chairman of the Central Committee and First Secretary of the Communist Party, virtually drops out of sight. Before we know it, Foreign Minister Dmitri Gorodin has taken his place at all Party functions. Gorodin also retains his hold on the Foreign Ministry, and with it, Soviet activities abroad. At the same time Gorodin's making inroads at home. Within three weeks there are shakeups in the party secretariat in Moscow, Leningrad, and Kiev. Gorodin is moving fast, placing his personnel as high up as he can.

"On the other hand we have Oleg Kobalevsky. Kobalevsky is an engineer by training. His base is the middle level of the Party, made up of technocrats. Over the last twenty years the character of the regional and urban wings of the Communist Party has changed. The Stalinist leftovers and the Brezhnev hangers-on are fading. A new breed is emerging, the long-awaited postwar generation. Technological." Telford stretched out the word. "Better educated, broader in experience and training, able to assimilate the party line while filtering out the propaganda. They have become, in spite of their lackadaisical attitude toward the Party machinery, the new Soviets. Technocrats. Kobalevsky himself is one of them. Although he's older, he realized early in the game that if world socialism was to hold its own against the West over the very long haul it would have to replace adherence to isolationist dogma with an acknowledgment that in the coming years engineers, technicians, and scientists would be the new Heroes of Socialist Labor, not the miners in the Donbass coalfields or the enforcers at Kolyma. All right so far?"

"I think you're one of the few people who read my last book."

" 'The mediocre borrow, the brilliant steal.' T. S. Eliot." Jonathan Telford smiled, then resumed pacing. "In the late seventies, this difference between Party theoreticians and zealots and Kobalevsky's technocrats begins to simmer. The elders— Brezhnev and his crew—are too busy keeping themselves alive to pay much attention. In the early eighties, the situation changes with the death of Brezhnev and the ascendancy of the military in response to the Reagan buildup. It was you who predicted that after Mr. Brezhnev the military would make its move, and they did. But they did not reckon on a fellow called Sergei Bibnikov, who got wind of the coup. Chairman Komarov then slapped them down, using Marshal Pavlichenko, who is now the Minister of Defense. When the dust settled, Chairman Komarov was on top of the heap. But the debate between his subordi-

nates, Kobalevsky and Gorodin, continued, each vying for territory, each staking out claims, raiding the other's larder, trying
to steal away, blackmail, or otherwise line up talent in the best
capitalist fashion. Chairman and Party First Secretary Komarov
belonged to neither. He was above them and rode the country
as Ben-Hur did the chariot. Kobalevsky and Gorodin were his
horses. Sometimes Gorodin got free rein, sometimes, Kobalevsky. But neither won out. Only Komarov." Telford chuckled,
shaking his head. "Then the old son of a bitch just recedes.
Everything went through Foreign Minister Gorodin. Since our
network in Russia is in the process of being rebuilt, which is to
say it's for shit at the moment, we've relied on the Israelis to
keep us abreast of things. Traditionally they've had the best
lines into the country anyway. And what have we learned? That
no sooner was Chairman Komarov taken ill than Minister
Gorodin made his bid. Not a man to shed crocodile tears, he
went for the top, working around Komarov's people as best he
could. He's an infighter, and this is where he has the edge on
friend Kobalevsky, who's something of a wimp when it comes to
hard backroom brawling."

"And it's Kobalevsky we want to succeed Chairman
Komarov," Laine Compton said.

"Naturally. But it's also Kobalevsky, the technocrat, who's
losing ground fast. Gorodin's pounding him from all sides. The
weaker Chairman Komarov becomes, the bolder Gorodin gets.
Kobalevsky's running out of time. If Komarov were to die tomorrow, guess who'd be making a grand tour of the Siberian
goldfields?"

"So we're going to help Comrade Kobalevsky."

"Don't ever say such a thing," the President rebuked her.
"That's like saying the Soviet Union has the power to influence
our choice of our next president. But . . . yes. That's exactly
what we're going to do."

His cold, unfeeling resolution made Laine Compton's skin
crawl. This was the other part of the man, the dark side—potentially vicious, uncompromising. It fascinated, attracted, and
repelled her all at the same time. It was the catalyst that trans-

formed this otherwise modest man into the President of the United States.

But then the United States over the last century had been responsible for ninety-five changes of government around the world. It was a fact Laine Compton was well acquainted with. Destabilization, assassination, blackmail, economic intervention —covert and otherwise—sheer, brute military force, all these were at Telford's command. The blueprints only needed to be dusted off, and fresh ones could be drawn up on demand by think tanks across the country. But that was not the reason for her anxiety. This time the target wasn't some banana republic or some Southeast Asian country that had lost its identity and become a domino. The issue was not oil, a strategic piece of real estate, or the support of a valuable though morally repugnant ally. This was the only other superpower in the world.

"Komarov will not permit himself to die without grasping at every available option," Telford said. "He's a fighter. He'll hang on for as long as he can. What about us? Are *we* ready?"

"Any time at all." Laine Compton ran a finger over the crystal of her watch. "Farraday will be calling soon."

The President of the United States walked to the long rectangular windows, looking out at the silent towers of the World Trade Center jutting up over the fog.

"The Russians have a crisis in Poland," he said. "Komarov brought it to a head because of Cardinal Stanislawski. Something Stanislawski knew." He turned back to her. "But the real question is whether Komarov's failure in Poland will be the signal for the jackals to move in."

4

Dr. Michael Franklin Turner was sitting in an alcove of the Metropolitan Museum's Bennett Wing. The time was half-past eleven, Christmas morning. Beside him on the bench was a package of Marlboros, already two-thirds empty, an electronic pager. Turner took a last pull on his cigarette and ground it out in the small ashtray he carried with him. The alcove was a nonsmoking area. Several people who wandered in to study the half-dozen paintings on the walls gave him pointed looks. They would have said something to him if they had not felt the intense concentration, warning against interference.

His physique added to this impression. Turner was a heavy man, even for six feet, with a well-developed chest, broad shoulders, and strong forearms. The fifteen extra pounds he was carrying were lost on his frame. His brown hair was shot through with gray, and his eyes were a brilliant blue, but his fingers were not long or slender, as one might have expected of a famous surgeon.

Michael Turner snapped the ashtray shut and slid it over by the pager. For an instant he wished it would sound its beep and give him the excuse to get out of there. He suspected it wouldn't. Neurology staff at Wilder Penfield Memorial usually made certain there was no reason why he should even think of coming in on Christmas. Examinations were taken over by residents, and chief of staff Weizmann made a point of being available for any emergencies. It was unwritten policy that Christmas Day was Michael Turner's. Everyone knew that late this morning he; his wife, Jeanne; and their ten-year-old son, Christopher; would be at the Metropolitan Museum's Junior Art Exhibit, a seasonal event at which the city's most talented youngsters exhibited their work.

This year had been no different. The exchange of gifts was a quiet, intimate affair. While Jeanne helped Christopher dress, Turner looked after breakfast—flapjacks, crisp bacon, an egg for topping, specially prepared jams and preserves sent over at Christmas from Jeanne's parents in London. After breakfast the three of them began the ten-block trek from their apartment to the museum, arriving a few minutes after the doors opened at half-past eleven.

Michael Turner first made a complete tour of the exhibition with his family, then moved off and sat down on a bench to study his son's two paintings, the exhibit's centerpieces.

They're grotesque, Turner thought, spellbound by the first picture.

Is this where he lives? Turner thought to himself. Is this what he *sees*, what he *feels*? Others could talk to him about the immense power of his son's work, the surrealistic vision and profoundly disturbing spirit that infused those scenes. *But, Christ Almighty, they're talking about a ten-year-old child, not Hieronymus Bosch.*

Michael and Jeanne Turner had been married two years when Christopher was born. He had met her in London, during the year which saw his perfection of a laser surgery technique that had become known as the Turner Bypass. Jeanne Harrington was the daughter of a retired Harley Street ophthalmologist. She herself was a Laurier Research Fellow in one of Europe's best cancer research centers, Haddon Hall at the University of London. Introduced to the young American at a party given by her director, she had fallen in love with Michael Turner then and there. To say that the feeling was reciprocal was an understatement: their courtship lasted all of two months.

Jeanne was thirty-one when she became pregnant. She stopped smoking and watched her liquor intake, mapped out a careful diet, and attended prenatal exercise clinics. Labor was short, the delivery flawless, the baby male, seven pounds, two ounces, and perfectly normal. At least normal until Christopher was eighteen months old.

Neither Michael nor Jeanne ever really knew what had caused the disease. Meningitis: inflammation of the cerebrospinal membrane. The cold came over Christopher in the last week of October. Then the hard projectile vomiting began, accompanied by drowsiness and a loss of appetite. After a series of tests the pediatrician at Penfield Memorial discovered that Christopher was suffering from photophobia. Even the softest light made him scream in pain. By the end of November the lumbar puncture had been performed. The conclusion was inescapable. There was nothing to be done but start an endless regimen of intravenous antibiotics. These would save Christopher's life, but they would never give him back his mind. Just before his second birthday Christopher ceased to develop mentally. His vocabulary consisted of the twenty-odd words he had learned to pronounce before the disease struck. For the next six years the only new thing he learned was how to dress himself. Beyond that he was utterly helpless.

Turner often wondered where it was that Jeanne found the strength. He marveled at the love and concern she showered on their son and at how much was still left for him, for their marriage. She never shared his anger over the injustice of what had happened but instead was there to comfort him. Her strength shamed Michael Turner, for there wasn't enough love in the world he could give in return.

Still, Turner had vowed to cut his schedule in half. His secretaries pruned his speaking engagements and reduced his lecture commitments by two-thirds. But Turner could not surrender the chairmanship of the neurosurgical department, and the demands on his skills at the operating table were as heavy as ever. Patients traveled especially to Penfield Memorial and would refuse to be treated by anyone else. Even though Turner himself no longer kept track of the latest developments in pathology, angiography, CAT-scanning, neurobiology, epilepsy, meningioma, and spinal-cord damage, he read the précis of journals his residents presented to him. When all was said and done, Michael Turner had been able to reduce the hours of his working day from nineteen to sixteen. To have given more would have meant giving up altogether the work that meant everything to him.

He heard her footsteps first, sharp echoes of bootheels, and he looked up, seeing the long, perfect legs between swinging halves of an open fur coat. A sheen of auburn hair fell across one shoulder. His eyes traveled up to meet her own, smoky blue eyes. Her scent made him breathe deeply, then she was sitting beside him. For a moment Jeanne said nothing, gazing at her son's paintings, then looked at her husband.

"Sometimes I remember having bought him that paint set. I didn't think it would come to this."

"Don't say that," Turner said. "Not ever. We don't understand the kind of world he sees through his eyes, but maybe we're just afraid. He's so young. We think children should have images of innocence, beautiful fantasies. But he's not that kind of child."

She understood that his frustration was directed toward neither her nor their son. Christmas, like her birthday or Christopher's—or for that matter, his own—was the worst time for him. That was when he remembered his unkept promises to spend more time with them, when the contradiction between the miracles he performed in surgery and his inability to help his own son was sharpest. She demanded nothing more of him than he already gave, but he was not satisfied with that.

From a box of paints to a place in the Metropolitan Art Academy; from charcoal to watercolors in less than a year. There was no question that Christopher was a prodigy. A boy who could neither read nor write, who spoke less than two dozen words.

"Where is he?" Turner asked suddenly.

"Michael, it's all right," Jeanne said quickly. What he could not give in time, he made up in concern. His protective attitude toward Christopher bordered on the extreme. "I left him with his instructor. He promised to bring . . ."

Her words trailed off, and Turner saw his son standing a

few feet from him, looking like any other ten-year-old, with longish blond hair, a smooth oval face that had his mother's lips and nose, the wide forehead and sharp eyes of his father. Except that there was no expression in those eyes. They were vacant, dreamless eyes, like the windows of an old abandoned house. It wasn't through them that Christopher Turner observed the world. He had other, different eyes.

"Professor Tobias?" Turner said, rising, his hand outstretched.

"Michael, that's not Christopher's instructor!"

Michael Turner reached them in one motion, taking the man's hand off Christopher's shoulder and placing himself between the stranger and his son. Although the man was several inches shorter, Turner felt the power in that compact body.

"Doctor Turner, my name is Stafford. Secret Service."

He offered Turner his credentials—a plastic card with photo, signature and countersignatures, and an embossed stamp that read *White House*.

"I wouldn't know a real ID from a fake," Turner started to say.

"Secretary Compton is waiting to see you, sir," the agent replied as though he hadn't heard Turner. "She's in a car in front of the museum."

"Compton? I'm afraid I don't know anyone . . ."

"Secretary of State Compton." Stafford smiled politely. "This is a matter of some urgency, doctor."

Turner looked down at Jeanne, who shook her head, brows knitting together. He looked over the agent's shoulder at the strollers going by. If he started shouting, museum security would get here fast enough.

"Look, Stafford, I don't know what's going on here—"

"My instructions are to escort you to Secretary Compton's car, doctor. Nothing more. As I said, the matter is urgent."

"And if I object?"

"Then I am to escort you to the nearest public telephone so that you can speak to the secretary yourself," Stafford said patiently. The implication was clear: one way or the other he would see to it that Turner kept his appointment.

"What the hell is going on here?" Turner demanded. "If it's a medical matter—"

"Michael, go with him." Jeanne was at his side, one arm hugging Christopher to her. "We'll be all right here. Maybe it's something that can't be discussed in public."

"You're sure?" Turner was annoyed.

"Yes, of course. We'll be fine."

"If you'd prefer, I can leave a man with your wife and son," Stafford offered.

"That won't be necessary," Turner replied, and swung on his coat as he followed the man toward the museum foyer.

The car was parked on Fifth Avenue, a Lincoln whose black finish was lined with salt streaks at the rocker panels. Stafford preceded Turner, moving quickly down the sand-covered steps. Another agent opened the door; Turner peered inside.

"Thank you for answering my request so promptly, Doctor Turner," Laine Compton said. "Please, come in. I'm sorry we had to intrude on your holiday like this. We waited as long as we could."

As Turner sat back the door was closed behind him. The Lexam windows were coated, so that while he could see out, no one could see into the vehicle.

"Would you care to examine my credentials, doctor?"

"No," Turner said. "What I don't understand is what you want. It's not the President?"

"No, not at all. The President is in perfect health. However, you're right in assuming the matter is of a medical nature. The President would like very much to meet with you."

Turner's reputation had brought him into contact with a number of heads of state. He had performed surgery on cabinet ministers and a member of the British Royal Family. No stranger to the wealthy and influential, he nonetheless found their power and privilege slightly offensive . . . or perhaps it was their presumption that they could use that power to command others to do their bidding.

"Yes, that would be convenient. I could come down to Washington tomorrow morning, after I've checked in at the hospital."

"No, Doctor Turner. The President must see you sooner, I'm afraid. And he is not in Washington."

"Now wait—" Turner started to say, but Compton held up her hand. She lifted the telephone receiver by the armrest and said: "Okay, David, we're ready for the call."

The Secretary of State passed the receiver to Turner.

"Is this Dr. Michael Turner?"

The voice belonged, without a doubt, to the President of the United States.

His family was safe. He had returned with them to their duplex condominium. At Laine Compton's insistence, two Secret Service men remained with his wife and son. She assured Turner it was a gesture only and not a precaution.

The limousine took them down to the financial district, making good time through the slush with the help of unmarked sedans that closed off the intersections. In the north tower of the World Trade Center an elevator was waiting. It took them to the roof. Turner ducked his head against the wind that rolled across the open expanse, following Laine Compton's lead. His eyes were watering by the time he made it into the Navy helicopter. Why, Turner wondered, hadn't they simply been picked up at the river's edge instead of atop the Trade Center?

The *Robert F. Kennedy* dwarfed the Statue of Liberty. Because of a fine winter mist rolling across the bay, the pilot banked to the left and came up behind the carrier, skirting the jets that rested on the flight deck, wings tucked up like falcons at rest. The helicopter's door was pulled back by a Marine guard who helped Turner out. There was nowhere to go but through the gauntlet of Shore Patrol personnel that led right up to an open door.

"Straight into the elevator, doctor," Laine Compton said, matching him stride for stride.

The descent was too quick to even guess how many decks they had dropped. When the doors opened, he was faced with walls covered by some sort of sheet metal, silver flashing off blue from the small but intense lights that burned in overhead wire nests. The floor was covered with a soft tile that added a slight bounce to his step. It gave off no sound as they walked into what appeared to be a never-ending tunnel.

Turner estimated that they had gone thirty yards before they came to the copper-sheathed door guarded by four Marines.

"Please, doctor, after you." Laine Compton waved him ahead.

The room was pale white and built in two tiers, with a sheet of clear reinforced glass separating them. From where he stood, Turner could see that the bottom level was lit only by the matsu-green phosphorescence radiating from the computer consoles that lined the walls. In the center stood four islands composed of silent readout terminals, their screens in constant motion. Above the islands, resembling a stock exchange digital toteboard, was a circular television monitor, flashing seemingly unrelated visual sequences. Behind the curved sheet of glass, on the upper tier, there was a single desk with one chair behind it and a battery of telephone circuits.

"This is the ship's Situation Room, doctor." The resonant voice belonged to Jonathan Telford, who rose from the leather chair. "What you see below is the primary analysis section of our satellite defense system. Computer-controlled and -operated, it's designed to alert the White House and all our military units, worldwide, of an attack. If the *Kennedy* ever found herself in the midst of hostilities, this is where her counterattack would be coordinated."

Was the ploy working? Turner hadn't said a word in response to the President's preamble. He stood very still, his eyes on the machines below. It was impossible to tell whether he was mildly impressed, awed, or simply indifferent.

Finally the surgeon stepped forward. He did not offer his hand to the President, because for the first time since leaving Manhattan, he was afraid. Here, in this room, faced with this man, he was suddenly aware of how totally out of his element he was.

"You mentioned that the matter was urgent, Mr. President," Turner said quietly.

"It is," Telford acknowledged. If offense had been taken, he didn't show it. "It's also sensitive, requiring an open mind on your part. Understanding. You appear somewhat upset. I know the meeting was arranged on rather short notice, but for security—"

"It's not the trip, Mr. President," Turner interrupted. "Nor the surroundings. But, yes, I believe I deserve an explanation."

Telford glanced at Compton.

"Very well, doctor, let me make this as brief as possible." Telford softened his tone. "I have a favor to ask you, an enormous professional favor. I assure you that for our part we have no choice as to whether or not to consult you. In fact no one in this situation has any choice.

"I want you to operate on the premier of the Soviet Union, Chairman Semyon Arkadyevich Komarov. His doctors have determined that he is suffering from an intracranial aneurysm. The Russians have their experts, of course, but they admit they lack experience. Dr. Andrei Razminsky, whom I believe you know, recommended you for the job."

Turner heard every word Telford spoke, but another part of him closed off the President's words. Without being aware of it, Turner began to look around the room. He imagined it to be the sort of place in which, years ago, his father had met another president. It was cold, airless, antiseptic. This is where he would have received his orders.

Turner was aware he was blinking his eyes rapidly, deliberately trying to ward off the memory. He didn't realize why he should think of his father so naturally, so quickly. It seemed almost an instinctive reaction, and somewhere in the recesses of his mind he heard warning bells toll.

"Is that Razminsky's diagnosis?" Turner asked. He had expected to hear the name of the Russian surgeon as soon as the condition was mentioned.

"It is."

The Secretary of State took over: "We have a full report on Komarov's condition available for you, doctor. As you must realize, time is precious. The equipment is en route to Rudin Hospital. Normal protocol has been observed. We are prepared to fly you to Moscow as soon as you're ready."

"Have you considered that I might have other surgery scheduled?"

"We checked." Laine Compton stood with her arms akimbo. "We know you don't have any pressing commitments at the moment."

"Of course." Turner pursed his lips. He wondered if they had given his father any choice, either. No, they hadn't. These were not people who offered choices. Dealing with them was a one-way street . . . a dead end. Turner looked directly at the President. "I will operate on Komarov."

There was no hint of excitement in his voice.

"We know you must have ambivalent feelings about the Soviet Union, about its government, now . . . and back then," Laine Compton said very quietly. She lit a cigarette and came forward.

"You were fourteen years old when your father, after spending a leave of one month with you and your mother, returned to Europe . . . on business. That was in 1959. As far as you knew, your father was a sales representative for a major computer firm, a position which required frequent travel. What you were not aware of was that his actual employer was the Central Intelligence Agency, that his destination was not Paris and Brussels, but Moscow. You learned of this only when you saw Peterson Turner on television, sitting in a cell in a Russian jail, reading from prepared notes. What he was reading was a confession of his espionage activities."

"He was a good man," Turner said. "But that was another time."

"The story in the press and television took the line that Peterson Turner had been apprehended by the Soviets while actively spying for the United States." Laine Compton was watching him very closely, trying to see a response, the tiniest flicker.

"Yes, and the Eisenhower administration saw to our needs after his death."

"Your mother signed over the settlement to you on your seventeenth birthday. She died four days later. The half-million dollars remained in the Dreyfus Fund. It paid for your university studies: UCLA, Harvard Medical, and postgraduate work in London, during which time you devised, at the age of twenty-eight, what is now known as the Turner Bypass. This achievement has made you a leading authority in the field of laser surgery. Since then no one has matched your talent, or your ability."

"You make it sound so easy, but it wasn't like that at all. I buried Mother in a small cemetery outside Boulder, Colorado, at the foot of the mountains she loved and painted. Then I sold everything we had and left for Los Angeles."

Laine Compton looked away. "Two things puzzled people about your reaction. First, in spite of an enormous workload, you nonetheless studied Russian history and language, becoming quite accomplished—fluent in Russian. Second, even with the Freedom of Information Act, you never made any effort to obtain documents pertaining to your father. We thought this very curious."

"Why have you gone through all this?" Turner asked harshly.

Laine Compton picked up a thick dossier, the cover slashed with twin red bands.

"The President signed an Executive Order this morning for the release of this dossier from Agency archives. Officially it did not exist. It would not have been made available to you through the Freedom of Information Act, nor will it ever be released . . . except in this one instance. The dossier is about your father, the operation he was running in Czechoslovakia when arrested, the sacrifice he took it upon himself to make—"

"I don't want to know," Turner said. "Do you understand? I don't care!"

"I can give you a brief summary," Compton went on, ignoring his angry outburst. "Peterson Turner was in Moscow to arrange the final details of a defection, a *major* defection. The defector was a scientist who had perfected the means by which laser power could be applied to satellites. And what's more, he had devised a method of building energy modules which would make nuclear reactors obsolete."

"Dimitroff." Turner nodded.

"Your memory is remarkable. Lavrenti Dimitroff had to be brought out. Your father had been working on it for over three years." She opened her hand, elbow braced against her side—a helpless gesture. "We never learned what went wrong. Your father had a network for moving Dimitroff, passing him through a series of shelters until he was in the West. From what we were able to learn, Peterson Turner spotted his surveillance just as he sent Dimitroff into the tunnel out. At this point he made his choice: He could have followed Dimitroff and risked letting KGB counterintelligence pick up not only him and Dimitroff, but the entire network as well . . . or he could throw them off the track, go off on his own, force them to follow him. Peterson Turner had nowhere to run, no help—nothing. He played the red herring for as long as he could. By the time the Soviets got to him, Dimitroff was safe." She flipped open the file. "The whole story, as the agency pieced it together from Dimitroff and other sources, is here—medical reports on the drugs your father was given to force his 'confession,' his resistance, his bravery until the very end."

"They didn't bring him back, trade him, *save him,*" Turner said. "You had something, someone the Russians wanted!"

"We did, yes," the President interrupted flatly, and cleared his throat. "We had Dimitroff. The Russians would only settle for him in exchange for your father. They couldn't hand Dimitroff back to them. They couldn't acknowledge that he was even *alive*, much less that they had aided and abetted his escape. The Russians were never to be certain we had him at all."

There it was, the whole ugly story, neatly tied up in flaming red ribbons designed to conceal the truth forever. Turner felt empty—drained—and suddenly very tired.

"Why have you told me this?"

Jonathan Telford walked along the instrument-lined wall. "As I mentioned before, there is only one Michael Turner. If the Russians had a choice, if they could have found someone in their own country or in Eastern Europe to perform that surgery, they would have done so. And the same goes for us. You were the last man we wanted. But you are the *only* one." The President paused. "And, yes, we knew all about Peterson Turner and the tragedy that his work made for your mother . . . yourself. We knew that you owed us nothing. We couldn't appeal to your patriotism, we couldn't buy you. You didn't need us. There was only one thing that we could offer you—an explanation. Your father was a patriot. We wanted to admit how helpless the men guiding him had been. We wanted you to know that he *chose* to serve his country to the very end. He could have come out and could very well be alive today . . . but *he* chose the alternative. Above all, we wanted you to understand that."

"Did you expect me to be grateful, Mr. President?" Turner said. "Did you think that in some noble way this truth would free me of all the pain and indignity I hoped I had forgotten? On the contrary. You told me the truth—now. Not last year. Not five years ago. But now . . . because you need me. Sir, my father has been dead for over twenty-five years. Where the hell has this file been all that time?" He looked up at them and shook his head. "I don't know where you get off playing with people's lives as though you have some blessed authority to do so. You haven't told me anything I don't already know. Not about *my* father. If you want me to operate, then let's get on with it. Please spare me the history lecture."

"Open up the phone line to Rudin Hospital in Moscow," said the President.

5

Security updates continued to pour into the Special Investigations bureau throughout the night. Acting on verbal instructions from the bedridden Chairman Komarov, Sergei Bibnikov made preparations for Michael Turner's safety and anonymity.

Intercepts of Telexes exchanged by the Soviet Ministry of Health and the U.S. Department of Health and Human Services in Washington contained no mention of Turner. Since 1974 this system had linked the Soviet and American medical communities. Used to coordinate all official exchanges, conferences, and delegation details, it was also programmed to handle security communications in emergency medical cases, such as the time Nikita Khrushchev had been treated by A. McGehee Harvey of Johns Hopkins University. However, there would be no such record of Turner's ever having been summoned to Moscow.

Bibnikov's informants at the KGB's New York station reported that Penfield Memorial's chief of staff had been notified by the FBI of Dr. Turner's sudden departure for the West Coast. The Bureau discreetly noted that the President's mother was currently being treated at an undisclosed location in California, leaving Dr. Weizmann to draw the inference that the President had personally enlisted Turner's cooperation.

From London, one of his units confirmed Turner's arrival

on a scheduled British Airways Concorde from New York. Subsequent reports indicated that while Turner was being driven along the normal M4 route to London, the limousine changed course at the last minute, skirting the city and taking the surgeon toward the RAF base at Lidendown Fields. Another supersonic, this one with no markings, lifted off as soon as Turner was on board.

Bibnikov's domestic units took over at a Soviet air force base 70 kilometers outside Moscow, where, unlike at Sheremetevo or Vnukino, the city's civilian fields, security could be total.

Dr. Turner was met by a senior official of the Foreign Ministry. They shook hands and walked to a waiting car. With an escort vehicle leading the way along the restricted center lane, the drive to the Nachalstvo Clinic on Kalinin Prospekt lasted less than forty-five minutes.

"What the hell is he doing going out?" Bibnikov muttered as he listened to the surveillance reports being radioed in. "I would have thought he'd confer with Dr. Razminsky right away."

The reunion of Drs. Turner and Razminsky had been what one would have expected of two friends—warm and affectionate. But no sooner had Turner examined the special equipment that had been flown in ahead, and explained to Razminsky exactly how it was to be installed, than he took the Russian neurosurgeon aside and whispered something to him. A few minutes later the two men reappeared on Kalinin Prospekt, strolling down the avenue like a pair of tourists.

"Damn."

Aleksandr Roy emptied a third bucket of water into the office humidifier. He glanced at the television screen, which was receiving a transmission from a mobile surveillance truck on Kalinin Prospekt.

"They have a shadow." He indicated the Chaika sedan that was crawling after the two men, its running lights glowing through the snow.

"Sasha, go over to their hotel and check the arrangements."

Roy looked at him.

"I know our esteemed KGB chief, Comrade Suslev, is a very capable baby-sitter," Bibnikov said impatiently. "But indulge me in this. When I speak to Komarov later, he will ask about this. I really wouldn't want to lie about such a significant detail. Then check with our people in Warsaw and see if they have anything more on our tattooist. Perhaps by some miracle they have managed to find some trace of the cardinal they've misplaced."

An indigo tint had crept into Moscow's night sky. Beyond a thin veil of clouds, the stars pulsed in erratic rhythm, their wintry brilliance unchallenged. Over the ancient walls of the Kremlin drifted a pale-fire moon, uncaring and unconcerned. It was the kind of night that brought peace over the land, lulled children to an early sleep, and lifted the inhibitions of hesitant lovers.

Doctor Michael Turner was standing on Khudozhestvennaya Street, directly in front of the brilliantly lit façade of the Moscow Art Theater. He marveled at the soaring architecture before him, his concentration unimpaired by the slamming of a car door.

"They've checked with the powers that be." Andrei Razminsky laughed. "Apparently it won't be a breach of state security if we continue our walk to your hotel."

Turner tugged off his fine chamois gloves and brushed the snowflakes from his hair. Magnificent hands, Razminsky thought. In his forty years of surgery he hadn't seen anyone with the skill, no, the extraordinary brilliance of this American. Razminsky grew puzzled as Turner knelt down and scooped up some snow. He pressed it into a small, hard ball, then swung his arm back like a child and flung the tiny projectile as high and as far as he could, watching its trajectory until the snowball disappeared from sight.

"You're not at all tired, are you?" Razminsky said.

Turner brushed the snow from his hands. "Not tired, Andrei. Drained," Turner said. "Completely and utterly drained."

"A walk in this air will clear your head," Razminsky said. "You'll sleep like the dead. Come on. The hotel is a good eight blocks further."

The Chaika's rear tires spun in the icy slush, the engine turning over with a particular *ping* to protest being pushed along in low gear.

Turner lengthened his stride, moving effortlessly through the snow that was building up along the sidewalks. Khudozhestvennaya Street was silent at this hour, devoid of traffic and pedestrians, the newly fallen snow sparkling under the steaming sodium arc lamps.

"Are you still annoyed with them, Michael, and angry with me because you are here?" Razminsky asked, matching his friend's pace.

"Not with you, Andrei," Turner shook his head. "With Telford and the rest of them? Yes."

Turner threw an arm around the smaller man's shoulder. Walking alongside him, the churning fear he had felt when he arrived was dying by degrees. He longed to tell Razminsky about his father, the hatred he felt for the men who had killed him, the surprising affection he had come to feel for a people he had only studied about. He understood that Razminsky was curious. But how could Turner explain it to him when he himself had not worked out the puzzle?

For his part Andrei Razminsky cherished their relationship. He remembered Turner from London, the fierce competitive energy that had created the bypass. Even then Turner had been an outstanding surgeon. Inexperienced to be sure, but daring, innovative, successful because of the meticulous preparation he insisted on for every operation. Some bond between them had transcended their professional respect for one another. It was a meeting of souls, Razminsky thought. During the decade they had known each other, the Russian had often regretted Turner's inability to express what was in his heart, and to share and thus perhaps to come to terms with his great sorrow. But Razminsky was a patient man.

Michael Turner maintained his pace, breathing deeply in the crisp night air, feeling it drive out the stale taste of the long journey. As he turned the corner onto Petrovka Street, with the Bolshoi Theater a shining landmark three hundred yards away, the words came to him. They were not the ones he wanted to say, but they were all he could manage at this moment.

"After they had told me about you, Andrei, I couldn't refuse to come. They knew that."

Razminsky laid his gloved hand on Turner's arm, stopping him. The streetlights glazed his spectacles.

"Thank you for coming," he said. "You've managed to keep part of yourself very secluded, Michael, for all your honors and very public life in medicine. I knew I would be intruding on that very private life of yours. If there had been any alternative, anyone else I could have turned to, I never would have suggested you. But I pray you will believe me when I say that you were my one hope."

Razminsky's apology faltered, and he was silent.

"I came here because of you," Turner said. "You're Komarov's doctor."

Turner looked past him, at the white silence of the street. Up ahead he could make out the aura from the floodlights trained on the Metropol Hotel. They had another fifteen minutes to walk, at most.

"I have always found it ironic, Andrei, that you of all people should be his doctor," Turner said.

"Because I am a Jew?"

"Because you're a Jew, and the man whose life we are trying to prolong is an anti-Semite who would have done the czars proud."

"Yes, he is that," Razminsky agreed, "but as you say, he is also a man, a human being."

"Your conscience doesn't trouble you?" Turner persisted. "The anguish he has brought to this country?"

"You are right that I serve the man who holds my people in bondage," Razminsky said quietly. "Yet every time I take the temperature of a Politburo aide, the gesture is worth one exit visa. When a ranking army officer enters my office to have a particular narcotic prescribed for his mistress, six more are free. A new Central Committee member desiring an excuse for a

Black Sea sojourn receives his 'medical convalescence' slip for twenty new passports issued families whose relatives are awaiting them in Jerusalem. As for Chairman Komarov, or anyone of his stature, well, that, my friend, is worth a writer, a scientist, even a dissident physician, someone who would otherwise never, never leave."

Michael Turner walked on, the thick soles of his boots plowing through the gray, crystalline slush.

"Some things don't change," Turner breathed, his stride steady.

"No," Razminsky echoed, his words barely audible above the soft wind. "Mine is a small contribution, but sometimes it has made a difference. That is the way we must proceed, at least for the time being. People like myself are needed here, to serve, to demand payment in whatever coin we can. We have a little bit of leverage, a sliver of influence, so that, yes, the bargains are kept. I would perform surgery on the Devil himself if a few more families could be gotten out. It is wrong before all God's laws, to reduce medicine to barter, but there is no other way. Sometimes even slaves dream of dark justice."

Michael Turner clasped his hands behind his back. He had not meant to challenge his friend's activities. He had no right to sit in judgment; he had never worked under conditions which demanded such compromises.

"We'll do fine with Komarov," he said. "Nothing will happen to him."

"I never thought anything would."

"What about yourself, Andrei?" Turner asked. "Will there be a day for you . . . to come out?"

"Perhaps," Razminsky said dreamily. "To tell the truth, I do not think of it. My wife and I were never blessed with children. We have only ourselves." He shrugged. "I will work as long as I can, as best I can. And when I can do no more, then I will leave."

"If you need help, anything at all, you'll call me," Turner said suddenly. "If there are any problems, I'll remind Komarov who saved his life."

"That is very kind of you," Razminsky said. "But Chairman Komarov will probably be long dead by then. We're going to give him a little time, nothing more."

"Jeanne and Christopher send their love," Michael Turner said, changing the subject.

"You must give them mine, and Zina's. Will you be bringing them to London for the Clarke-Bennett conference? We'd love to see them."

Because he was a physician, Razminsky understood better than anyone the agony Turner lived with because of his son.

"Promise you'll be there," Turner said.

The older man patted his younger colleague's arm.

"What's Komarov's status at the moment?"

The question almost caught Razminsky off guard, although he had been expecting it. He and Turner were friends. There had been the opportunity and the need for this quiet exchange. The operation had begun, however. Between now and the time Turner stepped into the operating theater, he would think of nothing but the surgery ahead. Even in his black and dreamless sleep, his brain would be smoothly, silently preparing to probe a human mind—the brain.

"He's had a chest X ray, an EKG, a urinalysis, kidney and liver tests, and a series of blood tests." Razminsky counted off the procedures. "The coagulation profile is normal, he is resting comfortably, if somewhat impatiently. Komarov's like a peasant that way: if he doesn't feel sick, he believes he isn't."

"When is scrub time for your people?"

"Nine o'clock."

"Which means I'm on at eleven . . ."

The Metropol Hotel glittered before them, a massive, vainglorious Stalinist cathedral basking in the spotlights clustered around it. These were so bright Turner could see the sparkle of the quartz chips embedded in the giant, rectangular stones.

"Time for a drink before bed?" he asked.

Razminsky shrugged. "I'm not driving," he laughed.

Turner glanced around at Razminsky, but he never saw him. From across the street his eyes were struck by a blinding light.

The Zil parked there was a military vehicle, heavy and cumbersome, with a massive front grill welded onto the bumper. It had been stolen earlier in the evening from the depot at Zorensk outside Moscow. The driver released the brake and let the heavy car coast forward, tires crunching the frozen snow. As the surveillance sedan approached, the Zil reached the edge of the wall that was shielding it. When the surveillance car crept into view, the Zil's driver gunned the engine, spinning the oversize tires. The vehicle swerved, its grill aimed at the cab of the Chaika. With a gnashing of metal on metal, the Zil rammed the smaller vehicle. The Zil's driver did not hear the screams from inside nor did he see the agent in the passenger seat desperately trying to get at his weapon while the driver fought to steer clear of the monster that had gored them. The Chaika was hopelessly outmatched. Inexorably the heavy Zil pushed it from the street onto the sidewalk.

A small Volga raced around the corner, skidding to a halt before Turner and Razminsky. Two figures leaped out through the wildly swinging back doors and instantly fell upon the American. One brought him to his knees, then both grabbed him under the arms, dragging him toward the car.

Razminsky snapped free of his astonishment and started after the men. But his abductors had Turner halfway into the back of the car before Razminsky reached them. A third man had seized Razminsky from behind, pressing a massive forearm against his throat.

"Don't interfere!" he hissed, and flung the surgeon away as easily as he might have a mannequin. Razminsky slipped on the ice, falling heavily, his fur hat gone, skull striking the icy stone.

Turner's heavy coat had absorbed some of the blows, and he was kicking back, hearing a grunt of pain. He was trying to twist around to get some leverage with his legs when from behind a hand reached under his jaw and viciously jerked his head back. There was the sound of escaping gas . . . and something that smelled of apricots.

His assailants piled back into the Volga. With a grinding of gears the smaller car fishtailed off down the dark street.

Only then did the Zil give the surveillance car one last push and back off, dragging with it a piece of the Chaika's fender. The twisted metal drew a stream of sparks in the furrows of snow along the street as the Zil made a tight turn and roared after the Volga. One of the surveillance team made it out of the Chaika and, though reeling wildly, he managed to squeeze off three shots before the target was out of range. Not that he could have harmed the military vehicle. Its tires, gastank, and windows, he knew, were completely bulletproof.

6

It was half past three in the morning, yet Foreign Minister Gorodin was still at his office at the ministry, working on a rough draft of a plan to maneuver one of his protégés into the Leningrad party secretariat. The task had occupied him most of the night. He wanted to finish it before going home for an hour's sleep. Then it was on to Rudin Hospital, to the observation gallery to watch Komarov undergo surgery.

One of his six telephones whirred softly, his private line, checked every day by a special detail from the Guards Directorate.

"Dmitri." The voice was Viktor Suslev's. "Can you meet me in the underground garage?"

"Of course."

Nothing more was said. Nor had Gorodin expected any elaboration, even over secure telephone lines. What they had to discuss would be said in the security of Suslev's massive Zil limousine. It was armor-plated and impenetrable, a three-and-a-half-ton mobile office protected by a complement of Suslev's personal staff. Minister Gorodin gathered up the papers he had been working on, deposited them in his safe, setting both the time lock and explosive antitampering device.

Minutes later he was downstairs in the vast underground parking lot, flanked by two internal security escorts, watching as Suslev's vehicle came to a stop in front of them.

"Good morning, Dmitri."

"Morning, Viktor."

Gorodin did not see Suslev until he was actually seated. A faint light came on automatically as the door closed, bathing Suslev's jowls in a pale yellow glow. Slowly he turned toward Gorodin, the eyes sparkling in their pouches like sapphires in cotton batting.

"Turner," Suslev said. "Doctor Michael Turner has been kidnapped."

"When?"

Suslev gazed at the clock embedded in the veneer above the work table.

"Twenty-two minutes ago."

"I think you had better give me what details you have," Gorodin said.

As the car dipped across the sidewalk and onto Smolensky Boulevard, Suslev explained exactly how the abduction had been carried out. The great car moved effortlessly toward the circumferential highway, one of the two that ringed the entirety of Moscow. It would stay on that roadway, cruising in circles until Suslev gave other instructions.

"Who took him, Viktor?" Gorodin asked. "As soon as the Americans find out, they will certainly want an explanation."

Suslev reached forward and pulled out a bottle of Bulgarian brandy he was particularly fond of. He poured out two shot glasses and handed one to Gorodin.

"I have no idea," he said. He raised his glass to Gorodin. "I think the question we must ask ourselves is who would have, no, *who is* going to benefit by Turner's absence from the operating room?"

"And what am I to tell the Americans when they call?"

"Perhaps *you* should take the initiative," Suslev suggested. "Call Ambassador Farraday and tell him the truth. Turner has been kidnapped. One of our surveillance team has been killed trying to protect him. We are questioning the survivors of the incident, and will share whatever we have as soon as it is available."

"But you know what their ambassador will be thinking," Gorodin said.

"Undoubtedly the same thing as President Telford and his cabinet." Suslev nodded. "That someone within the Soviet government or our security services has engineered the kidnapping."

"I shall have to try and disabuse them of that notion," Gorodin said. He threw his head back and laughed. "You know . . . you know, Viktor, it couldn't have worked out any better for us even if we *had* planned Turner's abduction. With the American out of the picture, who is left to operate on Komarov?"

"Whoever the sons of bitches are they deserve a medal from you," Suslev said. "Unfortunately, if I get to them before Bibnikov, all they will get is a bullet in the head."

At six fifteen A.M. the duty officer at the American Embassy on Chaykovsky Street logged a call from the office of the Foreign Minister. Gorodin himself was on the line, his voice worn and strained with fatigue, his manner brusque.

The duty officer put the minister on hold and buzzed the ambassador on the house line. At six seventeen Ambassador Farraday came on the scrambled line. Upon being informed of the caller's identity, he rushed to the bathroom to splash cold water on his face. Coughing, he returned to his bedside, fumbled for and lit a cigarette while arranging a pad and pencil in front of him.

"Good morning, Minister," Farraday said, speaking in perfect Russian. "You have my undivided attention. . . ."

Ten minutes later the ambassador hung up, and donned his blue jogging suit and Morland slippers. Leaving his quarters, he descended the three flights of stairs to the central reception area. In the company of the Marine guard he stepped into the elevator that provided the only access to the basement and stared at the crack between the doors during the eight-second descent. The door to the communications center was open; the two technicians on the graveyard shift were already clearing a secure electronic path for the message between Moscow and Washington.

"Lock us up," Farraday ordered his Marine escort. When the door was sealed, he took out the notes he had made during Gorodin's monologue and began to dictate.

Gastronom Number One at 14 Gorky Street was still known throughout Moscow by its prerevolutionary name, Yeliseyev's. The premier foodstore in the city, specializing in meats, fish, and delicacies from around the world, Gastronom was the real thing. Turn-of-the-century chandeliers glittered from their moorings three stories overhead, sparkling down on stacks of tins lined up along gleaming white marble counters. Stately fluted columns separated one department from another. Gastronom opened its doors punctually at seven o'clock. Among the first inside were the legation cooks, always searching for any specialties which might please their employers' palates. Although Sergei Bibnikov shopped at Gastronom regularly, he had never found it necessary to come so early. His security card ensured him a wide choice withheld from even extraordinary shoppers. Nonetheless he was there when the doors opened, having waited a full ten minutes outside in the blistering morning wind.

Inside he made for the pastry counter, where the aroma of fresh coffee gently erased the chill, and the smell of baking brioches reminded him he hadn't eaten properly for twenty-four hours. He had looked for Thompson outside but hadn't seen him. Yet Bibnikov knew the man he was supposed to meet must have been in that small crowd.

"Did you have a look at the lobsters today? God, I swear they're straight off Clarence Point."

Bibnikov looked down at the man who had come up beside him and watched as Charlie Thompson, Passport Officer at the American Embassy, reached up and snatched a warm pastry. The blond attendant behind the counter caught the motion out of the corner of her eye. She was about to intervene when Bibnikov pushed some English money at her and ordered two coffees.

"Obliged," Thompson drawled. "Let's get back to the fish counter. I want to get some of those beauties."

They were of a particular breed, this bulky Tatar and the

seemingly frail New Englander, whose tortoiseshell spectacle frames magnified his eyes to owlish proportions. Both had learned their craft during the Cold War; both had begun their careers in the European theater, where their paths first crossed. Later Thompson moved on to Southeast Asia, while Bibnikov, having provided the crucial evidence which brought Khrushchev down, formed the Special Investigations bureau. Theirs was an indiscriminate rivalry of the kind found between artists, whether it involved espionage or another great love—cooking.

The seafood counter was thirty feet long, enveloped in an aroma that made Thompson smile. He turned his attention to the assistant in starched overalls, who was deftly lifting the skin off a whole salmon.

"A *tour de force*." Thompson grinned as the skin came off with a flourish.

"You've heard what's happened," Bibnikov said, sipping his coffee glumly and watching the attendant slice up inch-thick steaks.

"Very disturbing," Thompson said, shaking his head. He hunched to get a better look at something in the glass display case.

"I want to get a message through to Telford."

"Seryosha, now don't tell me the moment's finally come. Great day, do you really want to come over to us?"

"As far as anyone's concerned, *I'm* trying to convert *you*."

"Ah, yes, I see. What is it you want the Great White Father in Washington to be apprised of?"

"Suslev is playing his cards very carefully." Bibnikov casually examined a packet of crackers. "He and the Foreign Minister are coordinating the operational details. Three units from Petrovka are conducting the search. No general alarm has gone out."

"I wouldn't have expected anything less," Thompson said, munching the last morsel of pastry. "You can't get away with a full alert in this village without the entire diplomatic corps hearing about it from their maids."

"Granted, but I want your superiors to understand that *I* will be going after Turner as well—independently of Suslev."

"Is that right?" Thompson considered what the Russian had just said. "That's real decent of you. Do you believe Suslev wasn't completely delighted to hear that Dr. Turner was operating on the old man?"

Bibnikov frowned and did not answer. The question was out of bounds, and both of them knew it.

"I can circumvent Suslev's objections," Bibnikov said. "My department answers directly to Chairman Komarov. I clearly have the authority to conduct a separate search."

"Seryosha." Thompson glanced at the produce shelves. "Believe me, I can appreciate what it means to have you on the case. But I've got to tell you, everybody is shitting bricks—the White House, State, National Security, even the desk fliers in Virginia. Everyone has hit his panic button." Thompson looked at his old adversary. "You gotta understand how bad this looks. Hell, Turner was brought over here on less than twenty-four hours' notice. No sooner does he land than someone snatches him. Now if you were in my position, what would you think? Your security is highly rated, and with good reason. It's damned hard for anyone to believe that Turner could have been snatched without official complicity. Sure, we know that you have dissident movements and underground movements, but they're nickel-and-dime outfits, Seryosha. You're going to have to talk hard and fast to convince my bosses that one of those groups had the wherewithal to grab Turner and, more important, that they somehow *knew exactly where he would be, and when.* His coming over at the invitation of the Ministry was probably the best-kept secret since the Man in the Iron Mask. He didn't really even *want* to come here. Even President Telford might not have been successful without this Dr. Razminsky's help."

"What are you telling me?" Bibnikov asked.

"I'm thinking out loud." Thompson raised his eyebrows. "I'm letting you know what the word is both here at the embassy and in Washington. Right now the White House is looking at two theories: Either there was one hell of a leak on your side, a leak which translates into high-level penetration of your security services, or else you've got yourself a renegade bunch within the KGB or somewhere else." Thompson paused. "Seryosha, if you have another scenario to suggest, then let's hear it. Give me something I can take back to Langley. Changing the guard is one thing. Involving an American guest like this is quite another. Makes all those first-strike types mighty nervous."

Bibnikov raised his eyes. "I don't know what to say to you," he whispered. "There is that possibility." He took Thompson by the arm. "But what I want you to understand is that I'm going after this Michael Turner. I will do whatever I have to. We both want Komarov alive." Bibnikov pinched a head of lettuce. "The President must be dissuaded from taking any rash action. Chairman Komarov drifts in and out of consciousness. If any substantive decision has to be made and he is not capable, then the Politburo will be convened. They will try to resolve any crisis collectively, and you, better than most, understand the kind of thing that can result from that. Don't let them act precipitously in Washington."

"I'll do what I can," Thompson said, as though he were talking to himself. "I'll convey the message and the urgency. Somehow I don't believe you'd be jerking me around on this. No, sir, not on this."

Bibnikov's hand dipped into his waistcoat pocket and he flashed his identification to the attendant.

"Six Maine lobsters," he said. "For him."

"Now that's *real* decent of you, Seryosha," Thompson grinned. "You figuring I ought to lay on some kind of spread? You're invited, naturally."

"I can't stand those animals," Bibnikov told him. "You know that."

"Not animals, crustaceans," Thompson corrected him. "Don't you love those little sickle things they're wavin' at us?"

They stood there with their hands behind their backs and watched as the attendant plucked the lobsters out of the salt-water tank.

"Hey, Seryosha, don't you think that one looks like Beria?"

7

His first sensation was of bitter cold covering him like a shroud. The dankness was broken by breath warming the edge of his face, the scent trailing along his cheeks, then disappearing. Michael Turner groaned and opened his eyes.

"You are all right. Quite safe."

The accented voice belonged to a woman. Turner squeezed his eyes shut against the glare of the overhead light and turned his face to one side. He started to speak and broke into a fit of coughing. His throat was terribly dry.

The woman, with her arm around his shoulder, helped him to sit up, and brought a metal cup to his lips. The water was tepid and sweet, and she held it too high, so that some of it trickled down Turner's chin. He craned his head around, trying to catch a glimpse of her face. Her hair was russet, with streaks of deepest brown, pulled back tightly and tied. The face emphasized high, slanted cheekbones that dipped past a delicate nose, full lips, and a small but prominent chin. Her eyes were dark gray.

Turner drank the water and lay back on the hard cot. From the reflection of the light he saw that the walls of the room were white, glossy tile. Embedded in the ceiling were high-intensity bulbs that gave a luster to the sinks along the far wall. There were cabinets above the sinks, with doors missing. He recognized an odor, a disinfectant, a surgical disinfectant.

"Where am I?"

"I can't tell you that."

"Why not?"

The girl leaned forward and raised his eyelids. "The effect of the drug has almost worn off," she said, "but don't try to stand up yet."

"Why shouldn't I know?" Turner repeated.

"It's for your own protection."

Turner tried to sit up, but his stomach muscles deserted him.

"You know better than that, doctor," she admonished.

"Kidnapped," Turner muttered and closed his eyes. "Goddamn, kidnapped . . ."

"It was the only way we could reach you without their interfering," the girl said.

"You know who I am, I presume," Turner muttered.

"Yes. And why you have come to Moscow."

"You must have the government's blessing," he said, running his tongue over his lips. The cot was hard, the slats dug into the base of his spine.

"Wrong, doctor, we are far removed from official circles."

Through the red haze that fell over his vision as he peered at the lights, he saw her open the door. Then nothing made any sense anymore. The man who entered, although dressed in black turtleneck and heavy padded trousers, had a crucifix on a chain around his neck.

"I am Father Gregory Rowitz," the visitor said, coming toward him. "You have nothing to fear from us, believe me."

Turner managed a short, guttural laugh. "Nothing to fear! What the hell are you trying to do to me? I'm scheduled to operate. Dr. Razminsky—" He stopped short. What had happened to Razminsky!

"Andrei Razminsky is not with us. We had no need of him."

But Turner had scarcely heard. If Razminsky was safe, he would get to the authorities, the American Embassy. She leaned forward to check his pupils.

"I take your silence to mean that you are working out the

situation in your mind, doctor. Obviously we were correct in our dilution of the Methazine."

"The dose was correct," Turner retorted coldly. The numbing effect was melting away from his muscles. "You'd have a corpse on your hands by now if I had a heart condition."

"We knew that you did not suffer from such an ailment."

"May I get up?" The dampness in the room had crept under his skin. He wanted to walk to shake off the chill.

"You may stand up, but do not move around."

"It's too damn cold just to stand!"

"We have certain amenities," the priest said. He reached over and depressed a switch. Almost immediately a current of warm air flowed underneath the cot.

Carefully Turner swung his legs off the cot and stretched his arms out wide. He rotated his head, working out the numbness of his neck muscles.

"Are you nauseous, doctor?" the girl asked.

"No."

"Very well, if you're up to it then, we can talk. The sooner we can come to terms, the sooner you can leave."

Turner looked at the priest. He was an older man, but he appeared to be fit and strong, more like a farmer than a clergyman. Still, it was two against one.

"You have a captive audience," Turner said.

"Bravo, Doctor Turner." The girl smiled tightly. "Your sense of humor is encouraging. To begin with, this man is Father Gregory Rowitz, late of the parish of St. John in Warsaw. We wish to assure you that we are not terrorists, although you might object to such a disclaimer, given the treatment you have received at our hands. If there had been any other way to reach you, to speak with you without risking our lives or your own, we would have used it. That was not feasible. You'll have to accept our apologies."

"Go on," said Turner.

The girl nodded to the priest, who took over.

"Are you familiar with the name Karol Stanislawski?" Father Rowitz asked.

"Stanislawski? You can't be serious."

"Perfectly serious, doctor. Karol Cardinal Stanislawski."

"Christ Almighty," Turner said, his shoulders slumping forward.

"Yes, we have him—here, doctor," Father Rowitz said. "You must have heard of the tragedy in Warsaw on Christmas Eve. The massacre. We managed to get the cardinal out."

There was a gap in their logic: Move a fugitive from Warsaw to *Moscow* in order to save him?

"The other fact you may not know about," he said, "is that His Eminence suffers from a disease. Idiopathic hypertrophic subaortic stenosis. You are familiar with it?"

"Yes."

Rowitz came toward him. "Then you can appreciate why we have gone to such lengths to reach you," the priest said, his voice wavering. "His Eminence was to be moved to the West as soon as possible. However, all the routes were watched. Every avenue of escape, overland, by ship or by plane, was denied us. The situation was critical; we could not bring His Eminence to the West, and he could not remain in Poland much longer without being discovered. There was only one course to take, and that was to move him where no one would ever even dream of looking. We could not move him west, so we went east."

"To Moscow."

"Yes. However, the privations he has been subjected to during these various transfers, the conditions of these . . . well, they were the best possible under the circumstances."

"I don't understand," Turner said. "What is it you want me to do? I'm not a cardiologist."

Rowitz nodded. "We know. But there is no one else. The cardinal is a figure who stands up for those who dare not stand up for themselves, who speaks for those who cannot be heard, who prays for those whose prayers have never been answered. If he is allowed to die, the barbarians will have won. There is no other Stanislawski. We are asking you, doctor, to save him."

Turner was struck by the vehemence of the priest's words, but he could not give them false hope.

"And how do you expect me to do that?" he demanded.

"His condition isn't something I can prescribe a pill for. Stanislawski needs hospitalization—immediately. From what you say, surgery may be inevitable."

"None of which he will receive here," the girl interrupted.

Hope, he thought. Sometimes hope can be so pernicious.

"I will examine him if that's what you want," he said. "As long as you're aware there's nothing I can do."

"There is a great deal you can do, doctor," the woman corrected him. "Which you *must* do!"

She took a folded paper from her pocket and extended it toward Turner. He took it, puzzled.

"Go ahead. Look at it."

The drawing was that of a cemetery with rows of headstones. There was a circle around one of them.

"What is this place?"

"A cemetery, doctor. The circled grave belongs to your father."

"It was the only thing which we could *offer* you as payment," the priest said.

"What could you know about my father?" Turner said. "He died over twenty-five years ago."

"I know Peterson Turner was never released because of Komarov's personal orders," she said. "At the time of your father's arrest Komarov was the ranking officer in state security."

"What are you saying?" Turner paled.

"How else do you want me to say it? Komarov murdered your father? He stood up to Komarov for three months. That is too long for anyone. In the end Komarov had nothing to trade with, even if he had wanted to, and your father's heart gave out."

"That's hard to believe," Turner said. "If Komarov had caused his death, he would never submit himself to a scalpel held by his son, would he?"

"Wrong, doctor. You did not know until this moment that Komarov was responsible. Your people might have suspected his complicity at the time, perhaps even knew of it, but they never told you. They never say anything that is not absolutely necessary."

"Is there any proof?" Turner said, his words scarcely audible.

"There are no records. Even if there were, we could never get to them."

"Who are you?" Turner demanded. He was sweating profusely, his throat parched and hoarse. He looked at the woman, studying her features, memorizing them, trying to fit a nationality with the facial features and accent. And the priest, what role did he play? A misguided man of God, whose faith had run out like the sands of an hourglass, to be replaced by desperate politics.

Neither made any reply.

"Every moment we waste, His Eminence suffers."

Turner sat on the hard iron-frame cot and brought his hands out in front of him where he could see them clearly.

"I think the drug has worn off," he said tonelessly. He looked across at the priest, who was watching him closely. "Take me to Stanislawski."

With the woman in the lead they descended two flights, coming out into what appeared to be an old underground garage. Overhead, the ceiling had cracked under the weight and erosion of moisture, the water dripping silently onto the poured-concrete floor, creating rivulets of rust-streaked water. Rats scurried somewhere beyond the light cast by a few weak bulbs.

"What is this place?" Turner asked.

Neither one answered him.

The priest led them over to the far wall, to a metal-faced fire door, which he rolled back. The room beyond was large, forty by twenty feet, and in much better condition than the outer room. The concrete floor and cinderblock walls had a fresh coat of whitewash. The air was clear, though sterile and odorless—obviously filtered. The faint hiss of a compressor or generator muffled all other sounds. In the center of the room was the medical equipment—all of it, according to Turner's fleeting appraisal, first-rate. There was also a single standard hospital bed.

Turner wouldn't have expected much better if he had been shown this arrangement in a regular hospital, but in this godforsaken pit it was truly amazing. The time and grinding effort it must have taken to set this room up, feed in enough electrical power to run the equipment without anyone above-ground becoming suspicious. The machines themselves—Swiss, German, even American—where had they gotten them? And all this obviously accomplished in secrecy.

"Temperature control?" Turner asked.

The woman looked back at him. "Sixty-eight degrees Fahrenheit. Humidity twenty-two percent. The air is recycled through a Weber filter driven by an independent generator."

"Equipment?"

"One ELG, a Bausch-Roderer life-support system, Timoli surgical lights, the standard oxygen units, full dispensary."

Turner examined the equipment piece by piece, then came over to the bed, adjusting a surgeon's mask over his mouth and nose.

Karol Cardinal Stanislawski was a large man, six feet three inches, with the physique of a drayman, the massive chest rising and falling regularly as the respirator kept feeding him enough oxygen to keep the body alive. A tiny tube made its way down his throat and was taped to the bridge of his nose.

Karol Cardinal Stanislawski . . . When he had time, Turner preferred biographies to any other reading. Jeanne had brought him a copy of Stanislawski's life, and once he had started reading he spent three consecutive nights with it. Since then he had returned to the biography time and again, rereading passages he had marked, trying to work his way into the mind and soul of the man whose words had so profoundly marked him. A man larger than life, bearing a name known to the farthest corner of the earth. The child who had cheated Auschwitz to become the apostle of defiance and brotherhood in a sealed-off world that at once suspected and cried out for them.

At the age of eighteen Stanislawski published a critique of religious arguments, two years later his "Christian Response to the Holocaust" had brought down on him the censure of Rome itself. Yet his history of the Catholic Church in Poland was impeccable, bringing him to the attention of Bishop Wyzinski, who became the youngster's mentor and protector. Ordained at age twenty, he spent nearly nine years in the provinces before being recalled to Warsaw and elevated to monsignor. By this time he was known throughout Poland as a champion of human rights, heir apparent to such as Mindszenty of Hungary, who had fought the lonely battles of conscience against Soviet tanks and occupying armies.

At the unheard-of age of forty Stanislawski was made archbishop of Warsaw. Five years later the whole world came to know of him when the Nobel Committee awarded him the peace prize for his writings and sermons. Knowing that he might not be permitted to return to Poland if he left, Stanislawski did not journey to Oslo. Instead, protected to some degree by the archbishop's mantle, he made himself a rallying point for those whose lives and dreams had been ground down by the Communist regime. Too late the successors of Gierek and Brezhnev learned that such a man should have been seduced into exile, where, away from his native soil, his words would lose their potency. Recognizing Stanislawski as a charismatic figure who had won the allegiance of the millions of Catholics in Eastern Europe, Rome had bestowed upon him the cardinal's red hat, placing him squarely in opposition to the secular authorities for the remainder of his natural life.

Turner's eyes flickered over the life-support system. The readings indicated that the patient was exhibiting considerable ventricular irritability. Gently the surgeon took the cardinal's head between his hands. His eyes opened briefly, his fingers moved under the sheet, seeking human contact. He attempted to speak, but no words came. From behind his mask Turner's eyes tried to convey reassurance. When he drew his hands back, his fingers were covered with blood.

"What's happened to him?" Turner whispered to the girl. "He's *pumping* blood out!"

"The head wound," the girl said. "He was slightly injured in the explosion at the cathedral. I dressed it as best I could."

"Do you have *any* kind of detailed history on him?"

The girl shook her head. "We couldn't get to his doctor in time. He was arrested. The clinic was closed by internal security, the files removed."

"You've been letting him bleed to death," Turner said. He went to the improvised sink and began scrubbing his hands.

"Intravenous xylocaine and propanol," he called over his shoulder. The girl was reaching for the solution when the buzzer went off. Turner's head jerked around, eyes riveted on the monitor screen. Ventricular fibrillation. Failing pulse.

Turner walked back to the bed, his gaze never leaving the cardiac monitor.

"He's all right?" the priest asked weakly.

"No. He isn't. Think. Has he been ill in the last few weeks? A bad cold, the flu? Fever, muscle aches, a bad cough, shortness of breath? Give me *something* to work with!"

The girl glanced at the priest.

"Yes, he's had a cold," Father Rowitz said.

"What about dizziness?"

"Yes, he's complained of that," the priest said nervously.

The woman was watching Turner carefully, almost feeling the possible diagnoses being called up, scrutinized, rejected. The surgeon, domineering and callous, was in his element.

"X rays," Turner hammered on. "There had to have been X rays."

"But they didn't show *anything*," the priest protested. "Wait. I remember something about a silhouette—"

"That's it," Turner muttered. "Pericardial effusion."

"What is that?" she said.

"Fluid in the sac surrounding the heart, restricting the heart's ability to pump blood in and out." He looked at her with complete calm, she thought. "A situation complicated by his wound." Turner held out his hand. "Cardiac syringe."

"What are you going to do?" the girl demanded.

"I don't suppose you have an ultrasound echo cardiogram?"

"I don't even know what it is."

"A monitoring unit that plots cardiac echoes over time and gives a graphic readout of the internal heart structure. If I had that, I could tell you if he does have pericardial effusion."

"I'm sorry—" the girl started to say.

"So am I. Give me the needle."

"What are you going to do?" she persisted stubbornly.

"Drain that sac."

"But you can't be sure of your diagnosis!"

Turner let his hand fall to his side.

"All right, *you* decide," he said coldly. "Without a defibrillating unit, the next attack could kill him. Better than a fifty-fifty chance. If I go for the sac, relieve the pressure, we can buy him time."

"And if there is no fluid in the sac? If you're wrong and injure him even more?" she challenged.

"Then I could kill him."

She stared at him, incredulous at the ease with which he had spoken the words.

"You're willing to risk that."

"Not a question of risk," Turner said. "There really isn't any choice. So, go ahead. Decide."

She snatched up the needle and held it out to him in her gloved hand.

As soon as the instrument was in his hand, Turner's mind cleared. He concentrated on nothing but the heart, hidden under a few square inches of skin. He tried to imagine it, visualize the sac clinging to the outer wall, pulsating in time to the feeble rhythm. He unsheathed the six-inch needle. He was staring down at the chest. Pulling the skin back between two fingers, he slid the metal into the space between the third and fourth ribs.

"Sponge."

The entry was clean, the welling of the blood slight, manageable. He closed his eyes, feeling the syringe pass through the thin layer of fat, then the more substantial muscle. It was in about two inches when he felt resistance. Either the sac or the heart.

"Have the shocks ready . . ."

He drove the needle home, at the same time retracting the plunger. Rich, dark blood swirled into the capsule.

"Come on," he whispered. "I didn't miss."

The blood continued to pour in, then abruptly turned pink and finally stopped. The rest of the syringe was filling with a clear, viscous liquid.

"Lucked out . . . check the blood pressure."

"Ninety over sixty."

"Still too high." He retracted faster.

"Dropping . . . eighty over sixty."

Turner checked the amount of fluid in the syringe. Three hundred sixty cc's, almost twelve ounces. The sac must have been distended enormously, exerting unbearable pressure. He withdrew the needle, dropping it into a tray where it clattered, rolled, and finally lay still. His face was burnished with sweat, the perspiration stinging his eyes.

"Here, use this." The girl handed him a towel. Turner pressed it hard against his face.

"I'll stay with him as long as I can," Turner said. He checked his watch. A quarter to eight. A little over seventy-five minutes before Komarov was to undergo surgery. "Find a way to get me to Rudin. To Komarov."

As he turned his attention to the monitors, Turner felt a hand on his shoulder. He turned around to see the priest beside him.

"We will not forget this."

The woman had held up better than he had dared hope, but it was Stanislawski who had helped him most. Turner had never seen a constitution as strong. Somewhere in that awesome body the man's sheer will to live had kept the heart beating in spite of surgical trauma. As though it had a sense of its own, the heart, and body, had responded.

"Thank you," said Father Rowitz.

Michael Turner arched his stiff back. "You're welcome."

8

In the half-light of the morning sun Moscow lay like a city under siege. To the thousands of citizens who plodded their way to work through the gray coldness nothing appeared to be amiss. But behind the façade, the city was churning.

From the vast underground holds beneath Dzerzhinsky Square, waves of official cars swept into the streets. Their destinations predetermined by the computer at communications control, they made for the railway stations, bus depots, airports, and roadblocks which had been set up along the major highways leading to and from the city. Supplemented by manpower from other directorates, surveillance division agents spread out across Moscow. Using the Metropol Hotel as their command post, they fanned out in all directions, a remorseless army that left nothing unturned in its path. Hotels, churches, synagogues, were all systematically searched. Intourist groups about to begin their daily itinerary were infiltrated. All departments having anything to do with foreigners were ordered to cooperate with KGB liaison teams. Agents rode the trolleys and buses, rounded up all the taxi drivers who had been on duty at the time of Turner's kidnapping, and a special squad was assigned to cover every station within the Moscow metro system.

In the Metropol Hotel itself the entire fourth floor had been given over to KGB forensic experts. The body of the dead agent first had been carefully scrutinized for any clues that might lead to the identification of the kidnappers. At Dzerzhinsky Square headquarters bystanders who had seen part of the kidnapping were desperately trying to absolve themselves. The KGB inquisitors were not easily convinced; pawns were to be brushed off the board as needed. There would be no consequences for the investigators. Their overriding concern was the whereabouts of the American doctor, now missing for ten hours.

Minister Gorodin stepped out of his limousine into the cold dawn that clung to Moscow. He made his way into the ornate nineteenth-century building and hurried up the magnificent spiral staircase to his flat on the third floor. Neither the hour nor the previous night's events seemed to have had any effect on him. On the contrary his energy was bordering on the manic. He marveled at the way fate was weaving his destiny, eliminating the obstacles between himself and his goals with such flawless ease. He was certain that it would not cheat him now. Turner would not be found in time to perform the operation. He might not be found for hours or days . . . and with every hour that passed Komarov came closer and closer to death. In Komarov's death Gorodin saw his own rebirth and the dawn of a new era for his country.

Gorodin let himself in, left his coat in the hall closet, and silently walked down the corridor that ran the length of the suite, pausing only when he reached the bedroom. She was still asleep, as he knew she would be, with only a sheet covering her, the blond hair spread over the pillow, a curve of breast rising and falling as she breathed. The girl was only eighteen, an understudy for one of the dancers with the Kirov Ballet Company. Gorodin had watched her dance and knew that she would never leap over the line that separated the mediocre from the great. Even though she was tall and muscular, her movements lacked courage and imagination. But she suited his purpose. He enjoyed women who were lean and hard.

Quietly he walked to his study and slumped into his favorite armchair. Behind him in the glass case were his mementos and medals. He felt at ease, despite the events of the previous day that had kept him at his desk all night.

If only Komarov had died a year ago instead of wasting away; if only surgery had been out of the question, then, in a matter of weeks following the chairman's death, Gorodin would have become the next chairman of the Central Committee, Komarov's successor, and sole heir. As it was, Marshal Pavlichenko, the Defense Minister, was a partisan of Kobalevsky's. He controlled the majority of the Politburo, since eight of its members were as indebted to Komarov for their positions as was Pavlichenko. Had the old man died, the debts would have been canceled. Pavlichenko would retain control over three, perhaps four members, but the rest would have raised their noses to the wind, sniffing out Komarov's successor. And there were only two possibilities. Pavlichenko himself was ruled out because he was a military man; Suslev was too violent and tainted, and the Politburo would never choose him. The choice came down to Gorodin or Kobalevsky. The remaining members of the Politburo eventually would have to line up behind one of them.

Gorodin glanced over at the photograph of himself and the bulky man beside him. They were disparate figures, Suslev and himself, examples of extremes not only physically but emotionally. Yet they were bound by common threads stronger than their differences: an insatiable thirst for power, and a certain vision of Russia. Suslev had leaped into prominence at the beginning of the Stalinist purges. His hands had been washed in more blood than could ever have been imagined, yet he had not wavered in his attempt to subjugate an entire nation and bend it to the Party's will. For years Suslev had stood behind Stalin, then Malenkov, and finally Khrushchev; he had exercised great power while never really appearing to. When Suslev at last stepped out of the shadows, he did so reluctantly. But by then he knew there was no one to challenge him.

He found his *tabula rasa* in Dmitri Gorodin, a bezprizornik—waif of the devastating collectivization program carried out in the Ukraine in 1932—an orphan who had survived the war but whose horrible privations he never forgot. A specialist in the history of warfare and diplomacy, Gorodin believed that only as an insular entity could Russia survive and prevail over the West. She had to remain faithful to the Stalinist orthodoxy. She could never turn her back on the West or ignore the menace to the east. Internal discipline and military preparedness were paramount. Gorodin was ruthless with those who preached coexistence and disdainful of ideologues who did not recognize that even alliances with other Communist nations were only temporary accommodations. Gorodin was the purest of the Slavophiles. Self-sufficiency was the critical objective, and even exploitation of one's neighbors was the immutable right of the strongest.

In the eyes of Gorodin the likes of Kobalevsky were an abomination. Granted that science and technical genius had enabled Russia to hold her own against the West, even to overtake capitalism in some respects. But Kobalevsky, in his desire for further and greater advances, had acquiesced to a terrible compromise. To him the West was not the opponent but a vast repository of knowledge and gadgetry which could be mined for the sake of Soviet technological progress. He did not think in terms of the national will or his duty to the revolution, but rather improvement of the individual citizen's lot. He was a heretic.

Chairman Komarov had brought the country to a crossroads. Now Gorodin would guide it back to the powerful isolationism from which it would draw strength, just as the Americans had done until the world war. He would not permit Kobalevsky to expose Russia to the West. She had her industrial and military base, her own experts, scientists, inventors. What the postwar leadership had set out to accomplish had been achieved. Now was the time to consolidate, to strengthen internal power, to discipline the national will.

From a drawer in the coffee table Gorodin took out a sheaf of papers. The Foreign Minister once again reviewed the details of the plan whose genesis could be traced back to the last years of Stalin's reign. The memorandum outlined one of many contingency plans to be used in case of internal revolt. Drafted by a former KGB director, Yuri Andropov, read and annotated by Brezhnev and Kosygin, the memorandum outlined the step-by-step procedure for the suppression of certain national and

ethnic minorities within the Soviet Union. Gorodin was amazed
by its clarity. Every detail had been specified, down to the exact
number of boxcars and locomotives that would be needed to
transport the dissidents. The number of policemen and militia
needed in various cities for the roundups, the priorities of the
selection process—which factions would be picked up first,
the disinformation plans which would throw the foreign press
off the scent, the capacities of the various installations where the
dissidents would eventually be liquidated—all of this and more
had been anticipated.

It had taken Gorodin four and a half months of hard work
to put this new program together. During that time he had
relied heavily on Suslev to provide him with the minute details
needed to ensure success. Every day that he sat down with his
papers Gorodin realized the enormity of the risk he was taking.
If anyone were ever to discover what he was doing, he would
not live to see the next sunrise. Komarov would never believe
that Gorodin was not plotting against him. Pavlichenko and
others of his kind would be even quicker. They would see the
plan only as a demonstration of Gorodin's intransigence, intransigence they privately thought bordered on megalomania. Yet
Gorodin knew he had to proceed. The next ruler of Soviet
Russia would be the minister who acted decisively and without
pity at the moment Komarov breathed his last. Half-measures
meant certain failure. But what he had not anticipated was the
old man's hanging on like this. Every day that Komarov survived, the danger of exposure grew. The chairman lived, clutching at the remnants of his life, becoming more remote and
suspicious as age and illness took their toll.

Gorodin and Suslev had loyal cadres within the KGB and
its sister services, in the army, especially the eastern units, and in
all ranks of the Party hierarchy and the vast administrative networks that ruled Russia. These were men and women who had
committed themselves to Gorodin. A delicate balance of fear
and the promise of rewards assured their loyalty. Yet their patience and their courage were finite. He could not leave them
waiting much longer. If he could not activate his plan soon,
somewhere the masterly construction would give way. A few

untimely words from a labor camp administrator, and the proud edifice would begin to tumble. Unless he acted, he would lose control over his destiny.

But today it will all be nearly over with, Gorodin thought. Chance had intervened. The American surgeon who could have prolonged Gorodin's anxious vigil had vanished, and the chairman was in mortal danger. In a few hours the Politburo would meet without the chairman in attendance, and Gorodin would initiate the last phase of his campaign.

9

The emergency Presidium session was held not in the Kremlin's Arsenal, as was the custom, but in the new building constructed by the KGB in 1972 for its foreign operations unit.

The conference room on the sixth and top floor was swept for electronic implants. After the technicians had departed, the doors to the emergency fire staircase were sealed; two elevators were programmed to travel directly from the lobby to the sixth floor. At seven o'clock the commander of the security unit was informed by the guards at the entrance that the room was to be made ready. The Politburo was arriving. According to instructions, the commander unlocked the inner door and lighted the old Tiffany lamps. Walnut paneling gleamed under the soft light; the crystal ashtrays, glasses, and ice water decanters flashed their fire off the oval ebony table that dominated the suite. Thirteen leather wingback chairs were set out, with Suslev's heavily reinforced chair placed at the head of the table. The security unit commander had just enough time to flick away a dust mote from the table's gleaming surface before the first two of the Politburo's thirteen members arrived.

Slim and of average height, Dmitri Gorodin, at age fifty-five, had retained the compact, muscular figure of a gymnast, even after thirty years. Following Gorodin was Viktor Suslev, chief of the KGB. So overweight he used a cane, and a ferocious chain smoker, Viktor Suslev defied every medical precept. His body had degenerated to the point that it was physically difficult for him to move around, hence the cane. The two men moved into one corner of the room, away from the chief of staff who guarded the doors.

"What of Stanislawski?" Gorodin asked without preamble.

"Nothing yet." Suslev whispered hoarsely. "Warsaw is a sealed city. We will find him."

"What is the mood of the others? How has the situation with the Poles affected them?"

"Badly," Suslev said abruptly. "They're all skittish. Especially Pavlichenko. You can't blame him. I may have lost a few men from the Surveillance Directorate. He has a hundred times that many from his frontline units on the edge of the city. Since Komarov lost consciousness for an hour after making the decision to eliminate Stanislawski, no one knows where we stand."

"Perhaps that uncertainty should be remedied here and now," Gorodin said.

"These are not the right circumstances," Suslev said. "No one in the Politburo except you and I knows exactly why Komarov decided to neutralize Stanislawski. They have no idea you spent an hour convincing him that the cardinal would be issuing a call to rebellion. I can't believe Komarov appreciated half of the so-called evidence you put before him. He was too tired, too disoriented."

"But in the end he went along with my recommendation," Gorodin reminded him.

"True, but you did not convince him to act quickly enough. Now we have a would-be martyr on our hands. You can be sure that after this meeting the others, especially Pavlichenko and Kobalevsky, will start digging into the reasons why the chairman suddenly wanted Stanislawski out of the way. I suggest you do not permit them to use this meeting as a forum in which to start questioning you. Let us stay with the matter that we came here to discuss."

"You realize, Viktor, that I had no choice," Gorodin said. "Somehow Stanislawski knew something about our current project. There was no question that he had to be dealt with."

"He still has to be stopped," Suslev said. "Until we find

Stanislawski and rid ourselves of him, do not question Komarov's capacity or incapacity to act." He nodded at the other Politburo members coming through the door. Vladimir Pavlichenko stalked into the room like the old soldier he was, with long, confident strides. Five of the twelve members present could still be counted on to support whatever position the general adopted.

"They're following him like the sheep they are," Gorodin muttered, watching as the other ministers clustered around the marshal. The only one who did not join was Lapusnyk, Minister of Foreign Trade and Gorodin's favorite.

"Don't be too hasty," Suslev cautioned him. "Pavlichenko can't hold them forever. Eventually it will be a choice between you"—he paused, watching the last member enter—"and him."

Oleg Kobalevsky, Minister of Science and Technology, stood apart from the marshal's group and looked directly at Gorodin.

"I think it is time," the KGB chief announced.

As the senior minister present, Viktor Suslev greeted them all, moving through the assembly. He signaled to his chief of staff to close and lock the doors, then slowly lowered his great torso into his reinforced chair. One by one the others took their seats.

"Comrades, we are all aware of the reason for this meeting," Suslev wheezed. "You have all been informed that Chairman Komarov lost consciousness shortly after midnight on Tuesday. The latest medical bulletins state that he is not in any immediate danger and at present is resting. Therefore I suggest that we transact our business as quickly as possible so that we may return to our respective ministries and continue to monitor the crisis in Poland."

Suslev looked down the table and pressed a button underneath the table. To his right the door to the adjoining room opened, the guard standing aside to let Dr. Razminsky pass.

Three days earlier Dr. Razminsky had celebrated his sixty-first birthday. Today his eyes, usually sparkling behind the bifocals, were somber. There was no fear in them. Razminsky was not intimidated by his august hosts.

"Doctor Razminsky, welcome," Suslev said courteously. "We thank you for your cooperation. We are relieved your injuries were minor."

Their faces turned toward the physician as he stood at the head of the table.

"Gentlemen, you have asked me to personally explain to you the exact nature of Chairman Komarov's illness. Several weeks ago Chairman Komarov began to suffer from abrupt but severe attacks of vertigo, accompanied by vomiting, a hot swelling sensation in his face, and a lack of motor coordination. I subjected him to an intensive examination. The results were quite clear. Chairman Komarov was suffering from an intracranial aneurysm. A cerebral angiogram showed a saccular aneurysm, which is linked to the primary vessel by a stalk of variable caliber. In this case the intracranial aneurysm is compressing one of the adjacent cranial nerves. However, we have been quite fortunate. Thus far there has only been a minor leakage from the aneurysm, which has caused headaches, numbness, speech disruption, and general debilitation. If the aneurysm had ruptured then, the patient would have experienced agonizing headaches, immediate loss of consciousness leading to a coma, and some degree of permanent neurological impairment. And finally death."

"Doctor," Gorodin asked, "is there any way to calculate when, or even if, the aneurysm will burst?"

"None whatsoever." Razminsky poured out a glass of water. "Chairman Komarov is alive not because of any medical treatment, but because the aneurysm is only leaking and has not yet burst." He sipped the ice-cold water. "The only way to deal with such a condition is to remove the aneurysm. This requires a surgical procedure involving the use of a laser device. Quite simply, nothing *but* a laser will work because of the constraints imposed by the delicacy of this particular area of the brain. You have my reports concerning this procedure, as well as my comments on the facilities available. These are more than adequate.

All that is lacking, gentlemen, are the skilled hands to perform this operation."

"A point," Suslev interjected, raising a critical finger. "I find it curious that out of the thousands of physicians in our country you were not able to recommend even one who could perform such an operation. Instead we have had to embarrass ourselves by enlisting the aid of this American, Turner, who has been imprudent enough to be abducted."

"Laser surgery is a very new field," Razminsky replied. "Soviet medicine is advanced but not in the field of neurology. We simply do not have the experience or the expertise to attempt such radical surgery."

"You wanted to be certain there were no alternatives beforehand," Gorodin suggested.

"And are there any?" Pavlichenko asked, his hands folded in his lap.

"No."

"Then by all means, doctor, enlighten us," Pavlichenko said.

"I advised that a specialist from outside the Soviet Union be summoned to operate on Chairman Komarov." Razminsky spoke slowly. "There was only one man for the operation and he was, and is, Michael Turner, the foremost practitioner of laser surgery. He is also a neurosurgeon."

"He is also missing." Pavlichenko leaned forward, his elbows on the polished table.

Silence descended. Gorodin cleared his throat and spoke. "Surely another expert could be found, at least in Eastern Europe."

"Doctor Razminsky," said Kobalevsky, "*can* such an expert be found anywhere else?"

"No. Gentlemen, there is no one in the Soviet Union, nor in Europe or the United States or Canada who can perform this operation. If Chairman Komarov is to live, then Dr. Michael Turner must perform the surgery."

Gorodin rubbed his eyes. "How much time does the chairman have?"

"I cannot tell you that in terms of hours or days, or even

weeks," Razminsky said. "The only thing I am certain of is that the aneurysm is leaking. That is the only thing that has prevented it from bursting. But the pressure within the aneurysm is mounting. It is only a matter of time before the inevitable happens." Razminsky leaned forward, his hands on the table, fingers splayed out. "There is no other way. I urge you all to act with dispatch."

"Doctor." Gorodin looked exhausted. "I will not ask you how much time we have. I do ask what the chances of success would be now if we did locate Dr. Turner within a reasonable period of time. How much longer will Semyon Arkadyevich live as a result of the surgery?"

"With Dr. Turner the chances of success are perhaps eighty percent. It would give the chairman more than a year. For half of that time he may be incapacitated; the condition becomes more debilitating as time progresses."

"A year is a long time," Suslev observed.

If only Komarov had died, he thought. The surgery had a chance of being successful. Chairman Komarov would be granted a reprieve, as would Kobalevsky.

"I've received the most recent report," Suslev said, moving his empty water glass in a circular motion. "All measures are being taken to identify and arrest the attackers, and we are sparing no effort to find Michael Turner. There will be an open line between the Foreign Ministry and the American Embassy so that I may pass on word of new developments as they occur. At this point, of course, I cannot speculate on why Doctor Turner was abducted or by whom. The obvious conclusion, however, is that there has been a flagrant security breach. Time is running out, comrades. We must return to our posts and continue our work. Let us adjourn."

When Dimitri Gorodin came out of the building, Suslev's car was already waiting at the curb.

"I've spoken privately to Razminsky," Suslev began as soon as Gorodin was inside and the car doors closed.

"And?"

"As I expected, he was of little help," the KGB director

said. "What he said to me he had already covered, if not re-hearsed, with Bibnikov. He managed to give a description of the men who attacked Turner, but I doubt anything will come of that. He is keeping me abreast of Komarov's condition. At the moment the Chairman is under mild sedation, as you are aware. All preoperative procedures are being continued. Given that it was Razminsky himself who told us that only Turner could perform this operation, I believe it is our responsibility to decide whether to go ahead with it."

"I really don't see that there is any question," Gorodin replied. "Unless Razminsky is willing to perform the surgery, the operation must be postponed." He paused and looked at his friend. "The medical evidence Razminsky provided suggests that such a course would be far more hazardous to the chair-man's life than postponing. Dr. Razminsky has agreed to wait until eleven o'clock before canceling the operation altogether."

"So there is no possibility that he will attempt the surgery himself?" Suslev asked.

"None whatsoever," Gorodin assured him. "From Razmin-sky's interpretation of the facts, I think Komarov is in dire straits. Are there any new developments with Turner?"

"None."

"Komarov will die," Gorodin said flatly. "I can feel it in my bones. He will die."

"The moment could not be more propitious," Suslev said. "From the way Kobalevsky has been handling himself at Polit-buro meetings, you must realize that he's making up for lost time. He's taken a leaf from your book, Dmitri. He's pushed his own people into positions throughout the regional parties, re-placing heads of committees, expanding his power base. Now he must go after you."

Gorodin said nothing. He had his own sources on Kobalev-sky's activities, although these were not nearly as comprehensive as the reports Suslev provided him with. Kobalevsky was too late.

The driver knocked on the partition, and Gorodin leaned forward to slide open the hatch.

"It just came over the radio, minister. They've found the American."

10

"He hasn't said a word?" Thompson asked casually.

"Nothing," Bibnikov replied as easily.

"Telephone calls?"

"None requested."

"Has he spoken to anyone?"

"He asked for Dr. Razminsky."

"Has a room been arranged?"

"We have the administrator's office. My people have installed microphones and tape recorders. I have told Komarov that Turner is back. He wanted to see Turner right away, talk to him himself, but I convinced him to wait until we've had a chance to speak to him. I don't think he's under the influence of drugs or hypnosis, but I want your opinion."

Bibnikov and Thompson rounded the corner in unison, the staff scattering before them like frightened game.

"The big question is how did you find him, Sergei?"

"We didn't. Turner was coming to us. He was headed for the one place we thought he'd never go. Here, Rudin Hospital. Someone gave him a lift in a shiny new, albeit stolen, Moskovich."

"Jesus Christ on a sidecar!" Thompson exclaimed.

Bibnikov flipped his identification at the two sentries of the Kremlin Guards Directorate at the door. The administrator's office, as befitting a man of his position and responsibility, was decorated in Finnish style, Thompson noted: warm wood paneling punctuated by leather chairs and a divan, a Mirelli sculpture, and a LaBarge coffee table. The centerpiece of the room was a one-hundred-gallon aquarium filled with exotic fish. Michael Turner was sitting at one end of the luxurious sofa, his long legs stretched out before him. He looked exhausted, his clothes disheveled, his hair askew, eyes rimmed with black crescents.

Bibnikov closed the door to the administrator's office and followed Thompson to stand alongside Turner. The two men, hands stuffed deep in their pockets, loomed over the surgeon.

"You gave us quite a scare, doctor," Thompson said.

Turner's eyes fluttered open. He brought the palms of his hands to his face, rubbing his bristled cheeks wearily.

"Who are you?" he asked and sat up.

"U.S. Embassy." Thompson offered his consular card.

Turner did not even glance at the identification but looked at Thompson.

"Who's he?" Turned asked, indicating Bibnikov.

"Soviet security."

"Komarov—they wouldn't let me see him. I have to see Komarov," Turner said, getting to his feet.

"Sit down, doctor," Thompson told him, taking off his coat. "I understand your concern for the premier. But you've been kidnapped, held incommunicado for many hours, and now suddenly released. A worrisome situation. Many people have been very worried."

"My wife?"

"No."

"Thank God for that."

"Doctor, you've got to talk to us," Thompson said. "Please . . . tell us what happened."

"I have to speak with Komarov."

"Is his life in danger?" Bibnikov asked.

Turner glanced up at the man, well aware of the implication behind the question. "Only from the aneurysm, I would think. That's the only danger."

"Then why is it so important for you to speak with him?" Thompson cut in.

"I would have thought surgery would be your first consideration," Bibnikov said.

Turner looked from one to the other.

"Let me speak to Komarov," Turner repeated, and looked away.

"Doctor, be reasonable." Thompson held out his hand. "We don't know where you've been, what you've been through."

"I don't operate unless I speak with him." Turner rubbed his eyes. "You're the American representative here. If something happens to Komarov, you'll be responsible, not me."

Bibnikov's mind was working furiously. Whoever had taken Turner had told him something that had made an enormously strong impression on the American. But who was it? Komarov's enemies or the state's enemies?

"Why won't you talk to us?" Thompson thrust his hands back into his pockets. "Security agents were injured when you were kidnapped. Dr. Razminsky was hurt."

"Razminsky—"

"No, he's fine." Thompson allowed himself to smile reassuringly. "He's downstairs with the surgical team. But for Christ's sake, can't you see what you're in the middle of? Tell us something."

Turner shook his head. "I have nothing to say."

Bibnikov motioned Thompson over to the doorway.

"We don't have time to pry anything out of him," he whispered. "Komarov's room is equipped with listening devices. Perhaps we can overhear something that would help us."

"Someone has gotten to him," Thompson said. "You want to risk the consequences?"

"We have no choice." Bibnikov glanced at Dr. Turner. "If he wants to harm Komarov, he would have ample opportunity during surgery."

"Then Komarov will have to decide whether to trust him or not," Thompson said. He pursed his lips. "There doesn't seem to be any other way."

"Unfortunately not, at least not at present." Bibnikov pulled out his radio transceiver and spoke to the Guards Directorate officer stationed in the intensive care unit. A reply crackled back. Chairman Komarov wanted the American brought to him.

"Doctor Turner," Bibnikov called out. "Would you come with me? We shall introduce you to Chairman Komarov."

As he passed Thompson, the CIA man reached out and gripped Turner's arm. "We're on the same side, doctor. Please, remember that."

Turner took his arm away and followed Bibnikov out the door. Flanked by two Guards Directorate escorts, they made their way down the stairwell to the intensive care unit below.

"I want to speak to him alone," Turner said. "If you don't mind."

"Naturally," Bibnikov replied. As soon as Turner passed through the swinging doors, Bibnikov opened the door on his left.

The intensive care unit was a large room surrounded by three corridors where the security units were recording whatever went on inside. One-way mirrors mounted in the east, north, and west walls allowed surveillance from any angle. Cameras set in the top corners of the room could be focused to catch the slightest threatening movement a physician made over his patient.

"Raise the sound levels," Bibnikov told the technician sitting before the video screens. "Give me as much definition as you can."

"We have him coming in now," the technician told him, his fingers moving gracefully over the console.

"I'm going behind the north-wall windows," Bibnikov said.

From a wood-frame box Bibnikov lifted a long-barreled weapon, resembling a .22 caliber target pistol—except that it fired flechettes dipped in toxins which could totally paralyze a man instantly. He moved into position behind the one-way mirror, the tip of his boot touching a button on the floor. He was directly behind Komarov's bed, watching as Turner crossed the room. If the American gave him cause for the slightest suspicion, Bibnikov would step on that button, the mirror would drop instantly, and the flechette fire before Michael Turner knew what was happening.

Turner crossed over the smooth, frictionless linoleum to the oversize bed that stood like a clearing in the center of a forest of plastic IV sacs hanging from wheeled stands. On the left, near the climate-control unit, was a computer console with seven screens, each monitoring a different life function. Turner checked each one, pressed the readout button for an instant display on the patient's condition. Everything was normal, stable. If Komarov had been told of his disappearance, he gave no sign of it.

"Good morning, doctor."

Turner moved to the bed and looked dispassionately at his patient. Komarov was a slight man, but sinewy and resilient. Turner knew he exercised regularly, reserving one hour a day for calisthenics and weight-lifting. In addition he worked in the garden of his dacha, growing vegetables and fruits for his wife. Still his natural strength had drained from him, leaving his cheekbones gaunt, his mouth thin and bloodless. His hair had receded noticeably, and he had developed a tic over his left eye. But his eyes remained a cold, fathomless gray, disdainful of his body's weakness.

Turner stood over the bed and lifted Komarov's wrist. It was a wasted gesture, for the machines told him his patient's pulse rate with far greater accuracy, but he had to find something to do to avoid the man's glare, to try to form the words that suddenly caught in his throat.

"I wish to put a question to you, American." Komarov's words were firm but the strain behind them was obvious.

Turner looked into Komarov's eyes. "Pyatnitskoye Cemetery, plot six forty-seven."

Komarov had overruled Bibnikov's insistent requests that he be allowed to interrogate the physician. He knew well enough that whoever had kidnapped the physician wanted him kept alive. But at what price? He only had so much time in which to find out what it was and to strike a bargain.

But instead of a demand, the American had uttered incongruous words.

"What is this about? What cemetery are you talking about?"

"You know the cemetery. You should know the grave," Turner said hoarsely.

Komarov shrugged. "I have filled many graves, American. How am I to remember them all?" The Russian stared at the doctor. "Young man, what do you know of Pyatnitskoye?"

"My father, he is buried in plot six forty-seven," Turner said. The exhaustion he had managed to hold back was suddenly sweeping over him. "My father is buried in that grave," he repeated clearly.

"*You have an obligation to me!*" Komarov snapped at him, baring his teeth.

"I have an obligation to you," Turner said, "just as you have one to me. Fulfill yours, and I will honor mine."

"*Honor!*" Komarov rasped. "You dare to speak of honor when you are blackmailing a dying man."

"Don't talk to me of dying men," Turner shot back. "Not with all the blood on your hands!"

"You are *obliged* to save me," Komarov cried, his voice a high-pitched scream. "*Obliged*, do you understand? Your government will force—"

"Force what?" Turner asked him gently. "Can they stand over my shoulder and tell me how to save you? I came here because I have the most experience and have had the best results with this technique. I developed it and perfected it. So what can you or anyone else do?"

He thought that would have finished Komarov, made him back down, but the Russian had yet to show his mettle.

"If you do not operate, or if you make a . . . mistake, you are a dead man. My successor will see to it that you are punished. That your entire family is punished!"

"It's your decision," Turner said. "If the thought of revenge is that comforting to you, if your life means no more to you than that, then we have nothing further to discuss."

The eyes flickered uneasily. Instinct warned Komarov that his bluff had failed.

"What do you want?" Komarov asked, his face turned away. Turner looked back at the computer screens. Komarov's blood pressure had increased, but not dramatically. His self-control was considerable.

"Let Stanislawski travel to the West. Karol Stanislawski and a priest, Gregory Rowitz."

"Stanislawski." Komarov whipped his head back. "What do you know of that traitor Stanislawski?"

"I have treated him. He needs immediate medical attention he can only get in the West. I want you to authorize safe passage to Rome."

"What is this fantasy?" Komarov hissed. "Stanislawski cannot be in Moscow."

"Would you be willing to stake your life on that?" Turner asked. "Because that's what your refusal will amount to."

"Stanislawski," the old man muttered, his eyes flitting about the room in fear, confusion. No one had told him about this. Not even Bibnikov! What the hell was happening in his country?

"Where is Stanislawski?" Komarov demanded.

"Arrangements have been made," Turner said. "I will set them in motion after you have agreed to allow Stanislawski and the priest to leave the country."

"As simply as that?"

"For you nothing is difficult," Turner retorted. "Not even murder."

"You will refuse to operate on schedule unless this thing is done?"

"I will not lift a finger."

"Who else knows about Cardinal Stanislawski?"

"No one," Turner said. "And no one will ever know the truth of why he was permitted to leave."

"Fuck your mother. Get out of here, doctor," Komarov whispered. "Get out. Send me Bibnikov."

✤

Bibnikov caught up with Turner just as he came through the swinging doors.

"You heard everything," Turner said.

"I did."

Turner nodded. "Then perhaps you'd better convince him that I meant what I said."

"Wait for me here," Bibnikov instructed him. "I don't think this will take very long."

Komarov's eyes were trained on him as soon as he entered the room.

"Bibnikov. What the devil is going on here?" he rasped.

"Comrade Chairman?"

"Stanislawski! What is this business about Stanislawski? I thought the priest was dead."

"The last reports out of Warsaw state that the cardinal's body has not yet been found," Bibnikov answered. "That being the case, it is entirely possible that Stanislawski somehow survived the disruptions in St. John Square. How he came to Moscow—if in fact he is in the city—is a matter for further investigation."

"And this other priest?"

"Rowitz is a very close associate of Stanislawski's. It would appear that somehow both men have been able to find shelter in Moscow."

"This isn't like you, Bibnikov," Komarov rebuked him. "You're usually better informed."

Bibnikov did not react to the insinuation. His mind was still busy trying to arrange the information into some intelligible scheme. Who had gotten these details out of the closed KGB archives?

But the fact that someone had penetrated the KGB ironically absolved Suslev of any complicity in the kidnapping. Cardinal Stanislawski dealt with Polish dissidents. He had no connection with Soviet state security. Conversely the resistance network had shown itself to be much more resourceful than Bibnikov had ever imagined. It was no coincidence that Stanislawski was in Moscow at the same time as Turner. In addition to ferreting out the details about Peterson Turner, someone had leaked the information that Dr. Michael Turner would be arriving to perform an operation on Komarov. Someone had access to top-secret KGB memoranda as well as a connection with the Network. That someone had obviously eluded KGB chief Suslev.

"I know what you're thinking," Komarov rasped. "There is no way the Americans could have known where Peterson Turner's buried. Even if they did, they wouldn't have told his son." Komarov's eyes glittered. "A traitor, Bibnikov," he whispered hoarsely. "There is a woodworm in Suslev's house. A termite."

"I will deal with that," Bibnikov said quietly.

"But what is to be done about Turner's ultimatum?" Komarov shuddered.

"It should be heeded, the conditions satisfied," Bibnikov said at once.

"You, Sergei Bibnikov, are advocating capitulation?"

"Turner will not back down." Bibnikov shrugged. "We cannot force him to do anything against his will. I see no alternatives. We should let Stanislawski and Rowitz go."

"That is coercion!"

"That is life, Semyon Arkadyevich," Bibnikov replied.

Komarov stared at him balefully. "Are you aware of what a dangerous precedent we'd be setting? You of all people must realize what such capitulation would mean to our internal control."

"Things are not always what they seem," Bibnikov mused, as though he were working out a tentative hypothesis, when in fact he had already arrived at the only possible conclusion. "What if we were to arrange it like this: give Cardinal Stanislawski and the priest to Turner on the terms he has stipulated. Once they are on their way to Rome, announce to the world that the Chairman of the Presidium of the Soviet Union, in recognition of the efforts of Michael Turner, has permitted the renowned Karol Cardinal Stanislawski to emigrate to the West, where he may receive the treatment he needs. We present the whole business as a great humanitarian gesture, and so on and so forth."

Komarov's eyes burned with cunning and hope.

"What guarantee would we have that neither Turner nor the other two will tell what really happened?"

"I will inform Turner that if he breathes a word of this to anyone, I will exact a harsh price. I will also make certain the cardinal and his priest understand this arrangement. I doubt very much whether Stanislawski would wish to be responsible for any harm coming to the man who has risked his life for their freedom. Turner's memory of his father was obviously inflamed by the terrorists." Bibnikov leaned closer, feeling that Komarov was coming around. "By bargaining for Stanislawski, he will have had his revenge—on his own people as much as on us. The issue will have been settled."

Komarov considered this, twisting his skeletal fingers.

"Is there any alternative?"

"None that I'm aware of," Bibnikov said with finality. "And we are running out of time."

"Then talk to this Turner. If he agrees to *my* conditions, let the priests go!"

Turner was leaning against the wall by the stairwell door when Bibnikov emerged from the intensive care unit. He straightened up and shook his head.

Dead on his feet, Bibnikov thought. Will he *dare* operate on Komarov in that condition?

"We'll do it," Bibnikov said.

11

The announcer at the Moscow Central Radio Station had only been on the job for a few weeks. In that time he thought he had done an excellent job, partly because his supervisor seldom interfered with the programming, preferring to spend mornings with his mistress on Sadovaya Street. Therefore it was with genuine surprise that Yuri Matveiich Ivanov greeted his supervisor's disheveled appearance at the studio, surprise that immediately gave way to concern when he saw the man's frantic expression.

"Get this on the air at once," the supervisor yelled at him, thrusting a piece of paper at Matveiich.

"But what—"

"Don't ask questions, just announce it!" the supervisor said in a strangled tone. State security had met him just as he stepped out of the elevators. In another thirty seconds he would have been on his way to Ariana, blissfully unaware of the chaos that would have engulfed the station, or that he himself would have secured an indefinite posting to Radio Novosibirsk. Someone was looking after him.

Yuri Matveiich smoothed out the paper in front of him, swung the microphone into position, and glanced at the record that was playing.

"Get on with it!"

"But what am I supposed to say?" he asked helplessly.

The supervisor wrenched the microphone toward him and killed the record.

"This is a special announcement," he said, trying to keep his voice as neutral as possible. "The wind has shifted to the west. I repeat: The wind has shifted to the west."

He punched in the record again.

"Repeat this once a minute, do you understand?" he snarled. "Once a minute until I say otherwise!"

The girl was still asleep when the message came over the radio, but Father Gregory Rowitz heard it the first time.

"We have to go," he said eagerly, shaking her awake. "Turner's done it! I heard the message!"

She nodded, then she took out a cigarette and lit it, waiting for the sentence to be repeated. Only when she had heard it for herself was she satisfied.

"We've done it," she said, looking up at the priest. "Unless it's a trap, we've done it."

"It is not a trap," Father Rowitz replied.

"I wish I had your faith," she said. "If it is, there's nothing we can do about it. If we don't move him now, the cardinal will be done for."

She rose, then glanced back at the priest.

"Cover him as warmly as you can."

She opened the door and walked through the dispensary where they had first brought Turner, into a tunnel that opened onto the shelter proper. Anna Letelier knew Turner would never be able to say where he had been held. In fact, if he talked, his misleading conclusions would be helpful. Turner would never suspect that he had been taken to one of Moscow's first fallout shelters, built almost thirty years ago. Over a dozen shelters of the same design had been constructed, like the one beneath the Dynamo Stadium, until a major engineering defect had been discovered. The shelters had been emptied of their amenities and supplies, the entrances sealed off with concrete blocks, the names and locations erased from the official lists, the engineer packed off in disgrace. As far as the bureaucracy was concerned, they no longer existed. Yet for those who worked against the oppression above, they were ideal havens.

This is one of the best, she thought as she slipped behind the wheel of a small truck. Even the narrow concrete ramp which led up to the stadium's underground parking facilities was still in serviceable condition. But one day, perhaps after this operation, their refuge would be discovered. It would depend on how hard they searched. In the end everything was discovered.

She backed the truck up as close as possible to the dispensary, swung back the twin rear doors, and helped Father Rowitz slide the stretcher bearing Karol Cardinal Stanislawski onto the cold metal floor.

"Now he really is in God's hands," the girl said. "You know the route, father?"

"I've memorized it," the priest assured her. "May God protect you always," he whispered. "Bless you for what you and the others have done."

"Do not forget us, father," she called after him softly.

"Good-bye, Anna. Good-bye."

The blue exhaust hung in the air long after the sound of the motor had faded away. Anna glanced at her watch. There was just enough time to remove the traces of their presence and reach the nearest telephone booth, at the metro station on Leningradsky Prospekt, to dial the 111 emergency number of the Moscow police.

Unlike in other cities during a time of crisis, crank calls to the police were very rare in Moscow. Anyone who noticed or heard something unusual hurried home to wait out the uncertainty. No one wished to help or hinder the police; it was best not to become involved. Therefore the call received by Moscow's Municipal Police Headquarters was treated with the utmost seriousness, and a radio car was dispatched to the Kutuzovsky Prospekt, at the point where it crosses the Moskva River. Twenty minutes later the squad leader called in to say that two men had been found in a sedan reported stolen two weeks ago.

The police squad leader acknowledged the transmission

and began to issue very precise instructions to his units in the field.

The facilities at Sheremetevo Airport had been expanded for the 1980 Olympics, and it was the new runway, used by both the supersonics and the 747's, that Bibnikov now had closed off to all traffic save the Pan American L-1011 which was parked at the base of the macadam strip, engine warming up, poised for takeoff.

"We've cleared the air corridor through northern Poland, across West Germany, and down into Italy. Also, weather conditions are favorable at the moment and not as prone to sudden change."

The wind snapped at Bibnikov's coat, and he moved away from the backwash of the jet's idling engines.

"The crew is American?" Turner asked him.

"It's our plane," Thompson said noncommittally.

"I want to see the cardinal once more," Turner said.

"He's arriving now." Bibnikov pointed to the ambulance that was racing through the security gates, klaxons screaming, preceded by two police cars. The ambulance came to a gentle halt and backed up slowly to where Bibnikov, Turner, and Thompson were standing. The rear doors swung open and Turner saw Father Rowitz and Andrei Razminsky pulling one end of the trolley to the hydraulic lift.

"Andrei, how is he?" Turner yelled, climbing onto the platform.

"Doing as well as can be expected," Razminsky murmured, looking at the portable monitor which silently read out the cardinal's vital signs. "We've got to get him out of this cold."

"And you?" Turner asked.

Razminsky pressed Turner's forearm. "I'm fine, Michael. So much has happened," he said, dropping his voice. "It's all quite incredible. I really can't believe it, but, no matter, we are here, and he will be on his way to Rome."

Turner positioned himself on one side of the trolley and began wheeling it at a run. The hundred feet to the airplane were covered in silence. The medical team that would accompany the priest consisted of a doctor and a nurse, both American Embassy personnel. At the loading lift neither said anything to Turner but addressed their questions to Razminsky, who appeared to be embarrassed to speak for his colleague. The trolley rolled onto the lift.

"Thank you for what you have done."

From a reserve of will Turner could not fathom came a parched whisper from Karol Stanislawski. Turner motioned for the lift to stop and bent closer.

The cardinal reached for his hand and with trembling fingers took hold of Turner's watch. The eyes burned from fever, but the voice was lucid.

"You will come with me to the West," the cardinal said very faintly.

"No. Not yet. But I will—soon. I will see you in Rome."

"Roma . . ." Stanislawski sighed. "A beautiful word. A mirage . . ."

"No mirage," Turner said. "You will be in Rome in a few hours. You will be free. Rest, Eminence. You have been through so much."

"I will see you in Roma," the cardinal said, his head lolling. "In Roma . . . thank you . . ."

Turner motioned for the lift to ascend and stepped back, his eyes set on the hatch through which the body slowly disappeared.

Bibnikov and Thompson were standing sixty feet from the aircraft, watching the hydraulic lift.

"Hell of a thing that," Thompson said, his hands deep in his coat pockets. "I mean Turner's finding out about his father and all . . . how could it have happened, Sasha?"

"You know how," Bibnikov said without looking at him. "But I must say one thing—if he shows as much courage at the operating table as he did confronting Komarov, then the old man will live."

The American raised his hand to shield his eyes.

Bibnikov watched as Father Gregory Rowitz embraced Turner, holding him tightly for a few seconds. The priest took one final look at Turner, then hurried up the ramp.

A moment later, as Turner approached the two men, the plane's engines ignited, and the aircraft started down the runway.

It lifted off perfectly, banked gracefully to the west, and left a contrail in its wake. Michael Turner stared at the plane until it was out of sight, then walked past Bibnikov and Thompson to the waiting car which would take him at last to Rudin Hospital.

12

In spite of the fact that Sergei Bibnikov and Charlie Thompson were sitting on either side of him in the sedan on the return trip to Moscow, Turner focused his concentration on the dossier provided by the chief of surgery. Even as he was glancing through the sheets, Turner knew that the last phase of presurgical details was being completed at Rudin. As always, the neurosurgeon was the final component in the long string of preparations. Divorced from the mechanics of presurgery, he came onto the scene only when all the others had been assembled and their preparatory steps completed.

The anesthesiologist's report was straightforward. Komarov had no loose or cracked teeth. For the past several years his only serious symptom had been gastritis, for which Razminsky had prescribed a bland diet. There was no history of tuberculosis, polio, or rheumatic fever. To prevent Komarov from coughing and thus increasing intracranial pressure, a special solution would be fed through an IV. The chairman's arms would also be tied down so that there would be no possible interference with the arterial lines that would be installed during surgery.

Komarov's head had been shaved. After a heavy dose of Valium had been administered, the chairman slept.

The impromptu procession of outriders and cars came to a halt. They were back at Rudin Hospital.

As Michael Turner silently trudged through the snow to the front doors, the chief of surgery arrived in Komarov's room.

He plugged an IV into the patient's wrist to introduce steroids and thereby decrease the intracranial pressure. With the help of a nurse, the chairman was lifted forward and given an oral dose of Dilantin and phenobarbital, which would guard against seizures.

Turner walked through the vestibule in long strides. At the large swinging doors emblazoned with a No Admittance warning in Russian and French, he turned to Bibnikov and Thompson.

"This is as far as you go," he said. "I assume Andrei Razminsky is waiting for me inside?"

Bibnikov did not take his eyes off the surgeon. "He is."

"Excellent," Turner said curtly.

"Good luck, doctor," Bibnikov said.

Turner looked past him to Charlie Thompson. For an instant it seemed as though Thompson was about to say something, but the words never left his mouth. He watched silently as Turner closed the doors on them.

The old surgeon was waiting. Turner embraced Razminsky fiercely, their grips expressing their gratitude at being alive, at having survived the events that had been thrust upon them. Turner took a step back and looked closely at Razminsky.

"Andrei. Did they hurt you?"

"No, no, nothing bad." Razminsky smiled. "They left me." Turner sensed the Russian wanted to tell him more. He felt Razminsky's arms about him, shaking him lightly, then the Russian's fingers were touching his face, holding it tightly so that Turner looked directly at him.

"Later, Michael," Razminsky whispered. "You are safe, that is the main thing." Turner could feel the anxiety in Razminsky. He wanted so badly to tell him what had happened, where he had been taken, the incredible set of circumstances that he had found himself in, how he had actually risked the cardinal's life by treating him under diagnostic conditions that were nothing less than abominable.

Razminsky recognized the sightless cast of Turner's eyes, the first signal of a man withdrawing into himself, surrendering to the shocks his nervous system had been subjected to.

"Komarov," Razminsky whispered. "Komarov is waiting for us."

"Time," Turner said. "We're losing too much time." He was moving quickly now, discarding his jacket and tie as he almost ran for the surgeon's dressing room. By the time Razminsky had joined him, Turner was fully gowned although not yet scrubbed.

"I want to have a look at the OR," he said.

"They're not ready for you yet," Razminsky replied.

"Just a look," Turner insisted. "I know your staff can do its job, but I haven't even had a chance to meet them or talk with them. Let me see them working."

Razminsky hesitated. For the first time since Turner had arrived at Rudin, he permitted himself the conscious doubt: Could the American perform the operation? He was dead on his feet, he had not slept in over twenty-four hours. He had been conscripted in New York, kidnaped in Moscow—one continuous trauma.

"Andrei?" Turner asked. "Well?"

Razminsky knew he had to decide immediately. If he wavered any longer, Komarov's protectors, as well as the chief of surgery, would become suspicious. Razminsky reached out and gripped Turner by the arms, feeling the taut muscles beneath the skin. Slowly, without embarrassment, he scrutinized Turner's face, searching for any telltale sign of weakness, a fissure that would, during surgery, deepen, expand, and finally crack open. But all he saw was the aloof and arrogant self-confidence of the neurosurgeon.

"There is a small viewing room at the back of the OR," Razminsky said, and took the lead.

Operating Room Number 4 was thirty feet square, with a green tile floor that matched the paler green of the wall. Kettledrum surgical lights, manufactured by the Italian medical firm of Fuomi, were suspended from the ceiling. These could be moved on tracks as the surgeons deemed necessary and could light up the OR like a photographer's studio. There were no windows. On the right-hand wall, placed high enough so that observers in the gallery would have a clear view, was a television monitor and three video cameras, mounted at various angles on the ceiling for close-up shots.

"They will be making tapes of this," Turner said.

"Yes." Razminsky nodded. "Not only for the students."

Turner grunted and said nothing. He was used to being on stage, and he really didn't give a damn who would be watching. Instead he turned his attention to the scrub nurses, both of whom, as Razminsky had assured him, were the most experienced in Moscow. But unlike their American counterparts, who often had music piped into the OR while they worked, these two women moved swiftly and surely and with a minimum of communication. Their duty was to clear the path for the surgeons, to make certain that all the instruments were sterile and available as needed, and that whatever bulky equipment was required to be at hand would not be under foot. Most important the trepanning bits had to be sterile and sharpened to perfection. Although Turner would naturally have preferred to operate with his own team of nurses and residents, with whom he had developed an almost choreographic rhythm of surgery, he realized there would be very little difficulty with these people. The fact that he spoke Russian made everyone's job easier. From the way they handled themselves in the preparatory stage, he thought there was a good chance of a smooth working relationship.

"You have a lot of tangle on the floor," Turner said, glancing at Razminsky.

Razminsky shrugged. "This surgery is twenty years old. We have concentrated our expenditures on the latest technology rather than rewiring the entire operating theater."

Razminsky understood Turner's concern. Seventeen machines were going to be used at various stages of this operation, each one of them requiring a separate outlet. And the machines themselves were connected to probes, sensors, or foot pedals. Five separate feeds were required for the electrocardiogram alone, three more for the anesthesia machine, and a half dozen for the electrocoagulation equipment. In spite of every precaution, there was always a chance of a foot tripping a wire, someone falling, and the entire operating field becoming contaminated.

"They are bringing him in," Razminsky said.

The doors to the OR swung back, and the chairman was slowly wheeled in. Turner noticed that Komarov's eyes were still clear, darting from side to side, squinting against the glare of the surgical lamps, trying to focus on something recognizable. It was a familiar syndrome. This was when the patient realized he had reached the point of no return. He was in an alien environment in which he felt totally defenseless, of which he was wholly ignorant. At this point, more than at any other in the operation, the patient had to put himself completely in the hands of the specialists surrounding him. This was difficult enough for an ordinary patient, who might have established some rapport with the staff prior to surgery. For someone such as Komarov—bitter, suspicious, prey to an old man's horrors and fears—trust was clearly out of the question.

Komarov's entry to the OR galvanized the team into action. Turner was gratified to see that in spite of the awe in which the residents and nurses must have held their patient, the pattern of their movements conformed to standard presurgical procedure. In one motion Komarov was transferred from the gurney to the operating table. Immediately his dressing gown was stripped away and a sheet put in its place. Leather straps were fixed across his chest and thighs. At the same time that an IV was introduced into his left forearm, leads from the EKG were applied to his chest, and a blood pressure unit strapped to his arm. The anesthesiologist, Dr. Bauer, stepped into the room, gave his patient a quick glance, and rolled over his IV unit.

The anesthetic was on its way into his system. As soon as the sodium pentathol took effect—in less than four seconds—the anesthesiologist began to feed nitrous oxide through the mask. During the course of the operation, Halothane would be the principal anesthetic, administered through a drip IV. Dr. Bauer nodded at Dr. Razminsky. The patient was ready.

The resident surgeon opened Komarov's mouth with a tongue depressor that had a small but powerful light at the end of it. Lidocaine was administered through an eight-inch needle, which would freeze the vocal cords and prevent any convulsive reactions to the general anesthetic that was now seeping into his system. That done, a bitelock was clamped over the tongue and fixed into the main IV line, so that pancuronium, along with the Halothane, would immobilize every muscle except the heart. There was no chance now that he would move during surgery.

The head nurse took hold of Komarov's limp penis and painted it with Betadine solution. She slid a greased catheter into the urethra, then quickly taped covers over his eyes and introduced a needle into the femoral artery in the right thigh. In addition to verifying Komarov's blood pressure, this artery would be able to carry blood directly to the heart in case of a blockage in any of the other lines. A copper plate was placed under the buttocks to ground the electrocoagulation equipment and a rectal thermometer inserted so that the electric circuits could furnish a precise body temperature readout to the anesthesia machine.

"*Three minutes before entry,*" Turner said in Russian.

He turned and made his way to the scrub room. After the cap and mask had been comfortably adjusted, he began to wash. He used a small rectangular brush, generously lathering his hands, scrubbing each fingernail fifty times and each side of every finger twenty times. Toweled dry by a nurse, Turner stepped back into the operating room, arms held up so that any stray drops of water would flow down to the crook of his elbow, and held up his hands for the light green, skintight rubber gloves. Another nurse affixed a headlamp to his forehead and connected that to a transformer clipped to the back of his gown.

"*Good morning,*" Turner said in Russian, his voice still very clear in spite of the mask. His gaze rested briefly on each one of the eight members of the surgical team. In return he received deferential nods but nothing more. Turner looked back to Razminsky.

"Open him up," he said in English.

Razminsky moved into position at the head of the operating table. Because the sheet was pulled up to Komarov's forehead, his face was not visible. Razminsky placed Komarov's head on a red rubber cushion that had a hole in the center. The neck muscles were paralyzed, and this would keep the head in place.

Dr. Andrei Razminsky mapped out Komarov's skull with five small circles, which he then connected to form a pentagon, beginning and ending on each side of the ear and peaking just beyond the midline of the skull. He then etched the lines with a needle, drawing blood but also giving himself a clear grid over the layer of Betadine.

"Saline solution," Razminsky said. Quickly he injected saline into the scalp in half a dozen places, thus reducing its vascularity for the incision. In less than a minute Komarov's skull was disfigured with swollen knobs.

Standing four feet away, Michael Turner watched the procedure. He tapped the nurse on his right, indicating that the urine bag beneath the table was beginning to fill. To his right his ear could discern the regular pulsations of the oscilloscope. The readout of pulse and blood pressure was recorded in beautifully jagged lines.

"Ready for the first incision," Razminsky said.

Swiftly Turner moved over to the head of the table. He held out his right hand and felt the tight slap of a scalpel in his palm. Maneuvering the instrument between his fingers, he was about to make the incision, then he suddenly stopped, and leaning over the edge of the green sheet, looked down at the motionless Komarov.

I can let you die now, Michael Turner thought. I can take your surgery to a final step and then commit an error no one would be able to detect. I can take vengeance on you now, old man, and never again permit you to murder fathers, and husbands, and countless thousands of others. How much poorer would this earth be without you?

"*Michael!*" Razminsky said sharply.

Turner's head jerked around, and for an instant Razminsky recoiled at the hatred streaming from the young physician.

"Michael, we are ready," he said stiffly. Turner moved back into position.

The scalpel sliced along the forward line of the flap of skin and peeled it away from the muscle beneath. Three further layers of tissue were revealed: the scalp, the muscles, and the galea. All three had to be pulled back before the bone would be reached.

"How thick is the bone?" Turner asked.

"One point three seven centimeters," a resident answered at once.

It would take slightly longer than he had anticipated to actually lift the cranium. Turner set to work on the muscle, cutting the galea with a Bovie lub and pushing it back with the periosteal elevator. It was long and painstaking work.

Forty-two minutes later the bone was exposed. Turner stepped aside to allow the chief of surgery to drill six large holes some two centimeters in diameter. The pneumatically powered craniotome used a half-inch bit, and the tougher the tissue it encountered, the more power it generated. The skull was capable of withstanding up to fifteen hundred pounds of pressure per square inch, and the chief of surgery was bathed in sweat by the time all the holes had been drilled. Working beside him the nurse fixed beeswax into the cavities as they were suctioned and sponged out.

After all the holes had been bored and plugged, Turner glanced at the clock on the wall. Time was moving too quickly. The skull had been a lot harder to penetrate than he had anticipated. Ignoring Razminsky's startled look, he stepped forward and took up his place directly over Komarov's head.

"Craniotome," he said.

Michael Turner showed no hesitancy.

"The fan," Razminsky said to a nurse.

Almost immediately the imperceptible hum of the air-conditioning filled the OR, drawing away the smoke and some of the heat emanating from the skull as Turner cut across from one hole to the next.

Turner threaded the dural protector between the holes and separated the bone from the brain beneath it. He clipped the edges of the rongeur onto the holes closest to Komarov's ears and affixed the periosteal elevator.

"Blood pressure ninety-seven over seventy-one," a voice read out in accented English and repeated it in Russian.

Turner did not look up from his work. "I would like to drop him at least a couple of points." He glanced at the scrub nurse. "Chisels."

Cantilevering the one-inch blades, Turner pried the flap off the dura, and lifted it clear. Komarov's brain was swathed in a cocoonlike substance. The resident surgeon was at Turner's side now, cauterizing the meningeal artery that traversed the surface of the brain. This artery had been bleeding heavily since Turner lifted the flap. Turner stepped away from the table, allowing the nurses to pack the flap in moistened gauze, irrigate, sponge, and dry the dura, and finally drape the flap so that only the brain itself was visible.

Turner looked around at his colleagues. "Very nicely done," he said. "Now if someone would give me some orange juice, everything would be perfect."

He could see a few smiles behind the surgical masks. He beckoned Razminsky to come over to the tray wheeled in by a nurse.

"So far, so good," he muttered. "I like the pressure, I like his stability . . . I think we have a better than fair shot at it."

He felt the smooth rubber of the nurse's gloves pulling down his mask. A straw pushed its way to his lips, and he drank the iced juice greedily. Turner rolled his shoulders and flexed his arms, then slowly walked back to the table. Once again he looked around at his team, trying to reassure them, trying to infuse them with the same strength and concentration that was building in him.

"Malis scissors."

This was the part Andrei Razminsky had been waiting for. Everyone who was not engaged in some essential task at this moment gathered around him, watching the incredible speed and dexterity with which the American surgeon worked. The scissors cut through the dura, which then snapped away. No sooner were the scissors out of his hands than a scalpel had taken their place and a small incision was made. The bleeding was negligible. Quickly Turner looked around at the angiograms spread out on the wall only a few feet away.

"Microscope."

Overhead, an Ashley microscope, one of two that Turner had had to bring with him to Moscow himself, began moving along an inlaid track on the ceiling. Turner caught the periscope-type device jutting from the main stem, adjusted the focus, and trained the lens on a square centimeter of Komarov's brain.

"Activate the laser."

Attached to the microscope, so that the lens of the scope and the lens of the laser were lined up perfectly, was the electronic scalpel that Turner would use to go in after the aneurysm. Turner guided the microscope with very light touches of the foot pedal, whose calibrations permitted the microscope to move no more than one-quarter of a millimeter at a time.

"Still looking," he muttered. "Can't really see it yet . . ."

Komarov's brain looked very like a topographic map, crisscrossed with thousands of red and pale blue lines, rolling contours of muscle, that dipped into troughs only to rise once more. Somewhere within that landscape was the sac that, if it burst, would inundate the whole terrain.

Suddenly Turner's foot jerked up and down. The movement of the microscope was imperceptible to the human eye, but Razminsky knew that Turner had already found the aneurysm, that he was closing in, examining its contours, seeking out the stalk that connected it to the artery.

"Freeze it there!"

Without warning Turner stepped back from the operating table. He looked straight at Razminsky.

"The fucker's bleeding!" he whispered. "The goddamned sac is rupturing on me. Christ, Andrei, I don't know. If I move in there with the laser, I might just bust that sac like a balloon . . ."

Turner stepped away from the table, his whole body shivering uncontrollably. It was the kind of reaction that came upon him just before he was going to lose a patient.

13

The entire fourth floor of Walter Reed Hospital was reserved for the exclusive use of the President of the United States. In addition to the patient's rooms, the surgeries, and dispensaries, there was a large conference room at the far end of the south wing. The majority of this space was given over to medical computers, which were hooked up not only to the health-monitoring facilities at the White House, but also to similar units aboard Air Force One. The computers would keep abreast of the President's condition should a medical crisis befall him outside of Washington, D.C. These could also be linked up with their counterparts anywhere in the world the chief executive might be, thus providing a double-check on the local medical facilities. A special transmission—a video unit—was projecting relays from the National Health and Human Services Department that were coming from Moscow via satellite onto an oversized screen at Walter Reed. The President, his secretary of state, and the White House chief physician, Admiral Emil Washington, all had ringside seats for the operation being performed at Rudin Hospital, six thousand miles away.

Jonathan Telford felt he could almost reach out and touch Michael Turner, so close, so intense was Turner's face on the screen.

"What is Turner telling us?" Telford demanded, turning to Washington.

Dr. Emil Washington, a neurosurgeon seconded to the

White House by the Navy Medical Corps, said nothing. His eyes remained fixed on a smaller screen, which showed a close-up of Komarov's brain.

"What are you asking me, Mr. President?" he asked without turning around.

"What the hell can Turner do? Is he stalling us while Komarov bleeds to death?"

"No, Mr. President," the physician answered calmly. "Dr. Turner is faced with an extraordinary situation. It's not the stalk of the aneurysm that is beginning to separate. It is the sac itself which has begun to perforate. If Turner uses the laser now to separate it from the stalk, he could very well rupture the sac itself."

"And if he waits?" Laine Compton demanded.

"He might want to try to cauterize the sac before removing it." Washington looked up.

"Then why doesn't he try?" the President demanded.

"Because, Mr. President, the chances of his being able to seal the sac, as opposed to the chances of using the laser to cut off the sac entirely, are about the same," Dr. Washington said softly. "In either case he faces less than a five percent chance of success."

"Then there really isn't anything he can do," the President grumbled, glancing at Laine Compton. "None of this is his fault. It's not as if he's not doing everything that can be done."

Emil Washington shook his head. He could not believe what he had just heard. Although he was unaware of the precise conditions under which Michael Turner had been sent to Moscow, he was aware that certain complications had set in once the American surgeon had arrived. From the snatches of conversation he had overheard between the secretary of state and the President, the physician had reached the horrifying conclusion that they believed Michael Turner might not do everything in his power to save his patient, that he might actually allow the Soviet premier to die.

When Emil Washington spoke it was with an urgency that was almost pleading.

"Mr. President, you must believe he is doing what's best for his patient. For God's sake, don't even think anything else."

Six thousand miles away, Dmitri Gorodin shared the President's doubts. He and Viktor Suslev were the only spectators in the gallery high above OR 4. Both men watched Turner carefully as he turned and walked back to the head of the operating table, peering into the eyepiece of the microscope, his other hand resting gently on the lever that guided the laser unit.

Dmitri Gorodin leaned forward, his left palm covering his mouth. "He won't be able to do it, Viktor."

Viktor Suslev's bulk strained against the plastic frame of the lecture-style chairs. He noticed the excitement in Gorodin's face, the anticipation betrayed by a film of sweat that made his forehead glisten. Only forty minutes before Gorodin had been beside himself with fury, demanding to know what had happened to Turner since his sudden appearance at Rudin. He had savaged Suslev, had tried to bully Bibnikov into sharing whatever information the chief of Special Investigations had. His anger had brought him nothing. Now perhaps it would all work out as the fates had intended: whatever it was that had happened to Turner would have no bearing on the outcome of the operation. The American surgeon had arrived too late.

Through the glass frames cut into the operating-room doors, Bibnikov and Charlie Thompson observed the frozen tableau of the operating room.

"It's all too much for him." Thompson shrugged. "We should have known there would be no way he could operate, not in his condition."

Bibnikov shook his head but kept his gaze directed through the glass at Turner, as though willing the American to turn and look at him. "No one is dead yet," he said calmly. "You lazy shit, *move*! For the love of God, do something."

Michael Turner pulled back from the microscope lens. The sac was continuing to perforate, a fraction of a millimeter at a time. Its progress—inexorable, deadly—fascinated him. He felt a hand upon his elbow and turned to see Razminsky standing beside him. Slowly Turner looked around at the surgical team, all eyes upon him. They were waiting, they were expecting him to perform the miracle that his reputation made them believe he could conjure up. They were there to help him, but they understood that they could only act under his guidance. At that instant Michael Turner felt as alone as it was possible for any human being to be. In front of his eyes a human life was ebbing away. Inside him was a helpless rage contained within a body too tired, guided by a mind too confused. He wanted nothing more than to leave the operating room and sleep, just lie down and sleep.

"You must try."

Turner looked at Razminsky through glazed eyes.

"You can do it," Razminsky insisted. He turned to a nurse and beckoned her to bring him another container of juice. Pulling down Turner's mask, he shoved the straw between the surgeon's lips.

"Drink!"

The juice was sweet and heavily laden with vitamin compounds, Turner realized.

"Please, Michael," Razminsky was begging him. "Please, you must try for all of us. Do not abandon us, not now. If he dies—" Razminsky left the last thought unspoken.

Turner adjusted his mask and returned to his patient, gazing down at the shapeless gray mass. His eyes instinctively scanned the machines registering the vital signs. Komarov was still holding his own.

I can let you die right now, Turner thought. You're slipping through my fingers. May God forgive me, but I could let you die without the slightest remorse.

"Komarov," Turner said. "You're not going to get out of this life quite yet."

"Michael, perhaps instead of the laser, we can use the conventional procedure," Razminsky said at once. "Why don't we seal off the aneurysm, then perhaps cauterize the fissure. If we can get that far, then maybe we can cut the aneurysm away completely with the laser."

Turner shook his head. He was already moving, guiding the microscope to the precise location of the aneurysm, checking the final points on the laser, his foot already resting lightly on the power feed that would activate the beam.

"We're going to do it the way we said we would," he said. "There's no point in putting in the clip at the root of the aneurysm to seal off the link to the artery. In his condition we have no idea what the clip might do to the aneurysm. It might mean opening him up again, and *that* he won't survive. The arterial pressure will be too high. Even putting the clip in place is far too dangerous once the aneurysm has started leaking. Under the best of conditions I would have to guide the clip with a microinstrument, line it up with the base of the aneurysm and the surface of the artery, then snap it into place. But if I release the clip at the wrong angle, the vessel could burst. Or worse, it would cut into the fissure of the aneurysm."

"But with the laser—" Razminsky started to say.

"I'm going to do two things with the laser," Turner said coldly. "First I'm going to cauterize that goddamn fissure. I'm going to move the laser right along the perforation, right down to the aneurysm, then I'm going to excise it."

"Michael, you can't take that chance!" Razminsky almost shouted at him.

"Then you give me another choice!" Turner slowly turned. He looked at the rest of the team. *"Just follow every instruction I give you. Don't hesitate, not even for an instant."*

Turner positioned himself directly behind the laser, positioning the beam over the target area by means of the grid in the eyepiece of the microscope. Using the foot pedal, he delicately maneuvered the cutting edge directly over the base of the aneurysm.

"Blood pressure!"

"Ninety over seventy," the anesthesiologist said.

"Too high. Bring him down, Dr. Bauer."

"But if I do that—"

"Just do as I say!"

Andrei Razminsky watched as the pressure dipped to eighty-three, then to eighty, then past the danger point, into the high seventies. He knew exactly what Turner was trying to do. Twenty-five percent of aneurysms started to bleed during the course of surgery. The flow could be contained if the blood pressure was sufficiently low. The risk of this was the threat of the patient's going into shock. Razminsky also knew that hypothermia might have worked just as well, but in this case there was no time to set up the procedure.

"He's gone as low as we can let him," Razminsky said. He did not know if Turner heard him; there was no acknowledgment. But he saw Turner's foot touch the pedal once more. When the laser unit was focused, Turner switched on the power.

The beam that shot out from the laser was the purest white Razminsky had ever seen. The charge lasted no longer than a fraction of a second. Suddenly the smell of acrid burning tissue wafted up from the operating table. Razminsky leaned forward, expecting to see Komarov's brain covered with blood.

"Get back," Turner ordered.

Turner did not even wait to see if the laser had cauterized the fissure that had been perforating the aneurysm. With deft touches on the foot pedal, he guided the laser right into the base of the aneurysm and made a cut the shape of a scimitar.

"That's it. We're going to pull it off!"

Razminsky was at his side at once. Using a long microinstrument with miniature clamps at the end, Turner maneuvered the probes so that the serrated ends of the instrument clipped the truncated base of the aneurysm. In one motion he lifted out the blood sac, almost flinging it into the stainless steel basin.

Turner swung the laser away and peered through the microscope.

"We've got some bleeding," he said. "Give me the suction tube."

Moving the suction funnel around the base of the artery, Turner cleaned out the blood, then pulled back the instrument and watched intently. Because he had set up the laser so quickly there was always the chance he had severed another artery or burned away some healthy brain tissue. But the magnifying power of the microscope revealed nothing. There was a light red stain where the blood had spilled, but otherwise Komarov's brain was intact.

"Andrei, come over here and take a look."

Turner stepped back allowing the Russian surgeon a direct view. Razminsky studied the contours of the brain.

"That's it," he said. "The cauterization is complete, Michael! Michael! You've done it!"

A shout went up from the attending physicians and nurses. Razminsky took his friend by the arm and led him away from the table. "We'll finish up here. All standard procedure . . ." He looked up into the bloodshot eyes of the American surgeon, tears of fatigue, and something else which Razminsky could not understand, welling up in his eyes. "Please, Michael, you can leave the rest to us. You've done what you came to do."

"Has he done it?"

On the fourth floor of Walter Reed Hospital, Dr. Emil Washington turned to answer the President of the United States.

"Yes, sir," the White House surgeon said. "God alone knows what was guiding him in those few minutes, but, yes, he has done it. Komarov's going to live."

The President rose from his chair and came closer to the screen to watch Razminsky's team replacing the skullcap.

"Laine, cable Farraday at the embassy. Tell him to get Turner the hell away from Moscow as fast as he can. Under no circumstances are the Russians to hold him. Whatever happened during his disappearance"—the President paused—"God, whatever happened to him, perhaps it really doesn't matter anymore. If he wants to talk about it, we'll listen. But bring him home. Bring him home gently."

"He's got one hell of a lot of explaining to do," Undersecretary of State McConnell remarked.

The President shook his head. "I don't think so, Bill."

McConnell, about to put a cigarette in his mouth, stopped short. "Sir?"

"I know what you're after. A nice long debriefing, something just short of rubber hoses."

"Goddamn it, the son of a bitch almost blew it for us!" McConnell exploded. *"He coerced the premier of the Soviet Union into releasing a renegade Polish cardinal."*

"I think Komarov will forget it. He's alive, isn't he?"

"He's been humiliated!"

"I don't think Chairman Komarov is all that concerned about his pride," Telford said.

"We've got to debrief him," McConnell insisted. "He can tell us all about that Moscow tunnel he was taken to. And I'm willing to bet that we'll find a Jerusalem connection right there."

"I mean it, Bill," Telford said tonelessly. "No debriefing. Not by you, the Agency, not anyone."

"Why?"

"We never told Turner he was being asked to try to save the life of his father's executioner, did we?" Telford said. "We knew that, but we didn't say anything. Nor did we anticipate he'd find out for himself. But he did. If you thought he loathed us before, think of how he must feel now. Do you honestly believe he'll cooperate with you or anyone else at this point? He won't say a word. Which leaves us where? The truncheons and those funny chemicals that take your mind apart like a stalk of celery? I won't have it. We've got what we wanted: Komarov alive and time for the honorable Comrade Kobalevsky to deploy against Gorodin. In fact I think we're coming out of this damned well."

"What if Turner wants to talk to us?"

"That's another matter." Telford shrugged. "But I want the word put out: As soon as Dr. Turner lands in New York, make sure he's been given the standard security spiel about not talking to the folks at *The New York Times*, then leave him alone. I want no misunderstandings about that. If you and Langley are so God-all hot about the information Turner might have, then get the Agency to do some legwork in Moscow. We've done enough to Turner."

The President walked over to the coffee table and picked up one of the books Laine Compton was perusing.

"*The History of the Catholic Church in Poland,*" he read out loud. "Any particular reason?"

"Stanislawski," she said. "I have the odd feeling we're going to be hearing from him again."

"Well, keep me informed," Telford said.

"Count on it," she smiled.

14

Michael Turner retreated to the surgeons' dressing room. There he tore off his gown and stepped into a steaming-hot shower. Gradually his knotted muscles loosened, the stiffness in his neck disappeared, and the intense concentration that had held his body rigid for the last seven hours melted away. He was gratified to note that the clothes he was wearing when he arrived in Moscow had been cleaned and pressed. Dressing quickly, he made his way to the physicians' lounge, and from there for the next three hours he monitored the final steps of the operation.

During that time he allowed no one except Razminsky to disturb him. Neither Charlie Thompson nor Bibnikov, nor any of the half-dozen officials who tried, managed to reach him. Bibnikov, sensing that Turner would not give them anything, finally posted two Guards Directorate officers at the lounge doors. Only when Komarov was wheeled out of surgery and back into the special intensive care unit did Turner consent to leave. Waiting for him in the hall outside the lounge was Ambassador Farraday.

"Congratulations, doctor," Farraday said. "I want you to know that on behalf of the President—"

"I don't give a damn about the testimonial," Turner snapped. The man's expression, Farraday saw, was a mixture of exhaustion and annoyance. Farraday was familiar with the symptoms. Turner had been pushed too far. He had to get him out of there.

"There's a car waiting for you as soon as you're ready," the ambassador said. "I will take you to the embassy myself. An Air Force jet will fly you straight back to the States tonight."

Turner shook his head no and shuffled past the diplomat. Suddenly he stopped and looked back. "I want Andrei. Ask him to come to me. There is one more thing that has to be done."

Turner did not even bother to acknowledge the puzzled expression on Ambassador Farraday's face.

An hour later Drs. Razminsky and Turner drove off in a blue Oldsmobile that belonged to the embassy. In the quickly fading light they made their way to the edge of Pyatnitskoye Cemetery and walked along the frozen path to the paupers' graves and plot six hundred forty-seven. The wind coursed through the trees, rattling the ice-covered branches, depositing still another coat of snow upon the frozen Russian earth. At the foot of the grave, marked by a simple slab, Michael Turner placed a few lilies and violets that Razminsky had somehow miraculously procured. He bowed his head, his words barely audible above the wind.

"Promise me you will come here in the spring," he said to the older man and stared at the marker, which did not bear a date or a name—nothing to identify the man who lay beneath it. "Come and leave some flowers. . . . Make sure the grave is tended."

"I'll do that," Razminsky promised. "For as long as I'm alive, flowers will grow here."

The apartment they took him to on Panin Street belonged to a senior American official who was conveniently away on home leave. The debriefing began immediately. The Agency medical specialists, known as "the ghoul squad," led off, taking Turner through every phase of the operation, reviewing procedures, questioning him on the sophistication of Soviet equipment, urging him to omit nothing in his description of Komarov's illness, his chances for total recovery, the degree of his competency to govern. The "ghouls" kept him for only four hours, the easiest part of the debriefing, although Turner at first thought that was all of it. After the medical team stacked up its tapes and departed, the "hardhats" took over.

Playing on his fatigue and disorientation, his desire to return to his family, his anger at having unearthed the truth about his father, the inquisitors attempted to chip away at Turner's adamant refusal to discuss what had happened during the hours unaccounted for in his official Moscow itinerary. They wanted names and specific locations, details on the kidnappers and their association with Turner. Had Dr. Razminsky been involved? Was he one of their contacts? Was there any chance the kidnapping had been officially sanctioned, for some reason that only the Byzantine convolutions of Soviet politics could account for? Did they threaten him if he refused to treat Stanislawski? What was Stanislawski to him?

But Turner gave them nothing, did not supply a description of the woman, did not say a word about anything they had told him. He recalled Karol Cardinal Stanislawski, and his sudden smile only puzzled his interrogators all the more. Confusion erupted into anger before his vagueness. At the end of three hours with them, Michael Turner still had given them nothing.

"Let him go."

The words did not register either with Turner or the interrogation team, so the senior officer repeated them. The inquisitors protested, but the senior man gestured them out of the room, closing the door.

"We'll take you home now. You take off in forty minutes. A car's waiting downstairs to take you to the airport."

Turner looked up at him. "Thank you." There was no malice in his voice, only exhaustion.

"I'm sorry this had to be done," he said. "There was no reason we couldn't have waited . . . and no reason for you not to cooperate with us."

"I did what you asked of me," Turner said, rubbing his face with his palms. "Komarov's alive. As for the rest, it's really none of your business."

"Perhaps that's true. We asked you to operate on Komarov

because it was politically expedient for us to keep him alive. You walked into a hostage situation and came out with Stanislawski. The Russians' embarrassment is understandable, but it really isn't as great as you might think. They'll make hay of the fact that it was *their* idea to free Stanislawski—and who can say otherwise? No, all other things being equal, it would be nice of you to tell us what happened in Moscow, but not essential." The man searched in the inside pockets of his Harris tweed jacket and pulled out an envelope.

"I'm sure you could care less about this," he said, "but our accounting policy demands we proffer you a fee."

"Swell," Turner said. Tossing the government check on the seat of the chair opposite him, he made for the door.

PART
THREE

15

"How much longer?"

Doctor Federico Sabatini, Chief Physician to the Pontiff, lifted an emaciated arm he could almost circle with his thumb and forefinger, found the vein, and drove the needle in. As he depressed the plunger the morphine coursed through the blood, its deadening power taking effect almost instantly.

"How much longer?" the imperious voice demanded.

"Three months, four at most," he replied, discarding the syringe. The carcinoma had spread so quickly that it had proved impossible to contain it. As for the pain, he could only imagine how severe it must be. He had pleaded with his patient to allow the morphine treatment, but permission had not been granted, until now.

"Three months is more than ample," said the Pontiff. "Our work is almost done."

This pronouncement marked the beginning of the end, the doctor realized. The rule of Clement XV, Vicar of Christ, had entered its final days.

"You mustn't blame yourself, my friend," Clement said, his voice crisp and dry like winter leaves. "I needed all my faculties, every last particle of concentration I could command. Your nostrums would have denied me that."

Sabatini nodded and quickly packed up his medical bag.

"When His Holiness has concluded his affairs, perhaps he would be kind enough to grant me a few moments."

Cardinal Mirabeau quietly slipped into the room and patiently awaited the conclusion of the conversation between the two old friends.

Clement's lips creased into a faint smile. He too wanted some time alone with his oldest confidant and dearest friend, a specialist in pediatrics who had abandoned his practice to devote himself to the care of a single patient. A pediatrician. The idea never failed to amuse Clement.

"Later, Federico," he said to the physician. "And thank you."

He is tenacious, not to say stubborn, Cardinal Mirabeau thought. Sitting across from the massive bed in which Clement was lying, the French prelate, Secretary of State for the Holy See, watched this exchange. It pained him to see how wasted his body had become, its flickering life sustained by the blandest diet, reinforced with intravenous feedings of enriched liquids. But the face was the same: thin and sharp, with a cruel mouth that cut through arguments and objections, silenced dissent immediately. The mocking smile humbled the proudest critics and detractors. The disease should have borne him away within weeks, yet it had been held at bay for months. Clement had needed this time and refused to yield it in order to lay the groundwork for his final act: the choice of his successor. He would not be denied this last mark on history.

"You are becoming impatient with this old man," Clement said, his hands moving restlessly across the blankets.

"Never impatient, Holiness," Mirabeau replied. "But, I must confess, my curiosity is overwhelming."

Of all the prelates who served him, Clement trusted the Frenchman with the fewest reservations. Mirabeau, tall and thin, with black hair that highlighted disdainful Gallic features, was trained in the French tradition of service. He understood that one did not have to wear the mantle of authority to actually possess it.

"One moment, Mirabeau, while I catch my breath."

In his position Mirabeau combined the functions of prime

minister and foreign secretary. He had the last word on Vatican diplomatic policy. With a single word he could shift the political support of the Church from individual to individual, country to country. Prefect of the Council for the Public Affairs of the Church, Mirabeau had hundreds of nuncios, pronuncios, and apostolic delegates reporting to his office on the socio-economic circumstances of the countries to which they were accredited.

The secretariat was housed within the Apostolic Palace itself, one floor below the papal offices. Such proximity permitted Mirabeau instant access to the Pope and was a reflection of the importance Clement placed upon the workings of the office and his respect for the man who steered it. Clement conceived policy, Cardinal Mirabeau translated it into hard political fact.

It was generally said of Clement that he was more the general manager of God than the shepherd of the Agnus Dei, for under his guidance the Church had prospered considerably. He had scoured the seminaries for priests trained in computer science and modern communications. From the thinned-out ranks of the once-liberal Jesuits he had recruited the sharpest legal and diplomatic minds, capable of carrying out the most delicate financial manipulations and diplomatic maneuvers.

Mirabeau watched the Pontiff's labored breathing. And he will not permit any of his work to be altered, Mirabeau thought. He will not, as his predecessors have, simply consent to die. He realizes that he has guided the Church to a decision. By seeing to her material security he has made her strong and prosperous, yet he is not unaware of the price that has been paid, the waning of her influence in the poorer industrial countries, like Italy, and in the Third World. So which way is our Church to turn? Is she to continue to expand her gains in the temporal sphere? Or is she now to give full attention to that quarter which has been neglected, which is beginning to feel a bitter alienation?

"Are we to assume that in the last several days nothing has changed in the Vatican?" Clement asked, his eyes still closed.

"Nothing, Holiness," Mirabeau responded, and sat quietly awaiting further inquiries.

Three months ago, when the carcinoma had been diagnosed, it was understood by both men that even a rumor of the Pope's illness would spread throughout the confines of the Holy See. Behind overt expressions of grief, private negotiations would begin. Debts would be tallied, favors counted, the relative strengths and weaknesses of potential candidates determined, the various factions canvassed, the search begun by each camp for the *papabile*, the man with the makings of a pope.

"What is the status of the conservatives?" Clement asked. He lapped at the air as if he were desperately drinking in rather than breathing the oxygen.

The conservative wing of the Church was one of the two great factions that had emerged in the middle years of the decade: a fluid, sometimes uneasy alliance of cardinals from Italy, Western Europe, and North America, with token representation from the Far East. The conservatives believed that the Church could not afford to make any substantive change in either its governance or its dogma. The Church had successfully circumvented the demands for a married priesthood and for tolerance of artificial birth control, and had evaded the issues of homosexuality, abortion, the ordination of women. . . . In the end, time, not events themselves, had been in the Church's favor. Social attitudes had swung back to the right, and with them the fortunes of the conservative faction rose.

"They have decided among themselves," Mirabeau said when he saw Clement had opened his eyes. "I don't think there was ever much doubt about the selection. Picheli at seventy-five is too old. The younger candidates are American, and their time has not yet arrived. Even if circumstances had been different, the choice would have settled upon Joaquin Cardinal de Falla."

Clement lifted his head from the array of pillows that supported him and drew himself up. He appeared to be satisfied with the conclusion.

"As was to be expected," he said, wiping his brow with a lace handkerchief. "De Falla is young, very active in the Curia. With many allegiances and many allies throughout the Church. He has played Picheli wisely, using the old man to anchor himself to the Italian foundation, finally usurping Picheli's position to become more Roman than the Romans themselves."

"He has also managed the Vatican Bank very successfully," Mirabeau commented.

Clement fixed his gaze upon his secretary of state. Mirabeau had never agreed with his having ceded control of the bank to De Falla. Outside the Secretariat, the directorship of the Vatican Bank was the single most important post within the hierarchy. Mirabeau controlled only the Church's missions abroad and the finances of the Vatican City administration. The Administration of the Property of the Holy See looked after the "extraordinary revenues"—the many millions of lire which the House of Savoy had originally paid the Vatican as compensation for the See's territorial losses in Italy—and had been managed by the conservatives for many years. No sooner had De Falla become their favorite, than the control of this fund passed over to him. De Falla capitalized on his position and annexed the Administration of Property into his own fiefdom, the Vatican Bank, whose books had remained sealed for years and whose director answered only to the Supreme Pontiff. Clement leaned forward painfully.

The bank's power, and hence the authority of its director, stemmed from the fact that it alone controlled the Church's foreign investments. Its assets were never mentioned in the official Vatican budget. A justification of its accounts appeared only in one place: the annual report of the Bank for International Settlements in Basel. The report listed the foreign currency positions of banks in the ten largest industrial countries, including Switzerland and offshore banking centers. The Vatican Bank, for the year just ended, had netted the equivalent of five billion dollars and, uniquely, no new liabilities. Even Mirabeau had to admit, albeit grudgingly, that no fault could be found with De Falla's fiscal policies.

"He has built an extraordinary base," Mirabeau said. "If your decision is *not* to support him, then whoever his opponent may be, he will have a long and difficult struggle."

Clement reacted to that statement as a wise old trout might

survey a subtle but not totally convincing lure. He let it go by.

"What of the *arrivistes?*" he asked instead.

The second-largest coalition within the Church was made up of newly elected cardinals and those from the Third World. Having come into existence during the rule of John XXIII, this faction maintained its numbers and integrity as a separate party through the more conservative era of Paul VI. The reign of John Paul II increased their numbers, while under Clement their influence remained intact, because Clement needed their support to push through policies which the orthodox wing would have ground into dust through bureaucratic inertia.

"Their numbers are impressive," Mirabeau said. "And they have a cohesiveness which is to their credit. But their primary failing still remains. There is not a leader to be found among them."

"And that, my dear Mirabeau, brings us to you," Clement said delicately.

The third force within the Church had been carved out by Clement. They were the masters of the twelve Congregations which administered the Curia, the Vatican bureaucrats, each of whom wielded more power than a dozen Vatican ministers.

You selected us carefully, Mirabeau thought, respecting our strengths, taking note of our shortcomings. And what is more, you shared your vision with us, making each of us feel that he was playing an integral part, a sturdy pillar of the edifice you were constructing. We are waiting for a sign from you.

"Under your guidance we have gained influence that is disproportionate to our size. Our voice is respected as it has not been for a century. I have been given leave to speak for the other senior administrators of the Curia, Holiness. We wish to preserve what you have created. In that sense we are your proud creation. If we are able to retain our positions, if the core of the Curia remains in our hands, then no successor will be able to undo what you have accomplished. Self-interest, whether conservative or *arriviste*, will be held at bay. The *Church*, not the man, is everything. We have asked ourselves, however, if there is a *papabile* to be found who could at the same time provide leadership *and* preserve what must be preserved. We have not arrived at a choice. We pray that you have."

"What are the qualities you are looking for?" asked Clement.

"He should not be a manager," Mirabeau said bluntly. "For a manager would tamper with an already well-functioning entity. He cannot be a dogmatist—even a conservative—for dogma and expediency do not sit well together. An Asian or black seems out of the question; the Italians, let alone the Europeans and the Americans, would not stand for it. A South American is possible, but it is too soon for such a shift of power. There again social conscience might stand in the way of orderly progression.

"Whom are we seeking? A man whose presence sets him apart from, if not above, his peers. Who has prominence in the world, yet whose nature is tempered by a spiritual grace which lends itself to compromise rather than conflict. He must be a man who understands the true nature of what he has inherited."

"You are looking for a saint," Clement chuckled.

"I believe you had nothing less in mind," Mirabeau replied.

"No, nothing less . . ." Clement nodded.

In the last two months the ailing Pontiff had had Mirabeau bring him over a hundred dossiers. He had eliminated all but a dozen potential candidates in the first reading. The second time around he reduced that number by half. Now only four were left. Clement sensed that he could not delay his decision much longer; there were moments when he believed he could actually feel the disease feeding on him. It was only a matter of time before it began to overpower him.

"We trust our choice will meet with your approval," Clement said.

16

They were the Cabal. In past centuries they had taken, or had had bestowed upon them, different names. All but one of them were over seventy years old, but each knew that when he died his work would be carried on. Throughout their careers they had carefully selected not only their own successor but had also found able and eager disciples. These were now to be found in every stratum of the Church hierarchy, not only in Rome but in key dioceses in North America and Europe. Bound by an un-spoken allegiance, they formed a society of a thousand strong, a society even more disciplined and effective than the Jesuits themselves.

Yet the Cabal's guiding principles—to preserve the Church's sanctity, guard her independence, and defend her power—had not changed in over fifteen hundred years. The men in this room differed not at all from their predecessors—the cardinals who had crowned the mighty Charlemagne, the theo-logical politicians who had engineered the Fourth Crusade, which destroyed Byzantium, the ecclesiastical judges who had sent Dominic and his inquisitors after the heretics, or the princes of the Church who had blessed the Spanish conquista-dors before they sailed to the New World to baptize and pillage.

As they had been since 1887, when Leo XIII reigned, their meetings were convened on the second floor of what had be-come the Institution for Religious Works. Founded by Pius XII

in 1942, it was located in one corner of the Holy Office courtyard. The Institute was responsible for the administration of
capital investments whose proceeds were destined for religious
endeavors. On the face of it, it looked much like any normal
banking office with wickets and tellers, albeit in priestly robes,
handling accounts belonging to the residents of the Vatican
City state: diplomats accredited to the Holy See, members of
the Curia, the staff of religious schools, hospitals, and religious
orders, clerks, librarians, curators, accountants. Beneath this
level of overt financial activity lay another, whose beneficiaries
belonged to the sector of international society which maintained accounts with the Institute, whose positions and influence worked on behalf of the Church, and whose members were
in good standing with the financial controllers. These individuals and companies were permitted the use of Vatican
diplomatic immunity to initiate or consummate financial transactions. Such privileges proved invaluable when moving funds
in and out of a particular country, transferring hard currencies
across international borders, into offshore accounts, or to the
credit of dummy corporations in San Marino or Luxembourg or
the Principality of Monaco.

One function of the Institute was most secret. On this level
the Institute was referred to by its proper name: the Vatican
Bank. The officers, selected by De Falla and answerable only to
him, monitored the pulse of the international financial community, the channels through which church investments flowed
from market to market, common stocks to real estate, commercial paper to precious metals, from corporations dealing with
undersea research equipment to those that manufactured the
most advanced military and commercial satellites.

The office of Joaquin Cardinal de Falla overlooked the
courtyard, but the windows were disproportionately thick so
that not the slightest sound penetrated from below. As big as
the boardroom of a discreet but powerful private bank, it was in
fact modeled on the chief executive's office of one of the Bank's
most intimate financial partners: the investment house of Mor-
gan in New York. The Adam fireplace was flanked by portraits
of Pius XII and Gregory the Great. The walls were paneled

with fruitwood. The conference table seated sixteen comfortably. Along the wall stood the Telex printers, data-link terminals, banks of telephones with satellite hookups to all the stock markets around the world—Tokyo, San Francisco, Hong Kong, London, New York. Direct phone lines ran to the security headquarters next to the electric power plant, to the Secretariat of State, and one to De Falla's immediate superior, the Pope.

Joaquin de Falla was a prince among princes, with a family tree rooted in medieval Catalonia, an ancient Spanish kingdom his ancestors had ruled for centuries. To the house of De Falla the Church was considered a close relative, not an institution. Aristocratic in temperament, disdaining fools and weaklings, Joaquin de Falla brought to his marriage with the Church the political powers of his clan, ensuring that the privilege the Vatican enjoyed in his country would continue, even in a bedraggled democracy. Singlehandedly De Falla had protected the Church against the onslaught of the reformers when Franco died.

He was ruthless, tireless, and supremely confident of himself and his talents. It was De Falla who infused the Cabal with its determination to prevail. For too long the group had tolerated the policies of Clement without forming a coherent opposition. De Falla had changed all that. His name and prestige lent greater weight to their councils, and his connections in the lay world rivaled those of Mirabeau himself. De Falla held the promise that no other did: he had the makings of a pope.

The Cabal had to have one of its own elected pontiff. Then not only would the Cabal endure and be strengthened, but the Holy Church itself.

"Then we are agreed," De Falla said.

"We are agreed," came the response from several others.

Joaquin Cardinal de Falla looked around the table at each man in turn. Everything his birth had bestowed on him and everything that he had been trained for throughout his adult life had now come to pass because of a few words and nods of assent. He had expected such an acknowledgment for months; now formality demanded that he make his statement of fealty.

"Our task now is to take command of the machinery, to preserve Clement's work but to mold it to our purposes, to align it with the vision we have of the Church. For all of his achievements, I put to you that Clement has neglected to take into account the tremendous tide of conservatism that has swept over the Christian world . . . Western Europe, North and South America. He has permitted the Church to become allied with the liberal, or at best centrist, governments in the Western Hemisphere. In doing so he has ignored this essential change in the temper of the times. We have the means and the experience to be of great help to those who will soon be coming forth to speak for the more traditional values.

"However, I put it to you that before a strong, united voice can be heard abroad we must put our house in order here in Rome. If the voice of our faction prevails—and, God willing, it shall—we shall need the support of the senior administrators whose allegiance is to Clement. I believe that men such as His Eminence, Cardinal Mirabeau, have not yet decided which faction they will support. Indeed, they may be waiting, as we all are, for His Holiness to comment upon the choice of his successor. Should His Holiness be inclined to support my candidacy, then it is fair to assume that the majority of the senior Curia will vote with us. However, mere assumptions are not sufficient."

Joaquin Cardinal de Falla folded his hands in front of him. "Take nothing for granted," he said evenly. "Joseph," he said, turning to the diminutive cardinal from Chicago who was the Cabal's leading figure in the United States. "What are the present arrangements for the conclave?"

Joseph Cardinal O'Brian pursed his lips and looked up at the intricate molding on the ceiling, then rapidly began to recite: "The conclave will have one hundred and fifty electors. We of the Cabal can count on sixty-five votes, the *arrivistes,* fifty-five. The remaining thirty are controlled by senior members of the Curia. The majority for election: two-thirds plus one, or one hundred and one votes. Arithmetically we are thirty-six votes short of the mark."

"And practically?" Cardinal Picheli queried.

"Of the thirty in Mirabeau's camp, we have influence with twenty," O'Brian replied crisply. "I think we can count on them joining us, no matter whom His Holiness favors. Naturally if his choice coincides with ours, then we shall have at least five more, perhaps the lot."

"Which brings the total to somewhere between ninety and ninety-five," De Falla observed. "Between six and eleven fewer than a majority. Can we say there will be defectors from the ranks of the *arrivistes* once they realize which way the pendulum is swinging?"

"I would suppose there would," said the Jesuit Father General, Giancarlo Cardinal Silvestrini. "We know that there are several electors, principally from Eastern Europe, who are not completely loyal to the *arriviste* faction. They may not like the attitude of the conservatives, but they are more afraid of the radicals, whose histrionics will further erode the stability of the Church in the East. These fears can be played upon."

O'Brian's face flushed as he spoke. "There have also been several scandals concerning two cardinals from Brazil. Zhores of Santiago is facing possible criminal charges for certain activities undertaken in collusion with the leftist opposition in Chile. We have a firm understanding with the Chilean government. A timely intervention might be in order if the proper accommodation on Zhores's part could be guaranteed. In Paris Cardinal Villiers is said to have a certain fondness for young boys. Regrettable but human. Unfortunately he has also become the target of blackmailers. We know their identities. A word to the Minister of the Interior would not only defuse a potentially embarrassing situation for the Church but for Villiers himself, *if* he were to recognize the error of his position with regard to our candidate."

This candid exposition shocked no one. The history of the Church and the papacy was replete with such peccadillos. Stephen VI was strangled in his bed; Benedict VI was smothered in his sleep. John XII favored incest and practiced satanism but at least managed to die quietly in the arms of his mistress. Propriety demanded only that such transgressions be discreet.

"These are all possibilities," Joaquin Cardinal de Falla acknowledged. "Also it has come to my attention that some of the *arriviste* group have fallen on hard times, that they have used their office and their influence to help some of their radical countrymen trade in foreign currencies."

"It seems to me," Picheli said, "that as soon as Clement's choice is known we might consider meeting with some of these men, to discuss matters of common interest."

A faint knock on the door interrupted Picheli.

"Come," De Falla instructed, speaking into the intercom by his right hand.

A servant entered, bent forward, and whispered a few words into the cardinal's ear. De Falla nodded and waved his hand. When the door was closed he addressed the Cabal, the triumph in his voice evident.

"The Holy Father has requested to see me at once."

The Apostolic Palace was a maze of ten thousand halls, passages, suites, antechambers, meeting halls, and storage rooms. It housed the central offices of the Secretariat of State, the Prefecture for Economic Affairs, the secondary offices of the Institute for Religious Works, as well as the papal offices and apartments. Joaquin Cardinal de Falla walked across the Court of Saint Damaso and entered the palace through the west gate. A papal guardsman escorted him to the private elevator opposite the central staircase and, with a magnetic key, set the elevator to ascend directly to the third floor.

When the doors opened, De Falla was greeted by a second Swiss Guardsman who bowed to him, then preceded him down the great outer hall toward the already-open doors of the papal suite. A footman closed the doors behind the cardinal and hurried on ahead to the papal bedchamber. De Falla smiled at Sister Theresa, who looked after the Pope's private quarters, then passed through the simple double-frame doors and into the bedchamber itself. The footman withdrew without a word.

De Falla was not the slightest bit awed by his surroundings, either the Apostolic Palace itself or these intimate quarters. He knew the residence of the Pope as well as he did his own apartments. He had spent many hours in the library with Paul VI, he had walked with John Paul II in the gardens, had discussed state policy with Clement XV at his dinner table. Although he was well traveled and had spent months abroad on Church affairs, the Vatican was his true home, where he belonged.

Clement had not been asleep. He had closed his eyes because just as De Falla was shown in a wave of pain shot through his body, coming to rest in a burning ball in his stomach. He could all but feel the cancer closing in on him. But he would not cry out. He would not show any sign of weakness or despair.

"Joaquin, come forward, my son."

The cardinal did as he was bidden, kneeling on the padded stool at the apron of the bed, his hand searching for the bony fingers of the Pope, his lips pressing down on the Ring of the Fisherman.

"Sit there." Clement gestured at the imposing chair placed directly in front of the bed, close enough so that Clement could address his petitioners without having to move.

"We have accepted the advice of our physician," Clement said abruptly. "From this day, until the end, we will subscribe to medication. We trust you understand what this means."

"I do, Holiness," De Falla said clearly. "I regret that I have only my prayers to offer you."

"We thank you for them," Clement said. He had no doubt that De Falla's words and his prayers were genuine.

"We have asked you here because you have a right to know before the others what our decision is concerning the succession." Clement paused for breath. "It is known that before our death we intend to name one man whom we believe has the ability and vision to guide the Church through the years to come, a man the Church has great need of. We inform you, Joaquin, that contrary to your expectations or anyone else's, that man is not you."

It was a mark of De Falla's breeding that the only reaction he could not control was a slight widening of his eyes. Otherwise his composure held; his gaze did not waver from the old man's.

"You need not tell us whether you were anticipating our

support," Clement said. "We know you expected as much. In some ways you *should* have our support, for you are made very much in our own image: vigorous, strong-willed, a man who understands authority and influence. You have served us well, though not always faithfully. However, we have chosen to overlook this because your talents are too valuable. We hoped that through your work you would come to understand, far more clearly than we could expect others to do, where it was the Church required reform and what kind of man she needed to lead her." Clement turned his eyes away for an instant as the pain advanced, then receded. "But you have not been serving the body of the Church, Joaquin," Clement said. "You serve the Cabal. Instead of opening your eyes to the realities of the Church's role in the world, you have instead chosen the narrow path. We put it to you that special interests must never command a greater loyalty than the whole with which the Holy Father is entrusted. You are a skilled administrator, Joaquin, knowledgeable and shrewd, a seasoned diplomat. These are all qualities which should serve you well. But you lack compassion, my son. You seem to feel that ministering to the needs of the people means bringing back the old dogma, and refusing to take into account all the progress the Church has made, stilling that voice which speaks out on behalf of millions who are oppressed, turning one's back on blatant injustice when it seems inconvenient to challenge it. It is true. We have not paid enough attention to these matters. We too have fallen short of our goal." Clement sighed. "We cannot, we will not, deliver the Church into your hands, Joaquin. One day, perhaps, you may lead her. But not now."

Clement paused and looked at the cardinal.

"Have you anything to say?"

"I can only repeat what I have said before." Cardinal De Falla inclined his head. "My prayers go with Your Holiness. If there is anything I might do, any way I can be of service, I pray Your Holiness will see fit to call upon me."

A ghost of a smile came to Clement's lips. Blood will tell, in the end blood will always tell. But he would not hold out even a crumb of hope to De Falla, no matter that he believed him to be right in many ways, that his vision was representative of so many within the Church. He was not *papabile*.

"You may go now," Clement said.

Joaquin Cardinal de Falla rose, once more came to the foot of the bed, and made obeisance. Then he rose, and when he saw that Clement's eyes had closed, he withdrew as silently as he had come.

17

According to the specifications drawn up by the Sacred Congregation of the Ceremonial, a cardinal's quarters were to consist of a central staircase (as distinct from a service entrance and stairs) which opened on a vestibule and waiting room. There should be a formal reception area, as well as space for committee meetings, a throne room, and a private chapel. The door to the vestibule should have a baldachin lined with red cloth, while, within the vestibule itself, the benches should be covered with red wool and have their own baldachins trimmed with yellow silk. The doors leading into the waiting room were to display the cardinal's coat of arms and there had to be a special hatrack for the red biretta. The throne room, as befitting its title, would be carpeted in purple and on the far wall, under yet another baldachin, would hang the portrait of the Pope. All of this before the actual living quarters were even reached.

Karol Cardinal Stanislawski had no such quarters.

Every prince of the Church was required to have a retinue, the acceptable minimum being an ecclesiastical chamberlain, a gentleman-in-waiting, and a majordomo. Each of these was to be outfitted, at the cardinal's expense, with a uniform prescribed by the Ceremonial: black silk knee breeches, silk stockings, shoulder capes, silver-buckled shoes, and a bicorne with black ostrich plumes. The exigencies of the modern age also demanded that a chauffeur, with appropriate vehicle, be maintained. In theory a cardinal should never have to cross the streets of Rome on foot; if it so happened that the cardinal's private car was unavailable and one had no choice but to walk, the central thoroughfares were to be avoided at all costs.

Karol Cardinal Stanislawski had no such "family."

Even as orthodox a body as the Congregation of the Ceremonial recognized that in modern times, when cardinals who came from wealthy or noble backgrounds were the exception rather than the rule, a certain latitude in the enforcement of the regulations had to be permitted. Therefore the Vatican itself opened its doors to those who served her directly but who lacked the appropriate means. Hence more than twenty prelates were housed in the Palace of the Holy Office alone. Others had been made patrons of wealthy communities or prosperous monasteries and orders. Still others, if they had no pressing business in Rome or were of no immediate service to the Pope, were sent on legations, as representatives of the Holy Father, to be accorded all the privileges and perquisites which would be accorded an emissary of the Holy See. Thus Bartholemew Cardinal Mercier, from the Gaspé region of Québec, was kept traveling for almost a year, moving from Africa to South America and through the Far East before being summoned back to Rome, where at long last a benefice had been found for him.

Karol Cardinal Stanislawski, however, had come at the wrong time. There was no room for him either in the apartment house for resident foreigners or in any of the great palaces. There was no opening on a papal legation, nor were any religious communities able to look after his needs immediately. The man who had had the ear of millions, whose heart beat in time with those he had served for many years, who had stood as the bulwark of the Church against her Godless enemy, this man had arrived in Rome sick and bleeding, a pauper.

His first memory of Rome was of blue spinning lights, arcing across a sky strewn with diamonds, swept by a cold, low wind. He had heard men shouting, and gritted his teeth every time the gurney jarred or bumped. He remembered crying out but not understanding what was said to him. Father Rowitz's face flashed before his eyes. Suddenly a tremendous jolt pitched him into unconsciousness.

The next thing he saw was a series of overhead lights burning through his eyelids, the sharp antiseptic smell of a hospital burning his lungs, the rattle of glass jars that were feeding him life-sustaining blood.

Time ceased to exist for him. The minutes, hours, days all ran together. The only reality was within his own mind: snatches of distant conversations, flashing images of men and women whom he recognized but could not identify.

When Karol Cardinal Stanislawski at last awoke, he found himself in a large, bright room, the walls a pale hue, accented with yellow stripes. There were two watercolors hanging on the wall, and a simple crucifix over the door. On the left of the bed were several machines, with wires trailing along the floor, over to the bed, and sliding beneath the tape on his arms. The sun was streaming in behind him, warming the back of his head, throwing dappled shadows on the linoleum floor that smelled of pine. Beyond the night table with its vase of sunflowers were two men in white, beside them, Father Gregory Rowitz.

"Where am I?" the cardinal said. "Rome?"

"Freedom, Eminence," Rowitz answered. "You are free now."

The words stunned Stanislawski, overwhelming him. His head rolled to one side, and his eyes closed.

In the days that followed, Karol Cardinal Stanislawski remained conscious for ever-increasing periods of time. The physicians came first, explaining the details of the two operations he had undergone since his arrival. These had completely drained the pericardial sac, finishing the work begun in Moscow. They assured him there was every chance for a complete recovery, but that he had lost a great deal of his strength and stamina. Stanislawski was instructed to get as much sleep as possible, to rest and simply allow the natural healing process to do its work. If all went well, he would be able to leave the hospital in two weeks.

Father Gregory Rowitz spent most of each day by Stanislawski's side. Once the physicians had finished their morning examination, he drew up his chair and in a low voice went over every detail of what had happened in Moscow. He told Stanislawski about the American surgeon who had operated on him, of the conditions under which Turner had done so, of the arrangement Turner had made with Komarov, bartering Stanislawski's life for the chairman's. Finally he told the cardinal about Bibnikov's warning: If Stanislawski were to say anything of the events that he had witnessed in Moscow, it would not be the cardinal but the man responsible for his salvation who would suffer.

Time and again Stanislawski asked Rowitz to go back over details he did not fully understand. Then one day he looked at his friend and said, "So we are now in exile, you and I. We may never go home. Nor will the world know of the bravery and decency of those who brought us here. That is not right."

"Eminence—" Rowitz started to say. But Stanislawski held up his hand.

"I promise you, I will say nothing to jeopardize these arrangements," Stanislawski said. "But even if I am to remain silent, there is the work that I left behind in Warsaw. You know as well as I that that must continue. What has happened to me, to us, must not be allowed to interfere."

At the beginning of the third week the physicians pronounced the cardinal fit to leave the hospital. That morning another visitor arrived to see Stanislawski, a man he had been expecting.

"Do you recognize me?"

The Polish prelate looked up from his book at the ascetic face that was observing him.

"*You are Auguste Mirabeau, Secretary of State to the Holy See,*" he said, having difficulty forming the sentence in Italian. He paused, then said in English: "I pray you will forgive me, Eminence."

"The doctors tell me you will have a slight hearing problem for a time, the result of the surgery," Mirabeau said kindly.

"A trifling inconvenience, considering that I am alive . . . alive and in Rome." Stanislawski was smiling.

"Are you well enough for us to talk?" Mirabeau asked.

"I am, Eminence."

Mirabeau turned around and addressed his servant: "See we are not disturbed."

The room at the Hospital San Giacomo was one of several kept in reserve for the Vatican. Located on the twelfth and highest level, its windows overlooked the Via Rapeta. On a clear day one could see the Tiber and, beyond, the Ponte Cavour.

"I am glad that we have at last had an opportunity to meet face to face," Mirabeau said. "Although the circumstances might have been more agreeable. The doctors inform me that the surgery was successful. With rest there is no reason why you shouldn't make a complete recovery."

Stanislawski nodded. "I have been very fortunate."

Mirabeau paused as though Stanislawski's comment had upset the tempo of his prepared text. Before coming here the Vatican Secretary of State had made a point of reviewing Stanislawski's career, to prepare himself to meet this man who had descended upon the Vatican so unexpectedly. Yet he understood now that Stanislawski's dossier reflected only the facts about the man, and that these conveyed nothing of his extraordinary presence and strength of character.

Suddenly the decision that he and Clement had reached concerning Stanislawski seemed inappropriate. Yet Mirabeau understood that Clement had had little choice. Certainly the Vatican could not have turned Stanislawski away. But what to do with him was not a decision Clement had arrived at alone.

"I have come for several reasons," he said, picking up his train of thought, "not the least of which is to officially welcome you to the city, to our community. I want you to know that as long as treatment is required, you shall receive it. The Holy Father himself has asked me to express his wishes for a rapid recovery."

"Please convey my deepest thanks to the Holy Father," Stanislawski interjected. "That is more kindness than I could have expected."

"But there are other matters which must be put to rest," Mirabeau continued. "The political issue raised by your being here is one of them."

Mirabeau paused. During the time Stanislawski remained in the hospital, the Secretary of State had questioned Father Rowitz at length. Although the priest answered his questions with seeming candor, Mirabeau nevertheless felt Rowitz was holding something back, something which had to do with the reason the Kremlin had decided to arrest Stanislawski in the first place, why Chairman Komarov had risked so much bloodshed on Christmas Eve. He wondered how intimately the episode was linked to the agreement that the Vatican had made with the Americans and Russians concerning Stanislawski.

"Doctor Turner is a distinguished neurosurgeon who was called to Moscow to operate on a member of the Soviet government," Mirabeau said. "Before he was able to do so, he was brought to you. A bargain was struck, on what terms I do not know. The upshot was that you and Father Gregory Rowitz were permitted to leave Moscow."

Mirabeau regarded Stanislawski, waiting for him to elaborate.

"Father Rowitz has informed me that certain arrangements were made so that we both could leave Moscow. I know nothing of the details, and I'm certain he doesn't either, otherwise he would have told me."

"There is a great deal about your sojourn in Moscow that I do not know about," Mirabeau said. "To be frank with you, I believe Father Rowitz has not given me, or possibly even yourself, the full account of what happened. In some ways I suppose that scarcely matters now. Because, you see, the day after you arrived, I received the American and Soviet ambassadors at the Vatican. You can imagine my surprise when they arrived together, and more, when their accounts concerning your leaving Moscow were identical. They both informed me that Doctor Turner was able to postpone the surgery he had been sent to perform long enough to attend you, at least on an emergency basis. After the procedure was performed, and this was described in the vaguest terms, he recommended that you be brought here, to Rome. As a humanitarian gesture the Soviet Union agreed to cooperate. The ambassadors asked me to convey to you their request that you refrain from discussing what occurred in Moscow. They assured me that if you were to make any statement that contradicted the official communiqué already issued, it would be denied in the strongest terms. Furthermore they were relying on me to convince you that it was in the interest of all parties involved, including the Church, that this matter be laid to rest."

"I see." Stanislawski looked away. He knew that Mirabeau would come to him and say something of the sort. Rowitz had forewarned him. Yet the imposition of silence rankled. He felt as though he were betraying those who had risked themselves to save him. The truth would be buried by silence.

"Cardinal," Mirabeau said. "The Holy See is well aware of your political activities in Poland, that you have had contact with dissident groups, that you might even have been actively involved in their activities. It is to your credit that not once in all your years of service have you ever embarrassed or compromised the Church. There are those who believe that we in Rome could have done more to help you, others felt that even by standing by you we were doing too much. You were then, as you are now, a controversial figure. The Holy Father has not inquired too closely into the whys and wherefores of how you came to be here. You must trust me when I say that it is not necessary for him to know *all* the details. For us the important thing is that you have arrived safely, that your illness has been successfully treated. However, the press will want to question you as soon as you leave here. On this matter, the Holy Father has been very specific. You are requested to make no comment at all. This directive applies to Father Gregory as well."

"I shall do as His Holiness instructs, as shall Father Gregory. Neither of us will speak to the press."

"I trust you will also refrain from meeting with any of your former acquaintances, if they happen to call upon you, people whose political connections might cause the Church embarrassment," Mirabeau added.

"Those people are a thousand miles away, Eminence,"

Stanislawski said gently. "I doubt if I shall ever see them again." He paused. "What is to happen to my parish, to my flock?"

"The Holy Father has appointed as your successor Mieczyslaw Cardinal Kotarczyk."

"He is a good and decent man," Stanislawski said.

"You have left him a remarkable inheritance," Mirabeau said, and smiled. "No man could ask more. The Church could ask for nothing more."

The secretary rose and stepped closer to the bed.

"I should leave now. You must rest. If there is anything you need, my office can arrange for everything. And you needn't concern yourself with the future. The Church will provide. You are in her care now."

When Mirabeau departed, Cardinal Stanislawski once again turned his head toward the window. Massive, rolling clouds covered the sky. Winter in Rome. The days would be oppressive, with endless rain. Tears appeared on his cheek, tears that at last recognized that he was an exile, far from his native soil, destined perhaps never to see it again. Tears from the faces that came from his memory, one by one, for himself because he did not understand the mystery of the Lord and the final destination of his wanderings.

The following day Stanislawski left the Hospital of San Giacomo. His departure, in the company of Father Gregory Rowitz, was unceremonious. No representatives of the first or the fourth estate were waiting for him outside in the damp Roman mists. Up to that moment Karol Cardinal Stanislawski did not know where he would be taken, what—if any—arrangements had been made for him. He feared but did not dare believe that, contrary to Mirabeau's assurances, the Church would not provide.

The driver of the battered Fiat taxi relieved Father Rowitz of the suitcase and heaved it onto the luggage rack. He flung the straps across, then went around to the other side to fasten them. Stanislawski took a deep breath. It was good to feel the cold, sharp wind, refreshing after the scented air of the hospital. The engine started as they got into the car.

"My friend, where are we going?" Stanislawski asked as they got under way.

Rowitz glanced out the window. "Not far," he said.

The taxi had just turned onto Via del Corso and was passing the cathedral of San Carlo al Corso. The traffic thinned out along the Via della Carrozze. Just ahead were the Spanish Steps.

"We are almost there, Eminence," Rowitz said.

The Fiat swerved into the Piazza di Spagna, careened toward the Spanish Steps, then began to chug up what remained of the Via della Carrozza. It shuddered to a halt before a small town house on the left-hand side. The emergency brake was applied and somehow held.

"Eminence, we have arrived," he said. "Please go right in, straight upstairs. A friend is waiting."

Stanislawski was tempted to demand an explanation but concluded that that would spoil the surprise. He sighed and went up the stairs of the town house, his eye appreciating the masons' work on the sandstone columns.

The antechamber was cool and dark, white green-veined marble contrasting with the checkerboard stone floor. To the left, in what he took to be the drawing room, a fire was burning on the hearth; opposite was a dining table and a long, ornate buffet. Stanislawski heard a sound from upstairs. He climbed the smooth marble steps, which opened off the landing onto several bedrooms. The corridor led past veranda doors and out onto an enclosed terrace. In spite of the inclement weather, the doors were open and there was someone standing by the small fountain.

"Cardinal," the figure called out softly.

"Anna . . . Anna Letelier, is that you?"

"Come, let us go inside," Anna said. "The cold isn't good for you."

"No, I'm fine, and this terrace is so lovely."

The whole of the Spanish Steps were spread out before them, and the magnificent church of Trinità dei Monti beyond.

"It is prettier in the spring, as you shall see." She pointed. "There is hibiscus there, and roses, even sunflowers."

"Sunflowers . . ."

"To make certain you will always remember us," she said. "I know you love sunflowers."

"Anna." He spread his hands apart in a gesture of helplessness. "Anna, what is this all? I don't understand."

"This is your new home," Anna Letelier said. "This is where you shall live, indebted to no one."

"But I cannot accept this."

Anna drew her shawl around her and leaned back against the terrace wall. She regarded him with a faint smile. "Don't you like your new quarters?"

"They are exquisite, but—"

"They also have nothing to do with me."

"Anna, don't say such things."

"I know that the fact that I am a Jew means nothing to you. To others it might. The house is owned by one of the Solidarity chapters in the United States. It is their gift to you."

"You are a remarkable person," Stanislawski said. "How many times have I repeated that phrase over the course of the last several years?"

He still felt somewhat abashed by this woman, whom he had first met in his parish office in Warsaw. At first he had been somewhat scandalized by her brazen admission that she was connected with Israeli intelligence and that she was in Warsaw to propose an alliance between the Israeli network in Eastern Europe and the underground resistance network. Memories of the Russian destruction of the independent Polish labor movement were still fresh. Although he had heard her out, he did not give her any encouragement. Another meeting was arranged three months later. By that time Stanislawski had had an opportunity to satisfy himself as to her bona fides and was reassured that she had the authority to make the commitments she had outlined. Stanislawski agreed to be her spokesman within the ranks of the shattered Solidarity movement and the younger resistance network. It was he who brought Solidarity's leaders to her, organized the two clandestine conferences. As mediator, he pointed out to the Solidarity delegates that they shared a common goal with Anna Letelier. Both could only benefit from cooperation. It was the kind of help that Solidarity desperately needed. In the end Stanislawski himself guaranteed the integrity of this woman, with whom he already felt a certain kinship. Over the course of the next two years that sentiment had grown stronger.

Anna led him back to the house, closed the veranda doors, and led the way downstairs to the drawing room. In front of the fireplace on a round table was a vase with freshly cut flowers, a bottle of sparkling Frascati, and two glasses. Anna draped her shawl around the back of the chair, poured the wine, and took out a cigarette.

"You look so very different than I remember you in Warsaw," Stanislawski said. "You are a beautiful woman, Anna Letelier, yet there is a hardness within you. Almost invisible, but there nevertheless."

Her eyes flickered briefly; she was taken aback by the way he, a cleric no less, had perceived her.

"When did you come?" he asked.

She did not answer but instead raised her glass.

"*L'chaim.*"

"*Life,*" Stanislawski echoed.

"I came out two weeks ago," she said. "The situation is not getting any better, Eminence. In fact Foreign Minister Gorodin has made substantial inroads in the various party organizations. Old Komarov is holding his own, but only just. Dr. Razminsky has reported to the Central Committee that he will be dead by summer, perhaps sooner. Kobalevsky is still struggling to expand his base."

"And Solidarity?"

"Solidarity survives underground, as before," she said, her gaze upon the bubbles in her glass. "I'm doing everything possible to get you the information which will confirm the statement you were to have delivered on Christmas Eve." She paused and looked up at him. "I want hard evidence of their conspiracy against the Soviet dissidents and Jews."

"You mustn't think I'd forgotten about that," Stanislawski said. "But I was thinking about Dr. Turner. I can't tell you,

Anna, how badly it shames me not to be able to contact him, but I've been virtually silenced by the Vatican."

"There will be an appropriate time for that," Anna said. She hesitated. "I suppose Father Rowitz has told you everything?"

"Even that is not enough."

"It must do for now, Eminence. I also suggest that we never meet here again. In Rome the phones are tapped at random. Your calls will almost certainly be intercepted all the time. The Foreign Affairs department of the Roman Criminal Investigation Division has you under surveillance."

"Because no one really believes that joint communiqué issued by the Americans and Russians . . . or that the Vatican could have acquiesced in all this?"

Anna nodded. "Also, there's no telling whether your servants won't be coerced into making reports on you or planting microphones. It's happened before."

"How strange I feel," Stanislawski said. "Events have moved so quickly that it seems I'm still trying to catch up with them. What am I to do here, Anna? What good can I possibly do in this city, among these people who have no need of me? Who will listen to me now? Who will ever understand how or why I am here if I am not permitted to tell the truth?"

"Nothing has changed for you simply because you are here," Anna said. "You must not allow anything to change. In Russia, Gorodin is continuing what he has begun. You must never forget that."

Stanislawski nodded and looked over her shoulder, across to the windows and the cold Roman morning that lay beyond them.

"How long must I remain silent?"

"Until there is no choice but to speak out. I fear Gorodin will make that moment quite clear to us all. I only hope the Church understands your position then." She looked at her watch. "I must go."

"Anna Letelier, I thank you for your friendship and the risks you have faced so valiantly."

"Goodnight, Eminence," she said, and gathered up her shawl and shoulder bag.

When Anna was ready, Father Rowitz drove her to the gallery across from the Palazzo Ruspoli. The gray Lancia coupe she had arrived in had also been .purchased by the Cardinal's American sympathizers and would be left at his disposal.

Father Rowitz nudged the vehicle into the mainstream of traffic on the Via Condotti. Rush hour had begun, the madness compounded by the swirling fog descending upon the city from the river. The din in the street was hellish, a cacophony of klaxons, bells, and shrill blasts of policemen's whistles. Anna and Father Rowitz rolled up their windows tightly to prevent the exhaust-laden dampness from seeping into the car.

"You will have to look after him," Anna said. She turned to the priest. "It will take a long while for him to recuperate from the surgery and to adjust to exile. There were moments when I was speaking to him that I thought he could not believe he was actually here."

"You cannot ask a man to go through more than he has," said Father Rowitz. "On the one hand he realizes that he left an enormous task unfinished in Poland, on the other he is a thousand miles away from Warsaw. By the same token he has been silenced by the Kremlin on one side and by the Church on the other. So what in fact *is* left to him?"

Anna gazed out the window, oblivious to the beauty of the ancient city.

"We must make him believe that he has lost nothing," she said. "In time he can be effective here, and eventually in Poland as well. The one thing we can't allow is for him to despair. I have seen it happen to exiles before. They just wither and die inside. They become straw men."

"At least he has a fine place to live, and I am with him," Rowitz said. "Undoubtedly the Church will arrange some untaxing work, and that will help. And you can provide him with the information he needs on the Russian machinations in Poland. If Gorodin is not stopped . . . If six months from now, or whenever Chairman Komarov dies, this Gorodin takes power, then Poland and the satellites will be in great danger."

Rowitz took a sharp right-hand turn and slowed down the car.

"You can let me off here," Anna said.

When she got out of the car, she leaned down to the open window and said, "I won't stop working for what he wants. Nothing he has done has been in vain. Somehow, you must make him believe this."

They waved good-bye, and as Father Rowitz maneuvered the car back into the traffic, he wondered how true Anna's words were. There was much she did not know . . . there was much he had never told her. Something had held him back in Moscow, whether the sight of Stanislawski helpless or the aura of frenzied activity that surrounded Anna, who was desperately putting together the last pieces of the plan which would send both him and Stanislawski to the West. Or perhaps something else.

Withholding what Jaworska had told him had nothing to do with his trust in Anna Letelier. Like Stanislawski, he trusted her above all others in the Polish resistance fronts. But the implications of Jaworska's last words had shaken Father Rowitz. As he considered his friend of forty years' standing, Rowitz terrified himself, because he was thinking how much better it would have been if she had died quickly. Then what Jaworska had told him, what he now carried in his heart, would have been forgotten altogether.

Yet Rowitz knew he would pursue the slender clue Jaworska had left with him. He would search, and he would pray that at the end of his quest he would discover only a harmless reference which had somehow grown out of all proportion in a dying woman's mind. In these past few weeks, while Stanislawski was lying in San Giacomo Hospital, he had not been able to leave his side. But now he would slowly, very quietly, embark on a search for the man who, forty years ago, had brought Katrina Jaworska the condemned children she had saved with her stylus. She had left him a man's name—Telemann. Telemann was the one he would have to find.

Father Rowitz squeezed the Lancia into an empty parking space in a side street off the Via Condotti. He walked quickly past the fashionable shops to the KLM ticket agency. After a few minutes he emerged with an airline schedule. At the first opportunity he would set off to find this man who had saved young Stanislawski.

One of the three security men who were always on duty in the Letelier Gallery opened the door for her. During public hours they wore conservative suits and doubled as salesmen. After the gallery closed dress was strictly informal: black turtle-necks, crepe-sole shoes, silenced Ingram machine pistols in specially designed shoulder holsters.

"Good morning, Yossi. Everything in order?"

"It is, mademoiselle."

Anna cringed at his accent. Yossi had spent three years in Paris as the Israeli ambassador's personal bodyguard. During that period he had managed to kill three terrorists of Palestin-ian origin and five homegrown fascists of the Fatherland Front that had discovered the pastime of bombing synagogues. He had also produced two children, and learned French, or at least what he thought was French.

"I'll be working upstairs for about an hour. Any news?"

"A delivery," he said very quietly.

Yossi led the way through the darkened gallery, passing through exhibit rooms that held over a million dollars worth of contemporary and traditional paintings. In the vault below, next to the special viewing chamber, was a collection whose total value was three times that amount.

Only a handful of people knew that Anna Letelier, daugh-ter of the eminent South American art dealer, Emil Letelier, used her father's galleries as a cover for her activities as an Israeli intelligence agent.

Anna Letelier had spent her summers on Mediterranean yachts, autumns in English country houses, and winters on the slopes of Gstaad. She had gone to Israel just as the 1976 hostili-ties had erupted. By the end of that summer she had driven an ambulance across half the Sinai, helping to retrieve the bodies of young Israeli soldiers, most of them younger than she. Anna returned with running blisters on her pampered hands, skin burned nut-brown, and her once carefree spirit tempered by resolution. Anna flew back to Israel the following year and did not return to Europe until spring of 1980. In that time she had completed a basic course in covert operations at the Mossad training camp outside Jaffa, perfected her knowledge of seven Slavic languages, and had worked on the Soviet Desk at Mossad headquarters. From there she was recruited into an ultrasecret division that dealt with Eastern Europe and its Soviet masters.

In the last weeks of 1982, the Soviets had finally moved against the labor movement in Poland. Moscow had ordered the KGB to move into the major industrial centers and arrest not only the major leaders of the Solidarity movement, but by means of denunciations, mass roundups, and widespread terror, to disperse every last cell. The attack had been so well prepared and executed that Solidarity ceased to exist within a matter of weeks. It took months for the survivors to come out of hiding and make contact with one another, to reestablish a shadow organization underground. While the Russians ruled above ground, Solidarity worked to reorganize itself in secret. But its numbers had been drastically, almost fatally reduced. No one in its leadership believed that what remained of Solidarity could be organized into an effective force within the foreseeable future. The lone exception was the head of the new intelligence division in Tel Aviv, a man known only as Morris.

Acting on the orders of the prime minister, Morris sent Anna Letelier into Poland to consult with Cardinal Stanislawski. The plan she proposed to Solidarity was the most ambitious Morris and his department had ever undertaken. Israeli intelligence had a large number of cells operating in Eastern Europe. If Solidarity agreed, those cells in Poland would join the fragmented union. Overnight Solidarity's manpower would be strengthened, its access to weapons and communications systems would be assured. All Jerusalem was asking in return was that Solidarity would help transport Jews out of Eastern Europe.

Even with Cardinal Stanislawski acting as go-between, Anna understood that the risk of such a collaboration was great.

During the war Polish partisans had not hesitated to betray Jewish guerrillas operating against the Germans. The last pogrom had been in 1946, in Kelice. The enmity between the two peoples still simmered. Her only hope lay in the possibility that a new generation of Poles was less bigoted than their forefathers. The enemy was the same: the Russians. The Poles wanted to be rid of the Russians; the Jews wanted to get as many of their people out as possible. The alliance between Pole and Jew would be an uneasy one, but it was necessary. As long as the Poles understood this, as long as Stanislawski exercised his moral authority over them, she was certain that a working relationship could be kept in place, using the cardinal as the linchpin. She prayed that it would endure long enough for her to complete the second half of her mission Morris had sent her on, a part which no one in Poland but Stanislawski was privy to: to unearth the Kremlin's intentions toward Jews living in the East.

Anna opened the door of the gallery office and switched on the lights. She pushed aside the mass of papers and correspondence that had accumulated in her absence, clearing a working space for herself, then checked her watch and knelt to open the safe behind her desk. The time lock was accessible. From inside she withdrew an envelope and removed the contents. The four sheets contained the latest transmission received from her most valuable contact in the Soviet Union: VIPER.

Yossi had picked up the envelope earlier that afternoon from the Israeli embassy, soon after it had arrived from Tel Aviv by courier. She read the papers through, then reread them to make certain she had missed nothing. Anna dimmed the light. The digital clock on her desk had seven faces, corresponding to the time zones of the world's major cities. In Rome it was a few minutes after noon. In New York the day was just dawning.

Anna ground out her cigarette and dialed Yossi's extension downstairs. When she explained to him what had to be done, Yossi objected furiously, telling her that it was too late. It was the first time Anna ever screamed at him, ordering him to make the arrangements, to call the embassy in New York. Then she was on her feet, moving, throwing a passport into her overnight bag. Her eyes darted back to the clock, to the face that told her the New York time. There was always the chance, there was always hope. *Why* were the Russians always so vengeful?

The execution team—two men—had arrived in New York two days after Michael Turner had been reunited with his family. Since then one of them had visited their building a dozen times, in the guise of a delivery man; another had become a patient at the private rehabilitation clinic where Mrs. Turner worked as an occupational therapist and had observed her there. Within a week they had devised no fewer than a dozen ways to carry out the mission successfully but had stuck to their orders: At least twenty days had to elapse before they acted. Today was the nineteenth.

18

The snowstorm that had savaged New York City had gone down in meteorological records as one of the worst. Most of Manhattan ceased to exist as a civilized community, its streets clogged with snow. Parked vehicles buried under drifts that lined the empty street gave the city the appearance of a ghost town. Most New Yorkers were safely ensconced in their apartments; stranded commuters had taken refuge in hotel rooms snatched up during the first night of the storm. A kind of festive atmosphere came over the city, a rejoicing in the unexpected turn of events—and after all, the situation was only temporary. New York would be on the move again by morning. Day and night the rumble of enormous plows with their retinue of dump trucks, and the harsh grinding energy of tractors testified to the mayor's determination to clear the city's streets.

Most social functions had been canceled. Restaurants, nightclubs, and cafés closed their doors. But at the Plaza Hotel Dr. Michael Turner's evening proceeded on schedule. Turner had not canceled his reservation at the Oyster Bar. It would never have occurred to him to do so. As in years past, he would not permit anything to stand in the way of his and Jeanne's anniversary celebration.

Halfway through the meal a stranded guitarist perched himself on a stool at the far end of the copper bar and began to play. The melody was haunting, "The Umbrellas of Cherbourg." Michael Turner pushed his plate away and reached for his wife's hand. She intertwined her fingers with his and slowly brought her lips to his. The silken sheen of her hair, the faint scent of jasmine, exhilarated him. This was the song that they danced to so many years ago in London when they had first met. It was also the song she had played for him when he arrived home from Russia.

Dinner had been wonderful, and they were both in a playful mood. An outrageous tip to the Plaza doorman had somehow procured a taxi. But the driver was unwilling to take the chance of striking off across Seventy-second Street in the snow, and he dropped them on the corner of Madison Avenue.

There were almost no cars on the street. Half a block ahead Turner saw an orange snowplow swing into the other end of the block, its blade pushing the snow closer to the sidewalk. A small caterpillar tractor was working the other side of the bank, pushing the snow into a mound.

"With a little bit of luck they just might clear a path to our door," Turner said.

"I see you're as anxious to get home as I am," Jeanne Turner teased.

He hugged her and they continued on, past the antique shop on the corner, the wine shop two doors down, and a boutique. As they trudged on, taking deep breaths of pure cold air, both noticed that the plow and the caterpillar had stopped. The sidewalk, they realized, was still an impassable cornice of snow.

"Well, doc, are you about to carry your fair maiden to the castle?" Jeanne laughed. Turner cast a sour look at the two idle machines.

"Look, there's a bit of a trough on the outside. What if we just hold hands and take our chances?"

They could see the light above their doorway no more than forty yards away. The roar of a motor drowned out his words. Twisting violently on its treads, the small caterpillar veered away from the edge of the street and onto the sidewalk. Turner whirled around, not believing what he was seeing. The driver rolled down his window, a faceless mask behind a glaring light. The machine was almost upon them, its hideous yellow lights bearing down relentlessly, the blade swinging between its shafts.

"Get over there!" Turner screamed above the shriek of machinery and violently tugged Jeanne's arm. She couldn't make it over the furrow. He flung himself at her to push her out of the machine's path, but his heel sank into the slush, and he stumbled backwards, falling heavily on his shoulder, his hands digging into the ice as he tried to pull himself up. He was screaming but heard nothing. The roaring of the plow was all around him. He could smell the diesel exhaust from the caterpillar and twisted his head around, expecting to see the blade bearing down on him.

"Oh, dear God, no."

The caterpillar veered away from him, grinding toward Jeanne, the snow spewing from its treads.

"Get back!" he screamed. *"Back—"*

She was staring at him like one possessed, eyes pleading with him. Jeanne stumbled into a snowbank and scrambled to get away but could not get over it. She did not utter a sound as the blade smashed into her just above the hips. She recoiled from the blow and lay still. Her gaze was fixed upon her husband, her expression of pain and helplessness frozen. Even from where he was lying, Turner could see the dark blood pouring out of her.

"No," he whispered. "No, no!"

Turner scrambled over the snowbank on all fours. When he reached her, he was able to look at her only once. He fell to his knees, then rose, and knelt beside her again. Gently he rolled her head over and wiped some of the blood from her mouth. He would not look at her broken body but remained on his knees in the snow, cradling her face in his hands, staring after the orange snowplow that was trundling away down the street.

Anna Letelier had broken one of Mossad's cardinal rules governing operations in a foreign country by requisitioning four Israeli agents who were permanently assigned to the consulate in New York. But Turner had to be protected. There was no time to bring help all the way from Jerusalem.

It had taken her a full two hours to make her way into Manhattan from the airport, to the Israeli consulate on Forty-fourth Street. Ignoring the protests of the chargé d'affaires, she held an impromptu conference with her new recruits. By the time the Turners' dinner at the Oyster Bar was drawing to a close, two of her agents were waiting outside the Plaza.

That the streets were all but empty of traffic had worked to her advantage. The surveillance unit on the Turners had reported no unusual traffic around the vehicle carrying the neurosurgeon and his wife. Seventy-second Street, Anna saw, was lifeless. If Turner was to be taken, it could not be on the ground, through a kidnap attempt. Rather the killer would strike from above, possibly from the roof of one of the brownstones that lined Seventy-second, and his chances of success that way would be slim. With the gently falling snow, the darkness, and the wind, even the most skilled assassins would have a difficult target. Neither Anna nor her colleagues paid sufficient attention to the snowplow and the caterpillar, not until it was too late.

From her vantage point in the doorway of a town house Anna saw the caterpillar and the snowplow grinding their way through the snow, trying to make their escape.

"Oh, dear God. . . !"

Wrenching her communicator from her parka, she screamed to the backup teams to stop the driver of the orange plow roaring down the street.

"Get him!" Anna commanded her men. "Take him alive if you can!"

The agents realized that even their automatic weapons would be useless against the steel frame of the caterpillar. The man nearest the tractor drew out a small concussion grenade. He waited until the machine was almost parallel to him before he threw it, aiming for the treads. The tremor shook the street. The caterpillar lurched precariously, then tilted onto one tread and careened madly toward the opposite side of the street until it fell over on one side.

As Anna ran toward the crippled machine, she heard the sputter of gunfire farther down the street.

"Help me get this door open," she said. She leaped onto the tractor and grabbed hold of the door of the cab.

Scrambling over the hood of the tractor, the two agents pried open the driver's door and dragged out the motionless figure that was wedged among the levers and pedals. By the time they had pulled him clear of the smoldering caterpillar, the car carrying two other Israelis had slithered to a halt beside the wreckage.

"We couldn't take him alive," one of the agents called out. He pointed to a bloody heap in the back seat.

"Well, this one's still breathing," Anna said fiercely. "Get him inside, then let's get the hell out of here."

As her men worked to get the unconscious driver into the back of the car Anna looked back at Michael Turner, still kneeling in the snow, cradling his dead wife. She was seized with a desire to run to him, to help him somehow. Lights were coming on all along the street as residents were awakened by the commotion. Two doormen had run up to Turner.

"*Come on!*" one of the agents shouted at her. They could already hear the sirens wailing in the distance.

Anna took one last look at Turner and prayed he would forgive her.

"I didn't mean for this to happen," she said through her tears. "My God, what have I done to you?"

19

It took three attempts to get Michael Turner away from his wife's body. The whole of Seventy-second Street was in hellish chaos. Between Madison and Park, the street was cordoned off by police cruisers. Fire engines and support vehicles had moved up toward the wreckage of the caterpillar, the hoses trained on the smoldering engine. Scores of police in bulky blue parkas outlined with reflective stripes had surrounded the area. Detectives in plainclothes huddled about the overturned caterpillar while all along the street uniformed patrolmen kept curious residents from disturbing the scene.

As soon as the police department ascertained the identity of the victim and her husband, the New York FBI office on East Sixty-eighth Street was alerted. From there a message was transmitted directly to the White House. The message made its way through to the President's quarters on the second floor of the East Wing. By one o'clock that morning responsibility for the investigation of the murder of Jeanne Turner and the ensuing armed battle on Seventy-second Street had passed from the hands of New York's homicide division to the FBI. President Jonathan Telford directed the Secret Service to post a guard around the suite at Penfield Memorial where Dr. Turner had been taken. Additional security was arranged at Turner's condominium, where two agents moved in with the housekeeper to protect young Christopher Turner.

Dr. Theodore Weizmann was reached at the Dakota just as he was preparing for bed. An FBI team drove him to the hospital, where he assumed full responsibility for Turner's care. While Turner slept, heavily sedated with a massive dose of Demerol, Dr. Weizmann waited impatiently for news. All too aware that the White House itself was monitoring their efforts, the FBI intensified its investigation of the incident, yet it soon became evident there was precious little to go on. Neither the snowplow driver nor the operator of the caterpillar could be found. Both vehicles had been stolen from a garage on the East River. There were no fingerprints inside the vehicles themselves, no clues who the drivers might have been or what their motives were. But what puzzled and irritated the Bureau investigators most of all was that several other heavily armed individuals had apparently been present at the time of the killing. Fragments of a grenade had been found in the overturned caterpillar. Also several bullets had been extracted from the cab of the snowplow. All were being examined by forensic experts. Witnesses swore that they had seen at least three other people, possibly a woman among them, attack the caterpillar and remove a body. The anonymous attackers had driven off before the police arrived. The Bureau issued a three-state alert for the vehicle but the unit commander was not optimistic. No one had taken down the license number, not even a few numbers. The report the President received at his usual seven o'clock morning briefing infuriated him. The Bureau concluded that both Turner and his wife had clearly been the object of an assassination attempt, an attempt that had been only partially successful. It was also a fact that someone had had foreknowledge of the attack and possibly had tried to stop it. Who these people were, how they had come by this information, and what their motives were, were all questions left unanswered.

The new Israeli consulate on East Sixty-fourth Street was one of the most heavily fortified structures in New York City. The building was enclosed by a twelve-foot-high wrought-iron fence, the palings tapering into sharp spikes. The distance between the gate, which could only be opened electronically from inside, and the front door was only twenty-two feet. During the day surveillance cameras covered every square inch of this space, at night infrared cameras were supplemented by trained Dobermans. A passerby casually observing the consulate from the street would have noticed nothing out of the ordinary. There were no lights in any of the windows. Only at the rear of the building was there any sign of activity. To the NYPD patrolmen in the sentry box outside, the two figures patrolling the area around the adjoining garage were familiar—the consulate's security team. But the inactivity was deceptive.

"How *dare* you drop this . . . this carrion on our doorstep!"

The Israeli chargé d'affaires was beside himself with indignation. He had never seen anything like this: dead and wounded men hauled into this sanctuary, brought, no less, by a woman who had clearance at the highest level!

Anna Letelier lit her last cigarette and drained the last of the coffee from the paper cup. The lights in the commissary were far too bright. Her eyes were hurting, her arms and legs numb. But still she said nothing. Every once in a while she would look up at the diplomat and freeze his next words with a look.

"I demand to know what you people are doing with that wounded man!" the diplomat thundered at her. "We should have called a hospital, an ambulance. He needs medical attention!"

Anna regarded him languidly. "Believe me," she said. "He is receiving the very closest attention. Intensive care." Anna turned to the television set as it flickered to life. The early morning news was on.

"Watch," she said. "Watch and you will see exactly what happened."

Even though the camera crews had been held back behind the police barricades, reporters had managed to sneak through and get rooftop footage of the wreckage on Seventy-second Street. In some of the shots the blood of Jeanne Turner was still visible against the white of the snow.

"Palestinians," the chargé d'affaires hissed.

"Perhaps," Anna said. "In any case we will know shortly."

Just as she finished speaking the door to the commissary opened a crack and one of the agents beckoned to her. Anna slipped out into the hallway and moved toward the mailroom. Once inside, the agent locked the door behind them. On the rough concrete floor were two bodies in canvas bags. Surrounding them were other sacks filled with diplomatic mail, cartons, packages, and crates destined for Israel.

"What do you have for me?" Anna asked.

"They sent their best." The agent shrugged. "Fingerprints surgically removed, no labels on their clothing, no identification of course. The weapons they were using were purchased locally, impossible to trace. My guess is they were either slipped in some time ago or were part of a group being built up right here in the city."

"You still haven't told me who they are," Anna said.

"Iraqis." The agent shrugged again. "It didn't take very long to get to this one. He suffered terribly in the explosion. We were lucky to get him alive. If we ignore the usual ravings, then what the sodium pentathol brought out was very interesting: He kept repeating one word—Moscow." The Israeli shook his head. "It's almost impossible to believe that. Certainly we know that Russians are accustomed to using Iraqis, Palestinians, whoever they can get their hands on, but the orders are always placed by someone two or three stages removed from the operation. The field people never have any knowledge of who issued the orders or from where. So why the hell would he keep saying Moscow?"

But Anna understood. What the dead Iraqi had said made all the sense in the world to her.

"What about the target?" she asked. "Were they after Doctor Turner?"

If she could have the answer to that, she would know definitely if VIPER's information tallied with what she herself believed to be true.

"The target was the woman," the agent told her bluntly. "That was the first thing this piece of garbage spat out." The agent looked down at the lifeless form, the muscles in his forearms tensing as though he wished to shred the helpless corpse.

"We have to get the bodies out of here," Anna said. "It won't do for the mailroom clerks and couriers to see this, not to mention the rest of the embassy staff."

"It's being taken care of right now," the agent assured her. "We'll wait another hour, maybe an hour and a half, until dawn. The bodies will be taken out to the Hudson River by the meat-packing district."

Anna nodded and left the room. She did not have to ask why that particular location had been chosen. Across from the corner of Bethune and West Streets, right along the river, was an abandoned municipal garbage incinerator.

20

Michael Turner buried his wife at Mount Pleasant Cemetery. The day was bitterly cold, with gray clouds rolling across the sky like battleships. The graveside service was mercifully short. Only Dr. Weizmann and Jeanne's parents, the Harringtons, were present. Dr. Weizmann had told him that the entire neurological staff at Penfield Memorial wanted to pay their last respects; Turner asked the chief of staff to convey his thanks. Turner had been under sedation for many hours since the tragedy. Now, three days later, he was alternating between fits of manic activity and periods of silent depression.

"Are you sure you won't reconsider, Michael?" his father-in-law asked as the limousine was carrying them back into the city.

Sidney Harrington was sitting with his elbows on his knees, chin resting on his knuckles. Gone was his normally cheerful expression and the laughing sparkle in his eyes, so much like his daughter's. It appeared to Turner that Harrington's long black coat and homburg were like some cocoon into which his soul had retreated.

"Are you sure, Michael?"

"Yes, I'm sure."

"It would be easier for Christopher if you were there," Mary Harrington interjected. She was huddled in the opposite corner of the spacious back seat, clutching the sway strap above the door.

"Christopher doesn't know anything," Turner said. "Intuitively he will know that something is wrong. He will undoubtedly feel . . . Jeanne's absence. But he will have you, Mary, to take care of him. And Sidney. That's more than I can say for myself at this point."

"And don't you think you mean as much to us as he does?" she said.

Turner looked out the window at the bare trees that were blurring into a brown-gray smudge as the car sped toward Manhattan.

"I love you both very much," he said. "I'll come over as soon as I finish what has to be done here."

"And what is that, Michael?" Sidney Harrington asked. "We've talked to the police. We answered all their questions as best we could. So have you. It's gotten us nowhere. I have the strangest feeling that they're just going through the motions . . . that the police don't really understand what this is all about."

"Sidney." Mary Harrington pressed her hand against her husband's shoulder, making him sit back in his seat.

"A waste . . . such a bloody, meaningless waste," Sidney Harrington muttered. "We've lost her, Michael, and we don't want to lose you. Say you'll come with us. I'd feel you were safer with us."

The old man bowed his head, his eyes glistening with tears, while beside him his wife continued to look out the window, her expression pained and disbelieving.

The limousine dropped Turner off at his apartment. He did not want to ride on with the Harringtons, who would be picking up Christopher at Weizmann's home. Turner could not trust himself to confront his son.

For the next several hours Turner closed himself off from the world. He unplugged the telephone jacks and built a fire in the living room. He sat there staring into the flames, sipping whiskey, smoking quietly. When the mantelpiece clock chimed three, he knew that the Harringtons and his son were on their way to England. He rose and went over to the escritoire and wrote out three letters. The first named Theodore Weizmann as the executor of his estate. The second was a request for an indefinite leave of absence from Penfield Memorial, along with a suggestion that his lectures at Columbia-Presbyterian were to be divided up among the rest of the surgical staff. The third gave power of attorney to Weizmann with respect to banking transactions, mortgage payments, and outstanding bills and anything that had to do with the apartment he owned. He packed two suitcases and made certain that his general practitioner's case had everything he might need. He called the limousine service, then went downstairs, where he handed the papers to one of the security staff with instructions to have them sent to Weizmann's house. A little after five o'clock Michael Turner was on his way out of the city. Oblivious to the northbound rush-hour traffic, he settled back in the seat and closed his eyes. Even so, he could still feel his fingers trembling.

The house had belonged to a portrait painter named Philip Booth. What was originally designed to be a living room had served as the artist's studio. One entire wall was all windows, facing southeast for the morning light. Beyond them, during the night, Turner could hear the ice groan and crack against the little pier that ran out onto the river. Only now did Turner truly appreciate what Booth had done with this rambling old New England farmhouse. It had been converted for the explicit use of a single person. Every detail, from the finely polished hand-pegged floors to the delicately scrubbed marble around the fireplace, testified to the attention lavished on the place. While the house had been lovingly restored and carefully enlarged, the kitchen was ultra-modern, with enough freezer space for a man to provision himself an entire winter. Booth had been something of a cook. The real estate agent had also told Turner something else which until now he had forgotten. Booth had painted portraits of the last three presidents. Jonathan Telford had sat for him in this very room.

Booth's will had stipulated that the house could only be sold along with the furnishings. Jeanne had been very taken by the simple décor which the artist favored, and they had bought the place. Now Turner was simply grateful that he had nothing more to do than unpack his bags. The caretakers, a married couple who lived on a farm a few miles down the road, had seen to it that everything was in order.

Although there was a television and a radio, Turner ignored them. The only person he had any contact with was Theodore Weizmann, whom he telephoned punctually at eleven o'clock every Friday morning. It was a courtesy, nothing more. He was not at all surprised when Weizmann told him that not once had the police tried to contact him.

The days passed. Sometimes he thought he could stand back and actually feel the hours turning over. For the most part he was able to hold himself together. Only in periods of deep depression did he lose track of time, coming out of a reverie to realize that it was three o'clock in the morning and that the fire had gone out hours ago. His schedule remained irregular. It was not unusual for him to sleep until two in the afternoon or to have a corner of the immense studio brightly lit until dawn. As the days passed the sheets of yellow foolscap grew on the right-hand side of the desk, covered with Turner's swift, erratic scrawl. He read back sentences, then paragraphs, then whole pages, carefully excising words and phrases he felt did not express precisely what he wished to say. He knew he could not tolerate anything but the clearest possible account of what had happened. What he was doing was making himself a mirror in which he could see the events of the last thirty-eight days as they really were, not as his emotions had colored them.

This project took up ten whole days. When he felt he was cutting too close to the bone, he would swallow a few milligrams of amphetamine, as much to keep the remembered images at bay as to provide him with energy. At other times he felt he had gone too far and the memories threatened to overwhelm him. But even then he allowed himself only a few grains of a sleeping tablet. Not that they kept the nightmares away, or that he woke up feeling psychically rested. But at least he knew his body had had a respite. When he was satisfied with his mosaic, Turner began to examine every detail in it. On the thirty-eighth day Michael Turner had a visitor.

In the stillness of the country his hearing had grown sharper. He was sitting in the studio with his first cup of coffee when he heard the beating of helicopter blades. Turner rose and stood by the window. A moment later the aircraft came into view, flying low over the house. Through the branches he made out the markings of the U.S. Air Force as the craft hovered above the long front lawn and slowly descended, the blades kicking up a furious storm. The skids touched the snow, then lifted off again, then touched down and finally settled, sinking a foot before they rested on the ground. Two men jumped out, staggering to regain their balance. Turner recognized the woman who climbed down after them. It was the Secretary of State, Laine Compton.

"They don't want to come in?" he asked, still holding the door open.

Laine Compton took off her fur hat and slapped it twice against her suede coat. "I take it there's no one else in the house but you."

"Just me."

"Then they'll stay outside."

As Turner closed the door he could see the two men taking up their positions, one over by a tree from where he would have a clear view down the drive, the second one making his way around the house to the side porch. The helicopter blades never stopped their lazy spinning.

Laine Compton walked into the living room, stopped in front of the fire, then slipped off her coat.

"Is there any more of that coffee?" she asked.

He brought her a cup and put it on the table by the picture windows that overlooked the frozen river.

"I've been here before, you know," she said, staring out into the whiteness. "I came here with the President when he visited Booth during the New Hampshire primary."

"Why have you come now?"

Laine Compton withdrew a cigarette from her purse. Turner leaned forward to light it.

"We still don't know who killed your wife," Laine Compton said. She hesitated. "We don't know who killed her, we don't know why, and what we do know makes no sense and doesn't help us to understand anything else."

"You could have written that in a letter," Turner said rudely.

"In a way I did." She fished in her bag and came out with a thick sheaf of papers bound together with two rubber bands. She peeled off the papers one by one. "New York City police, Homicide Division report, FBI report, Secret Service internal memorandum . . . it's all there. And it all says the same thing: nobody knows why Jeanne Turner is dead or by whose hand."

"Is that why no one from the city police has come to me?" asked Turner. "The investigation was really being conducted in Washington?"

"It was, and still is."

"What you have there doesn't seem worth the effort of bringing it here."

"But there is a great deal more we *could* do," Laine Compton said. "If you were to talk to us, if you could trust us enough to explain what happened to you in Moscow, then maybe we could help."

"You know what happened in Moscow. You had your own man there. You had him at Rudin."

"I'm talking about the kidnapping, doctor." Laine Compton tapped the ash from her cigarette. "I'm talking about the hours that are still unaccounted for. You're the only one who could tell us what happened during that time. You're the only one who can help us help *you* understand what really happened to your wife."

Turner looked away, seemingly staring at nothing, yet his eyes were focused on the pile of yellow ruled paper on the corner of the desk, the mirror of his nightmare.

"I have the obvious part of the answer," he said. "You see, I operated on Komarov after I forced him to strike a bargain he didn't much care for. While I was bargaining for Stanislawski's life I never considered what the repercussions might be. Afterward I honestly—no, naïvely—believed Komarov would keep his end of the bargain. And when I saw Stanislawski on the runway, when I watched that plane taking him away, I thought everybody would be satisfied. That was my mistake. I misjudged Komarov. I didn't realize then the enormity of the ego I was dealing with. In a life-or-death situation Komarov found it convenient to strike a bargain. But I had defied his authority, and he wasn't about to let me get away with it. And so an old man reached out halfway across the world and touched me. That's why my wife is dead and my son has lost a parent."

"You think he punished you out of some senile vanity?" Laine Compton made a helpless gesture. "Stanislawski has been effectively silenced. That article in *The Times* . . . the tripartite arrangement among the Russians and ourselves and the Church. The Vatican has muzzled Stanislawski more effectively than we or the Russians could have." Turner did not speak. "You didn't do much to publicize the situation either." She looked at him. "What does that leave me with? What was Stanislawski to him that the cardinal's escape could have triggered such a vengeful reaction?"

Abruptly Turner rose and walked over to the picture window. He supposed that the man who had gone to the side porch had already put a tap on his phone by now. He supposed too that whatever mail he received would already have been read. Perhaps some new kind of microphone had been installed and they would be able to listen to him walking, piling logs on the fire, making breakfast.

"I don't believe there is anything further for us to discuss," he said to Laine Compton.

"Perhaps not right now." The Secretary of State rose.

"My life has been changed beyond recognition, and there is nothing you nor I can do about that. I feel as though someone has just dropped me down in a totally alien environment. There are no reference points, no landmarks, just an unidentifiable, faintly hostile presence. Out of this kind of surrounding I have to try to forge a life. Be good enough to inform the President to allow me to do this in peace."

Laine Compton slipped her coat on. "I don't think you realize how upset Jonathan Telford was when he heard about what happened." She sighed. "He wanted to see you. It was impossible for him to come to New York but he wanted you to come to Washington. I told him you probably wouldn't answer his invitation."

She waited a few seconds for Turner to reply but he did not even turn around.

He heard her footsteps on the flagstone floor in the ante-room, then the sound of the door opening and the soft click as she closed it behind her.

The drone of the helicopter's blades rose in pitch. In a moment they were fully revved up, and the craft rose and darted away across the meadow, climbing to cruising altitude, and the woods were again silent and cold.

PART FOUR

21

Spring came early to Rome that year. By the end of March the glass panels that enclosed the town house terrace on the Piazza di Spagna had been taken down. In their place the gardeners arranged a miniature landscape of flowerbeds and trellises around the flagstone terrace. Karol Cardinal Stanislawski not only oversaw the work but did much of it himself. He was gratified to feel the rich dampness of the earth, to minister to the buds that soon filled the terrace with a lifegiving scent. He needed this work. Aside from the enjoyment his labors gave him, they helped keep in check worries that preyed upon him.

As he had foreseen, the Church had found little for him to do. Throughout the remaining winter months his sole official duty had been to write a memorandum on the state of the Roman Catholic Church in Poland since the time he had assumed the office of Bishop of Warsaw. But unofficially there was other work, which the Church knew nothing about and which Stanislawski concealed from his superiors at St. Peter's. Using Father Rowitz as a conduit, Stanislawski kept in close touch with Anna Letelier. Hundreds of miles to the northeast, from within the nation he had left behind, Solidarity and the underground resistance network transmitted information to Rome. Not a single day went by without a package arriving for Father Rowitz at the Letelier Gallery. Spirited from behind the Iron Curtain through the resistance network, details of Soviet activities in Eastern Europe made their way to West Berlin, Vienna, Prague, and on to Trieste. The information was conveyed across the various borders by Israeli diplomatic couriers and forwarded to Rome, where Anna's people retrieved it from the embassy.

Night after night Karol Cardinal Stanislawski sifted through the memoranda, collating it with evidence already in hand. The accusations he had been about to make public on Christmas Eve were still valid. He regretted only that he had burned his own sketchy notes for his address, based on information Anna had procured for him in Poland and Russia. But Stanislawski was certain that the Soviet plan for a campaign of systematic repression, including wholesale persecution of Soviet Jewry, had matured well beyond that point. What he needed now was hard evidence of the devious scheme the Kremlin was about to conjure up. It was no longer enough to challenge the Soviets without irrefutable proof. Stanislawski knew that had he spoken as he had intended to on Christmas Eve, he would have thrown the Russian planners into disarray, forcing them to forestall their activities at least for a short while, on the off chance that Western intelligence services might also have got wind of their activities. But the agreement between Washington, Moscow, and the Vatican had effectively reduced Stanislawski's credibility. He was no longer the heroic solitary warrior, but merely one cardinal among many.

Since his arrival in Rome, Stanislawski had had no contact with journalists. When at last he agreed to give a press conference, he had refused to describe his return from Moscow in any detail. Countless times he refused to answer reporters' questions directly, turning them aside and talking in general terms about the situation in Poland. Though this approach met with Vatican approval, it reduced his effectiveness as a spokesman for the Polish nation. The incisive oratory that was his hallmark was not there. After a time reporters simply stopped calling. Obviously something had broken within this extraordinary man, but journalists had seen that sort of thing happen to exiles before.

Stanislawski was grateful that this humiliating charade had played itself out. He tried to put it out of his mind, concentrating on the information that was flowing out of Eastern Europe. Somewhere among these hundreds of scraps of information lay the thread that he was seeking, which, if he were to follow it, would lead him to the heart of the labyrinth.

The prelate's private work required only a little discretion, since by day his activities conformed to the obedience he had promised. By this time Stanislawski was speaking a bit better than passable Italian. His flawless knowledge of Latin was the base on which he and his tutor, a young seminarian from Milan, structured his studies.

So too his walks continued. Stanislawski understood that for better or worse he was now a resident of this city, not a passing traveler. He wanted to know it, to feel its pulse, understand its subtleties and intricacies, share its eccentricities and its history. Above all he wanted to discover that tiny but awesome state of which he was now a citizen—the Vatican.

Karol Cardinal Stanislawski regarded the See of St. Peter much as the simplest peasant from Calabria would: with an awe that bordered on incredulity. He did not believe a man could live long enough to see it all, for in every corner, every crevice, there was history, tradition, a subject one could devote hours if not weeks or years of study to. In the eyes of the Polish cardinal, the Vatican was nothing less than the repository of Church history itself, a monumental example of what men could aspire to, of all they strove to create so that one day they might behold the face of their Creator.

As one of the nine hundred and forty official residents of the Vatican, Stanislawski was free to cross the "border" of the Vatican city-state whenever he chose. His small red passport, issued in lieu of a permanent resident's card, opened every door. He discovered that the physical area was evenly divided into three sectors: the courtyards and piazzas, stunning in their geometrical perfection; the buildings themselves, ranging from the majestic Apostolic Palace to a small square building which served as the laundry-collection center; and the gardens, which during the spring mornings came to life before his eyes. Yet beneath this serenity was a bustling entrepreneurial energy. There was a grocery store, a haberdashery, a pharmacy run by the Fatebenefratelli, a small department store, and a hardware store. The post office dispensed highly prized Vatican City stamps, while gasoline could be purchased at the service station at two-thirds the price one would pay outside the Vatican walls. The bustle surprised him until he learned that, because of the bargains to be had at the various shops, citizens and residents often shopped for more than one family.

He leavened his day with one or two hours spent in the various museums and libraries, sometimes doing nothing more than walking the silent corridors of the Vatican Library, feeling the ages around him, running his hand over the spines of books, ledgers, and manuscripts hundreds of years old. He stopped by the glass cabinets and looked down on scrolls preserved in vacuum cases, written in Aramaic; he read from the first Gutenberg Bible. Such moments he savored as another man would a glass of the finest wine, content only to taste rather than to drink. The vintage was too potent. Invariably such moments of solitude and repose turned bitter for Karol Cardinal Stanislawski. But out of the depths emerged the memory of Michael Turner and what had happened to him—the terrible story he had seen on the front page of the *International Herald Tribune*.

He had sent Turner a letter of condolence, but there had been no response. Stanislawski sighed and resumed his routine.

Word that he had become a permanent resident of the Piazza di Spagna spread quickly throughout the quarter. Carried on the lips of his cook into the markets, the various shops, and cafés, news of this strange, silent man provided much grist for rumor and speculation. The denizens of the piazza were not intrigued because Stanislawski was a foreigner. The quarter had been a haven for outsiders since the sixteenth century. That he was a cleric, even a cardinal, was of no import. These streets had seen popes dragged down them in chains or borne aloft on the shoulders of princes. What fascinated the Romans was Stanislawski the man, his erect bearing, the way he dressed in plain black cassock and boots of undressed calfskin, which reached just below the knee, the way he walked, with long, even strides, taking no heed of the weather, his face thrust forward, hands held loosely behind his back. Although their greetings were courteous enough, the citizens of the Piazza di Spagna reserved judgment. They were waiting for something that would show them the measure of this man. Until then, they would continue merely to watch.

In the first week of April the sign appeared.

Although he ate sparingly, Karol Cardinal Stanislawski always took a constitutional after lunch. No matter what the weather, the people on the Via del Croce could expect to see him come out of the piazza no later than fifteen minutes after one.

On this particular day a thundershower descended upon the city without warning. The streets of the city, paved with small cobbles of lava that, when dry, were as hard as iron, now became treacherously slippery. The driver of a three-wheeled motorcart turned the corner of the Via Gregorio Magno into the Via della Carrozze. He had intended to park in front of the café on the right-hand side. He was carrying the afternoon consignment of fresh fruit for the bar but the motorcart failed to stop. It mounted the curb and hurtled toward the wall ahead, slamming down and pinning a small boy.

The street, which had emptied as soon as the first drops had fallen, was suddenly swarming with people. All that could be seen of the boy was his face, twisted with pain and horror as the cart slowly crushed the life out of him. Hands reached out but could neither pull him away nor get enough leverage to raise the vehicle. Stanislawski was one of the first to reach him. Quickly he waved the crowd back and stepped into the breach between the wall and the twisted metal. With both hands under the front bumper, he squatted down, then slowly began to rise to his feet. The shouting and the cries stopped. There wasn't a sound to be heard in the street. He ordered the other men to follow suit—to lift the front of the vehicle, engine and all. They groaned from the strain as they squeezed in beside him and pushed.

The wheel left the ground. Inch by agonizing inch the rear platform of the cart scraped back. The boy gave a weak cry as the crushing weight yielded and was suddenly gone. Hands instantly grasped him by the shoulders and pulled him free of the

wreckage. Cardinal Stanislawski and the other rescuers gave one
final shove and the motorcart lurched back onto the pavement.
With torn and bleeding hands, he staggered back against the
wall, his heart hammering against his chest.

This is the end, he thought to himself. God, what have I
done? Blackness threatened to overwhelm him . . . the sky was
spinning. He felt arms reaching out for him, men positioning
themselves under his shoulders, half-carrying, half-dragging him
inside the café. All the Rome dailies ran a photograph of the
cardinal slumped over in a café chair on their front pages.

And that afternoon the word spread from the Piazza di
Spagna. A remarkable man had been discovered in the quarter.
All of Rome should know. All of Rome should watch for him.

The cardinal's actions at the scene of the accident on Via
della Carrozze had marked Stanislawski among the people in his
quarter. They had also acted as a catalyst to draw clerics from
the more exclusive Vatican precincts to him.

The first visitors were simply curious to meet Stanislawski.
Most of them were close to his age, a few years younger or older.
They came from the poorer countries of southern Europe and
South America, or from Africa and the Far East. Politically they
represented the *arriviste* faction.

Like any good priest, Karol Stanislawski had the ability to
listen. He put people at ease, drew them out, tested the strength
of their ideas and beliefs. Soon the name of Stanislawski was
mentioned frequently in the offices and corridors of the Vatican.
Those who became regular guests at his apartment spoke with
unrestrained excitement of this man who had come from the
East, whose arrival was still cloaked in mystery, who appeared
calm, almost serene, even in the face of his exile and his en-
forced silence. They spoke of his generosity and his booming
laughter, the way he opened his home to them and the reputation he enjoyed in the neighborhood. They respected his writings and his commentaries upon the political role of the Church
and discovered that he shared many of their own feelings about
where the Church should be trying to go and how that road

should be traveled. They found that he possessed knowledge tempered by wisdom, the rarest of combinations.

Father Rowitz sensed that the more they spoke of the man, the greater the legend of the man became. It was the latter which had finally brought an element of urgency to Rowitz's preparations for his journey to Amsterdam, an urgency he could not articulate but which he sensed had to be heeded. The secret that Katrina Jaworska had passed on to him, if there was any truth to it, had endured for forty years. Another few months would not make any difference, he had thought. Now he no longer felt so complacent.

22

The April rains had washed away the grit and soot that had gathered over Amsterdam during the winter. In parks and along the canals sapling oaks braved the chilly air, sending out tentative buds and shoots. One by one the glass panels which had enclosed café terraces over the winter were coming down. Small metal tables and woven wire chairs reappeared, gleaming with fresh coats of white paint. The bookstalls along the canals were unshuttered and their shelves crammed with secondhand volumes unearthed during the winter months. Along the waterways the canalboats were cleaned and refurbished for another tourist season.

Father Gregory Rowitz arrived in Amsterdam on the early-morning flight from Rome. The address he gave the driver was in the Waag at Nieuwemarkt. As they were approaching the city limits the priest asked the driver to change direction and take him instead to Westermarkt, 263 Prinsengracht. The Anne Frank House. Gregory Rowitz crossed the street, imitating the zigzag movements of other pedestrians who were dodging the oncoming cars and weaving bicycles. When he finally reached the opposite sidewalk, he craned his neck to see as much of the narrow brown-and-white house as he could. He was not tempted to go inside. Although he had not actually been here before, he felt he knew exactly what he would find. Eight bare rooms, left exactly as they had been when the city was liberated by the Allies. The desk Anne had written on, the fragments of notes and poetry would be preserved, the last vestiges of a human being who was remembered as the *onderduiker*, "the hider." It was here that she had retreated from something so terrible that it had no place in the human imagination, yet that something, she knew, would overtake her also.

Rowitz bowed his head to pray, as much for himself as for the soul of that young girl in whom the suffering and brutality of the world was exemplified. At the last minute he had altered his route so that the spirit which dwelt within this place might reinforce the reason he had traveled to Amsterdam, for months had passed since Gregory Rowitz had first gone into the KLM office and purchased his ticket. Father Rowitz flagged down a cab, inhaled deeply, and set off toward his true destination.

The taxi dropped him off between the Kloveniersburgwal and Gelderskade canals. He paid the driver and slowly walked into the Jewish Museum. He lingered for a moment in the lobby of the greatest historical repository of Jewish culture in Europe, the time capsule which contained torahs and prayer shawls from the thirteenth century and Nazi documents outlining the deportation procedure for the Jews of Amsterdam. He could not read Dutch, but the intent and meaning was clear.

Father Rowitz pushed open the door of the Central Holocaust Archives and heard a tiny bell tinkle overhead.

"Good day."

Past the frosted-glass doors was a room that once might have been a front parlor. Now it was divided up by a counter near the doors and rows of metal filing cabinets, each at least six feet high. Behind the counter was a woman, no taller than a child. She was a hunchback with wispy white hair. When she looked up at Rowitz there was generosity in her smile.

Rowitz introduced himself, and the archivist said, "Yes, our Rome office telephoned us about you. Would you be good enough to show me a piece of identification?"

Rowitz tugged out his shiny Vatican passport and gave it to the woman.

"Would you move a little closer to the counter, please," she asked.

When Rowitz complied, the woman stepped up on a platform which ran behind the counter. She gave his passport a cursory glance, then reached out and calmly took his wrist. Without explanation or embarrassment, she pushed back his coat sleeve and cassock. With infinite gentleness, as though she were touching a fresh wound, she ran her fingertips over the blue numbers embedded in Rowitz's flesh.

"Auschwitz," she said.

Rowitz nodded and looked at her.

"My name is Hannah Levin. I hope you will forgive me, father, but we are obliged to be very careful here."

"I don't understand who would want to harm you," Rowitz said.

"You have not been in the West for long," Hannah Levin told him. "By comparison to what is happening in Eastern Europe and Russia, anti-Semitism in France and elsewhere in the West is mild. But there are times when it becomes virulent. Twice in the past we have had firebombs thrown at this office."

Rowitz looked past her to the rows of metal files. Hannah Levin caught his gaze and smiled. She motioned for Rowitz to come around the counter and led him to her office. Two things struck Father Rowitz: the large, gaily colored tourist posters of Israel and the wire-mesh grills bolted on the outside of the two windows, a precaution, he assumed, against rocks or firebombs. Hannah Levin cleared off several piles of papers and documents from the ancient leather sofa and asked him to sit down. When the priest declined her offer of tea, she settled down beside him.

"Now, father, how can I be of service to you?"

Father Rowitz had rehearsed his approach carefully. Choosing his words carefully, he managed to stay within the boundaries of the truth, beginning his story in Warsaw and the night a parishioner of his by the name of Katrina Jaworska had come to him. Her last wish was for Father Rowitz to contact a man called Telemann, someone Katrina Jaworska had known, had worked with in Auschwitz between the years 1943 and 1945.

The essence of the message that was to be passed to Telemann was privileged communication between penitent and confessor. The tiny woman looked thoughtful.

"Katrina Jaworska, was she certain that Telemann was here in Amsterdam?" Hannah Levin asked.

"That would appear to be the case," Father Rowitz said, nodding. "Whether she had had any contact with him recently, I have no way of knowing. But, yes, in her mind she was certain."

Hannah Levin rose and, placing her hands on the small of her back, began to pace over the threadbare rug that covered the creaky floor.

"I hope you understand, father, that we hear many such stories . . . people who have been told by others that someone they knew forty, forty-five years ago is alive and living in a certain place. In a great many cases we are unable to trace the particular person. Forty years ago a person *may* have returned to Amsterdam, *may* have resettled, and *may* have elected to keep his or her original name. Again, that is not often the case. Most Jews who returned to Belgium and France found they could no longer tolerate living in their former homes. In some cases they had no homes left. Some went to America, some to Israel, a surprising number to South America. And of those who remained, many changed their names. Some went further and would not permit their sons to be circumcised. All for protection, you understand. So it is only fair to warn you that this Monsieur Telemann may turn out to be a ghost. You mustn't misunderstand me. I have no doubt that Katrina Jaworska actually knew this person in Auschwitz. It is even possible, although doubtful, that she in some way kept in touch with him after the war. But we have no way of knowing whether the last message passed between them two months, two years, or two decades ago."

"I realize the difficulty of the problem," Father Rowitz said quietly. "Still, I hope you can appreciate that as a priest I did promise to discharge a certain duty to this woman."

"Every single inquiry that comes to us has the same importance," Hannah Levin assured him. "Whether it is a matter of conscience, such as your own, or a legal matter where millions are at stake, we do the very best we can. Who knows, Father, you may be one of the lucky ones."

"Is there anything I might do to help you," Rowitz offered. "Although I find this a beautiful city, I don't think I could enjoy it without contributing something to the search."

Hannah Levin gestured at the door to the right of her desk.

"Because the Auschwitz files are the most extensive, we keep them in the basements. There is also something in our microfiche records that might be of value. I will have a courier bring them around, but in the meantime your help would be most welcome."

"If I might use your phone to call my hotel and tell them where I can be reached . . ." Father Rowitz said.

"By all means." Hannah Levin went out to the main reception area. Over the intercom she spoke softly to the two other archivists who worked in the rear of the building. Then she pulled back a panel underneath the counter, revealing a console that controlled the elaborate security devices that blanketed the bureau.

Cardinal Mirabeau stepped from his chauffeured car and surveyed the town house he had come to hear so much about. This was his first visit to Karol Stanislawski's residence. Standing in the pale yellow light that filtered down from the streetlamps, the Secretary of State for the Holy See thought that it would also very probably be his last. He instructed his driver to douse the headlights, then quickly made his way up the steps, grateful for the lamp that was burning in the tall window.

Mirabeau heard neither the door chimes nor the approaching footsteps. But when the door drew back, it was not a housekeeper nor Father Rowitz who appeared but Karol Cardinal Stanislawski himself. Ignoring the cardinal's startled expression, Mirabeau quickly stepped inside. The door closed behind him.

"Is anyone else awake?" he asked without preamble.

"No one," Stanislawski answered him, perplexed. "My housekeeper is asleep, and Gregory Rowitz is away."

"Cardinal, I have come on behalf of the Holy Father. The end is near for him, and he has asked for you. I beg of you to hurry."

Even before the words fully registered, Stanislawski was moving.

"How much time is left?" Stanislawski asked as they hurried to the car.

"No one can say now," Mirabeau replied. "His Holiness has been losing consciousness for longer and longer periods. Dr. Sabatini believes that it is only a matter of hours before he sinks into a coma. Then there may be no recovery."

The drive across to the Ponte Cavour and the Via della Conciliazione took less than fifteen minutes. The car, with the yellow-and-white Vatican pennants fluttering at the end of each fender, was waved through the security checkpoints, and headed directly for the Apostolic Palace. Stanislawski took note of Mirabeau's silence in the car and so kept his own. When they arrived at the palace, Mirabeau led the way up the great staircase to the third floor, moving quickly; the minutes were precious. They passed the Swiss Guards in the hallway leading to the residential suites. At the door to the papal bedchamber, Mirabeau asked the footman whether the doctor was still with the Holy Father. He was informed that Dr. Sabatini had withdrawn earlier and was now in one of the spare bedrooms, where he had spent the last two nights.

In the papal chamber there were two lamps glowing, casting shadows the length of the room. On an immense canopied bed lay the Vicar of Christ. The sight of him paralyzed Stanislawski. Clement XV had been reduced to a living skeleton. He lay on his side, his knees curled up in the fetal position. The flesh of his face seemed to have melted away, sharply defining the bones and jaw, leaving great hollows for the glittering eyes, and a mouth whose yellow teeth were almost obscene. There was no sound except the soft, dry rattle of an old man's breathing.

Both men knelt by the side of the bed and pressed their lips to the papal ring, loose now on a clawlike finger.

"We are pleased that you have come," Clement said, his

voice soft. "You will sit there, in that chair. Mirabeau, we ask you to stay. What will be said concerns you as well."

The secretary bowed and settled himself on a seat next to Stanislawski.

"You understand, Cardinal, there is little time left to us," Clement said. "Therefore you will listen carefully to what we say. When we have finished, a simple answer will be required of you. Is this understood?"

"It is, Holiness."

"Cardinal, you should know that we have held you in great esteem for many years now. The Church has been the beneficiary of your scholarship as much as your ministry in Poland. You have defended her heroically; you have never permitted vanity to cloud your actions. The world has accorded you great honors, yet when you came here you abided by our instructions not to speak of what had occurred in Moscow. You remained obedient. You came to us a man alone and in pain; we see now that the intervening months have done their work in restoring you. However, while the body may be whole again, your spirit suffers. It is difficult, not to say impossible, for a man to accept the fact that he may never see his land again. Yet you have tried to make this city your home. You have been seen within these walls daily. It is said that even in Rome itself, which is a suspicious, sometimes jealous village, you are highly regarded.

"We have been watching, Cardinal. The political eddies of the Vatican have swirled around you, yet you appear to take no notice of them. You have entertained your brother cardinals at your table, yet not once did you make mention of the seeming indifference that was shown to you—that the Church seemed to have forgotten your very existence. You maintained your faith in the Church. In part, we presume, your silence was founded upon that faith."

Clement drew a handkerchief to his bloodless lips and wiped them. His eyes were beginning to burn brightly, as though all of his energy was concentrated within them.

"We have striven to create an independent Church and believe we have succeeded. But nothing is gained for nothing. Signs of schism have appeared, the inevitable results of some of our policies. The conservative element has grown estranged, not to say hostile. And we fear them because they are dogmatists entrenched in ideological positions that are no longer defensible. Their position is strengthened by the avenues of finance they control. They have allies in the highest places, inside and outside the Church. They have become formidable opponents that my successor may not be able to appease. He will be obliged to work with them yet keep their power in check. A delicate balance must be struck if the whole is to be preserved.

"Opposite them are the newly created cardinals, men who, we might say, are closer to you in spirit, who have endured and lived in the midst of suffering yet who believe it is time for the Church to show more of the Cross and less of her political flag.

"Our successor, Cardinal, will be a man who understands this and who can act to bring harmony out of discord, who has the patience to allow these two groups to see, each in its own way, that their aim should not be unto themselves but unto the common weal. He must be a humanist like yourself, yet a pragmatist; a man of compassion but not without cunning and a firm hand. He will be a man who is dedicated to the Body of the Church and not to the office of the Papacy.

"In the months gone by, we have reviewed the dossiers of many men, seeking among them the one who is truly *papabile*. There are learned men, men who are capable administrators. Some are Romans like ourselves and understand what this state is. Still others have a purity and simplicity which have endeared them to the faithful. But you, Cardinal, have exhibited most of these qualities and one other which is lacking in the rest. Courage. We will be candid with you. You were among the first to be considered, but we believed that you were too far removed from Rome and the workings of the Holy See to understand the true responsibility of the Supreme Pontiff. We confess to you that there is still doubt in our mind as to whether you can overcome this obstacle. You may accept it as the truth when we say that it takes even more than the wisdom of Solomon to guide the Holy Church. Yet perhaps that is how the Lord intended us to see you, as an unfinished man. He has placed us in a position in which we can either do nothing or entrust His church to our faith. And we cannot simply do nothing, Cardinal. Therefore we put this question to you: Are you willing to accept our support for your candidacy for the throne of Peter?"

Anna Letelier saw an opening in the traffic and twisted the wheel to push the Ferrari into the left-hand lane. The car whined across the Tiber into the Via del Leone. At the end of the street Roman midday traffic piled up again.

Anna shifted into first gear, then turned to Father Gregory Rowitz sitting in the passenger seat, an overnight bag on his lap.

"You're sure he didn't tell you anything?"

She knew the question was gratuitous. She must have asked it a dozen times, but Father Rowitz's patience appeared to be limitless.

"I got the impression that he didn't want to say anything over the telephone," the priest replied. "He said he wanted me to come back to Rome as quickly as possible."

"And when did he call you?"

"A little after five this morning."

Anna released the clutch and the car edged forward. "Six hours . . . was there some kind of problem at the airport, a baggage handlers' strike?"

"I don't know," Father Rowitz said. "But I could not get a flight out of Amsterdam until ten o'clock."

Father Rowitz looked away. He was ashamed to have to lie to her, just as he had been when Stanislawski had called him that morning. The cardinal had been very agitated, but in spite of Rowitz's persistent questions he had refused to say why. He repeated again that Rowitz had to return to Rome as soon as possible. He would see to it that Anna Letelier met him at Leonardo da Vinci Airport and hung up before Father Rowitz could register the slightest protest.

"I see that we're not going to the town house," Rowitz remarked.

"He didn't want us there," Anna said tightly. "He will meet us at Il Cembalo."

Rowitz knew she was very concerned. Early on Anna Letelier had made it clear that only in the gravest emergency should the two clerics come to her house in Rome, as the cardinal was now doing.

Maneuvering the car along the Via del Leone, she headed for the Piazza Borghese, veering sharply to the right and heading for the tall gates that closed off the Palazzo Borghese from the outside world. On electronic command the gates parted, gravel spurting out from tires as the car sprinted up the private drive toward Il Cembalo, "The Harpsichord," as her stately house was known. But instead of turning right along the main drive, the car sped straight toward the rear of the estate where, by the wall that ran parallel to the Via di Clementino, sat a small guesthouse. One of the seven bodyguards on the grounds opened the door, inclining his head as the driver alighted.

The ground floor was one very large room, partitioned with Chinese screens, the décor mandarin, the predominant colors jade-green, ivory, lacquer-red, and sandstone. By the French windows which opened on the garden, Karol Cardinal Stanislawski looked gravely at the arrivals. Rowitz was shocked by his appearance: color had fled from his face, leaving it a pasty gray, and the prelate's fingers were white.

Rowitz knelt and pressed his lips to the ring on the fourth finger of the right hand. When he rose, he heard Anna Letelier saying, "Eminence, what has happened?"

Cardinal Stanislawski closed his eyes tightly, trying to organize his thoughts. Instinctively he had reached out for the two people he trusted above all others. The burden demanded to be shared; he needed to hear their reactions, their opinions. If nothing else he had to hear the sound of his own voice telling them the story of this sudden change in his fortunes.

He began to speak, slowly at first, then, as the words gained momentum, he became animated, his features reflecting the entire spectrum of emotions, from intense expectation to puzzled disbelief. He told them of his audience with Clement and the offer the Pontiff had made him.

Rowitz and Anna Letelier were dumbstruck.

He described Cardinal Mirabeau's magnificent suite of offices, where he and the secretary had gone after the audience and where Mirabeau had outlined what the election process entailed. Mirabeau had provided him with a detailed précis of the various political groups within the administrative Curia and the Sacred College, the relative strengths and weaknesses of each, how the campaign on behalf of the conservative candidate was already under way, the background of Joaquin Cardinal de Falla, the inability of the *arrivistes* to bring forward a candidate. He delineated Stanislawski's strengths and how his name had to be put forward before possible supporters.

"The man was quite incredible," Stanislawski said. "His feeling for the political pulse of the Church is so accurate." He turned to Rowitz.

"So this is where the road has been leading," Father Rowitz said.

"Possibly," Stanislawski said quietly. "But the proposal was made so suddenly . . . I never expected anything like this."

Anna took out a cigarette and struck a match. "There has been a great deal going on within the Curia over the last few months," she said slowly. "There have been rumors that Clement had refused to name his successor, that Mirabeau was closeted with the senior Curia even more often than usual." She paused. "They must have been watching how the *arrivistes* were gravitating toward you, those informal meetings and evening discussions at your home. It seems to me that everyone in this city, clergy and layman alike, has underestimated the impact of your arrival. Everyone except the one man who was probably watching the developments from the moment you arrived. Clement."

"When I was with His Holiness, then later with Mirabeau, I felt as though I understood exactly what was happening," Stanislawski said. "Within that context I understood what it was they were offering me. But as soon as I have a chance to stand back, to reflect, the clarity dissolves, the immensity of what has happened overwhelms me."

"Eminence," Father Rowitz said. "I urge you to look back over what has happened in the last several months. At one time, everything seemed to be lost—your health, your freedom, all you had striven for. Then suddenly you were a free man. True, you were no longer in Poland, but you endured and persevered, and from exile God has led you to the gates of the Apostolic Palace. You *cannot* doubt that. You cannot doubt *yourself*."

"Can you imagine what effect your election would have in Eastern Europe?" Anna interjected, continuing Rowitz's theme. "You, who were meant to be destroyed, are now standing for election as Supreme Pontiff of the Roman Catholic Church!"

"That is one of the reasons I am so afraid," Stanislawski said, looking from her to Rowitz. "I am no longer the man I was. I have changed."

"You haven't changed," Anna said fiercely. "You have *not* forgotten. You have never stopped working for those you left behind. Don't you see? If you should be chosen, then the work *all of us* have been doing will suddenly mean so much more. Yours was a powerful voice in Poland. Think of what it will mean when you speak with the authority of Rome. No one will be able to threaten you, to silence you, to force you to hide or flee."

Stanislawski turned toward the French windows, looking out at the room that was reflected in the glass.

"There are two things you should be made aware of," Stanislawski said. "The contest for the Apostolic Throne may be a long and bitter one. You know as well as I that the man who is eventually elected does not necessarily inherit the full power of the office. He may find his actions thwarted, his directives and his aspirations curtailed by administrative bureaucracy of the Curia." Stanislawski paused. "There is a factor I have kept to myself. I have not shared it with either of you. Although the surgery in Moscow and here in Rome was successful, I have developed certain complications. I have been suffering from chest pains, periods of dizziness. I haven't said anything to the Vatican surgeons. Under the present circumstances I could not allow them to operate on me again. Not now."

"Eminence," Rowitz exclaimed. "Why haven't you said anything?"

"You have already been doing more than I could ask," Stanislawski said with great warmth. "Both of you have."

"There has to be an answer, some resolution."

"There is, I think."

Both men looked at Anna, startled by the insistence in her voice.

"There is a way," she said. "Something Michael Turner told me about in Moscow, a new technique, something called an AID, a device which was developed in the United States."

"What are you suggesting?" Stanislawski asked.

"That I bring Michael Turner to you."

"You're forgetting that he's a neurosurgeon, not a cardiologist."

"I know Dr. Turner's specialty," Anna said. "He may not be able to perform the surgery himself, but he could arrange for the best specialists in the world to treat you and in complete confidence. You must remember, Eminence, that in Moscow it was his skill and daring—"

"But even if I would consent to such a thing, the very fact that I would have to undergo surgery yet again would make me much less attractive as a candidate," Stanislawski protested. "How could they elect a man who might rule for only a short time?"

"The operation could be kept secret. It needn't be performed until after the election."

"I can accept everything you say, except that I do not see how I can bring myself to intrude on Michael Turner's life once more. Who is to say that he will even consent to come to see me, much less agree to treat me? What of the risks, the danger I would be placing him in if any connection were to be traced between us? What has happened to change all that?"

Anna understood the anger in Stanislawski's voice. "You are the same man, yet not the same," she said, her voice hard. "Before you were an exiled cardinal, a refugee, political liability. Now you are a papal candidate. That makes all the difference in the world."

Stanislawski considered her words and slowly nodded. "Nonetheless the question remains: Have I the right to ask him to come to me?"

"Would you be willing to do this if he did agree to help you?" Anna insisted.

Stanislawski looked away, then back at her. "Yes."

"I think we're all forgetting one thing," Father Rowitz interrupted. "It would be intolerable for us to demand that he help His Eminence without including him in our counsels."

"That is precisely what I had in mind," Anna said. "I believe we will have need of Michael Turner in more than just his medical capacity."

"And perhaps," Rowitz added suddenly, "Michael Turner has need of you, Eminence."

"I must decide now," Stanislawski said. "I cannot deny Clement the opportunity of choosing another man. And I must decide without being certain of whether it is truly possible, whether Michael Turner will consent to see me, whether in fact this technique you speak of will be of any value."

Stanislawski rose and bowed his head, his fingers running over the crucifix that hung around his neck. He looked back at Anna and Father Rowitz.

"I will call Mirabeau now," he said. "I will call him and ask him to send word to His Holiness that I will stand as his candidate."

"Eminence," Anna was saying. "I would like your permission to bring Michael Turner to Rome. He is somewhere in Europe."

"Go to him, Anna, and ask him."

23

"O most merciful Jesus, lover of souls, by the agony of Thy Most Sacred Heart and by the sorrows of Thy Immaculate Mother, wash with Thy blood the sinners of the whole world who are in agony and who shall on this day pass into the life hereafter. O agonizing Heart of Jesus, have pity upon the dying. . . ."

The Sacrista, the prelate whose responsibility it was to repeat the prayers for the dying, was alone in the bedchamber of Clement XV. Summoned by Dr. Federico Sabatini some thirty minutes ago, after the doctor had found the Pontiff's pulse ebbing rapidly, he had arrived to administer extreme unction. The Sacrista completed his prayers and rose from the side of the bed. The Holy Father was not moving. From his vestments the Sacrista withdrew a small mirror and, reaching forward, held it under the Pope's nostrils. The mirror did not fog up.

At four forty-three on the afternoon of April 15 Clement XV was officially pronounced dead. Present in the chamber with Dr. Sabatini was the papal chamberlain, the Camerlengo, who would, until the conclave had elected a new pope, head the caretaker government. The Camerlengo approached the bed and, leaning across the inert body, raised a tiny silver mallet, and gently tapped Clement XV on the forehead.

"Giuseppe Taranto, are you dead?"

Receiving no answer he tapped again.

"Giuseppe Taranto, are you dead?"

And again. "Giuseppe Taranto, are you dead?"

The Camerlengo paused, then lifted the withered hand and removed the ring of the Fisherman from the fourth finger of Clement's right hand.

The Camerlengo withdrew from the papal chamber. To those waiting in the antechamber, he announced, "He is dead." One by one the intimates of Giuseppe Taranto were permitted to enter the chamber, to kneel and kiss the ringless hand. The first was Auguste Cardinal Mirabeau, the fourth, Joaquin Cardinal de Falla, the last of the eleven, Karol Cardinal Stanislawski. When the intimates withdrew the doors were sealed, the cameriere segreto took his place by the bed, one of five who would take the first watch over the pope's body while the Camerlengo saw to the details of dressing the body. As the deacons of the basilica arrived to begin the mass, the body of Clement was washed, then attired in a cassock of white silk. A crimson cape trimmed with velvet was placed about his shoulders, while a soft cover of red silk was placed over the body, covering it to the chin, the arms placed outside and the papal ring set between the lifeless palms. Later the ring would be broken by the Camerlengo, as would all the seals of Clement's Papacy. A notary of the Apostolic Chamber drew up an affidavit testifying to all these acts, and the Camerlengo officially assumed the interim duties of his office. He, along with the College of Cardinals, would oversee the daily activities of the Church, but neither he nor that august group would be able to make any decisions that lay within the exclusive province of the Pope.

Sede Vacante. The throne is empty. Until the election of a successor, all coins minted would carry these words. All postage stamps, all seals struck.

Sede Vacante.

At the foot of Clement's bed, four candles were lighted. Two members of the Swiss Guard entered and took their positions on either side of the bed. Mass was sung continuously for three hours until the Camerlengo was finally informed that all arrangements for moving the body had been made. Clement XV was ready for the first stage of his final journey.

At seven forty-five a sergeant of the Swiss Guard arrived at the papal bedchamber to inform the Camerlengo that everything was in readiness. Clement's body was placed on a litter and lifted by eight officers of the Guardia Nobile. As the litter emerged from the papal bedchamber, eight prelates, Clement's closest advisers and friends, holding lighted tapers, turned to flank the cortege. As the cortege proceeded down the central corridor, members of the diplomatic corps fell in behind, representatives of the many religious orders brought up the rear.

The procession wound down the corridors of the Apostolic Palace, along the great interior hall that linked it with the basilica, and finally entered the candlelit Sistine Chapel. Beneath the figure of Christ in the *Last Judgment*, on a catafalque covered in red silk, the body was hoisted high above the mourners' heads. For three hours mass was sung, then everyone withdrew and the doors were closed so that the Penitentiaries of St. Peter might begin dressing the body for the Pontiff's final appearance before his people. A long white alb was placed over the cassock and over that a red-and-gold dalmatic. A pluvial—a cape of white silk and golden thread—was draped over his shoulders, a pallium of white wool adjusted around his neck and unrolled down the length of the body. The maniple—a strip of vestment hanging from the left arm, woven of silk and shot through with red and gold thread to symbolize the union of the Eastern and Western churches—was gently placed over the forearm. The tall golden miter was set upon his head while red gloves and red slippers were placed upon his hands and feet. Finally a ring of brilliants was slipped upon the fourth finger of the right hand, over the red glove.

Thus attired, the body of Clement lay in the chapel through the night, attended only by the Guardia Nobile and the Penitentiaries. Tomorrow he would be presented to his people for the last time, and from there he would be committed to the earth.

❖

Karol Cardinal Stanislawski did not sleep that night. He returned to his quarters only at the break of dawn, from the chapel at the Church of Trinità dei Monti where he had been praying. He washed, and dressed in his ceremonial red robes and hurried through the brilliance of the spring morning to the entrance of the Sistine Chapel. The whispers of the clerics he passed did not distract him. His mind was exceptionally clear, his devotion to the man he had served total.

Outside the Sistine Chapel the cortege was forming, a blazing panorama of color, yet strangely muted, even under the radiance of the morning sun. The whole of the Sacred College was present. All the officers of Clement's household bowed their heads. The earthly remains of Clement were lifted from the catafalque and accompanied by a murmured chanting of the Psalm *De Profundis;* the procession set off down the great gallery of the Sistine Chapel, leading into St. Peter's Basilica. When the procession reached the staircase, the litter tilted so that the body appeared to be standing upright against the red silk that surrounded it. The candles and torches, which continued to burn even though there was no need for them now, caught the jewels and precious metals of the miter.

The basilica was empty, its lofty, vaulted interior dwarfing even the hundred clerics who took part in the procession. The procession stopped at the Chapel of the Holy Sacrament. Here, beside Bernini's august columns, the Pontiff's body would repose in state for three days. Today the princes of the Church would deliver their eulogies. Tomorrow the people of Rome would crowd into the Basilica, moving from all points of the city as though through a funnel which emptied at the foot of the catafalque, ringed by twenty-four torches and sixty-six candles, surmounted by the papal tiara.

Karol Cardinal Stanislawski spent these three days in solitude. He gave instructions to Father Rowitz to admit no one to the house, to accept no calls or telegrams. He sequestered himself in a small chapel and, with only Rowitz to attend him, lost himself in prayer.

It was Rowitz who brought Stanislawski word that Anna's initial attempt to contact Turner had come to nothing. Stanislawski received the news without comment. He felt he no longer had any control over events. It was as though he was part of a grand design whose totality he could not perceive. And because he could not understand, he had only his faith to guide him. If Michael Turner was brought to him, it would not be Anna Letelier or anyone else who would do so but God himself. At the end of the third day, when he emerged from seclusion to take his place in the cortege that would move Clement's body to its final resting place, that was the only thing Karol Cardinal Stanislawski was certain of.

Just before dusk of the third day the great doors of the basilica were closed and the body of Clement XV was borne into another chapel. There, in the presence of the Sacred College, the Roman nobility, the diplomatic corps, and the closest friends of the deceased, Clement was draped in the red silk funeral shroud. A red velvet purse, containing an example of every coin and medal struck during his reign, was placed at his feet. Beside it was placed a metal tube containing a scroll which listed the signal accomplishments of his reign. Then, the body was placed inside a triple casket: the outer layer, of cypress, was lined with red silk, the next was made of lead, the last of simple oak.

According to tradition, the Pontiff could choose to be laid to rest near the tomb of one of his predecessors whom he had particularly admired. Stanislawski was later to learn that Clement XV had carefully reviewed the biographies of those who had come before him, looking for some special affinity. He had found none. So his tomb on the Vatican Hill was set well away from all others, proud, solitary, removed in death as its occupant had been in life. Seven hundred and eighty million Catholics mourned.

"The Pope who goes into the conclave comes out a cardinal. Have you ever heard the adage?" Mirabeau put the question to Karol Cardinal Stanislawski as the two were dining in the secretary's quarters.

Ten days had passed since Clement XV had died. The Novendiali ceased to be sung, a strange silence had descended upon the Holy See, a silence of anticipation. The pendulum had moved past the halfway point between the death of the old and the birth of the new. The yellow-and-gold Vatican flags flew at half-mast, but in Rome there was talk of nothing but the election of the next Pope. Romans were not a patient people. After the fifth day they had tired of the incessant requiem masses, had grown weary of the interregnum. It was time to move on to other business. The Pope belonged to them, and they were demanding their man.

"It is a Roman saying," Mirabeau explained, carefully slicing up his Dover sole, sprinkling the fillets with a lemon wedge wrapped in cheesecloth. "It means what it says—that the man most likely to become Pope never does. Tradition requires that the Romans must be surprised."

He chewed on the tender fish, swallowed, then added, "Such will not be the case with this conclave."

Karol Cardinal Stanislawski continued to eat. Tomorrow the path Clement had set him on would reach its end. Tomorrow the conclave would convene.

According to the constitution it had to begin no more than twenty days after the death of the former Pontiff. During the last five Stanislawski had been in the hands of Mirabeau, allowing the former Secretary of State to guide him through the rituals which preceded the gathering in the Sistine Chapel. He marveled at the way the character of the Vatican changed from day to day as the city swelled with the throngs of arriving cardinals, each of them with their retinues of servants, retainers, secretaries, translators, and factotums. Because of the fine weather, conversations among the prelates were often held outside. This severely restricted Stanislawski's normal routine. He could not walk in the gardens or on the terraces without bumping into a cardinal from Senegal, or Malaysia, or Los Angeles. He would pause and speak a few words to them but was seldom asked to join them. Stanislawski was *papabile*. He was there to be observed but was not included in the discussions and working sessions that were being held throughout the city by the various political factions and administrative departments.

As far as Cardinal Mirabeau was concerned, this was all to

the good. On the fourth day he had begun laying the ground-work. He had formally introduced Stanislawski to the twenty-nine other prelates who had constituted the leadership of Clement's Curia, and who spent that night debating the merits of Clement's chosen successor. At dawn Mirabeau emerged tri-umphant. Barring unforeseen defections, all thirty of them would support Stanislawski, at least on the first ballot.

Having had his staff work overtime for the last three weeks, Mirabeau had collected, condensed, and edited the best of Stan-islawski's writings. He reproduced the Nobel prize acceptance speech in toto because it seemed to him that in those words lay the gist of the man. This digest he distributed among the *arriviste* faction, summoning their representatives to his quarters and engaging them in long discussions of the man who had been chosen by Clement. Thus armed, the representatives greeted their own numbers as each arrived from abroad, making certain that every cardinal was taken aside and the *arriviste* position explained. Not surprisingly, there was little debate among the *arrivistes*.

The last phase of Mirabeau's strategy was to make appoint-ments with several of the conservative prelates to sound them out on their deliberations. Mirabeau knew that the Cabal, led by Picheli, had eavesdroppers within his own ranks; conversely he had his sympathizers among the conservatives. Until he chose to commit himself to Stanislawski, the secretary had been re-garded as a neutral. Now he had to rely on others' ears to keep him abreast of developments. Mirabeau did not like what he heard. The Cabal was proving to be very effective in manag-ing the conservative faction. Unless something extraordinary occurred in the conclave itself, the conservatives would vote en bloc for Joaquin Cardinal de Falla. There were also disquieting reports that pressure was being exerted on several of the *ar-riviste* cardinals, as well as the members of Mirabeau's own group. The way matters stood now, neither candidate could possibly win on the first ballot, and the conclave could easily last for quite a few days.

Stanislawski set down his knife and fork, jarring Mirabeau out of his broodings. Mirabeau sat back and spoke.

"The conclave will be traditional in the sense that the choice is obvious: you are the 'pastoral candidate' and De Falla the 'political.' This is a split between the worldly and the unworldly, between the administrator and the man of the spirit. I have tried to play down that distinction by presenting your past dealings with the Polish and Russian governments as evidence of your political experience. We shall see how successful I have been. But this conclave will be unique," Mirabeau mused. "I cannot remember a time when only two men so clearly had the field to themselves."

"Perhaps it is not too late for a surprise," Stanislawski suggested.

"No," Mirabeau said emphatically. "The Electoral College, the Romans, the whole of the Catholic world know by now that the choice is between you and De Falla."

"Isn't that all the more reason why a third man could be elected?" Stanislawski said.

"If the divisions were not so clearly drawn, I would agree with you." Mirabeau shrugged. "But you must consider that everyone realizes the Church has come to a turning point. Neither faction is going to yield. Each understands that if it is to survive, then its candidate must prevail."

"Eminence," Stanislawski said quietly, "I am saddened that we have reached this impasse, that we are talking in terms of factions and not what is best for the Church as a whole."

"That is why Clement chose you." Mirabeau smiled. "Because you *would* look after the body of the Church. You would be the physician. You would heal."

"And is that why you have shielded me from the College so far, because you are afraid my hesitation would cause concern among my supporters?"

"Neither you nor De Falla has taken part in the debates. The Cabal's strategy and mine are identical here. By setting the candidates apart, beyond the reach of the Cardinal Electors, we have allowed each Elector to review the candidate's record rather than deal with his personality. Both the Cabal and I understand that if the conclave is not to become unbearably long, it will be because of a single factor: when you and De

Falla walk into the Sistine Chapel, at that instant, as the Electors look upon you, votes may swing. That impression of you both will either tally with what they know of each man or else it will give them pause to reconsider. Everything they have heard, been told, and read of each man will crystallize. From that point on the election is beyond the Cabal's control or mine. Having seen both of you, the College will vote. If enough Electors have been swayed, then the matter will be decided on the first ballot, if not—"

A servant entered to clear the table. Coffee was brought in and a decanter of brandy. Stanislawski covered his snifter with his palm.

"I feel I have done nothing to help you," he said. "I have been passive, isolated from everything that's been going on."

"And I prefer it that way." Mirabeau smiled. "You have only one drawback as a candidate, Cardinal. Throughout all your years in Poland you have always fought for and defended others. You have never fought for yourself. You have always given of yourself, never believing that a day might come when you would have to put your own interests ahead of others'. I put it to you that tomorrow morning, when you enter the conclave, you must think *only* of yourself, because it will be through your victory that the Church will triumph. And I assure you, the scent of victory is unmistakable. It will be recognized—immediately. Each Elector, as he gazes upon you, must feel that passion, that pride within you. He must see in you a reflection of what the Church might be, for you will remake her according to your own vision. Show them your strength, Cardinal. Fortitude, and confidence. Fight for yourself and the prize that has been entrusted to you, as you have fought for others."

Because dinner had been served early and there remained nothing more to be said between him and Mirabeau, Karol Cardinal Stanislawski found himself completely alone when he stepped out into the Court of Saint Damasso. At half-past eight the Cardinal Electors were either still at table or continuing their discussions in the privacy of their quarters. He dismissed the driver who was waiting to take him home and elected to walk. The evening sky was a stunning collage of yellow running to pink, into purple. There was a gentle breeze that drifted over the city, cool and refreshing, lush with the scent of gardens in bloom. This night could be the last he would have to himself, to walk as a free man. Tomorrow, if God so willed it, he would become someone else.

So Karol Cardinal Stanislawski walked, with his long, almost loping strides, his hands held lightly behind his back, his face against the soft wind. He moved down the Via della Conciliazione past the Ponte San Angelo to the Ponte Umberto where he crossed the Tiber. He paused for a moment on the stone bridge, looking upriver, the sweet smells of Roman gardens replaced by the rank, oily effluvia that rose from the sluggish stream. He turned up Lungotevere Marzio and proceeded along Via Tomacelli which entered the Via Condotti. Oblivious to the frenetic noise around him, to the traffic which had begun moving again as the Romans prepared themselves for the evening, Stanislawski entered the Piazza di Spagna. He was no longer an anonymous pedestrian. People stopped along the sidewalk and looked after him. From the terraces they pointed at his passing figure and whispered to one another that the *papabile* had just passed by. One or two even bowed as he went by. Still others tapped the side of their noses, an expression of omniscience. He mounted the Spanish Steps, moving swiftly among the tourists who clattered alongside until he reached the first level of the Trinità dei Monti. There he turned around and beheld the city, which now had its collective eye upon him and was waiting for tomorrow, perhaps waiting to claim him for itself. At that moment Karol Cardinal Stanislawski was reaching out to his God as he had never done before. He needed guidance. He needed to penetrate the mystery his life had become. He longed to understand what inner voice had prompted him to accept the candidacy. He had been looking for the source of that voice ever since that moment.

As had become his habit, he took a glass of tea at the café on the Via della Carrozze, making light conversation with the barkeep and his daughter, who worked beside him. He played a single game of checkers with the old pensioner who always insisted on playing for money when he played with anyone else. He paid, as he always did, for his drink, but noticed that while his money was accepted it went from the barkeep's hand into the jar marked for donations to an orphanage, not into the register. As he got up to leave, silence fell over the café. Everyone else had risen along with him. They just stood watching him. Slowly Karol Cardinal Stanislawski raised his hand and made the sign of the cross, then left.

When he returned home, he noticed the lights were burning in the drawing room and, as he inserted the key, he wondered if Father Rowitz had returned from vespers earlier than usual. No sooner was he inside than the housekeeper bustled up and whispered in his ear. The cardinal had a visitor. When she opened the doors of the drawing room, he found Joaquin Cardinal de Falla waiting for him.

"Eminence," De Falla said, inclining his head, a half-smile on his lips. He came forward, hand outstretched. "I trust you will forgive this unexpected visit. Your housekeeper was kind enough to let me wait for you."

"Cardinal," Stanislawski said, the tone betraying his puzzlement. He turned back to his housekeeper. "Please leave us now and see that we are not disturbed."

The housekeeper backed away, closing the doors after her.

"Cardinal, if you sent a message, forgive me, I never received it," Stanislawski said.

De Falla held up his hand. "There was no message. I only thought that as long as everyone else was preoccupied with meetings, private discussions, and the like, we might as well have one of our own." He paused. "Unless, of course, I've come at an inconvenient moment."

"No, not at all," Stanislawski said. "Please, sit down. Perhaps I can offer you some coffee, or something a little stronger if you prefer."

"No, thank you."

He watched as De Falla crossed to the other side of the room and settled himself on one corner of the couch. A book with a protruding leather marker was lying on the cushion beside him. Stanislawski recognized the volume as being one of his own, a short treatise published many years ago.

"I took the liberty of reading a few pages from one of your works, to refresh my memory," De Falla said easily. "You are a remarkable writer. Lucid, with a simple narrative style for a topic as weighty as the future of the Church in Eastern Europe."

"It is, I think, a question of how one perceives the situation," Stanislawski answered. "In some ways matters are more clear-cut in Eastern Europe. The Church finds herself in an alien, hostile environment. She walks a thin line between demanding too much and not enough, of antagonizing the civil regimes beyond their tolerance or of not doing justice to the faithful by stilling her voice. She must survive for herself, and she must survive for her flock."

Stanislawski went to the small round table in front of the fireplace and gently ran his hand over the tops of the flowers. What does he want? he asked himself. Why has he come here?

De Falla lifted the slender volume and flipped the pages open to the marker.

" 'The Church,' " he read aloud, " 'must not permit the policies of the secular authority to undermine her own. She cannot tolerate this authority's indirectly encroaching upon her domain by subjecting her communicants to laws and decrees which would effectively remove them from her fold. Every act of the State must be carefully examined not only to ascertain its immediate impact upon the Church but for its ultimate impact upon the community of the faithful. The Church is engaged in a struggle with the secular power. The Church must be prepared to counter her adversary's every move. She is always on the defensive, because for her the nature of the contest is different. She does not envisage the destruction of her opponent by any means; her only goal is to protect herself and the faithful.' "

The Castilian set the volume down, carefully replacing the marker.

"You wrote that some fifteen years ago," he said. "Do you still believe your analysis is accurate?"

"In Eastern Europe, more so than ever."

"And for the rest of the world?"

"I cannot say," Stanislawski said, coming around and sitting down in the leather armchair opposite his visitor. "I have not had enough experience in dealing with the West."

"You are a candid man," De Falla said. "Therefore, I am sure you are surprised to see me here. You are wondering why I have chosen this night to visit you," he finished delicately. He paused, staring at Stanislawski as though trying to fathom what lay beneath the calm, curious exterior.

"Let us admit, Cardinal, that both of us are aware of the situation we find ourselves in," De Falla continued, speaking with a familiarity Stanislawski found disquieting. "We are to be the two candidates. I hope you won't go to the trouble of denying this."

"Go on."

"Our respective supporters have seen fit to rescue us from the usual politicking which surrounds the election. For each of us the rules are the same. In that respect we are completely equal. I ask you to believe me when I tell you that I came here tonight of my own accord. No one knows I am here. I have asked your housekeeper not to mention my presence here tonight, and I have no doubt she is a godfearing woman who will abide by my request. I have come, Cardinal, because I have a proposal that I wish to put before you. I ask you to accept my words in the spirit in which they are intended, and to listen to my explanation before you reply. I want you, Cardinal," De Falla said slowly, "to withdraw your candidacy before the Electoral College."

In the momentary silence that followed, De Falla saw no reaction in Stanislawski's face.

"You have asked that I not interrupt you," Stanislawski said calmly. "I trust you have more to say."

"I do," De Falla answered, inclining his head slightly to give added emphasis to his words. "We are both aware that tomorrow the Camerlengo will exhort the Electors to look to their consciences and decide which man—not necessarily either of us—is best suited to lead the Church. That is the prescribed protocol. He will ask that God help guide the decision of the College, that somehow His Will manifest itself so that all may choose wisely. In practice we know that far more pragmatic considerations are involved. The Church must deal with harsh realities, as you yourself are aware. We are very different personalities, Cardinal. Each of us has his strengths, his weaknesses. But the cardinals should not take these into account. The fundamental issue is whether one of us should withdraw now, because what he represents is unsuitable for the Church."

"You're suggesting that you and the conservatives best understand how the Church is to be led in the coming years?" Stanislawski asked. "You believe you are better able to see the future."

"The Church is an ancient institution," De Falla replied. "Our predecessor very much believed that preparation is everything, that planning was critical to the survival of the Church."

"Did I not say as much in my writings?" Stanislawski asked.

"Yes. But you would make the Church a political camp. I fear, Cardinal, that you would be applying your precepts of a defensive church to its workings throughout the world. You would permit the Church to lose the opportunity to take a leading role. I would prefer to see the Church as an active participant, a leader and formulator of those changes, not a spectator."

Stanislawski rose from his chair, walked round it, then placed both his hands upon the edge of the back.

"You are right in saying we are dissimilar men," he said. "You are a prince not only of the Church but here in this land. You have traveled, you are well read. You understand the concepts of power and the ways of the mighty. I, on the other hand, have arrived here a pauper. I live in exile and exist on charity. I came here ill and confused, a lonely man who had no thoughts of the future beyond what would happen the next day or the next week. You have been bred for the office you hold. I was chosen for mine by men who believed in me, who trusted me with the lives of hundreds of thousands, who believed in my judgment. As I speak to you I cannot help but think we are two sides of the same coin. But I am afraid of you, Cardinal. I am intrigued by the arguments you have put forward, by your concern for certain traditional values, your advocacy of accommodation with the lay world, your perceptive reasoning as to how the Church cannot only prosper, but as you say, take an active role in the leadership of the conservative, not to say chauvinistic, tide that is sweeping across the world. I fear you, Cardinal De Falla, because in you I see another man who led the Church many years ago. He too understood power, and accommodation. Whatever history has written of him, we cannot alter the fact that he *did* turn his back when he shouldn't have."

Karol Cardinal Stanislawski came from behind the chair and stood beside De Falla. He pulled back the sleeve of his cassock, baring the underside of the forearm. Imprinted on the skin, in blue ink, were six tattooed numbers.

"This is where accommodation ultimately leads," Stanislawski said.

Cardinal De Falla rose. "You are in error," he said. "One man can decide for himself, with whatever guidance he chooses, what is right and wrong, what he can live with before his conscience rebels. He has only himself to answer to, only his own life to place on those scales. But the pontiff is *not* a man. He is the custodian of hundreds of millions of people. He speaks for them and their volition. He is the Church."

"Yes," Stanislawski agreed, "and for that very reason it shall reflect the character of the man, shall be judged wholly on his actions, will have to bear them, for better or worse, long after he is gone."

"Cardinal, the hour is late. I see our discussion has reached an impasse. Therefore, I will make my plea to you. Tomorrow when the candidacy is offered, reject it. If you do not, then the conclave will be torn asunder. The proceedings will be lengthy, acrimonious. You will have become responsible for rending the fabric of the Church. You will have left her without a pragmatic leader at a time when a strong Papacy is desperately needed. I beg of you, consider this carefully."

"I thank you for your counsel, Cardinal De Falla, but I must bid you goodnight. We will both need all our strength tomorrow."

24

At seven o'clock on the morning of April 27 one hundred and fifty Cardinal Electors filed from the Paulist Chapel, where the Camerlengo had celebrated the Mass of the Holy Spirit and administered Holy Communion to each of them. Instead of dispersing to their apartments or offices, the Electors proceeded to the Sistine Chapel for the reading of the special constitution, whose articles were to govern their deliberations during the conclave. The decision to proceed directly to the chapel had been taken the night before in a straw vote. No one wanted to prolong the suspense; they all wanted to determine whether in fact the College was as closely split as the rumors suggested. In the case of a profound division the voting would go on for three days before a recess was called for prayer and further discussion. Should seven ballots be cast without a resolution, another recess would be called, in which case even more attention would have to be paid to the physical accommodations which had been arranged for the Cardinal Electors.

To all intents and purposes the Electors were removed from the world for the duration of the balloting. Natural or man-made catastrophes might occur, and they would know nothing of them. Once the conclave began, the entrance to the Vatican apartments adjoining the Sistine Chapel would be sealed off, the windows whitewashed. Food would be passed through turnabouts, pivoting cylinders once used in dungeons for prisoners who were being held incommunicado. Most cardinals had only a small cell, consisting of a simple bedroom and toilet facilities. There was a central dining area, chambers set aside for meetings and discussions, as well as several altars. No form of modern communication was permitted. The entire premises had been scrupulously checked by Vatican internal security for electronic listening devices, tape recorders, and unauthorized observers.

In addition to the one hundred fifty Electors who would do the actual voting, the recording secretary of the Sacred College, the Prefect of Apostolic Ceremonies, and several confessors were also present. If necessary, an Elector was permitted to bring with him his personal physician and a secretary and one assistant. The cardinal was required to vouch for the discretion and moral character of his retinue and was responsible for their actions. Thus, the total number of people filing into the conclave was almost double that of the Electors themselves.

As the Master of Ceremonies led the way into the Sistine, Auguste Cardinal Mirabeau stepped up beside Karol Cardinal Stanislawski.

"Is it true you had an unexpected visitor last evening?"

"It is." Stanislawski nodded.

Mirabeau's expression tightened. "Why did you not inform me of this last night?"

Stanislawski laid a hand on Mirabeau's arm. "There is nothing to be concerned about," he said quietly. "Everything is as it should be."

But Mirabeau did not relent. As they passed beneath the arches of the great doors he whispered, "The conservatives are saying that an accommodation has been made."

The Electors filed into the chapel, each climbing the few steps to his appointed row of pews, moving further along until he had come to his throne.

Just before he moved on, Stanislawski turned to Mirabeau.

"Nothing has changed," he said calmly. "There is no cause for concern. There has been no accommodation."

When all were seated, the Apostolic Prefect stood before the altar and, facing the doors, proclaimed, *"Extra omnes!"* Instantly the doors were closed from within by the Camerlengo, from without by the Marshal of the Conclave, the keys handed over to the Marshal-Warden.

The Prefect read the oath of the conclave. He then waited as each Elector in turn rose from his place and in a clear voice took the oath.

Looking across at the tiers of massive carved seats in the chapel, Stanislawski observed that over each one hung a canopy that could be unfurled at the tug of a sash. In the center of the fringe was a pin emblazoned with the cardinal's coat of arms. Stanislawski remembered from his first conclave, which had elected Clement, that it was not unusual to see an Elector relaxing on his throne, reading, chatting with his neighbor, or even catnapping. The first ballot was meant only to test the waters, to determine whether any real consensus had been reached. But such was not the case now. Even the eldest of the Electors was sitting up in his seat, fingering the ballots that had already been passed out. The sense of anticipation was unmistakable. There was something else that Stanislawski felt distinctly—an air of uneasiness, an undercurrent of fear. He could sense that at that moment one hundred and fifty minds were forming the question: What is the real choice we are about to make on behalf of the Church?

As soon as the oath had been administered to each of the Electors in turn, Pietro Cardinal Picheli rose from his seat and addressed the Camerlengo.

"I wish to submit, on behalf of myself and others, the name of a man we believe can lead our Church," he said in a stentorian voice. "I present before this august conclave his Eminence Joaquin Cardinal de Falla."

De Falla rose and remained standing for a few seconds, his hands clasped before him, his gaze steady, directed upward at Michelangelo's *Last Judgment*. Then he resumed his seat.

Mirabeau was on his feet.

"Cardinal Camerlengo, I too wish to put forward the name of a man who I and others believe has the strength, the courage, and the wisdom to lead the Holy Church. I bring before the Sacred College Karol Cardinal Stanislawski."

For all they had heard of the man perhaps few of the Electors knew what to expect when they saw him standing before them. Glances were exchanged, whispers coursed up and down the tiers as the cardinal slowly rose to his feet.

The Camerlengo, who had expected both nominations, looked around the assembly. He did not anticipate that any other candidates would be proposed, and none were. At this point he could have asked for a vote by the dropping of the canopies, but he did not even consider it. This was his fourth conclave. Each had been different, each had started and would proceed along its own particular lines.

"Cardinal Electors," the Camerlengo called out. "There are two nominations. I pray that the balloting begin. Please write: 'I choose as Sovereign Pontiff the Most Reverend Lord Cardinal _____.' "

One hundred fifty hands completed the sentence on the ballot. One by one the Electors left their thrones and proceeded to the chalice before the altar. The ritual phrases echoed through the chapel as each Elector stood before the altar in turn: "Our Lord Jesus Christ, who shall be my judge, is witness that I chose the one whom I believe should be chosen before God."

The ballot was dropped into the patten, the patten tipped, and the ballot slipped away into the chalice.

Rome did not sleep that night. Throughout the city cafés and restaurants remained open well past the usual closing time, the staff eventually joining the clientele, sharing tables and endless cups of espresso. In almost every apartment window the pale light of a flickering television set could be seen. At any given time at least one member of the family was awake and watching. Relatives who had come in to the city especially for the election snapped stories and broke bread with their city cousins while across the hall children slept three or four to a bed. In the editorial offices of the major dailies editors were waiting until the last possible moment before allowing the presses to roll, for there was always the chance that within the next hour, or even the next few minutes, the college would have reached its decision. In the studios of the radio and television networks, producers and directors, technicians, political analysts and anchormen prowled the studios, subsisting on cigarettes, smalltalk, and coffee. The regular staff announcers were ready to go on the air at literally a minute's notice; all they needed was something to announce.

In St. Peter's Square thousands kept the vigil. Some had arrived early that afternoon and claimed a vantage point on the cobblestone piazza. They came with food and drink and warm clothing to ward off the chill of the spring night. They came alone or with their entire families, having forsaken the usual evening's entertainment or made excuses for not showing up for the night shift. These Romans were no different from their ancestors. The election of a Pope was an international event, but for Romans it was also a rare local spectacle in which they were as much participants as spectators. For some their attendance was an expression of their faith, others assuaged their curiosity, still others simply had to be there if only to be able to say later on: "I was in the piazza when they sent up the white smoke."

As the first slivers of light crept into the eastern sky shouts erupted in the piazza. High above the square, along the left wall, was the chimney which would carry the signal. After the ballots had been read and counted, they would be burned. If a majority had been reached, then the paper would burn by itself and white smoke would pour out of the chimney. If there was a deadlock, then wet straw would be added to the ballots, and the smoke would be black.

For a moment the crowd in St. Peter's was confused. There was not enough daylight to make out the color of the smoke right away. But then the special floodlights which had been installed around the piazza wavered up the side of the building, working their beams along the chimney. A collective groan rose from the multitude. There could be no mistake now; the smoke was black.

25

A Grumman Gulfstream III corporate jet touched down on runway 303 at Charles de Gaulle, twenty-three kilometers northeast of Paris, outside the small town of Roissy-en-France. A sleepy customs officer met the plane after it had taxied into a rented hangar, made a perfunctory check of the plane's cargo bay, stamped the sole passenger's passport, and wished her a pleasant day. A company Mercedes whisked Anna Letelier into the city proper, the traffic catching up with it only along the Quai de la Tournelle below the Pont de l'Archevêché. The great car crawled over the bridge onto the Île de la Cité and past the gardens of Notre Dame, turning right onto the Pont St. Louis and across to the Quai d'Orléans. It drew up before the doors of a small eighteenth-century apartment block which had once been the home of Baudelaire, Gautier, and the Club des Haschischins, and now housed the Letelier Gallery. The private apartments of her father, Emil Letelier, were on the top three floors.

Between half-past nine and eleven o'clock Anna Letelier authorized the acquisition of two Modiglianis from the estate of the Comte de Lyons, one Degas sculpture from an anonymous party in the Bahamas, and three sixteenth-century icons from a source she knew represented the Soviet ambassador to France. She checked the final arrangements for a private showing to be held the following week, the début of a slightly demented contemporary artist whose work was created exclusively on glass and whose life was entirely in the hands of his mistress-pusher, who kept him supplied with heroin. A call was placed to the Beverly Hills agent of Sotheby Park-Bernet with a preemptive offer for a Ming Dynasty statuette of dubious provenance. That concluded her official business in Paris.

With the promise of a thirty-percent tip, the leering taxi driver she found at a stand by the Pont St. Louis metamorphosed into a true *chevalier,* allowing no obstacle to stand between his vehicle and the destination of his lovely passenger. Although the noon-time traffic was out in force, the driver shot down one-way streets, one hand on the wheel, the other on his horn, ran three red lights, then—as they cleared the melee at the Place de la Concorde—hunched over the wheel in the best French manner and pushed the accelerator to the floor. In the back seat of the swaying Citroën, Anna Letelier calmly smoked a cigarette, oblivious to the insults flung after the taxi by other motorists and pedestrians.

The American Hospital at Neuilly was at 63 Boulevard Victor-Hugo. A haven of mercy for those who dared not entrust themselves, for linguistic or medical reasons, to the Parisian hospital system, it had served the needs of the permanent and transient foreign community for forty-five years. Its staff was equally divided between North Americans, British, and indigenous Frenchmen who spoke English and were generally there because of the superior facilities. Anna Letelier presented herself at the main information desk.

"Can you tell me where I might find Doctor Turner?" she inquired.

"Doctor Turner is not on duty today," the receptionist said stiffly, and began battering the helpless manual typewriter into submission.

"Can you give me his address then?"

"We are not permitted to give out that information," she said, not bothering to look up. The pounding was formidable.

"I am a representative of an art gallery, the Letelier Group. Some time ago Doctor Turner left an order with us.

We've finally located the piece he wants. It's imperative that I contact him."

"No way she's gonna help you, ma'am."

Anna turned around to see an obese black man in hospital whites addressing her. His tag read Doctor Chambers.

"My name is—"

"I know." The fat man smiled, one of his jaws disappearing into the recesses of his chin. "You a friend of Doctor Turner's, ma'am?"

"As I said, he left an order with our gallery. The piece he's interested in has just become available. I must have his authorization to put in a bid—quickly. Otherwise the dealer will move on to the next buyer."

She offered him her card, which he glanced at and returned. His coffee-colored eyes flickered over her face, not unkindly, but there was something behind them, a kind of reserve . . . as though he were concealing something.

"Why don't you take a little walk with me for a minute, Miss Letelier."

For a man of his bulk he moved with exceptional grace, holding her elbow as lightly as he would a bird.

"I presume you work here, Doctor . . . Chambers."

"Chest-cutter," the physician said. Anna glanced down at his forearms, the diameter of the average man's calf muscle. Yes, he could open a chest with little difficulty. He held the door for her, and they moved down the steps to the gravel path, where Chambers extracted a battered Camel from his breast pocket.

"Only got one," he said shyly, offering her the limp cigarette.

"That's fine. Not my brand really," she said, taking out her own.

They lit their cigarettes, and Chambers led her to a bench which faced a small park.

"You a friend of Michael's?"

"Not really. Professional acquaintance."

"I suppose I could call him," Chambers mused softly. With anyone else Anna might have taken legitimate offense, but

Chambers had spoken so gently, and the concern behind his voice was so evident, that her anger was dispelled.

"Is he not well, doctor?"

"Not well? I guess that's a matter of interpretation."

"I heard about the death of his wife," Anna told him. "And . . . and how she died."

"Murdered, Miss Letelier. Jeanne was murdered," Chambers corrected her. "Michael hasn't been right since then, you know? All of us here, we kind of look after him, make sure he doesn't get into real trouble. We're waiting for time to do its work. Sometimes it's not so easy."

"I know."

"That's why we're all so protective about him. I mean, strangers coming up and bothering him. He doesn't need that."

"But he does work here."

"More or less, I suppose. If you call setting a sprained ankle or treating a peptic ulcer work for a surgeon. Tourist business, Miss Letelier. Some days though, you see the hands work. God, the talent in that man. But then there are other days . . ."

"Like his day off—today?"

Chambers nodded.

"You could always call," Anna reminded him.

"Think I'll save myself a few francs. You have something to write on?"

"I'll remember."

"Seventeen Rue Norvins, just off the Place du Tertre."

"Montmartre?"

"Could have picked a worse street in that neighborhood. The place isn't so bad, being so close to the church and all. Dynamite view. You know Paris pretty well?"

Anna sensed what was coming. "We have an office here. The last address I had for Doctor Turner was in London, his in-laws." Now the lie: "They didn't have his home address. I gather all his mail is being sent to the hospital."

"That it is, ma'am, that it is."

"Doctor Chambers—"

"Call me Willie."

"Willie, what's happened to him?"

"I can't answer that for you. All I know is the loss cut deep, the hurt is still deep. So if it's just business you have with him, don't worry. He'll handle it. Anything else . . ."

"Why did you give me the address?"

The physician's face broke into a smile. "Because you shine, honey. I think he'll be glad to see you. Just treat him gently and don't make any judgments. You know where he's coming from. Just remember he has a ways to go yet." Chambers rose to his feet. "Call you a cab?"

"What is it you want?" Turner asked as he reached the bottom of the stairs. The dog, pricking up its ears at his tone, growled softly in its throat.

"Hello, Doctor Turner." Anna Letelier glanced down the corridor as a door slammed. "Might I come in?"

"No."

"There are things we must talk about. Very important things."

"You're wrong, there is *nothing* for us to talk about!"

She did not back down. "You are needed in Rome, doctor," she told him. "Karol Cardinal Stanislawski needs you again. Give me twenty minutes to explain. Then, if you like, you can send me away. But at least give me that much."

"I don't owe you *two* minutes," Turner said.

"You owe me nothing, doctor. The man whose life you saved is an altogether different matter, don't you think?"

He closed the door behind him and locked it, and without a word started down the stairs, ignoring Anna, who followed behind. He was moving as though he wanted to run from her. A *deux chevaux* squealed just before its bumper hit his legs, the driver screaming obscenities. Turner ignored him, swinging through the doors of the Café Skrip. He glanced at the barkeep, jerking his head in the direction of the back room.

"It's available."

"A coffee for the lady. Brandy—a bottle—for me," he said shortly.

One by one the men rose from their chairs as Anna strode by. When Marcel the pimp reached out and patted her ass,

Anna swung about, gripping his hand and bending it back at the wrist. Marcel's head snapped back at the pain. He slid off the chair, falling to his knees on the dirty floor.

"How long do you think you'd last out there with a broken hand?" she asked softly, in perfect argot. She paused. "I'm sorry, I didn't hear you."

Marcel whispered something unintelligible, and Anna slowly released him. "You're lucky there's a doctor on the premises," she told him, and continued toward the back, to the corner where the pinball machines were lined up. The barkeep bustled up with their order, a smirk on his face.

"*Tigresse!*" he said approvingly. Turner gave him a fifty-franc note and waved him away. He poured himself a small brandy and then held up the open bottle.

"Just a touch, please," Anna said. He poured her a drink, then downed his, refilling his glass immediately.

"You have something to say to me," he muttered, searching through his pockets for a cigarette. He did not want to look at her.

Disgust welled up inside her. She decided on the direct approach.

"Karol Cardinal Stanislawski would very much like to speak with you," she said.

"I don't do surgery anymore," Turner answered brusquely.

"Yes, that's what I was told. These days you prefer to minister to distraught tourists."

For an instant anger flared, a white light glowing in his lifeless eyes. Then it was gone.

"That's no concern of yours," he said, the voice dangerously quiet.

"I'm afraid it is," she answered. "Because it's possible that Stanislawski has chosen the wrong man."

Turner shook his head. "I don't understand you people," he said, a trace of genuine amazement in his voice. "You act as though you have some God-given right to jump in and out of people's lives, not giving a damn about whom you hurt, what the consequences are, all for something you've decided is of the utmost importance. Well, maybe it is that important, maybe it's incredibly vital for you, but not for me. I don't need you or your explanations. I've already paid for listening once."

"Michael Turner, I can't tell you what it is Stanislawski wants with you," Anna said. The aggressive tone disappeared, to be replaced by concern. "I can't speak for him. But do you honestly believe I would have intruded upon your life again if I thought he really played dice with men's lives? That's not true. Your wife's death—"

"I don't want to hear a word from you about my wife," he said. "Not one."

Anna sat back against the wrought-iron frame of the chair. "Is there a telephone here?"

"Just before you get to the washrooms," he said, gesturing toward the rear of the café.

"Stay here while I make a call . . . please."

He nodded, raising his glass.

The stench from the W.C. was overwhelming. Anna fumbled with the change, managed to work it into the slot, and began dialing. Almost four o'clock. She prayed that it wasn't too soon.

When the switchboard operator at the Israeli embassy answered, the coin dropped. Anna identified herself and asked for the First Secretary. Two minutes later she was back with Turner.

"Is there a television in this place?" Anna asked.

"What the hell is going on?" Turner demanded.

"Is there a television?"

"Over the bar."

Anna went over to the barkeep. She said something to him and he coaxed the old black-and-white set to life, flipping through the channels until she told him to stop.

"Leave it on that station," Anna told him and came back to Turner. "I want you to see something. If you still feel the way you do now after seeing this, I promise I'll leave you alone. You will never hear from me again."

For a moment he didn't get up, and Anna could see the struggle within him. The brandy was acting quickly, churning up the memories, tearing open the wounds. Finally he gripped the bottle by the neck and came over to the bar.

"Look there," she said.

The camera must have been placed very high up, for it commanded the whole of St. Peter's Square. The camera zoomed across the heads of thousands of people at the balcony just as a figure stepped out dressed all in white. The camera settled on the features of the man on the balcony, his arms held out before him in the sign of benediction. The roar of the crowd was deafening.

"Can't be," Turner whispered hoarsely. "It can't be."

The barkeep, a good Catholic, crossed himself, then looked sharply at Turner. "The new Pope," he said proudly.

Turner gripped Anna by the forearm.

"Stanislawski," she said. "Now you know why it's imperative you come to Rome."

"Nuntio vobis gaudium magnum: Habemus Papam!"

"I announce to you tidings of great joy! We have a Pope, the Most Reverend Lord Cardinal Stanislawski!"

"Quo nomine vis vocari?"

"By what name do you wish to be called?"

"Innocent. The fourteenth of that name!"

Immediately after Stanislawski had spoken, the Prefect of Apostolic Ceremonies drew up a notary's instrument for the name while the Secretary of the Sacred College and two Masters of Ceremonies acted as witnesses. Innocent XIV accepted obeisance from the members of the Sacred College, embracing each prelate in turn. He then was led by Mirabeau to the small dressing room where the tailor made final adjustments on the robes. So outfitted, Innocent had begun the journey his predecessor had last made in death, carried on his throne from the Sistine Chapel to the Chapel of the Holy Sacrament, on to the tomb of the Apostle, a sheaf of *flabelli,* enormous fans, serving as a canopy. The Master of Ceremonies, walking before the procession, his silver baton tipped with smoldering hemp, turned back toward the Pontiff every thirty steps and intoned: "Most Holy Father, so passes away the glory of the world!"

On the balcony of St. Peter's the new pontiff had his first chance to gaze upon the people of the city who were now his charges, belonging as much to them as they did to him. He was crowned with the triple tiara that once graced the brows of the Great Kings of Persia, and then he raised his arms in his gesture of first benediction.

26

The small van from KGB Technical Services Division pulled up at the service entrance to Number 17 Kutuzovsky Prospekt. After being cleared by the Guards Directorate security detachment, the three-man team disappeared into the building, pushing a small trolley laden with electronic equipment toward the service elevator. Admitted by Gorodin's personal bodyguard, they conducted an electronic sweep of the Foreign Minister's apartment. Three quarters of an hour later they were packing up their equipment. After the team left, the bodyguard posted himself outside the door. The Foreign Minister would be arriving on the hour. He was a punctual man.

At precisely six o'clock in the morning the limousine bearing Dmitri Gorodin eased to a halt before the apartment block. The minister stepped out into the black Moscow dawn and quickly made his way upstairs. He paused briefly at his doorway to hear his bodyguard's report, then issued a new set of instructions and went inside. Gorodin indulged himself with a long hot shower, donned fresh clothing, and had time to glance at his personal correspondence before KGB Director Suslev was announced.

Gorodin greeted the director and led the way down a spacious corridor, the walls adorned with small landscapes illuminated by wall lights. He turned left into what had originally been a living room and parlor but now served as the library. The double glass doors had been removed, the windows facing Kutuzovsky Prospekt taken down and replaced with one-way glass. Gorodin had also insisted that the glass be armored. Two walls had built-in bookcases, whose contents ranged from geopolitics to astrophysics; by the handsome desk stood a large globe which Gorodin liked to spin very very slowly when he was deep in thought. A smart leather sofa, two comfortable armchairs, and a coffee table on a cantilever base rounded out that half of the library. The other had two large working tables set in an L shape, a teleprinter, and the prerequisite battery of phones. There was also a high-speed shredder with a built-in incinerator.

"I take it my people were here earlier," Suslev said, settling himself on the couch and propping his cane in the corner. Like Gorodin, he too had been up all night, but from the look of his rumpled clothing it was obvious he hadn't been home.

"Everything has been looked after," Gorodin said. He sat down behind his desk, as much to establish his authority over his meeting as to distance himself from the smell of the obese man.

"It seems to me, Viktor," Gorodin opened delicately, "that the unfinished business of Stanislawski has come back to haunt us."

"Stanislawski? Innocent XIV," Suslev barked. "It is somewhat ironic that he chose that particular name."

Both men had been watching the satellite-relayed broadcasts of the Papal election.

"I am always amazed how a small error, a seemingly insignificant oversight can, in time, grow out of all proportion," Gorodin said. He leaned forward across the leather blotter on his desk. "We can't ignore him any longer, Viktor. What he threatened to do to us last Christmas pales by comparison with how much he can hurt us now." He paused. "No, not hurt. Destroy. As an exiled cardinal, Stanislawski had been effectively neutralized. As Pope—"

"You're suggesting we move against him," Suslev said.

"I submit to you that we have no choice. In fact, Viktor, it is your own foresight that leads me to this conclusion. You had your people in Rome keeping watch over Stanislawski and Rowitz. All reports from that station indicate that Rowitz has been a frequent visitor at the house of the Israeli woman Letelier. There can only be one reason for that."

"There is also something else," Suslev whispered. "On one occasion Rowitz went to Amsterdam. The field report indicates that he visited the Central Holocaust Archives. The only reason anyone goes there is to trace the whereabouts of a camp survivor."

"I fail to see the connection," Gorodin said.

"Rowitz is a survivor of Auschwitz," Suslev continued. "One might think that he's simply trying to track down someone he knew there. But two things made his visit curious: The trip seems to have been arranged surreptitiously; that is to say, from the way Rowitz handled the travel arrangements, I don't think the Vatican knew exactly where he was going or why. Secondly, Rowitz had to leave Amsterdam in a great hurry. The reason for this now becomes obvious. Stanislawski must have summoned him back to discuss the election. But even under such pressing circumstances, Rowitz did not leave for Rome immediately. Instead he flew to Geneva and there spent about an hour and a half in a lawyer's office. Only then did he return to Rome."

"Go on," Gorodin said. Suslev's narrative clearly intrigued him.

"Think back to that Christmas Eve," Suslev prompted. "From military intelligence reports we know that Rowitz barely escaped Bibnikov and the armed security units. But the report also states that Rowitz could have easily gotten away before they arrived. Yet he stayed on in Warsaw. According to the report on the Holy Trinity Clinic, he did so because of a woman who had sought him, the woman Katrina Jaworska. We don't know—and neither does Bibnikov—what passed between Rowitz and her. But it was obviously sufficiently important for Rowitz to be willing to risk capture. Let me put the following question to you:

Who or what would be so important to Rowitz that he would risk his life by staying with her until the last possible moment, knowing that Stanislawski had either been taken or was missing?"

"Stanislawski," Gorodin said immediately. "Stanislawski is the most important thing in Rowitz's life. Whatever it was this Jaworska knew, it had to do with Stanislawski."

"Therefore the reason for Rowitz's trip to Amsterdam and Geneva may indeed be connected with Stanislawski," Suslev put in.

"I still don't see how this helps us deal with Stanislawski now, as Innocent XIV," Gorodin objected.

"You can't move against the Pope openly," Suslev concluded. "If *anything* were to happen to him, suspicion would fall on us immediately. His history here is too well known. But perhaps Stanislawski is not the key. Perhaps it is Rowitz. Perhaps there is something about Stanislawski which no one knows, something which Rowitz is either trying to find out, or to conceal. I think the first order of business is to increase surveillance on Rowitz."

"I think there is a great deal in what you say." Gorodin put the pencil down. "But I also think that the election of Stanislawski has brought us to a crossroads. We cannot take the chance that he won't speak out immediately. We have no way of knowing how much he has learned from the Jews. I agree that we cannot move against him directly, that Rowitz might be our answer. But that will take time, Viktor, and that is a luxury we can no longer afford."

Gorodin sat back in his chair and looked closely at the KGB director.

"To all intents and purposes the country is ours. In the last few months Komarov has initiated no new programs, and none, as far as I know, are being planned. There has been no discussion of treaties which would limit our development of inner-space weapons. Our agricultural policy is a shambles. Once again we are buying heavily from the Americans and Canadians, yet our gold production has not been increased to match the demands on our foreign-currency reserves. The last five-year plan expired two months ago, but no new quotas have been set. I have to ask myself what Komarov is waiting for. He cannot govern but he refuses to step down. And every day that the situation remains unchanged, Kobalevsky grows stronger. Add to this the unexpected element of Innocent XIV, and you have the makings of destruction . . . our destruction, Viktor. Everything that we have worked for over the last three years."

"There is also another factor," Suslev said hoarsely. "You have to take into account the effects Stanislawski's election will have in Eastern Europe. The 1981 revolt in Poland germinated from the election of John Paul II. Poland still remains undisciplined, a threat to the unity of the Warsaw Pact."

"So I think you can see that it is incumbent on us to take action," Gorodin said with finality.

He allowed Suslev a moment to consider the implications of these words. As well as Gorodin thought he knew the KGB director, as close as they were ideologically and politically, he still had to wait for Suslev to commit himself openly.

"I presume you have some proposal concerning all of this," Suslev said. He crushed out his cigarette and looked up at Gorodin.

"Yes, I do," Gorodin said.

When he started to speak there was no hesitation . . . even though he knew that what he was advocating was treason.

They appeared to be a perfect, ordinary family even though the man wore the light gray uniform of the KGB, with lieutenant's bars on his shoulderboards. The woman, who could have been mistaken for his wife, was markedly older than he, a thick torso giving way to massive thighs and protruding rump. She could have made an excellent caricature, had it not been for the silent despair that scarred her face. The boy was a handsome lad of ten or eleven, with shaggy hair and a quick laugh. They were coming out of Number 17 Ulitsa Vernadskova, near the intersection with Lomonosovskii Prospekt, the thirty-four-hundred-seat arena that housed the Moscow State Circus. Aleksandr Roy, who had been sitting two rows behind them, shouldered his way through the crowds that were streaming out to the broad plaza, intent on his surveillance. He felt a little sad. He hadn't been to the circus in over twenty-five years, yet the performance had still moved him. He felt sorry for the little boy.

As the crowds fanned out across the plaza, he followed the KGB lieutenant, the woman, and her child across the street to the car park. Roy knew the officer had a legitimate reason to be with the woman: he had served with her husband in the East. He could easily explain that afternoon as one friend's looking after the widow and fatherless son of another. That would even account for his taking them home in his car.

Roy was wrong. The lieutenant opened the door of his midnight-blue Moskovich, but instead of reaching around to open the rear door, he brought out a package in brown wrapping. Roy was standing thirty feet away, under a sodium arc lamp. He saw clearly what was happening beside the Moskovich and knew that at the same time anyone looking his way would be blinded by the glare of the sunlight.

Poor tradecraft, Roy thought. He really should have taken them home and passed the package on the way. He must be in a hurry, a very great hurry.

Of all departments within the Committee for State Security, few were watched as closely by Sergei Bibnikov as Jewish Affairs. This was not because there were Jews in the forty-one man unit; there wasn't one. The officers in this unit were primarily Ukrainians. All had received extensive training in Jewish history, folklore, philosophy, and religion. Several were expert linguists, fluent in Yiddish and Hebrew. Their responsibilities were twofold: to maintain strict and constant surveillance on known Jewish dissidents, including such routine tasks as supervising mail intercepts and debriefing informers in factories or laboratories where the number of Jewish workers was substantial. Secondly, to infiltrate the tightly knit Jewish communities in Moscow, Leningrad, and Kiev, with the object of ferreting out and closing down the intelligence links between the Soviet Union and Israel.

Always the older ones, Roy thought. We don't have to worry about the young careerists. We know too much about them. Their chance for corruption hasn't come. But those like Valerian, with better than ten years' service, sometimes found their beliefs changing, and with them, their loyalties. They were only human. Indoctrination could tell you over and over again that the Zionists were the enemy, but how long could you consider people so helpless, so put upon, to be dangerous? After a while it was difficult to keep the edge on one's work. After that the doubts would creep in, like the wind under the door; then the first betrayal, a small one, a fact omitted from a report to give someone a second chance, a remark overheard but the obvious connection not made, an analysis misinterpreted and evaluation rejected. Minuscule deceits, seemingly without import, until one day one looked back and saw the miserable heap of fear and treachery they had accumulated into.

That was the point that Lieutenant Arkady Valerian appeared to have reached at this precise moment. He didn't know when Valerian had been turned or by whom; he had had the officer under surveillance for only sixty days. But he had been turned. At some point, probably not too long ago, someone had tapped him on the shoulder and confronted him with his treachery. At that point Valerian had two options. He could either inform Special Investigations and let himself be used as a ferret, sent into the underground to see how far he would get and whom he would encounter, or he could make his change of loyalty complete, betray his country, and start working for Jerusalem.

Roy had evidence of two dead drops Valerian had carried out, both in the Moscow metro. He could have taken the lieutenant at any time he chose. But he held off, trusting his instincts, which told him to play Valerian lightly. Four months ago someone had managed to learn that Dr. Michael Turner would be arriving in Moscow to operate on Chairman Komarov. Someone had passed that information to Solidarity, for it had been Solidarity that had gotten Stanislawski out of Warsaw. It had to have been Solidarity that had snatched and held Turner and taken him to Stanislawski. Someone who had access either to the files or the conversations of a half-dozen of the most powerful men in the Soviet Union, who knew why Turner had come, what his itinerary was. Someone who also had access to the pipeline into the Jewish underground. The go-between. Someone who had been turned. Lieutenant Arkady Valerian.

Roy watched as the lieutenant set the package down on the roof of the car and began to remove the brown paper wrapping. The woman was looking at him without a trace of a smile, oblivious to the child's excitement. Valerian opened the box and brought out a small-scale model of a Soviet warship, fending off the boy's hands and patiently explaining something about the construction, running his fingers along the hull. Suddenly he squatted on his haunches, disappearing from sight. All Roy could see was a pair of arms holding the toy boat and beyond that a child's excited face. The woman looked around listlessly. She wasn't trying to spot surveillance. Roy could almost smell the resignation that emanated from her. Valerian finished explaining about the boat and let the boy put it back in the box. He leaned forward, his lips brushing the woman's cheeks, hands on her shoulders. Whatever it was he was saying to her, she must have understood. Her head bobbed up and down like a doll's. Then the woman took the boy's hand and began to walk away, threading her way through the other cars in the parking lot. The boy turned back and with his free hand waved back to Valerian, who in turn raised his arm. Roy watched the mother and child walk across Vernadskovo Prospekt to the Universitet metro station. The lieutenant also watched them until they were out of sight, then finally slid in behind the wheel and started up his car.

Roy got into his own car, a standard gray police vehicle. He drove for twenty minutes along Sadovaya, then turned off along Kutuzovsky Prospekt. A quarter of an hour later the woman and boy, the package held tightly under his arm, got out at that stop and walked toward Number 17. The plainclothes security guard nodded to the woman and let her pass without any inspection. Roy did not bother to get out of the car. Number 17 was the apartment building that housed twelve of the thirteen Politburo members.

Roy returned to his office and went downstairs to the computer section. In twenty minutes he had the names of all the occupants of Number 17 Kutuzovsky Prospekt, including the live-in help. The woman and boy were among them.

By half-past four Irina Mikhailova had finished cleaning up the tiny kitchen, folded up the ironing board, lifted it into the recess in the wall, and shut the door behind it, locking the board in place. She took a last look around to make certain everything was as it should be, then went into the small parlor. Her son, Lavrik, was still asleep in the other bedroom of their two-room flat in the basement of Number 17 Kutuzovsky Prospekt. A short, thickset woman, Irina Mikhailova looked a decade older than her thirty-seven years. But time was cruel to widows, especially those who had not remarried and never would. She sat down at the dining room table, which also served as her desk, and glanced over the grocery list. As the yellow-faced clock chimed the half-hour, she realized that the special state store where she shopped would be closing in three-quarters of an hour. Irena Mikhailova was scanning the list a second time, trying to remember if she had made a note of everything Gorodin's pantry required, when there was a knock on her door.

"Kuragin" was Irina Mikhailova's first thought. Since her front room was directly underneath the main staircases leading to the suites above, she had heard the distinctive tread of Gorodin's bodyguard twenty minutes earlier. Kuragin knew that she did her shopping today. It was not unusual for him to have her bring home a few delicacies for himself on Gorodin's account.

The man standing at the door was not Kuragin. He was younger, in his late thirties, slim, with the build of an athlete. His hands were held loosely by his side, his eyes steady, without pity or remorse. The moment she had dreaded, though she knew would inevitably come, had arrived.

"Irina Mikhailova?"

She knew there was nowhere to hide, and she wanted to face her inquisitor with the same dignity that had given her the courage to commit the action which now condemned her. Yet at the final moment her courage seemed to have deserted her. It refused to speak for her, and she could only nod her head.

"I am from Special Investigations," Roy said. He did not offer to show any identification. "May I come in?"

She let him in. He watched as she locked the door behind him.

"Is your boy here?"

"Yes," she whispered.

"Is he still asleep?"

"Yes."

The man nodded. "Perhaps we should go into the kitchen then," he suggested.

She noticed how his eyes took in the details of the room at a single glance: a small table, the short counter beside the refrigerator, the knife rack above the stove. Irina Mikhailova sat down at the table and folded her hands in front of her. The man from Special Investigations pulled back the chair opposite her.

"You know an officer by the name of Lieutenant Arkady Valerian?"

She knew she could deny it, tell him nothing. She could stand mute and watch as the man walked into the bedroom and brought Lavrik out with him. The boy would be sleepy. He would be looking at her, not understanding what was happening. Then the man's grip would tighten on Lavrik's arm, and he would begin to cry, then scream. . . .

"Yes, I know him," Irina Mikhailova said quietly. Did they have Arkady? Was he already in prison? Was he even in Moscow? And why only this man? Why not a full investigating team? Why in the afternoon and not in the middle of the night? Did Gorodin know?

"I asked you if you met with Valerian today at the Moscow Circus?" Roy repeated.

"Yes. We met at the circus."

"He gave the boy a toy, a model ship."

"Yes."

"That ship has been hollowed out to accommodate a recording device. This morning, when you cleaned Foreign Minister Gorodin's apartment, you removed a similar device that was ready to be passed on. You kept the boy home from school because you needed a reason to go to the circus, which was where Valerian passed you a fresh unit and the model ship. Sometime during the day you were going to damage the boy's toy. Using this as a pretext, you were to contact Valerian, who would offer to fix the boat. Tonight you would have given him the boat . . . and with it whatever you had taken from Gorodin's apartment . . . a tape, perhaps."

Irina Mikhailova bowed her head, her hands clutching for the locket at her throat.

"I want you to come upstairs with me and show me exactly where you put the device."

"It's in the study—"

"I want you to show me."

"The boy—"

"He will be all right. No harm will come to him."

The man got to his feet and stepped aside to let her pass. Irina Mikhailova hesitated by the closed bedroom door.

"If he wakes up, and I'm not here . . ." she started to say.

"Then we had better hurry."

Roy guided her away from the stairs to the old-fashioned elevator, swinging back the brass gate. He pressed the button for the fourth floor.

"How long have you been working for Valerian?"

"Three years."

"Since your husband was killed on the Chinese border."

"My husband was *murdered*. He was killed by his own men because he was an officer . . . and a Jew."

"So you ended up with a military pension and this job, which is enough to get by on comfortably. You were approved by state security because you were the widow of an officer, killed in the line of duty."

"Murdered."

"Yes, murdered," Roy agreed. "And to get your revenge you started working for the Zionists."

The lift glided smoothly to a stop, and he pushed the grill

back. He was watching her hands as she reached into the pouch of her apron and pulled out a ring of keys. Their footsteps made no sound as they walked down the hall to the polished walnut doors with the gleaming lockplate. Irina Mikhailova inserted the key and opened the door. Silence reigned in Gorodin's apartment, the faint odor of lilac hung in the air. She went directly to the library and over to the wall behind Gorodin's antique desk. On the third shelf from the top hung framed commendations, two for military service, two Orders of Lenin, a commemorative medal struck when Gorodin was admitted to Politburo. That was the one Irina Mikhailova reached for. She snapped out the back plate and handed it to Roy, who examined the microrecorder, no larger than a matchbox.

"Ingenious," Roy murmured. "Voice-activated timer, otherwise the unit remains inert. A sweep never finds it. Where are you to meet Valerian today, to give him this?"

"A dead drop at the Bolshoi metro station. There is a kiosk just before the turnstiles. He'll be there, watching."

"What time are you to be there?"

"Half-past six."

"Will he speak to you?"

"No. We'll meet again, at the Ponds, tomorrow evening."

Roy removed the recording unit, snapped the back into place, and handed it back to her.

"Wipe it and put it back," he said, and escorted her out of the apartment.

"Are you planning to go out today?" Roy asked her when they were in the elevator. "Do you have shopping that has to be done?"

"I have to go to the market for the minister."

"Proceed as if nothing at all has happened," Roy told her. "Your telephone is being tapped. There is someone watching outside. You will be followed wherever you go. I will come back in an hour or so. We will talk again. I will tell you what you must do."

When Irina Mikhailova opened the door to her flat, she was greeted by Lavrik, standing in pajamas and bare feet, rubbing his eyes, smiling up at her. When she turned around, the man from Special Investigations was gone.

Roy left as he had entered—through the basement garage. In twenty minutes he was back in Bibnikov's office, fitting the cassette into a microrecorder.

"Where is Valerian?" Roy asked, without bothering to greet Bibnikov as he entered.

"At work, as usual. I take it you struck the mother lode."

"Four years," Roy said through his teeth. "Four fucking years!" He looked attentively at his prize. "We're ready."

For the next hour and fifteen minutes the room was silent except for the recorded voices of Gorodin and Suslev.

When Bibnikov finally turned the machine off, the silence was oppressive.

"He's insane," Roy whispered. "Completely and utterly."

"Is he?" Bibnikov said. "It sounds to me as though Gorodin has thought the whole thing through very carefully."

"We can stop him," Roy said, getting up and jamming his hands into his pockets. "We can get a voiceprint analysis and stop him. Him and Suslev both."

"You weren't listening," Bibnikov admonished him. "All we have on that tape is two men discussing a plan, purely hypothetical, nothing more. Do you think that's enough to go up against the likes of Suslev and Gorodin?"

"We can at least take it to Komarov and let him decide."

"Possibly," Bibnikov replied. "But I am much more interested in finding out about Gorodin's intentions, exactly what he proposes to do."

"He can't do anything as long as Komarov is alive."

"That's true, but how can he know exactly how long Komarov will live?" Bibnikov asked delicately. "After all, we now know Gorodin has a precise deadline to meet."

There was an awkward moment of silence in the room.

"What are we going to do?" Roy asked.

"We have our fingers on the thread that will unravel Solidarity," Bibnikov said. "We have Valerian and the woman. She is supposed to make a dead drop tonight. You will instruct her to do so. Valerian obviously has to pass the tape on."

"Without listening to it?"

"Oh, he'll listen all right. But don't you think he knows what's on it—or at least has a fair idea? After all he is in Jewish Affairs."

"What I don't understand is how he knew what Gorodin and Suslev would be talking about on that particular evening."

"We'll have to ask him about that," Bibnikov said thoughtfully. "Chances are he's been selective in his choice of when to listen. As with anything else, luck never hurts. But we must remember to ask him." Bibnikov thought for a moment. "Yes, Valerian will listen to the tape and pass it on."

"And he'll take us directly to his pipeline," Roy said. "Straight through to the other end, in Warsaw."

"That he shall," Bibnikov nodded. "That he shall."

"What about the cleaning woman?"

"We take her as soon as Valerian makes his drop."

"The boy."

"The boy's innocent," Bibnikov said. "I'm sorry for him."

The Mermaid was one of Moscow's most popular restaurants, even though it was located forty miles outside the city. Founded a century earlier as a writers' club on the banks of a tributary of the Moskva River, it was famous as much for the magnificent porch that encircled the entire house as for its cuisine. The Mermaid was a hard-currency restaurant. Dollars, pounds, Deutschemarks, and Swiss francs were as welcome as American Express cards. Rubles never sullied the till of the antique silver-plated register. Sergei Bibnikov grimaced when Roy called him later that evening and told him that surveillance had intercepted a call from Valerian's desk to the Mermaid. Meanwhile the drop made by Irina Mikhailova had been flawless. Valerian had appeared to retrieve the package exactly as she had said he would.

At half-past nine Aleksandr Roy followed Valerian out of the city along Route 43. They headed north past the industrial suburbs, through the forest that ringed the city, and finally into the countryside. Soon they both arrived at the restaurant, where Roy actually exchanged a few words with the officer from Jewish Affairs about the weather while the tall, cadaverous maître d'hôtel, who looked like some law clerk out of Gogol, examined the reservations ledger for their names. It seemed that Valerian was a valued customer, for he was led straight through the interior dining room onto the enclosed veranda and seated at a corner table. When the maître d' returned, twenty American dollars changed hands and Roy was led out onto the terrace and seated on the banquette that ran the length of one side of the porch. He was looking directly at Valerian, who was sitting four tables away, his profile turned toward Roy. By the time each man had finished his apéritif, the veranda was half-full. The sweet smell of timothy grass and hyacinth drifted through the air, punctuated by the sounds of the owl and the nighthawk. The smoke from fat Turkish cigarettes drifted over the tables. Soft conversations were punctuated by laughter, a slight touch of the hand, suddenly lowered eyes. Through this Arcadia moved stewards in clean, starched whites guided by the maître d', who watched each table with shiny black eyes, hovering over his guests. The musicians came in—an accordion player, guitarist, and bandurist. The songs were plangent, melancholy.

Perhaps not tonight, after all, Roy thought as he sliced through his tender rabbit in wine sauce. He had been certain Valerian would not wait, yet he seemed to have nothing more on his mind than the splendid meal and the wine. The exchange took place so quickly, with such dexterity, that Roy almost missed it.

A group of six—three couples—had been shown in. The maître d' brought them to three tables set together and one by one pulled back the chairs. Their conversation was in English. References were made to the Canadian Embassy. One of the men, a short, spry fellow with dark curly hair and a generous smile, removed his companion's shawl and, leaning across the aisle, asked Valerian in heavily accented Russian whether he could leave it on the empty chair opposite him. Valerian smiled, nodded. As the diplomat's hand brushed across the tablecloth, his fingers reached out and palmed the matchbox that was sitting next to Valerian's pack of Camels. The box disappeared when his hand was withdrawn. Roy didn't see where the diplomat had cached it—probably in the vest pocket of his three-piece suit—as he turned around to rejoin his friends.

There were any of a dozen ways Roy could have searched the Canadian, diplomatic immunity notwithstanding. But his instructions were to observe, nothing more. He would leave Valerian to the backup unit that was waiting down the road and follow the Canadians' car back to Moscow to make certain this wasn't a cutout. By midnight he would know the identity of the official who had made the drop, every move he had made since he was posted to Moscow, as well as the itinerary all diplomats had to file with state security. Roy had no doubt that the Canadian gentleman studying his menu was scheduled for rotation, perhaps a month's home leave or just vacation.

Where would he go? Roy asked himself.

When Roy saw that Valerian was finishing his coffee, he signaled for his check. He lit a cigarette and watched as Valerian strolled out to his car, got in, and started the engine. Roy could see the small Volga moving slowly along the narrow road that led away from the Mermaid.

He returned to the restaurant, taking a seat at the bar and ordered a cognac he didn't really want. He had to wait for the Canadians. He had scarcely tasted his drink when the maître d' materialized at his side. Two minutes later Roy learned from the surveillance team that Valerian had driven six kilometers down the country road, then pulled over to the side. The team moved in cautiously after his car horn continued to blare. By then Lieutenant Arkady Valerian had been dead for fifty seconds. There were traces of crushed plastic on his tongue. The leader of the surveillance team reported that Valerian had died with tears on his face.

27

Michael Turner stepped out onto the balcony of his room at the Hassler-Villa Medici and looked out over the teeming Piazza Trinità dei Monti below. It was five o'clock on a crisp, wind-blown day, and Rome was stirring once again after its mid-afternoon repose. From where he stood, he could see the Spanish Steps stretching out below him, the streets and avenues becoming congested as they approached the Vatican. The vigil at St. Peter's was nearly at an end. From the clerk at the front desk Turner had learned that the conclave would be over in just two hours. Anna Letelier had telephoned to suggest that they meet downstairs.

He picked up his English raincoat, then took the elevator to the lobby. Outside, under the portico, he paused to get his bearings, then stepped out into the street, alongside Anna Letelier. Together they headed west.

"Doctor, are you familiar with the geography of the Vatican?" Anna Letelier asked him.

"I think I could find my way, yes."

"There are several gates leading into Vatican City. One of them is on the Viale Vaticano. In exactly half an hour Father Rowitz will be waiting for us inside."

"Us?"

"Yes, doctor." For a moment he thought he saw a shadow of indecisiveness flit across her face. They stepped onto the sidewalk that ran alongside the high stone walls separating the sacred from the secular cities. Viale Vaticano was a busy street that evening, jammed with celebrants, vibrant with the cries of peddlers hawking everything from roasted chestnuts and skewered meats to small color portraits of Stanislawski. The portraits of De Falla were on sale at half-price. Romans, it seemed to Turner, never played only one horse.

Suddenly he felt her arm slip through his.

"The gates are about twenty yards ahead," Anna said, smiling up at him. "And for God's sake laugh—or at least smile. People are celebrating, and you look as though you just came from a funeral."

"We'll never make it through that," Turner said, pointing at the crowd pressed against the tall iron gates of the Vatican.

"We won't have to." She steered him along the wall. They moved on for a few yards, then stopped in front of a small gate. Someone had been waiting for them. No sooner had Anna paused and looked through the iron bars than the gate swung back. Quickly she stepped into the opening, pulling Turner after her. As soon as he was inside, the gate swung back into place and locked.

"We must hurry now," Father Gregory Rowitz said. "Welcome, Dr. Turner, and thank you for coming." The priest led the way, following a small path along the lawn that brought them to the drive that led to the central gates of Viale Vaticano. There he turned and made for one of the dozen entrances to the vast Vatican Museums. He climbed the steps, turning back every now and again to make sure Turner and Anna were still with him. It was obvious to Turner that his admittance must have been cleared beforehand. The two plainclothes security men who unlocked the doors to the museum gave only a cursory glance at his passport and medical identification.

Once inside, Father Rowitz turned to the neurosurgeon. "Before you is the spiral staircase to St. Patricius. We will follow it to the basement, which in turn leads to the tunnels."

At the base of the staircase Rowitz turned right, leading them to a cul-de-sac. Retrieving the keys from his girdle, he opened a door with a word, MAINTENANCE, stenciled across it. He led them quickly through the furnace room and past a massive air-conditioning unit that was dripping pools of water onto the concrete floor.

"In the past Popes hid in these tunnels on occasion or used them to get in and out of the city discreetly. They serve a somewhat different purpose now."

"It looks like it's going to be a long walk," Turner said.

"Yes, normally it would be." Father Rowitz pointed to an electric cart with a sign in Italian that read MAINTENANCE SUPER-VISOR. "However, we are thoroughly modern here at the Vatican." He turned to Anna. "I hope you know how to drive one of these oversize flashlights."

The tunnel below the Vatican Museums ran under the Court of the Belvedere and ended underneath the Court of St. Damasso. Anna parked the electric cart in one of the bays.

"We are now in the building in which the Cardinal Electors were sequestered for the night," Father Rowitz said to Turner. "There is an elevator that runs between this basement and the kitchens above."

Father Rowitz led them along a concrete corridor and inserted a magnetic key into the lock in the elevator panel. The elevator rose five or six floors. When the doors opened, he followed Rowitz into a small rectangular room, simple, almost spartan in its appointments. The walls were of whitewashed plaster, with a crucifix nailed over the door at the far end. There was a long refectory table with a half-dozen chairs pulled up beside it, a large sideboard with dishes stacked up on the shelves, and cheerful red curtains tucked to the side of the window sashes.

"This is where His Eminence—I mean His Holiness—has been taking his meals," Father Rowitz explained. "It is the only place where he can be alone for a few minutes." The priest indicated the room with a gesture. "This is where he will see you."

"Alone," Turner said. "That is essential."

"We have done what we had to do," the priest told him. "Rest assured that no one will intrude on the time you have with him. After His Holiness leaves, we will come for you.

Understand that the election and installation ceremonies are long and arduous. He will not have much time these first weeks."

With that Rowitz and Anna withdrew.

Turner took out his cigarettes, lit one, and went over to the window. He cupped his hands against the glass and pressed his forehead between them. Six stories below he could see the bright orange lamps that dotted a portion of the Vatican garden. Occasionally a shadow would fall across the cinder path and a moment later a Papal guard, his halberd slung over his shoulder, walked into view. He turned away and pulled back one of the chairs, the legs scraping against the pegged floorboards. For a few minutes he smoked quietly, realizing just how tired he was. While he was grinding out the cigarette into the lid of a tin can the door opened.

The nun looked up at him briefly, then bowed her head and lowered her eyes. She brought in a dish of cheese and cold meat, small bowls of marinated tomatoes and pickled beets, which she placed on the table. She left and returned with a bowl of fruit and an urn of hot water. After she had set out the plates, cutlery, and cups, she withdrew as silently as she had come in.

Turner pulled one of the refectory chairs around so that it faced the window, and sat down, elbows propped on the windowsill. This time he did not hear the door open behind him.

"Good afternoon, doctor."

Anna had warned Stanislawski, and Father Rowitz had confirmed her observation. Turner was not the same man who had operated on him in Moscow. Standing in the doorway Stanislawski was taken aback by his appearance. He had little memory of Turner—the moment the surgeon had leaned over him in the bunker, then a few distracted minutes on the windswept airport tarmac. Now he was not looking at the same man.

Stanislawski closed the door behind him and came toward Turner, his right hand held out. Turner rose and slowly came around the table. He offered his hand and felt it being enclosed by a hard, strong grip.

"There aren't enough words to express my sorrow about

what happened to your wife," Stanislawski said, still holding on to Turner's hand. "It may mean little enough to you, but I have prayed for her soul every night, as I have for yours, and that of your son."

Turner nodded and moved away. He was struggling for something to say, but whatever came into his mind seemed feeble, inappropriate. The Pontiff spoke first.

"I don't think you had much time to eat properly, so if you're hungry . . ." He gestured toward the food on the table.

"I'm . . . I'm not very hungry," Turner said.

"Then perhaps some fruit, or a glass of wine?"

Turner shook his head. "Nothing."

Stanislawski pulled back the chair at the head of the table, sat down, and broke off a piece of the light, golden loaf. He sliced off some cheese and was reaching for the cold meat when suddenly he stopped and pushed his plate away.

"It seems I too have no appetite," he said ruefully. "But would you at least have some tea with me?"

Without waiting for a reply, he poured tea into two glasses mounted in silver-filigree and passed one to Turner. He waited until Turner was sitting beside him before he spoke again.

"Gregory Rowitz tells me that you did not know we were looking for you."

Turner pushed his cup away and gazed up at his host. "Why were you looking for me?"

"I have need of you again, as a physician," Stanislawski said. "In spite of what the College may think, or, for that matter, what my own doctors say, all is not well with my heart. When I spoke of this to Anna, she remembered your mentioning some sort of device. You must tell me, Michael, whether such an operation is possible for a man in my condition and whether or not it will have a desired effect. Will it allow me to work unimpeded and give me the time I need to accomplish what I must do?"

"Assuming there has been no further damage to the heart, then, yes, an AID unit would permit you to lead a perfectly normal life."

"You're certain of that?"

"I wouldn't say so if I weren't. Although you must understand, I'm not a cardiac specialist. The actual details would have to be worked out by a cardiologist."

Stanislawski sat back, a ghost of a smile on his lips.

"A few words," he murmured. "A few words can change so very much, Michael."

"I still don't understand what any of this has to do with me," Turner said. "The best medical treatment must be available to you now."

"Yes, that is so," Innocent agreed. "But there are other considerations."

"What have your doctors prescribed for this?" asked Turner.

"I haven't said anything to them."

Turner folded his hands across his chest and shook his head. "Vertigo, blackouts, chest pains. I hope you realize that you are in the process of killing yourself," he said flatly. "Without a thorough examination, the proper medication, and very likely another operation, I wouldn't give you very long . . . even less if you keep up the pace you obviously feel is required of you."

"But there is the possibility that another operation will allow me to do what must be done," Innocent said at once. "The AID . . ."

"An implant is probably the answer," Turner agreed.

"Can you explain it to me?"

"The AID is an automatic implantable defibrillator, the latest artificial aid for heart-attack victims." Turner gestured with his hands, illustrating the process. "Ventricular fibrillation, which means the uncontrolled contraction of muscle fibers in the chambers of the heart, cuts off the flow of blood to the brain. From what you say, you've been suffering from very mild fibrillation, resulting in the dizziness and vertigo. Before the AID was developed, a patient could not receive treatment outside a hospital. The available units were too bulky, and they not only took up space but required specially trained personnel to operate them. A few years ago the AID was developed by cardiologist Michael Mirowski in Sinai Hospital in Baltimore, in conjunction with Johns Hopkins. He worked with Heilman and Alois Langer at Medrad-Intec Systems of Pittsburgh, who developed the necessary microcircuitry. But it was Mirowski who conceived of a miniature defibrillator which continually monitors the heartbeat and can avoid a cardiac crisis by automatically releasing an electric charge which jolts the heart back into its usual rhythm.

"The defibrillator weighs two hundred and fifty grams and is surgically implanted just beneath the skin of the abdomen. Two electrodes lead to the heart, one through the veins into the right atrium, the other to the tip of the ventricles. The AID can be programmed not to interfere with the heart's normal rhythm but to respond to a severe arrhythmia. When this happens, it transmits a shock, something the patient would feel only as a slight tingle. If the heart doesn't respond at once, the AID will administer two additional jolts. The life-span of the lithium batteries is somewhere in the range of one hundred discharges . . . about three years on the average. As far as I know, only six or seven people in the States are using the AID implant, one a teen-age boy and the other a fifty-seven-year-old woman, so there seems to be no problem with age. All of them are living normal lives."

"Are you familiar with the implant operation?" Innocent asked.

"Just familiar. I wouldn't be able to perform the procedure."

"But you believe that such an operation would be feasible in my case," Innocent persisted.

Turner nodded. "From what you've said, and from what I saw in Moscow, it would be feasible. But you would have to have an expert opinion."

"And how long would such an operation take, from the time I enter the hospital to the time I can return to my work?"

"That is one of the side-benefits of the AID," Turner said. "The implant procedure takes only a few hours. Unless there are complications, the patient is usually ready to go home after two or three days."

"Then I don't see that there's any alternative. The operation must be performed." He looked fixedly at Turner, as though he were carefully selecting his next words.

"Now at last I can answer your question: Why I needed you, and still do. I ask you to remember that what I put forward to you now I do so in the knowledge of what you've already done for me. I will not think any the less of you if you should refuse. You must know that you and your wife and your child will remain in my prayers always." Innocent spread his hands on the table. "You see how we have to meet, almost like thieves in the night. Previously, Gregory Rowitz was able to serve as intermediary between myself and Anna. He was our trusted courier. Now that will be impossible. Father Rowitz is my secretary, and as such his activities will be almost as closely watched as my own. I cannot permit anyone associated with the Holy See to learn of my connection with Anna Letelier. That would be catastrophic. Yet I must have a channel to her, one that we can both rely on. This is where you can help us. You would be that link."

"Link?" Turner said in disbelief. "How can I be—"

Turner felt a hand upon his shoulder.

"You could be that," the Pontiff said urgently. "You could be of greater service now than perhaps you have ever been before. I have prayed for your wife and the child she gave you. I have also prayed for you because you have fallen. What you did for me in Moscow caused the death of the woman you loved. This loss has led you into the most pernicious vice. No, not drink, nor drugs, but sloth, the wasting away of your hard won talents. Of all things that is perhaps the most unforgivable."

"Some men are thought to be capable of more than they actually are," Turner countered, an edge to his voice.

"That is not true in your case. You know it as well as I."

Michael Turner rose. The pain translated itself into anger —at himself, at his condition, at the fact that even in his misery he was not free of the expectations of others, that he was still somehow involved in a world he had come to disdain.

"Holiness, I have the greatest respect for you, the man you were when I first met you, the man you have become. But, please, do not presume to know or judge me."

"You do not deny that you have permitted yourself to throw away everything that is good?"

"*Yes*, I do deny that!" Turner said. "I still have my son. Whatever sinkhole I may be living in, I'm still a father to him. I haven't abandoned him. Please don't make us compare suffering. You've experienced one kind, I another. You've survived yours, I'll survive mine. But I wish to God the world were decent enough to let me muddle through this alone."

"I did not seek to chastise you for giving in to self-pity, or to self-indulgence," Stanislawski said, his tone softening. "Nor do I equate your losses with mine. Before God they are equal, as are all men's."

He walked over to the man facing him, the man who still looked back at him defiantly, who refused to yield to the challenge of his words. He placed his hands upon Turner's shoulders.

"I am reaching out for you," Stanislawski said. "As the Holy Father, I will never know how many souls I have saved, if any at all. But I wish to reach out for you, to touch you, and help you out of this morass. Accept the offer of a man who stands forever in your debt, before whom, of all men, you can never feel ashamed or wanting. . . . I want you, Michael Turner, to be my personal physician, the Chief Physician to the Holy Apostolic See."

28

The sun poured through the wooden slats of the shutters, throwing diagonal strips of warm yellow light across the bed. Anna Letelier, her naked body half-covered by the crumpled sheets, swung a forearm across her eyes to shut out the sudden flare of light. The noise began to filter into her consciousness— the clatter of vehicles in the Piazza della Fontanella Borghese broken by the cries of the flea-market vendors and buyers as they jostled one another on the cobblestones, the din of children intermingled with the shouts of parents and the sporadic barking of dogs. The piazza, where students, artists, and merchants coexisted with the petite bourgeoisie, was well into another day. Anna knew she could sleep no longer. Her appointment would not wait.

She slipped from the bed and stretched, her breasts thrusting upward as she arched her back, the raven mane cascading along her spine, tingling. The deep-blue eyes opened wide, and the soft curve of her mouth twisted slightly with pleasure as her muscles tensed and relaxed. Then the coolness of the room prickled her skin. Shivering, she reached for the shirt that was hanging on the chair. Quietly she dressed and slipped out.

She had arranged to meet the Canadian diplomat at the Cavalieri, on the Via Michelini Tocci. At half-past nine the tables on the terrace overlooking the gardens were almost empty. Sam Waterman was sitting by the brick wall overgrown with ivy, the crumbs of a light breakfast in front of him, a pot of coffee on the spirit lamp beside him. Anna thought he appeared older than the last time she had seen him, two years ago in Budapest. His hairline had receded; bifocals had replaced the contact lenses. As she drew nearer, she saw that his waistline was running to fat, spilling over his trouser belt. The blue suit was rumpled as though he had slept in it for several days running. The tie was askew, spotted with stains. Even his fingernails had been bitten down to the quick.

"Good morning, Sam."

The young Canadian looked up at her with glazed eyes. His lips trembled as he tried to speak to her. But when the words at last emerged, they were little more than a whisper.

"Valerian is dead."

Anna sat down. Hearing footsteps behind her, she twisted around and shot a dazzling smile at the waiter, murmuring that she would help herself to some of Waterman's coffee. The waiter raised his eyebrows, grinned, and left them alone. Waterman was watching his retreating back as he spoke.

"Valerian is dead," he repeated. "It happened about fifteen minutes after he left the restaurant. We didn't see anything on the road. We were about a half-hour behind, no more. He killed himself. He knew they were watching him. That's why I didn't come out until now. You see, I was waiting. I had to be sure—"

"I want you to sit back and just relax for a minute," Anna said slowly. "Go ahead. Sit and think about what you have to tell me. Think. You're the only one who knows, Sam, and if you don't tell me what you know, then we won't know how to respond."

"I'm sorry," Waterman whispered. "It's just that we were all there at the Mermaid . . . and he was there, so alive."

"Don't think about that," Anna said sharply. "If you want to remember him, if you want to finish what he began, then think, think about what you have to tell me."

Waterman had no connection with Solidarity or the Resistance Network in Russia. He was an idealist, a volunteer who simply wanted to help. He first contacted the Mossad while on holiday in Israel, but they had turned him away, not wanting to get involved with an inexperienced diplomat from a friendly country. Anna had had no such qualms. She recruited Waterman while he was posted in Canada House in London. He was little more than a courier, who obeyed every instruction to the letter. He had little imagination and probably less daring. Yet every time he made a run, Waterman was putting his career, and this time his life, on the line.

"If they knew about me, they didn't follow up," Waterman said at last. He took off his glasses and cleaned them with a soiled handkerchief. "If they'd been there, they would have gotten me cold."

"You're certain you got away cleanly?"

"Yes."

"What about here, in Rome? Has anyone been following you, any unexplained messages?"

"I arrived late last night, spent the night at the embassy. The only message waiting for me was from my wife. She's coming in on a Canadian Pacific flight this afternoon."

"Give me the material."

"You're looking at it," Sam Waterman said, his eyes dropping to the matchbox. "That's the way it came. I haven't touched it."

Anna reached over and picked up the cardboard box. She looked at it for an instant as though trying to guess what its contents might be, then slipped it into her purse.

"All right, Sam," Anna said. "I want you to tell me what happened. Take your time. Tell me *everything* that happened."

A shudder ran through Waterman's body, as though he were ridding himself of some miasma. It took him a moment to connect his thoughts, and although his voice faltered in places, what he had to say to Anna was exactly what she expected to hear, except for the ending.

When Valerian had not shown up for work the following day, the alert had gone out. The VIPER network in Moscow shut down, suspending all activities until Valerian's backup learned that he had taken his own life. At that point VIPER stirred only once, to get a message to Waterman at the Canadian Embassy that his contact had been eliminated. After that, silence.

But what had happened to Valerian?

Waterman did not doubt the accuracy of the report. But why, if Special Investigations was on to Valerian, had he had the time and the opportunity to complete the drop, finish his meal, walk out of the restaurant, get into his car, and drive off? If they had been waiting for him. . . . Anna knew that it wouldn't wash. Sam Waterman had been there, the odd man out. If surveillance was on hand, then the suicide would have been all the excuse they needed to cordon off the Mermaid. Everyone would have been searched, diplomatic immunity or not. And they would have found the tape. Anna was familiar enough with the technique.

"Why did you wait almost two days before getting out?" Anna demanded. "With the network shut down, a possible breach of security—"

Waterman nodded miserably. "I wanted to get out sooner, but it was impossible. It took me a day just to convince the embassy doctor that I was really on the verge of a nervous collapse." Waterman laughed nervously. "Can you believe that? I nearly *was* headed for a breakdown, and the stupid son of a bitch couldn't see it. I'm sorry, I truly am, but I did the best I could."

"I know," Anna said. "I had no right to speak to you that way."

She took a long sip of coffee to steady herself. "How long will you be in the city?"

"A week, then on to Israel for ten days."

"And then?"

"Back to Moscow. I still have seven months left on my tour. One of the reasons the embassy didn't make a big fuss is that I have six weeks of leave coming to me anyway. But if I want to stay on in Tel Aviv, I'll have to give notice pretty soon."

"Will it make any difference to you?"

The sad brown eyes looked at her quietly.

"No, no difference. I'll stick with it if I'm needed."

Anna liked him at that moment. A slow, steady man who

wanted to help, who would go, without a murmur, wherever he was needed, knowing only that what he was doing would help.

"I'll speak to you in Israel, Sam."

"I'll say kaddish for Valerian."

Waterman was the first to leave. She gave him ten minutes, then almost ran out of the elegant hotel. Anna plunged the Ferrari into the midmorning traffic, pressing hard on the horn, her hand working the gearshift brutally.

What in God's name had Valerian recorded that had cost him his life? The thought was strangling her. At the entrance to the Villa Borghese she cut off a lumbering tour bus and sped through the gate even before the guard could turn around. Yossi was waiting for her as she ground the car to a halt in front of the carriage house.

"What's wrong?" he demanded.

"Later."

She went straight to her studio, which was crammed with photographic equipment she ostensibly used for her work. From the bottom case she removed a miniature tape recorder, a booster battery pack, and a large Uher tape deck. The tape was no larger than her thumbnail, no wider than a matchstick. Deftly she slipped the lead around another spool, then set the speed for ultra-slow. Valerian's tape would pass through the booster pack, the tracks augmented from thirty-two to sixteen, which was what the Uher operated on. The Uher would automatically speed up the transcribed tape.

She sat perched on a high stool for almost an hour, chain-smoking as the tape was transcribed from one reel to the other.

The miniature tape spun itself out. Anna punched the rewind button on the Uher and plugged in the headset. For the next seventy-five minutes she sat immobile, held motionless by what she was hearing. The tape had arrived too late. In Moscow the terror would already be upon them.

The hunting owls were out in force that night, the only creatures that had ventured out in the cold that had descended on the Sokolniki Hills, a hundred kilometers north of Moscow.

During the last week in April the frost still settled on the earth by night.

Semyon Arkadyevich Komarov leaned back in his rocker and propped his feet against the railing of the veranda that ran the length of the lodge.

"Why must I go back?" he demanded for the fourth time, sipping his lemon tea.

"You've suffered two attacks of vertigo," Razminsky said quietly. "Had those occurred while you were on a staircase, for example, the result would have been worse than a few bumps and bruises. You have been complaining of hot flushes on the left side of your face. Also headaches and drowsiness. These are symptoms that concern me."

"Go with him, Semyon," his wife said, not looking up from her quilting. She was sitting further down the veranda, making a comforter for her grandson. "Don't argue with Andrushka."

Komarov shot her a sour look but said nothing. He knew she was right. He should go to Moscow. In fact he should have notified Razminsky sooner. As it was, Asya had called him. The helicopter that had brought him was still waiting on the raised landing circle two hundred meters from the lodge.

"Tell me what this is going to involve," Komarov said.

"A close examination to begin with, diet restriction—although you've been very good in that respect—control of your fluid intake. I'll give you a Decadron IV to relieve the pressure on the brain. We'll do a scan, more X rays."

"Could it be something as simple as the cold?"

"Yes, it could," Razminsky admitted.

"If there's anything the matter—" Komarov started to whisper, leaning toward the physician.

"Speak up, Semyon," his wife called, never raising her head. "No secrets, please. You know better than that."

Komarov muttered under his breath. Did he think that after fifty years of marriage she wouldn't be able to tell when he was afraid?

"Is there anything else you want to tell me?" Komarov said in his normal voice. "If you're preparing me for further news, then you'd better speak up now, in front of both of us."

"Given your medical history, the symptoms are characteristically associated with the lateral medullary syndrome," Razminsky said, speaking so that Asya Komarova could hear. "I must find out if that's what it is. Then we can prescribe treatment."

He saw Komarov shudder in the gathering twilight. Razminsky could not blame him. Sometimes the treatment was worse than the disease. The patient simply became too tired to endure the abuse of drugs or operations which were preserving his life. For everyone there came a time to let go.

"If that is indeed what it is, I will tell you, both of you, immediately."

"I know you will, Andrushka," Asya Komarova said. She rose, carefully placing her work on the rattan chair beside her, and came over to her husband. "We both know what you can and cannot do."

Komarov felt her hand on his shoulder and covered it with his own.

"Asya, please telephone Kobalevsky and tell him I won't be able to meet with him tomorrow as we planned. Ask him to stop by the Rudin at ten o'clock in the morning."

He looked back at Razminsky. "Will I be able to take some work with me?"

"A little."

"There is no such thing as a little work," Komarov snorted, getting to his feet. "Will you pack me a bag, my dear?"

"It's all ready, Semyon."

Gently the chairman reached for his wife and embraced her, kissing her tenderly on both cheeks. He went inside, calling to his secretary to notify the security people and the helicopter crew. They would be flying directly for Rudin Hospital.

"You'll call me, Andrushka," Asya whispered to Razminsky, "if there's anything wrong, if there's any change in his condition."

"Asya, don't worry, please," Razminsky shushed her. "It's probably nothing."

"Do you really believe that?"

"If I rely too much on my intuition, I might as well drag

out the treebark potions and start grinding elephant tusks."
Razminsky smiled. "I think he's all right, Asya. But I want to be
sure. We all want to be sure."

"He's too proud," she said suddenly. "Too damn proud!"

The helicopter trip between the Sokolniki Hills and
Rudin Hospital took just thirty minutes. At ten o'clock
Komarov was walking down the halls he knew so well, and
which he had come to loathe because he feared that this lime-
green paint and gray tile would be the last colors he would see
in his life. The intensive care unit had been prepared for him,
the single bed standing in the center of the room, like a grand
piano on the empty stage of the Tchaikovsky Concert Hall. But
this impression of vast space was in part an illusion. Lined up in
rows in the shadows the machines waited, life-support systems,
portable oxygen tents, defibrillators, kidney machines, virtually
every device that could be called upon to preserve life.

And from behind the one-way-mirror windows, the security
people watched his every motion, the video cameras recorded
every action while the tape reels spun silently, capturing every
sound.

Komarov went behind the screen and changed into lemon-
yellow pajamas with burgundy borders and padded to the bed
in sheepskin-lined slippers. The only other people in the room
were Razminsky and Lydmilla Mayakovskaya, the head nurse of
ICU. A rather tall, sturdily built woman in her early forties,
with short curly hair brushed back and a generous smile, she
was one of Razminsky's favorites. She had a sense of humor.
Komarov got along with her as well. Two of her predecessors
had been reassigned when the chairman had complained about
them.

"Now, then, Semyon Arkadyevich, are you comfortable
enough?" Razminsky asked him.

"I need that working table, the one that comes across the
bed," Komarov replied.

"Planning to get up early?"

"No sooner than usual," Komarov said frostily.

"Lydmilla Mayakovskaya will see to it that you get everything you need in the morning." Razminsky turned aside and

lowered his voice. "Set up a two fifty cc, twenty percent Decadron solution." Lydmilla Mayakovskaya nodded and hurried off. "Would you like something to help you sleep, Semyon Arkadyevich?"

"That won't be necessary."

"All right, then. I'll set up a stand here for the drip. Nothing more than vitamins and a little glucose. I'm afraid you won't be getting much to eat in the next little while."

Komarov began leafing through a magazine while Razminsky checked the monitoring systems. Five minutes went by, and still the head nurse had not returned.

"What's keeping her?" Komarov muttered testily.

Razminsky was wondering the same thing. "I'll go see."

Razminsky went into the ICU booth and asked Mayakovskaya's junior aide where she had disappeared to.

"She's in the washroom, doctor," the girl answered. Razminsky saw her blush. "It's that time of the month." Razminsky nodded and withdrew. He was headed down the empty corridor when from around the corner there came two Guards Directorate officers, escorting Minister of Science and Technology Oleg Kobalevsky.

"Andrei!"

"Oleg, what on earth are you doing here?"

"Asya called me, told me they brought Semyon Arkadyevich here. She sounded a little nervous over the telephone, so I thought I'd stop by and check."

Razminsky slapped the younger man on the shoulder and continued toward the pharmacy, two doors down from the ICU control booth.

"Yes, he's here," Razminsky said. "I just got him settled in, so I'd appreciate it if you didn't disturb him."

"What's wrong?"

"Nothing. There are a few symptoms I don't like, but it's probably nothing at all. I have tests scheduled for tomorrow."

"But his secretary assured me he was going to see me in the morning," Kobalevsky said.

"He will, he will," Razminsky said soothingly. He opened

the stainless-steel door of the cooler and looked for the plastic bag of solution. "My eyes are going. There has to be some here."

"What are you looking for?" Kobalevsky asked.

"Decadron, half-liter, blue-and-yellow label."

"How about down there?" Kobalevsky pointed to a lone pack lying on its side on the bottom shelf. Razminsky squatted down to look. "That's it."

He closed the cabinet and stepped back into the hall. Lydmilla Mayakovskaya had just come out of the washroom.

"Doctor, I'm sorry but—"

"I know, I know," Razminsky said, handing her the Decadron. "Set this up for him, and as soon as you're done, lights out. No arguments. The Decadron should take effect in two to four hours. If the scanners don't show brain relief, call me. Otherwise he can get up as early as he likes tomorrow, so you had better get some sleep while you can."

"Yes, doctor. And thank you."

"It's nothing." Razminsky shrugged. He turned to Kobalevsky. "Oleg, as long as you're here, would you consider giving me a lift home?"

"Certainly," Kobalevsky smiled.

"Right then. Let me look in on him one last time, and I'll be right with you."

According to the security register, Doctor Razminsky and Minister of Science and Technology Kobalevsky both signed out at three minutes before eleven. The automatic timing device, which punched the video tape with a magnetic numeral every sixty seconds, concurred with the ledger entry.

At eleven thirty-three Komarov pressed the button on the frame of his bed. When Lydmilla Mayakovskaya appeared, he asked her to turn off the lights. He was ready to go to sleep. The head nurse wheeled back the reading stand, carefully stacking the papers Komarov had been perusing, and checked the glucose drip. Everything was normal. Lydmilla Mayakovskaya bid the chairman goodnight and returned to the control chamber, where she lowered the lights in the ICU and set the scanner which would automatically monitor Komarov's vital functions while he slept.

Behind the opaque shiny glass the video cameras switched on their infrared filters.

Lydmilla Mayakovskaya chatted with the other nurse, Sonya, until midnight, then went downstairs on her usual twenty-minute break. When she returned, Sonya went off on her rounds. At one o'clock, with two cups of tea in front of them, the nurses checked the vital signs readout before bringing out a deck of cards for a game of whist. At two o'clock the scanner readout was checked again. Everything was normal; the same at three. At three forty-two Komarov went into cardiac arrest.

As soon as the red light came on and the buzzer sounded, Lydmilla Mayakovskaya was out the door and into the ICU, where the lights were now blazing. In the control unit Sonya was summoning the director of the hospital, the intense, chain-smoking Valery Antipov, who was always present in the hospital whenever Komarov was there. The emergency stand-by team—a cardiologist, anesthesiologist, neurologist, and two surgical residents—was running down the corridor from the lounge at the far end of the wing. By the time they arrived at Komarov's bedside Lydmilla Mayakovskaya had the defibrillator ready. The cardiologist took three precious seconds to listen for a heartbeat before he ripped open Komarov's pajamas jacket and jammed the paddles against his bare chest.

"Stand back!" he yelled, and pressed the trigger, bearing down as the inert body jerked violently in reaction to the electrical charge.

Nothing.

The cardiologist, sweat streaming off his face, tried two more jolts with no results.

"Cardiac syringe!"

Mayakovskaya handed him the three-and-a-half-inch needle; it gleamed under the light. He pressed the plunger and a few drops of epinephrine spurted out, clearing the air bubbles. Mayakovskaya swabbed the skin directly over the heart with alcohol, and the needle began its descent. It cut through the skin cleanly between the third and fourth ribs, plunging through the thin layer of fat, reaching the more resilient muscle tissue, coming within a few millimeters of the rib. It sprang back slightly on touching the heart itself. The cardiologist forced it in the rest of the way, his thumb depressing the plunger. The needle came back up, dark with blood.

"*Live,* goddamn it, live!" the cardiologist snarled.

"*Time!*" Lydmilla Mayakovskaya shouted.

"Fifty-five seconds," Sonya replied over the speaker. As soon as the cardiac arrest warning had sounded, an automatic counter had started, measuring the exact time that had elapsed since the patient had gone under.

"No pulse," one of the residents said quietly.

Valery Antipov had arrived breathless. He had been watching his colleagues in silence for a few seconds. Now he checked Komarov's pulse for himself.

"He's gone," he said, shaking his head. "It's no use. He's gone."

Behind the opaque glass a security agent lifted the receiver, waited a moment, then spoke a few words. He lit another cigarette and checked once more to make sure all his equipment was functioning smoothly.

Andrei Razminsky was a light sleeper, but not even he heard the front door to his apartment open. It was the snap of the light switch in the hall that woke him. When he got out of bed, his wife, Zina, also awoke.

"Andrushka, what is it?" she asked sleepily, trying to prop herself up on one elbow.

"Doctor Razminsky?"

The man standing in the doorway of the bedroom was enormous. Razminsky could not see his face against the glare from the hall light.

"Who are you?" Razminsky coughed, trying to clear his throat.

"State security. There's an emergency at Rudin."

"Semyon Arkadyevich—"

"You're wanted immediately, doctor," the agent rumbled. "I suggest you dress as quickly as possible."

"Yes, yes, of course," Razminsky muttered. "Do you think you could wait in the hall . . . ?"

The agent did not move.

"Why didn't you telephone?" Zina Razminskaya called from the bedroom. "Why did you have to break into our home?"

"Zina, please," Razminsky whispered. "Not now."

"I want an answer from you," his wife persisted, her voice rising. She clutched at her nightgown and slid out of bed, gripping the night table, steadying herself. An ancient memory stirred within her, something far older than the Stalinist terror she had witnessed as a child, something that harkened even further back than the czarist pogroms. It was an instinct sharpened over the millennia that identified the oppressor, the executioner, even before he made his intentions known.

She fumbled for her glasses and shuffled to the door, staring up at the agent.

"Who sent you?" she demanded. "What do you want with my husband?"

Razminsky, who had stuffed his shirt into his trousers and was reaching for his jacket, heard his wife scream and turned around in time to see her being shoved back onto the bed by the impassive agent.

"What are you doing?" Razminsky shouted, rushing toward the KGB man.

The agent caught him with one hand, grabbing him by the shirt and pulling him off his feet.

"Come along quietly, doctor," he suggested in a soft voice. "There is no need to make a fuss."

"Andrushka, for God's *sake* don't go. Telephone Komarov . . . somebody. *I want to know what he's doing here!*" she screamed.

"Tell her to shut up, doctor, or I will break her neck. I promise you I will."

The grip was loosened, and Razminsky went over to his wife, throwing an arm around her trembling body.

"What in God's name is this?" he asked softly. "Has everyone gone mad?"

The man moved before he was even aware of it. He grabbed Razminsky by the arm, pinning it behind his back, and propelled him from the room. When Zina tried to run after them, a second agent, who had been waiting in the hall, caught her, spun her around, and threw her heavily against the wall, where she crumpled, her arm smashing against a light fixture.

"Zina!" she heard him scream. "Zina, call Komarov, call—" A sharp gasp cut off his words, then the slamming of the door. Zina crawled down the corridor and into the darkened parlor, clutching the window ledge, pulling herself up. In the dark, silent street she saw a shaft of light as the front doors opened, then her husband tripping and stumbling as he was pushed along by the agent who had gripped him from behind. She watched as Andrushka was heaved into the back seat of the waiting automobile and driven away.

"No," Zina muttered to herself. "Not like this. Not like this!"

She reached for the telephone, knocking it off the stand, and frantically began dialing the number of her closest friend, Lessia, the wife of Orlov, the other neurologist who was attached to her husband's staff. She closed her eyes in gratitude when the phone started ringing on the other end. Someone answered.

"Lessia ... Lessia, is that you? It's Zina."

No one spoke. All she could hear was bedlam. Someone screaming, the sound of glass breaking. A whimpering voice which seemed to be saying "Don't take him, please don't take him. . . ." Then the connection was broken.

Zina stared at the receiver, then dropped it as though it had burned her hand. She crawled up against the bottom of the sofa and drew her knees up to her chin, huddled up in her housecoat even though the flat was very warm. In her mind's eye she saw the terrifying scene that was being enacted at the Orlovs' household.

"Where else?" she whispered to herself. "Where else are they taking ..."

Zina Razminskaya snatched up the cord and dragged the telephone toward her. She had already dialed her neighbor's number before she realized the phone had gone dead.

As soon as Valery Antipov had pronounced Komarov dead, he dismissed both nurses and sequestered himself in the control booth of the ICU. The first person he called was Marshal Pavlichenko, who was now acting Chairman of the Politburo. The next call went out to Major-General Malyshev of the Guards Directorate. Within minutes Malyshev ordered an armed detail out to Rudin to supplement Komarov's personal security detail. Komarov's office in the Kremlin was sealed off, the hospital staff detained for the duration. The third call went out on the emergency line that linked Rudin with KGB chairman Viktor Suslev. The next call went to Dmitri Gorodin. The remaining members of the Politburo would be notified whenever Pavlichenko thought fit. Finally Antipov spoke with his friend of thirty years' standing, the venerable Pervushin, senior pathologist at Moscow Medical Institute. Pervushin had performed the autopsies on the last three Kremlin leaders. He had lived long enough to perform one more, but not alone. The standing rule was that three specialists, all acceptable to the Politburo, would perform the autopsy together, so that no one single opinion prevailed. As a precaution, the men chosen did not work together, quite often never knew one another except possibly by reputation, this to prevent collusion.

When Valery Antipov emerged from the control booth, he saw that his staff had been shepherded out of the ICU and the doors sealed. Again standard procedure. Whenever a Politburo member expired, the place was off limits to everyone except the investigating team from the KGB medical department. The staff who were present at the time of death, from the senior surgeons to the orderly who had been mopping the floor on the ward, was detained pending interrogation. The director went over to his staff, who were standing expectantly by the door to the ICU.

"You did everything you could," he said kindly, trying to

reassure them. I suggest we all go and wait in the lounge until the marshal arrives."

One of the two Guards Directorate officers who were standing in front of the sealed doors unslung his radio and alerted another unit. By the time the little group reached the lounge, three more officers appeared to follow them in. They were there to ensure that not a single word passed among the doctors and nurses. The time was four seventeen.

Dawn was just breaking when Marshal Pavlichenko returned to the committee room in the Arsenal Tower. All the other members of the Politburo were present. Pavlichenko had called them from Rudin Hospital after conferring with Suslev and Gorodin. He hadn't anticipated bringing them together so soon, but then the whole character of the present crisis had changed dramatically with Suslev's arrival.

Pavlichenko looked down at the letter in front of him, presenting a shabby contrast to the polished brilliance of the table. The paper was gray, of poor quality, the kind found in a child's exercise book, with a wide margin at the right, the lines spaced far apart. The right-hand side was frayed, indicating that it had been torn out of a loose-leaf notebook. The writing was small but meticulous, the mark of a disciplined mind.

"Viktor," Pavlichenko said quietly, "how long have you been running this agent?"

"Seven months," Suslev wheezed, shifting his bulk in the oversize chair. He was sitting directly opposite the marshal at the far end of the table.

"When and how was she recruited?"

The chairman of the KGB pushed a file along to Fadayev, the Minister of Nationalities, who passed it down the table.

"That is her dossier, from the hour she started working for us. You will note that it was *she* who contacted *us*."

"Why?"

"She was suspicious—as others were at the time—about why Razminsky was so insistent on having the American Turner brought in to perform the surgery. Her curiosity was alleviated to a degree after the chairman recovered, thus you will find a two-month hiatus in her reports. However, they become more and more frequent as the chairman's condition deteriorated."

"I was never aware that Semyon Arkadyevich had taken a turn for the worse," Pavlichenko observed. "I spoke with Razminsky on several occasions. He told me nothing of the sort. Neither did Semyon Arkadyevich himself, or his wife. I see an obvious discrepancy. How do you account for that?"

"Quite easily," Suslev wheezed, tugging out a cigarette from his silver case. "During the same time you will notice that Razminsky's appointments with the chairman *increased* in frequency. I have a list of all his visits here." Suslev pushed another file along the polished table.

Pavlichenko opened the folder and looked down at the dates.

"Very well, but what did your agent make of all this?"

"At first, nothing. However, on two occasions she called the Kremlin to make an appointment for Razminsky with the chairman's secretary. Each time, according to her, the chairman wanted to know why another examination was necessary."

"Razminsky is a very conscientious man. He was also, to a degree, the chairman's confidant," Pavlichenko commented.

"However, this was what truly frightened our agent," Suslev continued smoothly, as though Pavlichenko had not spoken at all.

From a third file he pulled out a single piece of paper, no larger than an ordinary prescription form, and passed that down.

"A release from the pharmacy at the Medical College hospital, where Razminsky teaches. The item requested is twenty centiliters of nitroprusside. That was duly released to the person whose signature appears at the bottom." He tapped the copy of the document. "Nitroprusside. It is used in treating hypertension and refractory heart failure. But it is normally used with extreme care because it breaks down into a very dangerous substance which, in the wrong dosage, can be lethal. I am referring to cyanide, comrades."

The form was passed along, each member taking a quick look at the signature, until it finally came to Pavlichenko.

"Has this been verified by comparing it with Razminsky's signature?"

"It has. You will note the date, Comrade Marshal."

"Two days ago," Pavlichenko said wearily.

"The day *before* Razminsky went up to the lodge at Sokolniki to bring the chairman back to Moscow for yet another examination," Gorodin observed.

Pavlichenko tossed the prescription onto the table and sat back in his chair.

"It's hard to believe," he murmured.

"We'll know for certain as soon as the autopsy reports come in," Suslev said, consulting his watch. "Which should be in the next hour."

"There are two things that bother me about this whole business," Oleg Kobalevsky announced, leaning forward on the table. "The first is the question of motive. Why would Andrei Razminsky, who fought so hard to *save* the chairman's life, who was willing to place his reputation, his career, perhaps even his life, in jeopardy by appearing before us and urging us to consent to the operation, why should he, four months later, be the prime suspect in the murder of the man he served so faithfully for so long?"

"I think—" Suslev started to say.

"Excuse me, Comrade Chairman, but I would like to finish," Kobalevsky interrupted. The chair groaned as Suslev shifted his weight.

"The other thing I don't understand is why Razminsky would have signed for this particular poison. Surely if a man is plotting the death of the Politburo chairman, he will take every precaution not to leave such blatantly incriminating evidence in his wake. I find it hard to believe that Razminsky could not procure this or any other substance without anyone's being aware of it. Certainly he had access to all sorts of places. Why then write a prescription and put your name to it? That doesn't make any sense at all!"

"The minister has a valid point," Suslev said. "I can perhaps answer his first question by pointing out that this substance is not obviously lethal. Only Razminsky himself will be able to explain the whole scheme."

"If in fact he is responsible," Kobalevsky interjected.

"Yes," Suslev said. "As to the second question, the prescription. It was sheer luck that our agent found it. You will notice that the paper is badly crumpled. Razminsky was going to destroy it, then at the last moment could not, for one reason or another."

"This letter from your informer bears the same date as the prescription," Kobalevsky observed. "At what point did you receive it, Comrade Chairman?"

"The following morning."

"It was delivered to you directly, along with the prescription?"

"Yes."

"How?"

"Through the internal mail."

"On the face of it this letter contains nothing but a series of baseless and possibly irresponsible accusations," Kobalevsky said, holding the letter by one corner, as though it offended him to touch it. "Your informer states, in somewhat hysterical terms, that Razminsky has been plotting against the chairman's life, using these examinations as a way of gaining time to devise a plan—a particularly inefficient one at that—for killing him. The prescription that was found was assumed to be an indication that Razminsky was on the verge of carrying out his plan. Now given the weight you seem to place on this so-called evidence, why didn't you inform General Malyshev of the Guards Directorate and have him deny Razminsky access to the chairman?"

"I placed Razminsky under twenty-four-hour surveillance," Suslev said, his voice tight. "He didn't go to the shitter without my knowing it. The Guards Directorate checked the ICU before the chairman arrived. Every piece of equipment was thoroughly examined. As for the time Razminsky was at Rudin, we have tapes to show that he himself gave nothing to the chairman, not even a sleeping pill."

"So why are you so certain that Razminsky had *anything* to do with the chairman's death?" Kobalevsky asked.

"Because Semyon Arkadyevich is dead!" Suslev whispered hoarsely, his calm façade exploding into blotches of red. "Dead not of an aneurysm but of heart failure! There was no problem with his heart. Not until the nitroprusside within the Decadron became cyanide!"

"Do you think Razminsky—if we presume for the moment he had anything to do with this—was acting alone or in concert with someone else?" Pavlichenko asked. He didn't want the young minister to start digging his own grave by pursuing the assumption of Razminsky's innocence too assiduously. The issue of Suslev's competence could also wait.

"That too is something that is yet to be determined," Suslev said, squeezing a fine spray of Riapin mist into his mouth to relieve his tortured lungs.

"Where is Razminsky now?"

"Across the street."

Marshal Pavlichenko nodded. He had expected as much. Suslev had virtually unlimited police powers. Lubyanka prison was across the street.

"And the rest of his medical team?"

"They're there as well, as a precaution."

"Were any of them present last night when the chairman arrived?"

"No . . ." Suslev said, but left the answer unfinished.

"Was there *anyone* with Razminsky last night?" Gorodin asked silkily.

"I was," Oleg Kobalevsky said quietly.

Pavlichenko looked at him, his expression one of incredulity.

"What were you doing there?" he asked apprehensively.

"Asya called me from the lodge earlier in the evening to tell me that Semyon Arkadyevich had just left with Razminsky. They were on their way to Rudin. Semyon Arkadyevich wanted her to telephone me and ask me to come see him around ten o'clock this morning. According to our arrangement, I was to have gone up there. Asya sounded concerned, so I thought I would stop by Rudin to see if there was anything . . . the matter."

"And did you notice anything out of the ordinary?"

"Nothing." Kobalevsky shook his head. "In fact, Razminsky wouldn't even let me see him, even though he was still awake. I gave him a lift home. . . ."

"Would you be willing to give us the benefit of your observations, Minister?" Suslev asked. "Sometimes the smallest detail can be of great significance."

"Yes, of course," Kobalevsky said.

"There's nothing to be done until the cause of death has been determined," Pavlichenko said. "In fact, I'll call Pervushin right now."

"Comrade Marshal," Gorodin put in smoothly. "I suggest that one item has been overlooked."

Pavlichenko's fingers released the receiver. He knew what was coming.

"And what is that, Minister?"

"According to our constitution, the interim government must remain in civilian hands," Gorodin reminded him. "Up to this point you have acted within the limits of your authority. However, I suggest that executive authority should now pass to the senior civilian member of the Politburo."

Pavlichenko regarded the seven members of the Politburo whom he controlled, controlled as long as Komarov had been alive. Why, why in God's name had Oleg Kobalevsky been at Rudin last night? And Gorodin, the son of a bitch, how cleverly he had maneuvered Kobalevsky into admitting he had been there. It all fit so beautifully: Kobalevsky was the last man to have seen the alleged murderer. He had even driven him home. Another thought struck the marshal: Who had told Gorodin about Kobalevsky's visit to Rudin? Who could have known . . . but *Suslev?* Pavlichenko gritted his teeth. The power play was about to begin. Gorodin was well within his rights to demand a transfer of authority. And he had chosen his moment beautifully. Suslev was accusing Razminsky of complicity, at the very least, in Komarov's death. Kobalevsky had been at Rudin Hospital only hours before Komarov died. Accusations had been made, but would that be enough to sway the others? Pavlichenko would not give up yet.

"Are we all agreed that this question should be put to a vote?" Pavlichenko demanded.

One by one all their hands rose, without hesitation, giving him no indication of how his bloc would vote.

"Both the Foreign Minister and the Minister of Science and Technology have equal seniority," Pavlichenko said. "I assume there is no dispute here."

There wasn't.

"All those in favor of Comrade Gorodin assuming the post of interim chairman, so signify by raising their hands."

Six votes were needed since Gorodin, as a nominee, could not vote for himself. Suslev raised his meaty arm. The old Komarov clique followed obediently, led by Fadayev. Goddamn you all to hell, Pavlichenko thought furiously, but he was helpless.

"Shall we make it unanimous?" Suslev suggested. Neither Pavlichenko nor Kobalevsky raised their hands.

"No," Kobalevsky said. "The vote will not be unanimous."

Pavlichenko shook his head, indicating that he too would not vote for Gorodin. As Marshal of the Army, Pavlichenko was too powerful for Gorodin to remove or replace. But Kobalevsky's position was far from secure. Now that Gorodin had one foot in the door, he would use all the leverage of his provisional office to secure a quick vote of the Central Committee ratifying his election. Never in the history of the Party had an interim chairman failed to be elected officially.

The telephone sounded softly, two short whistles. Pavlichenko looked at it, then pushed it toward Gorodin. The transfer was complete. Gorodin lifted the receiver, identified himself, and listened.

"That was Pervushin in the pathology laboratory at Rudin," he said almost conversationally. "*They* have reached a consensus," he added ironically. "Beyond any doubt the death of Chairman Komarov can be attributed to cyanide poisoning."

Gorodin allowed a few seconds to go by before he spoke again.

"We must now decide whether or not to make a public announcement of Chairman Komarov's death. I believe we should but should not mention the cause of death. Simply place emphasis on his operation, and let the people draw the obvious conclusion."

"It's unthinkable to allow even the suggestion of foul play," Suslev chimed in.

"That is true," Kobalevsky agreed. "But you have two problems, Minister," he said, addressing Gorodin. "The first is what you will tell the people—indeed, the world—once we are certain who the killer or killers are. Secondly, what are you going to say to Asya Komarov?"

"One more point, Minister," Marshal Pavlichenko said. "If foul play is a consideration, then standing orders demand that I put our armed forces on full alert, without delay. Bear in mind the Americans will immediately learn of this by means of their satellites, and Jonathan Telford will be on the direct phone in less than thirty minutes. What are we to tell him, Minister? I suggest you consider this carefully, because there are only three contingencies in which we can go to condition red: Either we are preparing for war, there has been a nuclear catastrophe within our borders, or," Pavlichenko paused, "something unthinkable has happened to the leadership and we are, for the time, without a government. Under the circumstances which possibility do *you* believe the Americans will think of first?"

Gorodin listened very carefully to the marshal. Even while Pavlichenko was still speaking, he was trying to calculate the ramifications of the Americans discovering, at this point, that something was not right in Moscow. It was too soon for such information to come out.

"I suggest we forgo the red alert," Gorodin said, realizing that some of the initiative had been snatched away from him. To keep Kobalevsky off balance he had to maintain a crisis atmosphere. "But the investigation of the circumstances of Semyon Arkadyevich's death will go on all the same."

✦

Auguste Cardinal Mirabeau, Papal Secretary of State, found it odd that Innocent had not taken over the official residence one floor below the papal offices in the Apostolic Palace. He said as much to Gregory Rowitz.

"You must give him time, Eminence," the priest advised. "His predecessor's library is much too grand a place for him to feel comfortable in. Perhaps in a while he will use it, but not immediately. As for the bedroom, he will never go there. He will never sleep in a room where a man has died. At Auschwitz he not only slept with the dead, he was embraced by them."

The seal had been set upon the doors leading to Clement's quarters. When he saw this, Mirabeau knew they would remain locked for the duration of this reign.

The rooms on the fifth floor had been a jumble of storage rooms, offices, and bedrooms reserved for visiting friends of the Pope. The Papal study was a small two-tiered room, with the bottom level dominated by a large conference table surrounded by large chairs. There was a fireplace in one corner with an oil portrait of Clement hanging over it. On the second tier were the bookshelves, half of them still empty, and the large desk at which Innocent worked. Mirabeau noticed that the windows had finally been washed. The sunlight helped dispel some of the gloom, although a certain mustiness still lingered.

Innocent entered from a door set into the wall that connected the study with the small bedroom behind it. He dressed now as he always had, in a simple black robe with the unadorned crucifix hanging from his neck. Mirabeau looked carefully at the strong features. There was no change in them, nor in the quiet gray eyes observing him.

"Holiness," Mirabeau said.

Innocent embraced the secretary and led him over to the table.

"Will you take coffee with me?"

"Thank you, Holiness."

Mirabeau settled himself at the table so that the sun would not shine into his eyes and began to arrange the papers in front of him.

"Can you tell me something about what you have there?" Innocent asked. "Give me a general overview before we come down to details."

"Of course, Holiness."

As Father Rowitz poured out the fresh, strong coffee, the Secretary of State settled back in his chair, his points falling into place, one by one, until they were deployed as neatly as a general's battle order.

"I would like to begin with the international reaction to your election, which has on the whole been cautious," he said. "The Americans and Western Europeans have been polite in their congratulations but reserved. There have also been more inquiries than I would have expected about the nature of the foreign policy you intend to pursue. Naturally no comment has been offered. Here in Italy the government greeted your coronation with something less than enthusiasm. The left-wing coalition keeps harping on your career in Poland. They're concerned that you may adopt a rather uncompromising posture with respect to the Soviet Union. As for Eastern Europe, the reaction of the people has been overwhelmingly positive. All our reports indicate that. In Moscow your election was accorded three lines on an inside page of *Pravda*. The Russians have held back on their reactions; not even their usual intermediaries have approached us. They're waiting for you to make the overtures.

"As for South America, the story is much the same as in Eastern Europe: both civilian and military governments have expressed concern, the people are still celebrating. Africa, the Far East, much the same. In short the situation we are facing is generally what one would have anticipated, not unlike the reaction which greeted the elevation of John XXIII. You are regarded as a populist with limited experience in the international arena. Your strength lies in your personal appeal rather than a substantial base within the Church. You are not a Roman so conflict within the predominantly Italian Curia is anticipated. I think the next sixty days will prove pivotal. Your policies will be under scrutiny. Everyone will be watching to see whether you implement your programs with authority. Will you be master within your own house? Will you be obeyed, or merely tolerated?"

Mirabeau sipped at his coffee, aware of the dust motes that were dancing above the ceramic vase, creating a halo above the sunflowers.

"And what of my own house?" Innocent asked.

"If a house be divided against itself, that house shall not stand," Mirabeau answered him, "to quote from St. Mark."

"And are we divided, Auguste?"

"We are, Holiness," Mirabeau told him. "You feel it as strongly as I do. While it is true that each and every cardinal made his obeisance before you, we must remember that the conservative faction held firm for the first three ballots."

"You have never told me what happened before the fourth ballot."

"I spoke with Picheli while the first ballot was being counted. I pointed out to him that our party would continue to vote as Clement had wished us to, that the *arrivistes* would not falter. He could either continue to press for De Falla or he could release the handful of electors who would decide the issue. I argued that the rival factions were too firmly entrenched, that no provision had been made for a compromise candidate. In effect I made him the Pope-maker."

"What else?"

"There was no compromise, Holiness, if that's what you mean to imply. No one could possibly compromise the Pontiff-elect."

"But there was an understanding."

Mirabeau hesitated. "Yes. There was. Picheli told me, to my face, that he would abide by my suggestion, that he had no wish to see the Church endangered by this internecine strife. However, he also made it abundantly clear that the conservatives still controlled better than half the administrative departments of the Curia. That was all he had to say, Holiness."

Innocent smiled wanly. "They elected me, but at the same time left me weak."

"Holiness—"

"I understand exactly what Picheli meant," Innocent said.

"If I initiate policies which are not to the conservatives' liking, I will find inertia and perhaps outright hostility. The age-old problem returns: who controls the Church—the man who is at her head or the administration which, like any bureaucracy, serves itself first and the master second, when it so pleases it to do so?"

"Your Holiness asked me to summarize the situation," Mirabeau shrugged. "I regret I have to be the bearer of such information."

Innocent pushed away his coffee and placed his chin upon his knuckles, regarding the Secretary with a faint smile.

"What is in the dossier, Auguste?"

"Suggestions for the middle road."

"Is it a road you feel the Church would do well to travel?"

"It is a road on which she will survive. Better yet, she will hold her own. It is a continuation of the work Clement began, the work he bequeathed you."

"Auguste, I want you to understand what I am about to say." Innocent looked up at the portrait of his predecessor. "I believe Clement made a tremendous contribution to the independence and stature of the Church. I do not intend to meddle with his creation but nourish it, and watch it flower. You, and others who helped him, will remain, guiding the administration. I intend to invite Picheli, De Falla, and others, who call themselves the Cabal, to help me guide the Church. I do not like secret societies or private interests within the Church but I am enough of a realist to understand that I will not be able to do away with them. I *must* have their cooperation, if not their respect."

"Those are strong words, Holiness," Mirabeau said uneasily.

The great hands came apart, the long thick fingers flat upon the table.

"They are words which reflect the reality," Innocent said, his voice cold like iron. "From some I will receive friendship, even love; from others obedience; from others no more than tolerance. I cannot be all things to all men. I will seek, with every fiber of my being, to work with the conservatives. But I will *not* be led by them."

Mirabeau pursed his lips. He had heard three Popes utter similar words. Innocent was no different in insisting on his ability to set his personal mark upon his rule. What was different about this man, Mirabeau thought, was the purity of the fire within him. He was one who could not be denied, whose faith would feed him as naturally as a tree draws sustenance from the earth. Mirabeau understood that he was looking at a rock which would not be eroded but only broken. That was why, he realized, he feared for this man.

"Would his Holiness consider examining the details?" he asked.

"Very much," Innocent answered. But there was no smile behind the words.

Anna Letelier's first reaction was to call the Vatican. What she had heard on that tape had drained her of all her strength, leaving her frightened and oppressed by a terrible sense of isolation. She had actually dialed the first few digits of the number that would connect her with Rowitz's office, then abruptly she broke the connection. Reason told her that nothing would be served by speaking to Innocent now. He deserved at least one final night of uninterrupted peace. She prayed that he would draw as much strength from it as possible, because the demands that would be placed upon him would be intolerable.

The rest of the evening she spent on the telephone. Over a secure line at the Galleria Letelier calls went out to West Berlin, Vienna, Munich, Stuttgart, and Geneva. Tersely worded instructions disrupted the everyday affairs of men and women who, on the surface, were nothing more than solid, law-abiding citizens, respected members of their professions and their communities. Two were lawyers, another was a banker, the contacts in Munich and Stuttgart were small industrialists. Yet there were two common threads that bound them together: they all traveled to the Soviet Union on business at least a dozen times a year. Each of them controlled one agent, whether in Moscow,

Kiev, or Leningrad. All of them were Jews. All responded immediately and without question to Anna's instructions. Thus, the first of these agents, all Jews, all recruited and controlled by her in the same way as Sam Waterman, would be arriving in the Soviet capital later that night.

At half-past eleven Anna arrived at the State Opera House. At the door to the Israeli ambassador's box she met the Israeli cultural attaché, took him to one side, and explained what she needed. Thirty minutes later an official car with blacked-out windows passed through the gates of the embassy compound. Using the service entrance, Anna slipped inside, heading for the communications chamber. Within the hour she had gotten the go-ahead from Morris in Tel Aviv.

Dr. Turner's first official act as Innocent's personal physician was to pack him off to bed for a minimum of ten hours' rest. After he had received Rowitz's assurance that his instructions would be carried out, Michael Turner was escorted by the Swiss Guards to the third floor of the Apostolic Palace, which housed the dispensary, a small pharmacy, and adjoining surgery. There, for the first time, he met his predecessor, Doctor Federico Sabatini. The old man introduced Turner to the nursing sisters he would be working with and then proceeded to show the American exactly how the small facility functioned. Equally informative was the advice Dr. Sabatini passed on regarding how the physician to the Pope was viewed by the rest of the Curia.

"Although you may not perceive it as such, the position of Papal physician is a highly political one," Sabatini remarked. "Most Papal elections, as this one was, are founded on compromise. That means there is always a faction, sometimes greater, sometimes smaller, which will be ever alert for some flaw. Since most Popes are at least well into middle age, the question of health, both physical and mental, can become an issue very easily. You must be very careful as to what you say about a Pope's health or suddenly the world press will have the Pontiff on his deathbed. I am leaving you a list of specialists here in Rome who are available on a moment's notice."

"Father Rowitz tells me an official announcement of my appointment will have to be made," Turner said. "I wonder if the first criticism won't be that I'm a neurosurgeon."

"Think nothing of that." Dr. Sabatini laughed. "You mustn't forget that I'm a pediatrician. This is one of the few occasions on which the Holy Father needn't consult anyone about an appointment."

After Sabatini had left, Turner shut himself away in what was now his office. For an hour he worked without pause, drawing up a list of names and institutions. Reading these over, he realized he would not have to go outside the continental United States in search of expert cardiologists. There were two in New York, one in Chicago, and three in Houston, including Michael DeBakey. He was certain that any of these men would be able to supervise the team that would perform the AID implant procedure on Innocent XIV. But since the surgery had to be performed more or less clandestinely, Turner had to obtain an operating schedule for each of them. With that in hand he could approach his first-choice candidate. If he accepted, then the rest of the team could be put together quickly, the necessary equipment flown to Rome from Switzerland. Turner glanced at his watch and calculated how soon it would be prudent to phone Theodore Weizmann in New York. Weizmann would be his jumping-off point. He could contact each of the others without questions being raised. Once he had made it clear that he was inquiring on behalf of an important but anonymous patient, Weizmann would have little difficulty in obtaining the necessary operating schedules.

Watching the moon's progress across St. Peter's Square, Turner leaned back in his chair, his arms clasped behind his head, and wondered what Dr. Weizmann's reaction would be. So much had happened that Weizmann was unaware of. So much would happen that he could never be told.

It was nearly morning before Michael Turner returned to the Hassler-Villa Medici. He called Anna Letelier's number at the gallery twice, but each time a male voice told him that she had not yet arrived. Whoever answered would not divulge either her home address or her private number. All through his

dinner of cold chicken and a fine red Bardolino, Turner wondered what had become of that strange woman. She was the last
person he thought of before sleep finally overtook him and the
first he remembered when the telephone woke him up later that
morning. Anna Letelier arrived at half-past nine, following a
breakfast trolley Turner had not called down for. Her makeup
did little to conceal the lines of fatigue drawn across her face.
Her eyes betrayed her anxiety as she paced and smoked. When
he came out of the bathroom, she handed him a cup of coffee
and asked, "Are you with us, then?"

"I am."

"I can't stay," Anna told him, refusing his offer of breakfast. From her bag she pulled out a white envelope and handed
it to Turner. "You must get this to Innocent right away. It's a
tape. Make certain that Gregory Rowitz is there to hear it as
well. What we have been waiting for is finally coming. Tell
Innocent this is VIPER's last transmission."

"But you—"

"I have to get back to the gallery. There are a great many
arrangements to be made. Call me there later in the afternoon.
We'll talk then."

Turner tore upon the envelope, and a cassette fell into his
palm.

"There is one other thing," Anna said, standing by the
door. "Komarov is dead. The announcement won't be forth-
coming until this evening at the earliest. That gives us a little
time, but not much."

Auguste Cardinal Mirabeau and Innocent XIV were standing in the doorway of the papal office, exchanging quiet comments about the policy briefing that had just ended, when
Father Rowitz came up and announced that Michael Turner
was awaiting the Pontiff in his surgery two floors below. He reminded Innocent that this half-hour had been set aside for a
preliminary physical check-up, the results of which would be
communicated to the Curia and which doubtless would find
their way beyond the Vatican's walls. It was the necessary first
step in assuring not only the Church, but the whole world as

well, that the man who headed the Catholic faith was of sound mind and body. After promising to send Mirabeau a copy of the report, Innocent and Gregory Rowitz made their way to the infirmary. But when they arrived, they found Michael Turner not in the surgery but in his office. His desk was bare except for a tape-cassette player. Only after the door had been locked did Turner speak.

"Anna delivered this to me this morning," he said, tapping the cassette. "I don't know what's on it, but she wanted you and Father Rowitz to hear it immediately. She said it's from VIPER."

"Play it," Innocent said sharply.

Turner depressed the button. There was a faint hiss of static, then Anna Letelier's voice came through.

"The tape you are about to hear was recorded several days ago, secretly, in the apartment of Dmitri Gorodin, Soviet Foreign Minister. Two of my people died getting this tape to us. Perhaps even more have been picked up . . . I don't know. I haven't had a chance to authenticate the voices, but I'm certain you will recognize Gorodin's. The other speaker is Viktor Suslev, director of the KGB. The original of this tape is with me. After you have listened to this copy, please make absolutely certain that it is filed away in a very secure place. Once you hear it, you will understand why."

There were a few seconds of silence, then the voices of Suslev and Gorodin filtered into the room. It mattered not at all that the speakers were Russian. Everyone in the room understood every word.

"So when Komarov dies, the blame for his death will fall upon the Rudin doctors. They are all Jews, led by that Razminsky who brought the American over. The accusation will come from a nurse. To support her contention, she will offer documentary evidence that Razminsky was tampering with the drugs he prescribed. Although these notes will not be signed, experts will later determine that the handwriting on them is Razminsky's. An autopsy will be performed immediately, traces of poison found."

The voice was Gorodin's. "Razminsky and his staff will be immediately taken into custody. At this point I would expect the newspapers and electronic media to resurrect the Doctors' Plot that Stalin intended to use as the pretext for his last purge. We must keep reminding the people that all the blame for Komarov's death lies with these Jewish doctors, that had it not been for their treachery the chairman would be alive today. Precisely two weeks after Razminsky and the others have been arrested, the Prosecutor General will announce that the suspects have all confessed. Once their confessions are published in the newspapers, I would expect a massive public outcry, which will open the door to the expulsion of Jews from all university faculties, managerial positions in industry, from every post which could be considered sensitive. They will not be permitted to travel abroad. Internal passports will be revoked as well. Any resistance will be met with overwhelming force . . . The police in various cities, especially in the Ukraine, will uncover evidence that groups of Jews have been banding together illegally and forming subversive cells and forging secret links with Solidarity hooligans and other antisocial elements. By exposing these cells we will galvanize public opinion. Citizens will form vigilance committees to monitor the activities of the Jews. Some of these committees might become somewhat overzealous in discharging their civil obligations. So much the better.

"It is anticipated that a few Jews, primarily the young ones, will fight. Daytime violence must be kept to a minimum. After we give them a taste of what's in store, they will go underground. We must be right behind them, taking them in darkness, moving them out in darkness. Adverse foreign reaction can be anticipated, but nothing your department cannot cope with. I think we can rely on a number of our nationalists to support what we shall call containment."

"You realize of course that American satellites will

discover the locations of the camps as soon as they become operative." Suslev's voice was unmistakable.

"We can dispute the interpretation of satellite photographs until doomsday if we have to."

"Israel will not stand by and watch her people being destroyed."

"There is nothing Israel can do. You don't seriously expect her to attack us? Also, can effective sanctions really be imposed against us by anyone? The answer is no. We are almost self-sufficient in fuel, and we pay in gold, which helps. Thus far we have had to supplement our harvests and we will continue to do so in the future, but if the United States will not sell us grain, the Canadians and Argentinians will. Israel will be left without an effective counterstroke. She can only stand by and watch. Finally there will be heavy reliance on a KGB disinformation campaign to supplement our other efforts. The Israelis must get nothing in the way of concrete intelligence. What they manage to get from their own networks here will be what we allow them to take out."

"I presume the Prosecutor General will be preparing for a lengthy trial."

"Of course. With the world press in attendance— assuming the accused can be properly handled in an open courtroom."

"That has been done before, Minister. I also assume the confessions will incriminate certain ethnic Russians as well as clandestine groups working with the Jews, who had all been waiting for Komarov to die."

"As you know, there are a great many Jews in the technical services—Kobalevsky's territory. I'm certain the confessions will have a great deal to say about him and his kind."

"We have four million Jews in this country. You propose to deal with all of them?"

"We take the dissenters and the males from the professional classes first."

"Yes. All right. But *how* do you intend to deal with them, physically that is. What are they to eat? Where are they to live?"

"I don't believe I said anything about their living."

"I see."

"You know your camps better than I. You can judge how much labor you need and how much is surplus. You have the resources and manpower; you have the transport and holding facilities. It is simply a question of getting on with the job."

From somewhere in the boughs of the great oak that framed itself in the window of Turner's office came the sweet warble of a bird. Another joined it. The singing was all that could be heard, that and the soft hypnotic ticking of the Lefarge clock over the mantelpiece. A match snapped, its flame bright for a second, then fading in the sunlight. Michael Turner cupped his hands and lit his cigarette.

"I can't believe it," he said. "*No one* can believe that. The idea's insane. It's too monstrous to even imagine, let alone believe."

Innocent came over to the recorder, his face set, the lips bloodless. He removed the cassette and passed it to Gregory Rowitz.

"See to it that this is locked away in my personal safe."

Father Rowitz's hands shook as he accepted the cassette.

"That was certainly the voice of Dmitri Gorodin," Innocent said. "And of Viktor Suslev. As God is my witness, I will not permit it!"

"But you don't have to act alone," Turner said. "You now have the authority to make them listen . . . the President, the United Nations, anyone! You can play that tape for the world, and the Russians will *have to* back down!"

"It won't work that way, Michael." Innocent shook his head. "You do not understand Russia as Gregory and I do. You do not really understand the meaning of expediency. The tape can be challenged on a dozen levels. Experts will refute experts; accusations and counteraccusations will be hurled back and forth. But in the meantime the Gulag trains will begin rolling, and no one will be the wiser. Right now we have the advantage. We know what their intentions are. If we plan carefully, we can find the exact means to strike, because we will only have that one chance."

"And Komarov is already dead." Turner gestured helplessly. "He is dead . . ." He looked at Innocent and Rowitz with terrible comprehension. "Dear God, Razminsky—it's all going to come down on him!"

Innocent looked pale. "The inaction of the West during the Hungarian Revolution. Prague in 1968, Warsaw and Gdansk. Afghanistan. Freedom and dignity—these have always been subordinated to political expediency. It will happen again. It will happen this time if we permit it. And we cannot."

29

"Where is Suslev?"

Sergei Bibnikov looked decidedly uncomfortable in the passenger seat of the Volga that Aleksandr Roy was driving with reckless skill through the evening traffic on Ulitsá Arbatskaya.

"He is having dinner with Gorodin in the club room of the Foreign Ministry," Roy said, not taking his eyes off the road for an instant. He shifted smoothly into third gear and made a screeching turn past two Moskoviches. "He'll be there for two hours. All you'll need is twenty, twenty-five minutes, possibly less."

"What about the guard?"

"He's a fellow by the name of Gugarin, no relation to the cosmonaut," Roy said, catching a yellow light. "It took some doing, but I managed to unearth a few unsavory facts about his past. He's greedy, our Gugarin—has a mistress to support in a certain style. He sells drugs on the black market."

"Who is his source?"

"One of the doctors who works the Lubyanka. He gets whatever Gugarin wants right out of the cabinets. There's no shortage of pharmaceuticals in that place, and the control is nonexistent."

"I trust you have reacquainted this Gugarin with his past indiscretions."

"I showed him some home movies."

"We've got to do this exactly right," Bibnikov muttered. "Borgatov is still thinking of you as a prospective son-in-law. He'd never forgive me if anything happened to you."

"Nothing will." Roy paused and looked across at his chief. "But we have another problem."

Bibnikov regarded him warily. The bantering tone was gone.

"Suslev's medical team filed its report twenty minutes ago," Roy continued. "The bottle of Decadron solution that Razminsky had hooked up to Komarov before he left . . . the inside was coated with nitroprusside."

Bibnikov rubbed his face with both hands. "What else?"

"The security around Razminsky and the others at the Lubyanka has doubled. No one gets in to see them without Suslev's written permission."

"Now he's acting like a fucking schoolmaster! Have you tested this famous security?"

"As a matter of fact, yes."

"And?" Bibnikov waited impatiently.

"There's a way in."

"You're improving. What about Suslev's informant? Which son of a bitch was after Razminsky's hide?"

"Not a he—she. Lydmilla Mayakovskaya."

"I want everything we can have on her," Bibnikov said tonelessly. "Where is she now?"

"The entire staff is out at the Rudin. The Guards Directorate is still interrogating the lot of them. There's more. Something arrived for you from the directorate office." Roy brought out two video cassettes from his briefcase.

"Very good," Bibnikov smiled.

"Would it spoil the surprise to tell me?"

"They're duplicates of the surveillance unit tapes."

"From the Guards Directorate at Rudin?"

"The same."

"But how did you—"

"A friend of a friend."

"And I suppose they have Komarov's last hours."

"That they do, and here we are."

They had arrived at the prison. Parking in the official lot, they entered the Lubyanka through the Dzerzhinsky Square gate. At the first checkpoint their names were checked against the duty sheet. Within the cavernous, turn-of-the-century foyer their credentials were examined once more while both men signed in.

"Central Registry?" the duty officer asked.

"Yes," Roy said.

"Shall I call down?"

"No, you shall not," Roy told him softly. "This is an official investigation. You would do well to keep this to yourself."

The duty officer paled and closed the ledger. He had heard about the headhunters from Special Investigations.

Both Bibnikov and Roy presented themselves at the counter which ran the length of the room two floors below. They waited until the duty clerk came up to them and asked what it was they wanted. Roy started to speak, then Bibnikov interrupted.

"Where are your facilities?" he demanded brusquely.

The girl told him he would find the washrooms out in the corridor. Bibnikov departed, leaving Roy to carry out his part of the deception.

In the corridor Bibnikov turned right, toward the elevator which could be operated only with a magnetic key and ran only between the two lower levels of the basement and the reception area where the prisoners were held prior to interrogation. The entire plan could die here if there was someone in the elevator.

There wasn't.

He stepped in, and the doors slid closed. Thirty seconds later, Bibnikov emerged on the lower level, the deepest part of the Lubyanka, which contained the torture chambers. There was no one in the glass booth to his right, where the duty guard should have been.

Cameras, Bibnikov thought. What if the son of a bitch set up cameras? His eyes flitted to the corner where the walls met the ceiling. Nothing. Bibnikov was not altogether relieved, but there was nothing he could do. He was committed. His only consolation lay in the fact that if Suslev ever came to hear of his nocturnal sortie into his lair, the absent guard would be the first to die. Small consolation. Bibnikov took the three steps into the corridor between the cells and moved quickly along to Number 473. He inserted the key that Roy had provided him with and opened the door.

The first thing that struck him was the bright light shining from a thousand-watt lamp in the mesh basket high above the floor. The second was the smell of human excrement and rancid sweat. But to Bibnikov even more powerful, more pervasive, in that cell was the palpable despair.

The figure lying on the pallet did not move. He was dressed in the clothes he had been taken in, a light brown suit. His belt had been removed, and his shoes had no laces.

"Razminsky," he called out softly. The figure stirred, rolling over on his side. One look at Razminsky's haggard face told Bibnikov all he had to know about the methods Suslev was using on this man. Razminsky was not being beaten. He was being fed enough to keep him alive. In all likelihood the actual interrogation hadn't even begun yet. Suslev was softening him up for the confessions in the cruelest way imaginable—by slowly causing Razminsky to go blind in the searing light that burned in the cell twenty-four hours a day.

His hands were handcuffed behind his back, and he had probably been given a moderate dose of amphetamine, just enough to keep him awake, without seriously endangering his heart. There was no way Razminsky could keep from opening his eyes some of the time.

"Stand up," Bibnikov said, pulling Razminsky to his feet. The physician's face was contorted with pain. He squeezed his eyes shut against the light.

"Hold still. I'm not going to hurt you," Bibnikov said. "Stand still."

Gently he placed a pair of heavy sunglasses over Razminsky's eyes, slipping a pair on himself. He did not want to think about how Roy had anticipated this particular selection from Suslev's repertoire.

"Open your eyes." He could tell by the softening of Razminsky's expression that he had done so.

"Who are you?" Dr. Razminsky asked, his voice dry.

"I am not from Suslev."

"Then who are you?"

"Who I am is not important. I am here to ask you to help me."

"Help you?" Razminsky said woodenly. "Help *you*?"

"This is not a ploy," Bibnikov said. "And I don't have time to convince you that I'm telling the truth."

"You mean to say Suslev is not standing outside that door?" Razminsky's muscles were quivering.

"Suslev doesn't know I'm here. I've taken a tremendous risk by coming here. What more of a guarantee do you want?"

Razminsky moved back to the wall and leaned against it, his head arched back against the stone.

"What do you want?"

"Do you know why you are here?" Bibnikov asked.

"I—we—are accused of killing my patient, Semyon Arkadyevich Komarov," Razminsky said in a dead voice. "My entire staff has been accused."

"Have you been asked to write a full confession?"

"Yes. But I haven't. I'm certain the others have not consented. But I don't know . . . I don't know how much longer I can stand the light. What must they be doing to the others?"

"You're right, doctor," Bibnikov said brutally. "You will not hold out much longer. The pain will become intolerable. You know better than I how quickly a man's cornea can be burned away. But you are wrong in one respect. One of your team has already confessed."

"That is not possible," Razminsky breathed. "It's me Suslev wants—"

"And he will get around to you, believe me. But one of your people has already given him a confession. Voluntarily. It states that you intended to murder not only Komarov but other members of the Politburo as well. A much wider plot against the leadership and the state."

"What are you saying?" Razminsky demanded. "That's insanity. How could anyone even think that?" He swallowed. "Who was it who confessed?"

"That is what you must tell me."

"How can I? I don't know."

"Dr. Razminsky, we will have only one chance to uncover the traitor. That's right. You have had an informer there for God knows how long. I don't know who he is or how Suslev got to him, but I think he must have been there for some time, since you did not suspect him. It has to be someone you trusted, someone whose loyalty you would never question."

"But it can't be," Razminsky protested. "God help us that it's come to this."

"God is of little use in this place," Bibnikov whispered. "I am the only one who can help you. And to do that I must have the name of the man who betrayed you."

"Why should you help?" Razminsky demanded suddenly. "You're with state security, otherwise you would never have gotten into this place. What difference does it make to you?"

"It is not you that I am concerned with," Bibnikov said. "It's what will happen to all of Russia if this scheme is allowed to grow to fruition."

"You are asking me to condemn a man I have probably known for years." Razminsky shook his head. "I have worked with most of these men for the better part of forty years. How am I supposed to discern treachery after forty years?"

"Let that work for you." Bibnikov stepped closer. "You know each one so well that anything out of the ordinary would be meaningful. Concentrate on each and every one of them. A minor incident, off-hand remark, out-of-character behavior, something like that is bound to come up."

"I will never be certain, you understand," Razminsky said.

"That's a chance we'll have to take," Bibnikov said. "I can only risk coming here so often. As the need for confessions becomes greater, it will be impossible to gain access to you. So the name you give me will have to be the one. Do you understand, Razminsky, *it will have to be the one*."

"How much time do I have?" Razminsky asked.

"Four days at the most," Bibnikov said. "Suslev will start the interrogations then. There is nothing I can do to prevent that. You must have the name for me before he starts."

"To serve the greater good you spoke of?" Razminsky said.

"There is no good," Bibnikov said. "Some things are less worse, less evil than others."

"I wonder if you truly believe that."

"I do."

"When will you come again?"

"If I can, four days from now. It may be sooner or later by a day. I have no idea what sort of problems I'll encounter next time. So take three days, look for me on the fourth. If not, then the fifth."

Bibnikov reached out to take the glasses and Razminsky stepped back.

"I'm sorry," Bibnikov said. "Believe me, I wish I could leave them with you. But they would be found. And that would be the end of everything."

"Three days," Razminsky said, squeezing his eyes shut against the light. "Three days. No more."

30

A discreet, monotonous murmur circulated through the lobby of the Bernini Bristol Hotel. On his way to the dining room Michael Turner passed Count Lemanteza, leading a blue-black panther toward the elevator. The maître d' met Turner at the entrance to the interior courtyard. After his reservation was verified, he was led through a forest of candlelit tables toward the salon doors. Turner gazed around the room at the women in evening dresses, their escorts in perfectly tailored suits beckoning to waiters in blue uniforms accented with yellow braid. Exotic perfumes and expensive scents mixed with the piquant aromas drifting up from the chafing dishes. The flames of cognac leaped up to illuminate a caress, a furtive glance. Michael Turner saw Anna Letelier looking at him from across the room, the candles changing the color of her hair from dark brown to russet. He walked toward her. When he reached her table, her fingers were cool to his touch and tightened around his own, accenting her welcoming smile. As the physician sat down his champagne flute was filled.

"*L'chaim,*" Anna said.

Turner raised his glass. The champagne was dry and ice-cold.

"We have no cause to celebrate today," Anna said softly. "So I am drinking this simply for its own sake."

"There's no better reason."

"Thank you for joining me tonight."

"Thanks for inviting me. Frankly it's been one hell of a day, and it's not over yet."

"Have you spoken with Weizmann?"

"I don't know how he did it." Turner shook his head. "Howard Berger, from UCLA Medical School, is on his way. He was the last one I would have thought that Weizmann could get to. He operates only with a hand-picked group, and, as I recall, his schedule is booked up years in advance, not months."

"He'll be bringing in his own people?"

Turner nodded. "They're due to arrive at ten tomorrow morning. The equipment Berger wants is coming in by charter from Basel in about three hours. I have to be there to meet the plane."

"What about the actual site of the operation?"

"Castel Gandolfo. I wanted to stay away from any of the Roman hospitals. The surgery in the Apostolic Palace is too small, and it's doubtful we would have been able to get the equipment in there without anyone knowing about it."

"Castel Gandolfo is perfect," Anna agreed. "Private." She hesitated for a moment. "What time to you think the operation will begin?"

"That will depend on Berger," Turner said. "From what I know of him, he's a very fast cutter. It's unlikely that the trans-atlantic trip will take so much out of him that he won't want to go in at once."

"Does he know yet who he's to operate on?"

"No. Because he's a good friend of Weizmann's, he didn't have to tell him that. Berger simply assumed that the operation had to be performed with no delay. Besides, Berger may well have guessed."

The waiter came by and set plates of antipasto before them, refilling their glasses. When he left, she said, "I took the liberty of ordering for both of us. These are house specialties that shouldn't be missed."

They ate prawns in garlic sauce and, as the main course, *abbacchio alla Romana*. Anna said, "You know that tomorrow there won't be any peace for you. One way or the other the press will ferret out the story."

"I haven't been told how Innocent intends to handle that," Turner said.

"He will give the official announcement of Komarov's death as the reason for his retreat," Anna said. "Naturally Cardinal Mirabeau will have to be told about the operation." She hesitated.

"Still, his absence at Papal ceremonies will cause speculation. If all goes well at Castel Gandolfo, then I can have Innocent back in Rome within two days," Turner said. "If necessary, I can hold a press conference and explain exactly what the AID operation is all about. The media can check with any medical experts they want. The answer will be the same. The surgery is neither critical nor radical. The records of past cases are there for anyone who wants confirmation."

They continued to eat and to chat about the details of the procedure. When the meal was finished and their coffee before them, Turner asked, "You don't believe Gorodin will back down, do you?"

"No. I don't," Anna said, extracting a cigarette from her case.

"That means you'll be leaving," he said.

She looked away, and in the candlelight he could see the tears in her eyes. He lifted her head with a finger under her chin.

"I have to be at the airport," Turner said. "I'll be taking the equipment directly to Castel Gandolfo. I've made arrangements for Berger and his people to be driven there directly. Innocent will be arriving tomorrow morning . . . and there is really no need for me to come back into the city."

"I know," Anna said tenderly. "I will stay with you at Castel Gandolfo tonight."

At five o'clock in the morning, half an hour before he was scheduled to leave for Castel Gandolfo, Innocent called Mirabeau to his chambers and informed the Secretary of State of the

real reason for his departure. He apologized to the cardinal for
not letting him know in advance but made it clear that it wasn't
until the last minute that he was certain the physician and the
surgical team would be available. After Mirabeau was satisfied
that the operation was not a critical one, he assured Innocent
that court circular would be revised accordingly while scheduled audiences would quietly be postponed. An announcement
to that effect would be issued four hours hence, at the same time
that an internal memorandum would be circulated to the senior
officials of the Curia. All inquiries, both internal and external,
would be handled by Mirabeau's office. Father Gregory Rowitz
would remain in his office, monitoring internal Vatican reaction, deflecting the most persistent queries to Mirabeau. Innocent XIV embraced Mirabeau, thanked him for his prayers, and
assured him he would return to the Vatican within a few days.
The cardinal escorted him through the galleries to the car that
awaited outside the enclosed portico.

At the same time as the papal limousine quietly nosed its
way into the Roman dawn another private car was already
hurtling along the *autostrada* toward the papal summer retreat. Dr. Howard Berger and three other American surgeons
were reading a copy of Innocent's medical file.

At Castel Gandolfo, Michael Turner was checking the final
placement of the equipment. The surgery was larger than the
one in the Vatican, its wiring and lights refurbished two
years earlier. Dr. Berger would doubtlessly want to go over it all
a second time, but Turner was satisfied that everything the
cardiac specialist could possibly need would be on hand. When
he returned to his room to freshen up, Anna Letelier was still
asleep in his bed.

At half-past seven Michael Turner met the doctors from
the United States. Dr. Berger, a tall, thin man with a shock of
wiry hair, greeted Turner warmly. He introduced the rest as
they walked through the main entrance of Castel Gandolfo and
up the stairs to the Papal apartments. By the time Innocent and
Gregory Rowitz entered the study, Turner had heard enough
from Berger to know that there would be no last-minute hitches
with the surgery.

By nine o'clock, after they had given Innocent a thorough examination, the cardiology team was finally satisfied that he was physically capable of undergoing the operation and that Turner had followed the appropriate preoperative procedures.

"If I remember correctly, it wasn't so very long ago that I was looking up at you in exactly this way," Innocent murmured, his lips in a faint smile.

The Pontiff was being wheeled to the elevators with Turner on one side and Berger on the other.

"I'll be with you," Turner promised. "I'll just be observing, but I will be there."

Innocent's eyes glazed over and his head rolled to one side as the massive dose of Demerol began to do its work. At the entrance to the surgery, the gurney was transferred to Berger's team, which was already scrubbed. Because there had been no chance to recruit the necessary surgical nurses, two of Berger's residents would perform those functions.

As the two chief physicians donned their gowns, Turner said, "We can't have anything go wrong."

"It's going to be a cakewalk." Berger winked.

Turner knew what he meant. The offhandedness was characteristic of the man. To Berger the Pope was simply another patient—a series of charts and graphs and scribbled notations. That was the safe distance Berger and all who wielded a scalpel maintained from the identity of the human on the operating table. But just this once Turner wished he would make Berger think otherwise.

As soon as Innocent XIV was wheeled into the operating theater Father Gregory Rowitz returned by car to his office at the Vatican. There was no point in sitting and waiting. Time would go by much more quickly if he kept himself busy. The mail that had been delivered still awaited his attention.

Cardinal Mirabeau had forewarned Father Rowitz that the offices of the Pontiff would receive fifteen hundred letters and parcels daily, but only after each one had been subjected to fluoroscope examination by a special detail of the Vatican security office. Mail bearing diplomatic or diocesan seals or the imprimatur was forwarded directly to him, the Papal secretary. It was he who decided what would reach the desk of the Holy Father immediately and what could be left until the day's work was over. To ensure the confidentiality of correspondence from close friends and relatives, Mirabeau had suggested to Rowitz that these privileged correspondents be supplied with a three-digit code number; a letter with this number marked in the lower right-hand corner of the envelope would only be opened by the Pontiff himself.

Today the volume of mail could be dealt with quickly. Two envelopes were addressed to Rowitz personally. The first was a telegram from Amsterdam. Rowitz noticed immediately that Hannah Levin must have sent it from her home, since the address of the Central Holocaust Archives did not appear anywhere. The text of the message was simple enough. Hannah Levin wanted to see Father Rowitz as soon as possible. It was essential that he come in person. No mention was made of Telemann, if he had been found, or how far the search had progressed. But the urgency of the telegram was unsettling. The second envelope bore the strip seal of the British Embassy in Rome and contained within it a second envelope, bearing the red waxed seal of the British Embassy in Prague. It was an invitation from an old friend.

For the next few minutes Father Rowitz considered what had to be done. There was no question but that he would have to leave Castel Gandolfo for at least twenty-four hours, perhaps longer. That would mean he would not be present when Innocent regained consciousness. If there was only Amsterdam to consider, then certainly he could have gone there and come back in a day. But not to Prague, and it was Prague that demanded his presence most urgently.

From his safe Father Rowitz removed a thick sheaf of papers which he carefully wrapped in a padded air-freight envelope before he affixed the seal of his office. He made his way back to his private quarters and packed a small overnight bag, taking care to include his Vatican passport. For the first time he was grateful that Michael Turner was preoccupied with the surgery and that Anna Letelier was nowhere to be found. He had no answers to the questions they would surely have asked him.

Father Rowitz arrived at Leonardo da Vinci Airport at half-past eleven, going directly to the Swissair travel assistance desk. He presented his Vatican credentials and was assured that the package he had brought would be out on the next flight to Geneva, in three hours. The airline guaranteed delivery into the city and would obtain a receipt from the addressee.

Next the priest went to the post office in the main concourse. From there he sent a short telegram to Hannah Levin, acknowledging receipt of her message and informing her that under the circumstances he could not get in touch with her for another twenty-four hours. He would call as soon as possible, or else come in person.

Then Father Rowitz hurried to the office of Czechoslovak National Airlines and asked to speak with the supervisor. Over the clatter of teletypes and typewriters he explained that he had to leave for Prague on the first available flight. He had no visa, but under the circumstances such a formality could surely be waived: he had been called to Prague to attend at the deathbed of a British Embassy official. The supervisor stiffened. He excused himself and closed the door of his glass-walled office. Father Rowitz waited patiently while the supervisor dialed the number he had been given and noted the mild expression of surprise which came over the man's face. He returned to the ticket counter. There was no CAS flight for Prague today. However, a scheduled Aeroflot jet was leaving within the hour for Moscow, with a brief stopover in Prague. A seat was available, as well as a hotel room in the Czech capital.

The British Embassy stood in the shadows of the magnificent spires of Hradčany Castle on Thunovka Street, a tall, narrow building in the neo-Gothic style. When Father Rowitz arrived at seven o'clock, only the consular office remained open. His Vatican passport gained him entry to the small waiting room on the ground floor while the guard telephoned the duty officer. The embassy official greeted the priest politely enough, but there was no mistaking the tone.

"I don't suppose that, in the circumstances, you've come to escort the good archbishop to Rome?"

"No, that is not the reason I am here."

"I'm afraid I can't offer you accommodations," the embassy officer announced with ill-concealed satisfaction as he stared down at the priest's modest overcoat and shoes.

"I have made arrangements to stay at a hotel," Rowitz answered. "I don't intend to be with the archbishop for more than an hour. Perhaps less."

The British official's relief was evident. "Right. In that case, you will find the archbishop in the garden," he said. "Eleven o'clock in the morning, half-past seven in the evening— regular as clockwork. That's his constitutional. If you'd like, I'll announce you."

"Thank you, but there's no need. We know each other . . . from another time."

The official feigned a smile. "As you wish. It's just over there."

Rowitz nodded and walked over to the double doors that opened onto the flagstone patio.

The courtyard of the embassy was enclosed by a high brick wall, laden with ivy. The sweet smell of budding rosebushes drifted through the air, mixing with the scents of the violets, gardenias, and rhododendrons that bloomed in brilliantly colored beds. In the center of the yard was a massive oak, with clots of black tar where the lower branches had been chopped off and the wounds covered over. A figure in a black cassock, wearing gardener's gloves and a broad-brimmed hat, stepped back from the beds to survey his handiwork.

"Ladislas," Rowitz called out softly.

Ladislas Bittmann, the archbishop of Prague, looked around, his head turning as sharply as a bird's. He gasped when he saw his visitor and took a tentative step toward Father Rowitz, then broke into a run, holding up the hem of his cassock so as not to stumble.

"Gregory," he cried, flinging his arms around Rowitz.

Stepping back, he looked at him in wonder, then embraced him once again.

"It's been a long time," Rowitz said.

Rowitz saw the hope in the monsignor's eyes, the hope that had sustained the archbishop throughout his ordeal, that one day he would be able to walk out through the gates of the British Embassy and into the streets of his beloved city, to reclaim his rightful place on the episcopal throne of the Prague cathedral. Archbishop Bittmann had been one of the leaders of the Czech Spring of 1968. Unlike the others, whom the Soviets had sent off into the backwaters of Czech society, Bittmann's condemnation of the Russian-backed government had been too vituperative. He could not be trusted simply to fade away. But the Czech secret police had missed him, and by a miracle Bittmann had managed to cross a hostile city and request asylum in the British Embassy.

In time Archbishop Bittmann became a permanent resident on the fourth floor of the embassy. Subsisting on a nominal stipend from Rome, he did what he could by celebrating mass for the faithful, acting as interpreter when the occasion warranted, and in his free time working on his memoirs and in the embassy garden.

"Ten years," Bittmann said, his voice rising with incredulity. "Ten years it's been, Gregory."

Rowitz nodded. He was one of the very few who had visited Bittmann in his exile. Stanislawski, when he had first been made cardinal, was another.

He looked up at Rowitz. "It's so good to see you, my friend."

Rowitz smiled. "I received your note. Coming when it did, I thought it very disturbing. You say, Ladislas, that the Russians are making inquiries into Innocent's past life. I'm not sure I understand what you meant."

"I never commit too many details to paper," Bittmann said, taking off his gardening gloves. "I think we both share that modest form of paranoia." He glanced up at the windows encircling the yard.

"Gregory, you know how difficult it is to read the flight of straws in the wind. But even though I have not been outside the embassy gates in years, a good deal of information still reaches me. This particular item is above suspicion. Moscow has sent out a directive to all intelligence services within the bloc to check their files for anything having to do with Stanislawski."

"The directive applies to all Warsaw Pact intelligence services?"

"Yes. I can't comprehend why something like this should apply to Prague as well. Innocent was never associated with this city. But"—he shrugged—"I thought you had better be informed."

Rowitz nodded. "Yes, of course. What, I wonder, are they searching for?"

"Anything that could be construed as derogatory or inflammatory. A scandal, anything of that sort."

"I don't understand what it is they're looking for."

"They are wary of him. They realize that their own propaganda might not be enough to discredit him."

"It's patently foolish for them to take on something like this," Rowitz said, dismissing the Communists with a wave of the hand, but he did not want the conversation to end here. He had to get every last detail from Bittmann . . . and in such a way that the archbishop would suspect nothing. "It's puzzling though. Would they be expending so much effort and time if they didn't believe that *something* would eventually turn up?"

"I think they are simply afraid," Bittmann said. He reached out and touched Rowitz's arm. "I'm sorry if I misled or frightened you. I truly did not expect you to come here in person simply on the strength of my note."

"These are not normal times," Rowitz answered. "Everything must be investigated, no matter how farfetched it seems. Besides," he added gently, "it is good to see you again after all these years."

"The Russians can behave very strangely," Bittmann mused. "They're almost as clever in hunting out the truth as they are at fabricating lies. But what can they do with Innocent —try to prove that he was once a Communist? Certainly he was too young to ever be a Nazi. Or maybe because he has taken up the cause of the Jews, he is a Jew himself?" Bittmann chuckled.

Father Rowitz sniffed appreciatively at the fragrant air of the garden. He knew now he had acted correctly in coming to Prague. He knew too what had to be done.

He had dinner with Bittmann in his rooms, the archbishop being much more concerned with Father Rowitz's conversation than with the food. He was a man starved for news of the outside world, particularly of Rome, the city he missed most of all after his beloved Prague, and his old friend Stanislawski. He detained Rowitz until eleven o'clock, when he reluctantly saw him to the front gate and embraced him in the foyer.

"Will you come by again before you leave?" he asked.

"I can't," Rowitz whispered. "I must get back to Rome. There is a flight that leaves early in the morning."

Bittmann nodded, then suddenly smiled. "Give His Holiness my warmest regards," he said. "The prayers of all of us go with him. And next time don't wait so long to come visit me."

"Next time it is you who should come to Rome," Rowitz said.

"Yes, my dream," Bittmann said, smiling. "But I will not go unless I return as a free man."

Father Rowitz declined the guard's suggestion that a taxi be called to take him to his hotel. The U Tri Pstrosu Hotel was only six blocks away, on Narudova Avenue. He wanted some time to himself, to think about what he would do next.

They would have found him no matter which route he took. Two mobile units covered Thunovka, one a block east, the other a block west of the embassy, just out of sight of the guards at the gates. Another car was stationed on the street behind the walled-in garden; a fourth was positioned on Snemovi Street. They waited until Father Rowitz had walked fifty meters along Thunovka and had reached the intersection of Tomasska Avenue. There was almost no traffic on the street. Spring evenings in Prague were spent in the parks and forests outside the city.

Father Rowitz was thinking of what he would do when he landed in Rome. Innocent would have missed him by now.

Somewhere in the back of his mind a warning was signaled by the slamming of car doors. By the time he had turned to run back toward the embassy, one of them was already behind him, cutting downward with a swing of his club, striking at the nerve centers behind the ears.

31

Bells tolled all across Moscow, punctuated by the dull roar of the artillery pushing their echoes far across the mourning land. A hundred thousand hands made the sign of the cross while a million feet shuffled across the cobblestones of Red Square, giving off the sound of summer thunder, distant but discernible. Huge banners streamed overhead while the morning sun glinted off the fixed bayonets of the rifles of the honor guard. From loudspeakers affixed to lampposts and the cornices of buildings drifted down the tinny echoes of Chopin's *Funeral March,* then Tchaikovsky's *Pathétique.* Once every hour the national anthem was played by the Soviet army orchestra.

Semyon Arkadyevich Komarov had lain in state for several days, on a catafalque in the Hall of Columns, surrounded by flowers from every corner of the Soviet Union. The procession that wound its way past his tomb never ceased. Allies and enemies alike beheld him for the last time, lying beneath the glass that covered the coffin, his expression firm but not as imperious as it had so often been in life. While the diplomatic corps expressed its condolences to his widow, who stood beside Gorodin, the Orthodox churches, at the behest of the Patriarch, offered up their prayers for Komarov's soul, candles sputtering in the hands of old women draped in black shawls, tears streaming from their eyes as the chant of the Office for the Dead was sung. The mausoleum had not yet been completed, so his name, underneath that of Lenin, Stalin, and Brezhnev, was carved into the tomb. At the moment the body was laid to rest within the massive marble confines, all human activity in the land halted for the final memory.

For hours Andrei Razminsky had been lying on his back, unable to move his body more than a few centimeters. He did not hear the door opening, nor the sharp intake of breath as the person who entered recoiled at the stench and at the sight of Razminsky lying in his own excrement, his swollen eyes tightly shut against the light. The first thought Roy had was that he had come too late, but he saw Razminsky's fingers moving slightly. Quickly he bent over the beaten man.

"We want the name," he said, his lips almost touching Razminsky's face.

Andrei Razminsky's lips parted. Once he had discovered he could neither move nor dared to open his eyes, he had focused all his mental energies on searching for the name. No matter that his visitor could have been part of a terrible hoax, no matter that he would in all likelihood die before the next time the door opened, through the pain he continued to search his memory for that one detail which would tell him who had betrayed him, and he had found it. Through cracked lips Razminsky whispered the name—Bauer.

Roy drew back, staring down at Razminsky. He had killed men in his line of work. He had watched others die during interrogation. But those he had killed and those whom he had seen suffering had been traitors or spies, men who had known that no mercy would be shown them if they made the cardinal error of being taken alive. But this, the horror he saw before him on the pallet, was the work of a demented mind. It was a portent of things to come—if the troglodytes were permitted to have their way. It was the track that Gorodin had set them on. It took all his self-restraint not to loosen the strap and turn back the screws on the wooden blocks.

"A little while longer," Roy whispered. "You must live a little while longer. Don't let them get you now."

Even against the glare of the light Roy thought he could see Razminsky smile.

Once outside the Lubyanka, Roy took a circuitous route around the city, making certain he wasn't being followed. His meanderings took him to the Dynamo Stadium, where Bibnikov was waiting for him in the announcers' booth, high above the playing field.

"How is he?"

"Barely holding his own. He gave me the name—Dr. Bauer."

Bibnikov shook his head. "One of the last ones I would have suspected."

"Shall I do the honors?"

"No, I think you should leave that to me," Bibnikov said. "You are going elsewhere."

32

The surgery was concluded at one seventeen in the afternoon. Drs. Michael Turner and Howard Berger were the first to leave the operating theater.

"If every patient I've operated on had that kind of constitution, there wouldn't be a single rejection of the AID implant," Berger said as the two surgeons shed their sterile gowns.

"Prepare yourself for a hero's welcome," Turner replied, and laughed.

Back in his office, Turner telephoned Mirabeau to inform him of the successful conclusion of the operation. He was rather surprised that Father Rowitz was nowhere to be found, either at Castel Gandolfo or the Apostolic Palace, but there was too much that still had to be done for Turner to be particularly concerned about the priest's absence.

At precisely four o'clock Turner and the entire surgical team were presented at a press conference presided over by Mirabeau. After the press had been repeatedly assured that the prognosis was excellent and the Pope wasn't in the slightest danger, Turner accompanied Dr. Berger and the others to the airport. He returned to Castel Gandolfo early that evening, and after a light supper fell into a deep sleep on the couch in the makeshift recovery room.

Innocent XIV did not stir the whole of that night and Turner slept well into the next morning. When he awoke, he saw that the effects of the anesthetic had worn off completely. The Pontiff's eyes were clear. He appeared to be strong and alert, eager to get out of bed and move around.

"Surely it won't be any great tragedy if I simply take a few steps," Innocent grumbled after Turner had forbidden him to get up.

"Karol Stanislawski, I want you to rest at least one more night," Turner said firmly. To allay the Pontiff's concern he explained how well the press reception had gone, about the thousands of phone calls and telegrams that the Holy See had received wishing him a quick recovery.

"And Gregory, where is he?"

Turner frowned. He hadn't heard from the Papal secretary in over twenty-four hours. "He's probably in Rome. If you like, I'll call him and have him come down tonight."

"And Anna?" Innocent asked, with a faint smile.

"She is no longer in the city."

"Any complications?"

"Nothing, Holiness. Anna promised she would be back soon. If there was any news, you know she would have contacted me. For now, please listen to your eminent physician and rest."

Innocent smiled and nodded, his eyes closing as he drifted back into sleep.

Searchlights arced across the sky as Anna Letelier stood in the middle of the Friedrichstrasse in West Berlin, squinting up at the roof of Number 44, a dozen meters from the American military's demarcation line that marked the beginning of Checkpoint Zulu. She had been eight years old when the Wall had gone up, sixteen on her first visit to the city with her father, twenty-two when she had first taken part in a refugee-escape operation. But she had never believed she would witness such horror as confronted her now.

Even though it was well past midnight, the Zone was lit to a stark white glow. A million candlepower flowed from the klieg lights mounted on tractor trailers and rooftops overlooking the perimeter from the western side. Steam rose in incandescent clouds, the heat of the lamps fighting against the

chilly night air, bathing the West German and American on-
lookers in fog. Looking up, Anna could see the rifle barrels of
the snipers posted on the roofs overhead. On either side of the
Friedrichstrasse stood columns of armored personnel carriers,
their engines idling.

"Here, drink this, ma'am. If you're going to stand out here,
there's no point in freezing too."

Without taking her eyes off the strip of asphalt that led
into East Berlin, the barriers raised high to provide a clear field
of fire, Anna accepted the cup. The warmth seeped through her
gloved hands. She took a deep draft and coughed.

"Schnapps," the American intelligence officer said. He was
an older man, perhaps fifty, with a sharp chin and glasses that
were opaque in the glaring light. He stood with his hands behind his back, staring into the Zone. Nothing moved. Under the
lights the pavement sparkled as if the street were inlaid with
diamonds.

"Thank you for the coffee," she said.

"Were they yours?" he asked casually.

"Yes."

"What they tried was an old trick. You can go to the same
well only so often."

Anna drained the cup and held it upside down in her
hand, the last drops falling onto the street. Slowly she moved
across the white line to Checkpoint Charlie, her eyes squinting
against the light. She stopped just short of the double line,
painted in luminous green, and looked across into East Berlin.

"Do you know the building, Number 44?" the American
asked her.

"No."

"Ministry of Health, of no strategic interest. That's why it's
so close to the Zone. They probably hid themselves in the johns,
or in a closet, until closing time. After that it was a simple
matter to get up there." The American gestured. Anna followed
his arm toward the roof of the building. "Getting the wire
across must have been the trickiest part."

She traced the taut wire, almost invisible, across the stretch of the Zone. Beneath were the pressure-sensitive mines, the electronic listening devices, the electrified grids, the Vopos armed with the latest Soviet weaponry. Anna looked to the east, back toward Number 44, where the other end of the wire had been fastened around the base of an air-conditioning cowl on the roof.

"We got the first infrared telephoto shots back a few minutes ago. There seems to be nothing wrong with their equipment—the pulleys, belts, or the cradles."

Finally she dared to look again. Suspended sixty feet in the air, silhouetted by the East German spotlights, were five figures, slumped like marionettes, heads bowed, arms hanging at their sides. The first had gotten halfway across the Zone. The rest were spaced out at twenty-foot intervals, as neatly as though they had been placed there by some giant puppeteer.

"Shouldn't their momentum and the angle of descent have taken them over the Zone?" Anna asked.

"Should have. We'll have to find out why it didn't work when we get them down."

"Sabotage—there had to be sabotage." Her voice stiffened, the words clipped. "The Vopos knew about it in advance. They must have."

"Of course they did. They don't usually post that many sharpshooters on their rooftops."

Anna could imagine the desperate hope building in those who were now dead. The line had been catapulted across successfully and secured. There must have been a last embrace between husband and wife as he slipped the hooks into the line, a final glance at the children, a boy and a girl, ten and eleven, who huddled back against the adults. The husband started down. The wife, seeing him slide away into the darkness, put the children on the line, then herself. Then the second man. When all were on the line, the lights had flooded the Zone and the marksmen squeezed the triggers, bullets racing toward the helpless bodies, every fifth round visible by its phosphorus tracer.

"Goddamn them," Anna whispered. "Goddamn them!"

The officer touched her elbow. "The Vopos have given the go-ahead for us to take down the bodies."

"That means it was a trap," Anna said dully. "The Vopos already know there's nothing on the bodies, no documents, no military plans, nothing. Otherwise they wouldn't surrender the corpses."

The American watched her as she walked away. He himself had lost agents in the Zone, over a dozen of them. There was nothing he could say to her now.

Anna entered the first building and made her way up the four flights of stairs to the roof. The American snipers were still there, their nightscopes trained on the tiny figures on the roof of the government building in East Berlin. She wondered about the East German sharpshooter who must have her in his sights by now.

An American captain in full battle dress glanced at her, then spoke briefly into the radio transmitter. He was asking for a chaplain.

"You want to step back, ma'am?" he asked her. "They're going to lift the wire from their end."

The guywire glinted as fifty yards away a Vopo helicopter slowly tugged it into the air. There was a sharp whine, metal scraping on metal, and a dull thudding sound against the ancient brick of the tenement. Anna winced.

"Get him up, fast!"

The first body was hauled over the edge. The soldiers leaned out to catch the next one. And the next. One by one they were laid out on the gravel of the roof. Anna did not look at the corpses. An army doctor quickly went over to them. She didn't see the face of the second man until the doctor rolled him over. The doctors looked up.

"This one wasn't killed by bullets. His neck's broken."

Anna Letelier knelt down and gently cradled the ashen face of Father Gregory Rowitz between her palms.

The West German police detained Anna Letelier until half-past three that morning. She accompanied the bodies to police headquarters and watched as the staff pathologist tagged each one.

"They were yours?" the police inspector asked. He looked over at the representative of the West German Foreign Ministry, a tall, dour civil servant who was fingering the flimsy, worn identity papers found in the clothing of the husband and wife and the school identification cards of the two children.

"They were yours, yes?" the inspector repeated. "Who is the other one?" He gestured at the supine figure of Father Gregory Rowitz.

"He is a priest," Anna said.

"What is his name?" the Foreign Ministry official asked immediately.

Anna turned away from them. If she gave them Rowitz's name and nothing more, it would still be only a matter of time before the West Germans linked Rowitz to Innocent XIV, which meant linking her to the Pontiff. Under no circumstances could Anna Letelier permit that.

"I would like you to release the body into my custody," she said.

The Foreign Ministry representative, Herr Jaunich, covered his smirk with a gloved hand. "That would be highly irregular," he said. "Unless of course you are related to him."

"I'm not."

"Then can you tell us if *he* is related to *them*?" the criminal inspector said impatiently, nodding in the direction of the four other bodies.

"No, they are not related."

"Why won't you tell us his name?" Herr Jaunich persisted. "Was it *him* you were waiting for? Was he using the other escapees as cover? Is that the way it was supposed to happen?"

"I don't know how it was supposed to happen!" Anna shouted at him.

"But you knew he was coming over the Wall," the criminal inspector objected. "You were waiting for him."

"Why won't you tell us his name?" Jaunich asked once more.

"Because it doesn't matter anymore," Anna said through her teeth. She stared up at the pitiless face. "Don't you understand? It doesn't matter anymore."

The two Germans sighed in unison. None of the escapees had been carrying anything. Their clothing had been carefully filleted for any papers that might have been sewn into the linings, the buttons examined for microreceivers and tapes. Each of the bodies had been carefully examined by police pathologists. Again, nothing. Whatever it was that this Israeli woman had been waiting for had not arrived.

The inspector exchanged glances with his colleagues. They would be able to verify the identities of the family soon enough. They might have even had relatives in the West, although neither of them really believed that. Their story would end in West Berlin's Grafstrasse Cemetery, where they would be interred beside others whose goal the Wall had foiled. But the fifth, the priest, was a loose end. He made the whole business very untidy.

"Fräulein, we have no wish to make this all any more difficult than it already is," the inspector said, "but you must consider our position. Technically this man became our responsibility as soon as the body crossed the Zone into West Berlin. If he is one of your people, then we need some official acknowledgment of that fact before you can claim the body. Otherwise"—he spread his hands in a gesture of helplessness —"we will have no choice but to conduct an autopsy, immediately."

"If you so much as break his skin, you can kiss your career good-bye." Anna flushed. She turned to the Foreign Ministry official. "The same holds true for you. I don't think your ministry would appreciate a diplomatic incident with Israel at this point."

The two men stiffened. Neither had any great love for the Jews. Especially this new breed, the Sabra, who held all things German in undisguised contempt. If they had no one to answer to but themselves, either of them would have authorized an autopsy at once. But they knew from the experiences of several of their colleagues that the Israelis could claw at a man's honorable career and reduce it to shreds. No Jew or Jewish sympathizer—and a dead one at that—was worth the trouble.

Anna knew exactly what they were thinking and it sickened her.

"Get me a telephone!" she said furiously. "Let me make a call, and then you gentlemen can run along to bed."

It took Anna a quarter of an hour to raise the appropriate official at the Israeli Embassy in Bonn. Another forty minutes elapsed before the Telex transmitted the message from the West German Foreign Ministry authorizing release of the unidentified body into the custody of Anna Letelier.

"He is all yours, Fräulein," the inspector said, and passed the yellow carbon copy of the Telex to his colleague.

"I have only one more favor to ask," Anna said. "I want to leave the body here, in the morgue. It will take me some time to make the appropriate arrangements."

"Any way that we can be of service—." The inspector forced a smile.

As she walked toward the door Anna Letelier looked over her shoulder. "And remember, both of you, not so much as a scratch on his skin."

The last leg of her journey, between Rome and Castel Gandolfo, was the most difficult for Anna. The faster she drove, the more concentric her thoughts became. She knew she would not be able to shield Innocent from the fact of Rowitz's death. Yet she was carrying such news that could break the Pontiff spiritually and she was carrying it without any hope of reprieve.

In her fury and frustration, Anna swept past the turnoff for Castel Gandolfo. She slowed down the car and, using the hand brake, whipped it around in a hundred-and-eighty-degree turn. The Ferrari clawed its way along the country road that led up to the gates at Castel Gandolfo. Handing the plainclothes security guard her passport, Anna explained that she had brought papers requested by Dr. Michael Turner. Given the hour, she expected to wait while security cleared her with Turner, but the guard returned her passport and waved her through immediately.

She found him in the small greenhouse at the end of the terrace adjacent to the Papal suite. As Turner got up from the chaise longue Anna noticed that his sweater and trousers were rumpled, as though he had slept in them. His movements were stiff, his face haggard, with a day's growth of beard. They regarded each other silently, then Turner came to her and pressed his lips against hers.

"You're cold," he murmured, swinging his arms about her.

She drew back her head. "Have you been out here all night?" she asked.

Turner nodded, looking down at her. "It looks like you haven't had any sleep either."

"No," she said.

Anna had called from West Berlin to tell him she would be arriving in a few hours. At first she thought the strain and disorientation in his voice was simply due to the late hour, but when he told her that he had been trying to reach her, she realized that something had gone wrong. Turner assured her that Innocent was all right, but that something else had happened, something he could not discuss over the phone. Anna had promised to get down to Castel Gandolfo as quickly as possible.

Her grip on his back tightened for an instant, then she broke away and came over to the white patio table where a coffeepot rested above a burning candle.

"He's sleeping now?"

Turner nodded. "Why?"

"The more he sleeps, the longer I can postpone what I have to do," Anna said.

"And what is that?"

She placed her cup back on the table.

"Rowitz is dead."

"What are you saying!" Turner exclaimed, his hand gripping hers.

"Just that," she said dully, not looking up at him. "He died trying to get across the Wall . . . in Berlin."

"But that's not possible!"

"Michael, it is. . . . I was there when they brought down the bodies."

Turner covered his face with his hands and slowly rubbed his forehead with his fingertips. "Berlin . . . what was he doing in Berlin?" He sat down heavily.

"I don't know. I've gone over it, over and over in my mind, and I can't find the answer."

"But why were *you* in Berlin?" he demanded.

"Our Bonn embassy received word that one of my people would be coming across," she told him. "Whoever supplied the information knew the time and the place where Rowitz would be crossing, except that no name was given. I didn't know who would be coming out until I got there."

"I don't understand," Turner said, getting to his feet, shaking his head. "I didn't know what to make of this when it came." He reached across the table and picked up a slim unstamped airmail envelope. "This came late last night by special courier. It's addressed to me, but I have no idea what it means. And it came from Geneva . . . I thought Rowitz must be there."

"Let me have it."

When he passed her the envelope, Anna turned it face up and saw the engraved letterhead of the law firm of Pallenberg et Fils.

"Do you recognize the name?" Turner asked her.

"Yes, of course," Anna said softly. "The Pallenbergs are lawyers, father and son. They've taken up the cases of a number of dissidents who have either left the Soviet Union or are still incarcerated. They're exceptional." She looked up. "I wasn't aware Rowitz had dealings with them."

"Read the letter," Turner advised.

Anna Letelier pulled out the single sheet, read it through quickly, then tossed it back onto the table.

"What the hell is going on?" She stood staring at Turner. "This"—she gestured at the letter—"this doesn't tell us how or why Rowitz wound up in East Germany, but it does show he considered the possibility of his never coming back. The papers he left for you in Geneva are to be picked up and read *only* by you if he did not return by a given date. *What papers, Michael?*"

"I don't know." Turner shook his head. "It's the first I've heard of it."

"Innocent . . . Innocent must have known."

Turner shook his head.

"Have you spoken with the Pallenbergs?" Anna asked. "Who knows what this could possibly be about?"

"I spoke with Louis Pallenberg at the end of the day." Turner put his hands in his pockets. "He confirmed sending the letter by courier, four days ago, as Rowitz had requested him to."

"And now Rowitz is gone. There was nothing on him—no papers, no microfilm, nothing at all. And if he already had some kind of information that he felt was important enough to entrust to the Pallenbergs, then what was he doing in East Berlin?"

"There is only one way for us to find out," Turner said. "One of the reasons I couldn't go back to sleep is that I'm going to be on the eight o'clock plane to Geneva."

"I'm going with you!"

He sat down beside her and once more took her hands in his own. "There's no point to that," he said. "I won't be gone that long. All I have to do is identify myself to Pallenberg and pick up the papers. One of us has to stay. That leaves you. You'll have to tell him sooner or later. Now would be as good a time as any . . . maybe the sooner the better. And I'll be back to do what I can."

She brought her face very close to his, and he could see the fear behind her eyes.

"Something has started, Michael," she whispered. "Someone wanted me in West Berlin, someone wanted me there to watch while Rowitz's body was brought over the Wall. They're sending us a message. Rowitz dies . . . and in the meantime someone sends you this." She ran her fingertips over the envelope. "Someone is playing a game with us, a vicious game, and this is just the opening move."

Anna rose to her feet. She ran her fingers through Turner's hair, then suddenly gripped it, raising his head.

"If you're going to be on time for that plane, then you

should change, and we'll be on our way. I don't want Stanislaw-ski to wake up and find neither of us with him."

Gorodin glanced impassively at the supine figure of Andrei Razminsky stretched out on the stainless-steel trolley in the morgue of the Lubyanka. Contemptuously he threw the gray rubber sheet back, uncovering the face, the mouth gaping open in the rictus of death.

Bibnikov and Gorodin were alone in the immense under-ground cavern, the white ceramic-tile dome gleaming from the reflection of powerful lights. The pathologists and technicians had been cleared out, with no reason given.

He is another Stalin, Bibnikov thought. He emerges in the middle of the night to gaze upon the victims that have been delivered to him like so many sacrifices. What does he read in their faces? Perhaps something the interrogators overlooked?

"Was he a good Jew, this one?" Gorodin asked.

"No. Not particularly religious."

"Interesting man." Gorodin suddenly gathered himself and turned away from the cadaver. "Thank you for accompanying me, Director Bibnikov."

"Not at all, Minister."

33

Innocent XIV awoke for the second time at noon.

He's dead, he thought. Dear Gregory, my friend.

The words seemed unreal to him, unintelligible. He could not reach out and touch the truth they expressed any more than an amputee can touch the severed limb, even though it continues to pain him.

Innocent forced himself to sit up, struggling against the mild paralysis of the sedative the male nurse had administered that morning, only a few minutes after Anna had told him. Slowly he swiveled his head from side to side, then rubbed the back of his neck. When he stood up, the blood rushed to his brain, and for an instant the vertigo threatened to topple him. But he regained his balance and went over to the mirror on the dresser. Somewhere behind him he could see the shaft of light coming through the gauzy lace curtains on the French doors and beyond them the morning sounds of the garden.

"He is dead."

The face that was repeating these words back to him was devoid of color. Since the operation he had eaten little. As a result his face was drawn, the cheekbones pronounced. Slowly he unbuttoned his pajama shirt and let it slip to the floor. On the left side of his chest was a fresh scar in the shape of a triangle. The crisscross stitches were angry red stings. Innocent raised his hand to the spot and gently moved his fingers over the scar.

The man of God, driven now by a machine . . . how much more can they do to me?

Innocent drew himself a shallow bath and, taking care not to wet the area over his heart, he sponged the rest of his body. He returned to his bedroom and from the closet took a fresh black cassock. By the time he stepped onto the terrace outside his bedroom, the last effects of the tranquilizer had dissipated. The morning wind felt fresh and cool. It carried the scent of a thousand flowers, and he could almost feel it sweeping away the stale, sour smell of sickness that still clung to him. He went carefully over to the stone balustrade and looked out over the fields of Castel Gandolfo.

He thought of Anna Letelier, remembered reaching out for her and cradling her face in his hands and pressing her to his shoulder and holding her. His grip had tightened as he felt a desperate need to pass some of his pain over to another human being. He had felt sick at heart that the man he loved above all others had not found it within himself to share the secret which had claimed his life.

She had explained to him as much as she knew of what had happened in Berlin, and of Michael Turner leaving for Switzerland.

Abruptly Innocent turned away and went to the chapel that was reserved for his private devotions. On his way he instructed his nurse that he was not to be disturbed. For two hours Innocent spoke with his God. In his prayers he retraced the lifetime he and Gregory had shared, he asked questions which he knew might never be answered and others which he understood it was pointless even to ask. Yet he had spoken them if only to hear the sound of his own voice and to expel them from his soul. Somewhere in the course of his communion, the bitter tears became resolve. He could not believe that Gregory's death had been necessary in order to goad him into action. Perhaps Gregory had paid because he, Innocent, had faltered.

"Holiness—"

He did not turn around, for he recognized the voice.

"I am going to do it," he said.

"What will you do, Holiness?"

"I am going to go to Berlin. I'm going to bring him home."

Anna shook her head. "It is too soon for you to travel. I know you feel you must do this, but, I beg of you, let someone else go in your place."

"I cannot permit that."

"But the arrangements that will have to be made," Anna protested. "The security—"

"I *am* my brother's keeper," Innocent said to her. "I will be traveling as a private citizen. There will be nothing of that sort to distract me."

"Would you at least consider waiting until we hear from Michael? The risk is too great."

He looked at her, and she felt him reaching for her, his eyes pleading with her to understand, yet at the same time telling her that any further argument was useless.

The Vicar of Christ rose and gently placed both hands upon the chancel rail.

"Whatever it was that took him from us, Anna, it is of no consequence now."

The Swissair flight touched down at Geneva at ten after ten. A Mercedes taxi brought Turner quickly across the city to the Quai Général Guisan. He presented himself at the desk set in the center of the cavernous nineteenth-century foyer, waited until the gendarme checked with Pallenberg's secretary, then stepped into the ancient cage elevator that bore him up to the third floor. A young woman greeted Turner, took his coat, and guided him through the reception area. She knocked softly on a paneled walnut door, and pushed it open to let him pass.

The setting was magnificent. Following the custom of the nineteenth century, the Pallenbergs had their desks placed one against the other, creating a huge square working space in the center of the room. Two walls had floor-to-ceiling bookcases. Along the third were windows that overlooked the Jardin Anglais and Lac Leman. Set on either side of the door were glass cabinets containing museum-quality porcelain and Meissen figurines. Turner judged there wasn't a piece in that room under a hundred years old.

"Dr. Turner?"

Louis Pallenberg, a short, spry gentleman with mutton-chop sideburns, rose from behind his desk and ushered his visitor over to a long, comfortable couch that was set beside the two lawyers' desks.

"Permit me to introduce my son, Alain," he said, nodding toward a tall young man who smiled faintly as he offered his hand to Turner.

"A pleasure to meet you," young Pallenberg said. "I hope you had a pleasant flight. Perhaps you would care for coffee. Or tea?"

"No. Nothing, thank you," Turner said, sitting back on the couch.

"In that case, we should proceed," the elder Pallenberg said. He went back to his desk and from one of the drawers withdrew a brown folder. He settled himself in his chair and drew out a pipe.

"This is the material that Father Gregory Rowitz left for you, monsieur," Pallenberg said. He handed it solemnly to Turner, who turned it over, his fingers running across the seals.

"Was there any indication as to why Father Gregory sent these to you?" Turner asked him.

"None whatsoever, monsieur," Alain Pallenberg said precisely.

"Can you tell me the first time Father Gregory sent you anything like this?" Turner asked.

"February twelfth of this year." The younger Pallenberg flipped open a buff-colored dossier. He looked at his father and received the signal to continue. "Additional material reached us in March and again in April."

"Is it all in here?" Turner tapped the folder.

"I assume so, monsieur, along with other papers that were forwarded to us five days ago."

"Can you tell me where this material originated?"

"The first three came from Amsterdam, by post."

Amsterdam. Father Gregory had never mentioned Amsterdam. Neither had Innocent. What was the connection?

"I take it the details don't mean anything to you, monsieur," Louis Pallenberg said.

"No," Turner said. "At least not right now."

"May I suggest, monsieur, that you examine these documents in our library." He gestured with the briar. "Have you a hotel?"

"No. I didn't think I'd be staying overnight."

Louis Pallenberg looked up at him. "After reading through all the material you may have questions with which we might be able to assist you. Sometimes these matters take a little longer than one anticipates. If you have no objections, we will reserve a room for you. I'm afraid that hotel space in Geneva is at a premium at the moment."

Turner considered the offer. "You're very kind," he said.

"In that case, I will have our secretary make the arrangements. Would the Hôtel de la Paix be satisfactory?"

"I'm sure it would. And again, thank you."

Alain Pallenberg escorted Turner through the conference room to the library and closed the door behind him. Like the office, the library was done in period furniture, dominated by an ebony table fourteen feet long. Turner sat at the head, brought out his cigarettes and lighter, moved the crystal ashtray within reach, and broke the seals on the leather pouch, flipping back the tongue. From inside he removed a sheaf of papers two inches thick. Whatever it was Father Rowitz had left, it would take some time to examine it all thoroughly. Turner leafed through a few of the sheets. They were handwritten, in English. Turner arranged the sheets according to the dates on the top right-hand corners. When they were in sequence, he lit his first cigarette and settled back to read. He was barely through the first paragraph when the universe exploded.

The first bomb detonated in the office next door, blowing off the door to the library; the force of the blast hurled Turner to the floor. Dazed, and bleeding from the splinters that had caught the side of his face, he crawled along the floor. He could hear the screams coming from the outer reception area. A woman. The receptionist or one of the secretaries. There were no sounds in the Pallenbergs' office except the crackle of flames. Turner was on his knees when the second explosion cut off the screams as cleanly as a knife. Turner staggered to his feet and stumbled over to the gaping door frame. Dust and smoke billowed all around him. The elder Pallenberg was at the far end of the room, only his torso visible. All that could be seen of his son were his legs, which protruded from beneath the wreckage of the twin desks. The flames had caught the curtains and were moving up the glass-enclosed bookshelf. The glass turned black, then shattered, the fire licking at the spines of the lawbooks on the shelves. The flames were fanned by the wind that swept through the shattered windows. In the outer office all Turner could see was flames. The smoke was beginning to choke him. He staggered back into the library, his mind reeling. What in Christ's name had happened? He stared stupidly at the flames that were approaching the door frame.

Before he realized what he was doing, he was on all fours, snatching up the papers that had been scattered across the floor. The heat grew more intense as the fire crept toward him. From somewhere in the distance he could hear shouting punctuated by the sound of alarm bells. From the quai below came the wail of a siren. He stuffed the papers back into the leather pouch, thrust the pouch into the waistband of his trousers, and made for the doorway. By now it was a solid sheet of flames. Turner made his way to the other side of the room and tried another door, which turned out to be a closet. Then another, which was locked. He stepped back and kicked it once, then again, his ankle cracking painfully. Finally he put his shoulder to the door and it gave way; he found himself on the landing of an interior staircase. Turner staggered out and, leaning against the wall, made his way to the floor below. The staircase was full of office workers hurrying down, the harsh cacophony of the fire alarm echoing up and down the shaft. He slipped in behind the last of them, trying to keep up, trying to ignore the pain in his shoulder. One of the secretaries glanced back at him, stifling a cry. Turner looked down at his jacket and realized for the first time that his chest was covered with blood. Somehow he got out the front door and through the crush of bodies in the alley that ran past the building. Pressing against the wall of the building, he ducked into a doorway to avoid being knocked down by a police sedan that was clearing a path for an ambulance, then staggered into the street and made for the Jardin Anglais.

He stopped running only when he could no longer hear the shouting, and the sirens were only faint echoes.

The troops withdrew from their positions on the rooftops and in the street, huddling against the chill in the canvas-covered trucks that took them back to their barracks. Only a water truck cleaning the street moved slowly down Belgrowstrasse. The armored units dispersed; the rattle of the clanking metal treads of tanks and half-tracks receded into the distance. The Wall, which had flared into activity for a few hours on the previous day, was dormant once again. Berliners, who had waited out yesterday's uncertainty, gave silent thanks. As long as the Wall slept, the city was secure.

He walked alone down the Friedrichstrasse, the sun at his back. His shadow stretched out ahead of him to touch the security booth at the American checkpoint. The army sergeant who was leaning against the movable arm of the striped barrier raised his eyes from his cup. Automatically the gun slung over his shoulder slid down into his hands. He stared at the approaching figure but couldn't make out his face in the sunlight. The cardboard coffee cup bounced off the pavement as the sergeant leveled his weapon.

"Halt."

"Please," Innocent said, "let me pass." From the sergeant's incredulous expression, he knew that the man had recognized him. He lifted the barrier. No sooner had Innocent cleared the Western Zone and stepped into no-man's-land than the East German sirens started winding out their eerie wail. But the Pontiff walked on, oblivious to the shouting behind him. He reached the double line, painted a luminous green, and watched as a squad of Vopos came running toward him. They slowed their pace when they realized he was only one man, alone, and their commanding officer came forward. He stopped a few feet away.

"*Mein Gott*—"

"This is where you killed them," Innocent said, his eyes fixed on the officer's. He looked up at the dirty-gray glass-and-metal building that housed the Ministry of Health. "That was how they tried to escape," he said, tracing a finger through the air. "You knew they were going to try, and you shot them."

"You must leave now," the officer said hoarsely. "We don't want any more trouble . . ."

Innocent's hand stretched across the green double line and came to rest on the officer's shoulder.

"Tell them that there will be no more killing. Do you understand? Tell your people and the Russians that there will be no more victims. We have had enough *victims*. There will not be any more killing, ever."

"Please go," the officer whispered, transfixed. "I will tell them but, please, *please* go, before any harm comes to you."

"No harm will come to me, or you, or to any other person." Innocent looked past him. "Tell them that I have come here because one man has been killed. Tell them to listen because I shall speak for millions."

The finger slipped away from the officer's shoulder. "*There shall be no more killing!*" he said loudly. Before the echo had died away, the Holy Father had turned and walked back to the Allied barricade, past the silent row of American soldiers, and back into the Friedrichstrasse, where Alois Keller, the bishop of Berlin, was waiting for him.

"The arrangements?" Innocent asked as he got into the back seat of a sedan with Italian diplomatic plates. The bishop followed, settling onto the seat beside him.

"They'll be waiting for you at Brandenburg Cathedral in one hour, Holiness," Bishop Keller said. The bishop kept his eyes on the road as they drove swiftly along the Kurfürstendamm, trying to keep up with the lead police car as it careered through the traffic, sirens screaming.

Sitting across the seat from the bishop of Berlin, Innocent felt his heart go out to the man. He had not informed the

bishop of his impending arrival until the Vatican jet had been
cleared into the air corridor leading to the city. At that point
the aircraft was only thirty minutes from touchdown. He had
instructed Keller to come out to the airport alone, and above
all, not to mention the impending arrival to anyone. Innocent
had been adamant on that point. That Keller had followed his
instructions explicitly was evident by the confusion at passport
control at Tegel Field. Finally Innocent walked through customs and embraced Alois Keller, then hurried away to the car
the bishop had brought.

The West German foreign minister in Bonn was receiving
word of the unexpected Papal arrival just as Innocent reached
the checkpoint.

On the way to the Wall, Innocent outlined to Bishop
Keller exactly what it was he wanted him to do. Again, Keller
asked no questions. He knew it was only a matter of minutes
before the West German authorities descended upon the
Friedrichstrasse with their security units. Because Innocent
would have to deal with them, Keller was left to make the
arrangements the Pontiff desired. The purpose of these arrangements remained a mystery to Keller, and he was at once concerned and frightened for his Pope, who had appeared out of
nowhere, who had dared to walk toward the territory of those
who had once tried to destroy him, who had uttered a clear challenge to them, and who was now racing to complete a mission
whose intricacies were known only to him.

"Are you certain, Holiness, that you do not wish to proceed
straight to the cathedral?" Bishop Keller asked. His eyes slipped
from the road to the rearview mirror and the black Mercedes
that was trailing them a hundred feet back.

"He was a lifelong friend," Innocent said. "He once gave
me back my life. I think you can understand my feelings—when
someone very dear has been ripped out of one's heart."

Keller fell silent. The shooting at the Wall had grieved
him, and he had instructed his secretary to find out whether
there had been any Catholics among the victims. If so, he would
say mass for them at the Brandenburg Cathedral. That service
had become a tradition in his parish during his twenty-one-

year reign as bishop. During that period he had presided over the funerals of one hundred escapees. He had seen to it that the Church looked after and comforted the survivors. But neither he nor the people of Berlin had any idea that this time one of the slain had lived in the heart of the Pope.

Bishop Keller's driver urged the car through the Potsdamerplatz toward the gray concrete monolith that was the headquarters of the West Berlin police. The surveillance escorts must have radioed ahead, because even before the limousine came to a full stop, three exceptionally tall plainclothesmen were at the doors, forming a shield for Innocent as he stepped out.

The phalanx swept up the stairs and through the heavy bulletproof doors. In the antechamber Innocent was met by a uniformed official whom Keller recognized as the chief of police. But the phalanx did not lose its momentum as it veered down the corridor to a waiting service elevator that could accommodate them all. When the doors opened, Innocent looked out at concrete-block walls, painted lime-green. At the end of the corridor were swinging doors, with heavy rubber pads at the center for the gurneys on which the corpses were wheeled into the pathology lab at the end of the corridor. One by one, Innocent's escorts dropped away, stationing themselves along the wall. The Pontiff paused for a moment at the doors, then pushed them open.

The room was empty except for a single body lying on one of the stainless-steel tables. The overhead spotlight left the rest of the lab in darkness. Slowly he walked over to the dissection table. There was still a trace of blood in the funnels that curved down and away from the shallow channels in the tabletop. Innocent reached out, his fingers curling around the blue sheet to pull it down.

"Oh, dear God."

Father Gregory Rowitz had taken four explosive bullets in the chest.

Innocent pulled the sheet over the gaping wound and tenderly touched the face.

"I loved you as I did no other man," he whispered. "What

we shared went beyond anything the word friendship means. Now you are with our Lord, but I must continue. Where did you go, Gregory? Why? What did you have to do that you could not tell me? I have need of you, my friend, but you will no longer walk by my side. I need to hear your voice, to listen to your wise words, to draw strength from the faith that filled you. May God forgive me, but I do not understand why He has taken you from me in this hour, why it is that I must stand alone before my enemies. I do not understand, Gregory, but I will do what I have set out to do. For the sake of your memory. Because in your death I see the deaths of millions of others. In your sacrifice I see the redemption of all those who have suffered. In some way I cannot comprehend, your death has released me to do what I must. It has led me to understand that I can do no other."

The doors behind him swung open. Innocent turned to Bishop Keller. "Would you see to the transport, please? I will not leave Berlin without him."

Innocent made the sign of the cross over his friend, then abruptly walked from the room. Keller saw no tears. But beneath the exquisite agony of these last words he sensed a terrible resolution.

34

Turner's face was smudged with gray from the masonry powder and black from the smoke, his left cheek streaked with blood from a host of minor cuts. His jacket, which had absorbed most of the blood, was beyond salvaging. He couldn't hope to wear it in the street. His shirt had somehow survived. Turner washed up as best he could, taking care to remove the splinters from his face, ignoring the persistent knocking on the door of the public toilet in the Jardin Anglais. By the time he was finished, most of the blood was gone. Quickly he removed everything from his jacket pockets, and ripped out the tailor's label on the inside pocket and flushed it down the toilet. He stuffed the jacket into the waste bin, forcing it down under the crumpled paper towels. Taking a last look at himself, he thought he could at least show himself on the streets without attracting attention. The weather was warm enough that a man without a jacket would not be considered an unusual sight, even in Geneva.

Turner opened the door and, with his head bowed, brushed past the man who had been impatiently waiting to use the facilities. He heard the man calling after him, yelling something about the smell of smoke. Turner didn't bother to look back, but started out quickly across the park, walking diagonally toward what he hoped would be the Quai Gustave Ador. From there he could get a taxi to the Hôtel de la Paix. For an instant the thought of going to another hotel crossed his mind.

He remembered what the man had shouted after him. He stank of smoke. He could not register anywhere without arousing suspicion. Certainly he could not get out to the airport and, dressed as he was, try to make it through Swiss passport control. He had only one choice and that was to go to the Hôtel de la Paix. Once there, he might have a chance to go through the papers Father Rowitz had left for him. If the police got to him sooner than he thought, his Vatican passport and quasi-diplomatic status would afford him at least some protection. But he needed time.

Turner flagged down a taxi on Rue Fatio. The driver looked him over but said nothing after Turner gave him the hotel's name and dropped fifty francs on the seat beside him. The driver told him there was a fire on Quai Général Guisan and that he would take the Rue du Rhône. Turner muttered something in broken French and rolled down the window. He gulped in the fresh air as the taxi moved across the river to the Quai des Berges, then along the Quai du Mont-Blanc to the Hôtel de la Paix. The doorman wrinkled his nose at him, but Turner brushed past, heading into the magnificent foyer toward the reception desk.

The desk clerk, a sallow-faced man of indeterminate age, blinked behind his rimless spectacles and checked Turner's reservation. Everything was in order. He rang for the porter to escort monsieur to his room.

The suite overlooked the quai and the Rade de Genève. Turner gave the porter his clothes to be cleaned and double-locked the door after him, ran a bath, and soaked for twenty minutes, letting the steaming water work into his muscles. He closed his eyes but all he could see was the bodies of the Pallenbergs, men dying violently. He looked past the open bathroom door to where he had left the leather pouch. Abruptly he got out of the bath, dried himself, then padded naked into the bedroom, snatching up the pouch as he went. He removed the papers, smoothing them out on the desk and arranging them as he had done in the Pallenbergs' conference room.

Turner forced his eyes to focus on the pages spread on the desk. For the next two hours the only sound in the bedroom suite was the rustling of paper and the distinctive snap of his cigarette lighter.

The last of the lunchtime crowds began leaving the park between the hotel and the waterfront. Secretaries, clerks, and even a few businessmen who had taken time out to meet their families, carefully bundled up their paper bags and, on their way out to the Boulevard Augustin, carefully dropped them into the wastebaskets. Out on the lake a stiff breeze billowed red, orange, green, and white sails as those more fortunate took to the open water, threading their sailboats through the inner harbor and into Lac Leman. Standing just behind the open balcony doors of his suite, Turner marveled at the tranquillity of it all. It was as though he was looking through a window onto a whole new universe, to which he had forfeited all hope of ever returning. As the breeze came in across the lake, he felt moisture on his cheeks. Only then did he realize that he had been crying.

Turner moved away from the window and went into the bathroom to splash some water on his face. When he returned, he dressed quickly, feeling the bite of the starched cotton of the fresh shirt. Carefully he gathered up the papers on the desk and stuffed them back into the portfolio. He knew exactly what he had to do. It was out of the question for him to remain at the hotel any longer. He could not afford to take the chance that the authorities might come to learn that he had been in the Pallenbergs' office at the time of the explosion.

Turner left his room and made for the staircase. He came out at the rear of the hotel, by the newsstand, then slipped out through the revolving doors into the narrow Rue de Rennes. He walked north for two blocks, then hailed a taxi, instructing the driver to take him to Geneva Airport. It wasn't a long ride.

The overseas call booths were located at the south end of the terminal, across from the security checkpoints on the departures level. Beside them was a counter at which the operators took the details of the particular calls. Turner gave his name and the number in Rome to a male supervisor and was told that the call would be put through as quickly as possible. Fifteen minutes later Turner heard his name over the loudspeaker system, a neutral voice instructing him to go to call booth ten.

"Michael . . . ?" Anna's voice rang in his ear, resonated as if it were an echo shouted from a mountain peak. "Where are you now?"

"At Geneva Airport. I'm heading out." He hung up.

Turner still did not know where Father Rowitz had disappeared to five days earlier. Perhaps he would never know now. But he knew the identity of the man who had contrived his disappearance, and although he had never met him, had never even set eyes upon him, Turner thought he knew him very well.

The concourse was filling up with businessmen hurrying to the gates of the short-haul flights that would take them back to London, Paris, Frankfurt, and Rome for the end of the business day. Turner stepped into that anonymous tide and made his way to the Air France counter. He asked the reservations agent to book him onto the first available flight to Amsterdam.

"Will that be a return, monsieur?" the ticket agent asked as her fingers flew over the computer keyboard.

Just as Turner was about to say "One-way," he realized that immigration officials were always suspicious of one-way ticket holders unless they happened to be returning to their own countries.

"Return."

"Your name, please."

Turner pushed over his passport and reached inside his pocket for a roll of Swiss francs. He was counting out the fare when the agent looked up at him.

"But you have already reserved your seat, sir," she said, flashing Turner her dazzling, pasted-on smile.

"That's impossible," Turner said immediately. "This is the first—"

They had known he would be at Pallenbergs'. They had known he would be staying at the Hôtel de la Paix, that he would be traveling to Amsterdam.

"Monsieur! Are you all right?"

"Yes," Turner said. "There must have been a mistake . . . I didn't think my friend would make the reservation." He paused. "When was the reservation made?" he asked suddenly.

"I will check . . . At eleven fifteen this morning. Do you wish to confirm, Dr. Turner?"

"Yes . . . Yes, confirm it. I'll be on that flight," he said.

Turner shoved his ticket into the breast pocket of his blazer and made for the escalator in the center of the concourse. He showed his reservation stub to a steward, who then pressed a button which opened the door. Decorated in copper tones, with an aquamarine carpet, the lounge looked just like an aquarium. Turner took one of the small tables by the windows and stared out at an Air France Caravelle that was being guided toward the mobile ramp.

How would they have known he was going to Amsterdam? He hadn't mentioned it to anyone. What in Christ's name was he supposed to do then? He had no weapons. He would not even recognize his enemies. They were faceless. What chance in hell did he have?

"Monsieur Turner?"

The man was wearing a light-blue Air France blazer, and in his right hand he held a small photograph, which he glanced at after looking at Turner.

"I'm Turner."

"Yes, monsieur. Would you be so kind as to come with me. There is an urgent message waiting for you at our courtesy desk."

Turner grabbed him by the arm. "The photograph," he said. "Who gave you that photograph?"

"It came with the message, monsieur," the agent said, pulling his arm away.

"Who brought the message?"

"I do not know, monsieur. The gentleman did not leave a name. He only said it was very important that you receive this message."

"Then why didn't you simply write it down and bring it to me?" Turner demanded.

"It is a telephone message," the agent said sharply. "Please, monsieur, if you think there is anything wrong, I will call airport security."

"No, no need for that," Turner said, realizing he had pushed the man too far.

The reservations agent walked him over to the desk, murmured a few words to the girl, who then handed Turner a small white envelope.

"You may avail yourself of the telephones there, monsieur," the man said. "If the call is long distance or international, the operator will see to the charges." He paused. "One thing, monsieur; if you are in need of assistance, you have only to ask."

"Thank you," Turner said. "And I'm sorry about being so rude. A family matter . . ."

"It is nothing, monsieur."

Turner went over to the comfortable lounge chair and ripped open the envelope. There were six digits written on a slip of paper—a local call.

Who were they?

He set the paper before him and started to dial. The connection was made, a phone was ringing on the other end. When the receiver was lifted, Turner heard nothing.

"Hello?"

"Turner?" The voice was male, thick and nasal, an ugly voice.

"This is Dr. Turner."

"Call home."

"What?"

"Call home."

"I don't understand—"

The connection was broken and the whir of the dial tone sounded in his ear.

Call home.

Where was home? Not New York. Rome? His home? The Vatican? Where was home?

He looked around. The lounge was about half-full. A steward was passing around a tray of champagne. There was a small buffet set up along the far wall; the odor of fresh, hot

canapés wafted through the air. A middle-aged woman noticed
him staring at her, crossed her legs and smiled back . . . Usual
thing, ordinary people. . . . It made no sense. Nothing was
ordinary anymore.

Call home.

Turner reached for the telephone and dialed the long-
distance operator and put a call through to the Apostolic Palace. While he waited for the connection Turner went to the bar
and asked for a coffee laced with brandy. He was on his second
cigarette when a hostess called his name.

The only answer he received from his apartment was that
of his answering service. There were no messages.

Call home.

What the hell did they mean? Not New York. He had left
nothing there. His son was in London, living with his in-laws
. . . *Call home.*

Turner's fingers were trembling as he dialed for the operator and asked her to put him through to a number in May-
fair. It can't be, he kept thinking to himself. They wouldn't
have gone after Christopher. Another ten minutes passed before
the cross-Channel connection was made. He heard the sharp
dual rings, praying that Sidney Harrington would answer.

"Hello?"

"Sidney? Sidney, it's Michael."

"Ah, Michael. We've been expecting to hear from you,"
Harrington said.

There was a pause. Michael Turner heard another voice in
the background, then his father-in-law came back on.

"Michael, the situation here is somewhat unusual. There's
someone here who wishes to speak with you."

Before Turner had a chance to reply, a soft, faintly accented voice was speaking to him.

"Dr. Turner, please listen very carefully. There are two
of us here. We will stay with the Harringtons and your son
until you have done what it is you wish to do in Amsterdam and
have passed that information on to one of our people. The
transaction will take place exactly twenty-four hours from now.
You will be followed wherever you go. Please do not even con-

template running from us. After all, we have your son, and your
wife's parents. Unless you comply with our request, we will start
killing them, one by one. If you remember New York, Dr.
Turner, you understand we are men of our word."

"Who are you?" Turner said harshly. "What do you want?"

"You know very well what we want, Dr. Turner," the
voice said smoothly. "You have twenty-four hours."

Sidney Harrington came back on the line.

"Michael, I'm afraid what they said about having us as
hostages is quite true. I don't understand what's happening,
what this is all about, but you must believe that these are very
serious, very professional men. For Christopher's sake you had
better—"

The connection was broken.

"Hello?" Turner said. "Hello . . . Sidney!"

But he heard only the operator's voice giving him the
charges for the call.

35

Brandenburg Cathedral was the vision of one man, Axel Rudolf Springer, who virtually controlled the West German communications industry. Springer had inherited his father's anti-Communist zeal as well as a profound Catholic faith. For years Springer searched for an appropriate site on which to erect a cathedral. Architects from all over the world submitted proposals. No idea was too fanciful. The subject of cost was never mentioned. In the end it was the Italian architect Pier Luigi Nervi who presented a scheme that met with Springer's complete approval. Nervi's Atlantean design called for a massive cathedral to be built within yards of the Berlin Wall, on a barren stretch of land no developer had dared to touch. The cathedral—which Nervi envisioned basically as an enormous stack of floating prisms—would rise seven stories into the sky; the effect on the observer would be that of beholding some majestic craft about to lift off heavenward toward its God. This image fascinated Springer. With the approval of Clement himself, the project was accorded the blessing of the Church. Two years passed from the day the site was consecrated to the day the first mass was sung by Bishop Keller.

There were two respects in which, at Springer's request, Nervi's original conception had been modified. The first was a massive balcony which overlooked East Berlin, the second was an interior design that allowed the actual sound of the mass to float high and free into the air over the city if the doors to the balconies were left open.

Bishop Alois Keller slipped out from behind the wheel of his car and looked up at the headquarters of his diocese for the past ten years. He could not reconcile the feelings of dread and joy that clashed within him. The soaring architecture of the cathedral reminded him of a gigantic springboard, waiting to launch something majestic into the skies over the city . . . over the entire land. Bishop Keller gathered his thoughts and hurried up the steps of the cathedral. There was little enough time to accomplish the tasks Innocent had requested.

In the presence of the director of the criminal police, the senior pathologist, and a representative of the West German Foreign Ministry, he formally identified the body of Father Gregory Rowitz. After he had affixed his signature to the appropriate documents he asked that the body be removed at once to the aircraft that was waiting at Tegel Field.

"Are we to presume, Holiness, that you will be accompanying the body to Rome right away?" the Foreign Ministry official asked quickly. He was present only because it had been his dubious good fortune to be in Berlin at the time Innocent had arrived. His superiors in Bonn had made it clear that he first determine exactly why Innocent had come to the divided city and second, if at all possible, spirit him out of Berlin as quickly as propriety permitted. If Innocent was planning to stay on in Berlin, then Bonn wanted to know why.

"No, you may not presume that," Innocent told them. "I realize that my unexpected arrival has been a cause for some concern. For that I beg you to accept my apologies. But Father Rowitz is only part of the reason I am here. I had hoped that the other gentleman I was to meet would have already arrived but—"

At that moment the office door opened and a tall figure swept past two protesting policemen. On catching sight of Innocent XIV, Axel Springer stopped short. He was a large, raw-boned man with an enormous chest set on short, almost bandy legs. His flaxen hair was perpetually askew, and he was perspiring freely, as though he had just run a great distance. This dishevelment was his trademark. It was rumored that Springer could not bear to sit for more than a few minutes, that he slept only two or three hours a night, and conducted most of his business either pacing in his office or dictating minutes to his secretary in his car, private aircraft, or on his yacht. Like the shark's, Axel Springer's metabolism insisted on perpetual motion. It was his intense, restless energy that now had the three officials completely flustered. But Springer took no notice of them; he almost ran up to Innocent and dropped to his knees before the Holy Father. Innocent accepted his obeisance and bid him to rise.

"Thank you for coming on such short notice," he said.

Having set his lips to the Ring of the Fisherman, Springer rose unsteadily to his feet.

"I am ready to perform any service you may require, Holiness," he said, his voice surprisingly soft and calm.

"Before we proceed any further, I would like to speak to you in private," Innocent said.

"Of course, Holiness." Springer's eyes darted to the other three men, sending them an unmistakable message. "I trust that the criminal director will allow us the convenience of his office."

The criminal-police director looked to the mayor, who looked at the representative from Bonn, who, after a second's hesitation, nodded. As soon as they had departed, Innocent gestured for Springer to sit and for the next twenty minutes spoke without pause. For his part Springer waited patiently until the Pontiff had finished. Then without wasting a moment he reached for the telephone and began making calls. Within a half-hour West Berlin's three major radio stations were in the process of carrying out Springer's instructions. In Frankfurt, Munich, Düsseldorf, and Bonn, television stations were preparing to receive transmission feeds from Springer's West Berlin headquarters. All the major dailies throughout the country had been alerted to an impending story. All wire services had been notified. Even the U.S. Armed Forces radio network had been contacted.

When Springer concluded his business over the telephone,

he excused himself and left the office. To the three officials who were waiting for him in the antechamber he calmly explained that Innocent XIV was now his private guest. As such Springer was obliged to extend him every possible courtesy. This included the use of his personal facilities, transportation from Springer's own fleet of cars, and a special security detail which would guard the Pontiff as long as he was in West Berlin. Springer finished by suggesting that if any of the three officials had any questions they should feel free to contact their superiors in Bonn. The implication was quite clear: Axel Springer was prepared to defend his actions and that of the Pontiff before anyone, including the West German cabinet and the chancellor, if it came to that.

Springer and Innocent XIV walked out of the West Berlin police headquarters side by side. Within seconds a contingent of private security guards had them safely ensconced in the magnate's Mercedes, hidden from sight by stained Lexan windows. With the help of outriders cleaving a path through the traffic of news vehicles, camera vans, and curious pedestrians, the Mercedes pulled out onto Rudolf Platz.

"Word of your arrival has already spread throughout the city," Springer said. "There will be crowds—"

"Let in as many as the cathedral can accommodate," Innocent said. "I wish the people to see me, not just to hear me."

"I will need between ninety minutes and two hours to have everything in readiness."

Innocent nodded. "That is soon enough. Until then I will remain in the sanctuary of the cathedral. No one will disturb my privacy there."

At the Brandenburg Cathedral Innocent XIV remained sequestered in the bishop's office. Refusing Archbishop Keller's offer to bring him food, he asked only for a pot of tea, and retired to the private chapel adjacent to the sacristy. There he remained for a full hour in silent prayer. This was the time Innocent had known he would dread most. As the minutes passed, he felt more and more the enormity of the decision he had made, the unforgiving and unrelenting burden of the actions he was about to undertake. At that instant a terrible aloneness seized Innocent and he experienced a bitter solitude.

Bishop Alois Keller intruded upon Innocent only to bring him a sheaf of messages, most from Rome. He watched as Innocent shifted through them, oblivious to their tone of guarded concern and foreboding as to what was happening in Berlin. What the Bonn government wanted to know was of little interest to him and the expressions of dismay and the explanations demanded by the senior members of his Curia left him unmoved.

Innocent glanced at his watch and rose to his feet. He left Keller's office, walked down the stone-lined corridor toward the door that opened onto the nave of the cathedral. The bishop of Berlin and the other priests in attendance fell silent when the Pontiff appeared in the sacristy.

"How soon?" Innocent asked Keller.

"No more than a few minutes, Holiness," the bishop answered. "Your vestments have been prepared for you."

Silently Innocent walked the length of the cathedral, looking up at the galleries on either side and the choir loft, where cameramen and technicians had interrupted their frenzied preparations to watch him. He looked at them and said:

"Whatever you hear, whatever you see, do not stop recording and transmitting."

Then Innocent climbed the spiral staircase in the left-hand corner of the nave and pushed open the door that led to the balcony, which ran the length of the Brandenburg Cathedral, the balcony that looked over East Berlin. He gripped the balustrade with his right hand and looked out over the ruin that was the Wall, into the heart of the divided city to the east. He stood there with the sun warming his face and the wind stinging his eyes. The sight he witnessed suddenly made his soul soar. As always, the Zone was empty, but farther to the east the streets, which were generally empty at this hour, were filled with people facing west. Beyond the original Brandenburg Gate, along the Karl Marx Allee, many thousands had gathered, many children among them. Seeing the Pope, the crowd surged and a cry went up. Children blossomed above the heads of the crowd as they were held aloft to see the Vicar of Christ.

He turned and walked the length of the balustrade, his arms held out in benediction. As he strode around the corner onto the smaller balcony overlooking the façade of the cathedral, he saw the Lindenstrasse jammed with humanity. A thunderous roar went up from the crowd. To the chant of the multitudes the Pontiff raised his crucifix and blessed them.

It seemed to be the greatest mass in living memory. A simple memorial to the dead was transformed into a moving, passionate aria, performed by one man. Within the cathedral the voice of the choir soared as never before. Outside, in the brilliant light, a silence fell over the tens of thousands who were listening to the loudspeakers, overwhelmed by the ethereal beauty of the ceremony.

Carried across the continent, across the world by satellite relays, Innocent's voice was heard by hundreds of millions. High atop the Brandenburg Tower, Springer's laser control disc beamed transmissions across Eastern Europe, battling the electronic screens that struggled to keep them out. When the requiem was over and the last words of prayer had died away, Innocent XIV took up his place before the altar and looked out over the sea of faces.

"The mass for the dead is over. I have prayed for the man I came here to escort back to Rome, a man whom I loved and whom I shall bury. I have prayed for the souls of the other unfortunates who were murdered because they believed in freedom and dared to reach out for it. I have prayed for all of you who live beyond this wretched Wall, for the people of my native land, for all who live in the great cities and plains of the East. I am one of you.

"But more than that, I have come to warn you of the great danger that faces us all. Conceived by ambitious men in Moscow, this danger has hitherto remained silent and unseen. But the moment is fast approaching when it shall creep into the light, and into your lives to warp and to destroy them. It will turn you against your neighbors, pander to your fears and uncertainties, goad you into thinking that, if you do not embrace it, it will in the end consume you.

"So I beg of you, listen to those words spoken by Dmitri Gorodin, Foreign Minister of the USSR, and Viktor Suslev, Chairman of the Committee for State Security. Listen to them and behold the vision of the future they have prepared for you."

Innocent descended from the altar and walked down the center aisle of the cathedral toward the technician waiting for him. From the folds in his vestments he removed a cassette and slipped it into the machine. The technician quickly checked the simultaneous-translation units which would convert the Russian dialogue into German, English, and French, and pressed the switch that began the tape.

For the duration of the recording Innocent stood with his head bowed while the thousands listened in rapt silence. When the tape had spun itself out, he retrieved it and walked back to the altar. The tension was almost unbearable.

"You have heard their words," Innocent's voice rang out. "I shall not permit such a thing to come to pass. I shall not permit history to repeat its ritualized butchery. May these few debase and destroy millions? I say unto the architects of this treachery, *no*. You shall not have your victims! As of this moment the Church stands prepared to receive each and every Jew who wishes to leave Russia, Poland, Hungary . . . wherever. This shall be the second Exodus, whereby a long-suffering people may walk out of the wilderness, leave of their own accord, and find the refuge vouchsafed them by their God. The second Exodus shall triumph. I say to those who would remain slavemasters, you have two days. You have two days to set your captives free. If, at the end of the second day, the first Jew does not step upon free soil, I shall, before all of God's laws, be compelled to intervene with the full might of the Church militant.

"I have come here, not only to pray with you but also to ask for your help. I tell you and all the millions who are listening and watching across the world that the horror is about to repeat itself. Even as I stand here, there are men in the Kremlin, in Moscow, who are preparing the destruction of the Jewish people in Russia, in all of Eastern Europe. They are cynical men, hard and brutal, who believe the world no longer cares for the plight of anyone, that it has forgotten how a people can be destroyed in full view of their brothers. I say to these men they are wrong!

"I demand—yes, *demand*—on behalf of the Holy Catholic Church, on behalf of *all* peoples, that Jews who wish to leave Eastern Europe and Russia be permitted to do so at once, without conditions, without reservations. I call for this second Exodus, by which an oppressed people might find the peace and tranquillity that is their right. The Exodus will have the full material and spiritual backing of the Church. If those in the Kremlin think that my words carry no weight, then I tell them that I will travel across the world seeking support from both religious and secular organizations. I will charge Catholics throughout the world to unite behind their Church. The hands of the faithful will do no work for the Kremlin! Commerce will come to a standstill until that which is God's—the freedom of His people—has been restored to Him!

"And you, if you ask me why I should place your Church in peril of your oppressors, risking their terrible revenge, I can only repeat those words which a fallen man whispered over forty years ago: 'When they came for the Jews, I said nothing; when they came for the Catholics and Protestants, I said nothing, and when they came for me, there was no one, no one left to speak for me. . . .'

"As of tomorrow, I am ordering a ban on all trade the Vatican carries on with the Soviet Union. It is insignificant, I know, but that will do for a start. I will then ask the Catholics of Italy, the Catholics of Europe, and of the world to join this boycott. No Russian goods are to be bought, no Russian ships loaded with grain, no Russian credits honored or contracts discharged. Not until the Soviet Union has publicly announced that it is willing to allow its Jews to emigrate as they wish.

"Funds will be disbursed to any persons who can help us—

broadcasting stations, the transfer facilities in Austria, the refugee camps in Western Europe. Special flights will be made available as soon as the emigration begins. *There!*" he shouted, pointing, "the time has come for us to clear the way. *Tear down the Wall!*"

36

The President was working on his fifth cup of coffee. Along the far wall of the briefing room adjoining the Oval Office a row of chafing dishes sent up a tantalizing aroma of coffee and breakfast dishes. For the last forty minutes no one had moved from the dining table yet breakfast had only been nibbled at. The conversation was being fueled by nicotine, caffeine, and adrenaline.

Jonathan Telford tapped his spoon against his cup.

"If we could just hold everything for a moment." He waited as the various arguments receded. "Thank you. There is no use in indulging in idle speculation. Let's start with what we know—or rather what we don't." He turned to the director of the CIA. "Toby, did you have any idea that the Pope was going to uncork something like this?"

"None, Mr. President," Toby Johnson said emphatically. "Every indicator we've had suggested that Innocent was trying to work out a compromise between the factions of the Church. I can show you details of meetings he's held with Cardinal Da Falla, his chief opposition, as well as Picheli, the leader of the conservatives. I even have a copy of the initial draft he made of a brief to be presented to the senior Curia, a kind of internal working paper on the direction of the Church. There is nothing in there—or anywhere else—to indicate he was about to confront the Kremlin."

"Laine."

"I'm afraid I have nothing to add to the director's analysis, Mr. President," the Secretary of State said. "Our embassy in Rome has been monitoring Innocent carefully since the election. There's been nothing amiss."

"We have a tape of Innocent's address," Telford said, looking at Johnson. "Is it possible to confirm electronically that Gorodin and Suslev are the men we hear speaking?"

The CIA director shook his head. "We might get an approximation of a voice print, Mr. President, but nothing more than that. Innocent had a recording that was already one stage removed from the original tape. And we would be working off a tape transmitted under good but far from ideal conditions. I wouldn't be able to tell you conclusively one way or the other whether that was actually Gorodin's voice—or Suslev's for that matter. The state of the art just isn't sufficient."

"Gut reactions?" the President said, looking around the table. "Was that Minister Gorodin and Suslev?"

"I say yes," Laine Compton volunteered.

"I would say yes, too," Toby Johnson added.

The Secretary of Defense and the Chairman of the Joint Chiefs also nodded their assent.

"If you think that, then you're telling me that the pogrom is also real—at least a plan formulated by them." There was a moment's silence. The President looked around him. "Well, doesn't that follow?"

"It does, Mr. President," Compton said.

"But?"

"But it's too damn much to swallow. I mean, if you believe Innocent, you have to believe that Gorodin and Suslev are planning an extermination that would make Hitler's camps look amateurish by comparison."

"And that is what you can't grasp, the enormity of that possibility?"

"I'm saying that even as big a gambler as Gorodin wouldn't dare something like that. What for? He has the Politburo in his pocket."

"Are we certain of that?" Telford interrupted. "Is he *really* in control? Are we selling Kobalevsky short?"

Toby Johnson knew the question was directed at him, so he released a puff of smoke to veil himself in.

"It seems that we've been caught with our collective pants down," the President said, his voice honing a cutting edge to the words. "Is there anything else coming down the pike I should know about?"

Laine Compton leaned forward. "I think the first order of business would be to reach Innocent and for you, Mr. President, to ask him where that tape was obtained."

"That's a very sound suggestion. And what if he asks me whether or not I support him? What am I to say to him then?"

"Considering the gravity of his statement, Mr. President, I would say you're well within your rights to ask for extrapolation," the Secretary of State replied. "I suggest that we find ourselves in a situation not of our making. Somehow it never fails to happen. Some minor power, in this case a religious force, makes a move which puts us at loggerheads with the Russians. It happened in Iran, Lebanon, Africa, the Far East. Each time the Chief Executive reacted quickly. Each time we walked away either beaten or disgraced."

"I do not intend to have this happen," the President interjected. "Let me also point out that there are sixty million Catholics in North America. It would be political suicide for me to talk to the Pope unless I'm willing to back him up. It's a case of being against him if you're not for him. Moreover, the whole issue of separation of church and state comes into play here. So until I have hard, and I mean very hard, information, nothing will be said or done by any member of this Administration. The press secretary will issue a statement to the effect that Innocent's accusation is being studied. Period."

Telford helped himself to another of Compton's cigarettes.

"As for priorities, it is important for us to know whether the tape is genuine. But it is much more imperative that we learn exactly what Innocent intends to do two days from now. He has issued the Russians an ultimatum. I do not believe Gorodin will move directly against Innocent. He will ride it out, probably counting on the fact that Innocent's own Curia might stop him. But I can't and won't count on that happening. Laine, Toby, you have to find out what it is Innocent's planning. I am not particularly concerned how you do this as long as there is no fallout. If you can't get it through diplomatic channels, then use contacts. If the contacts prove dry, turn the screws, if we have any left to turn. Apply some pressure. But let me caution you on one point—Innocent has made a lot of enemies within the Church, even before this afternoon. I have the odd feeling you'll be offered a hell of a lot of dirt. Let's make sure the bullshit screens are in place."

"Mr. President, there's one matter we haven't touched on," Compton said. She looked around the table. "That of Michael Turner."

"How do you mean?"

"We know Michael Turner is the Pope's personal physician. We also know that three days ago Turner, through Weizmann in New York, got hold of three cardiac specialists plus some extremely sophisticated equipment in Basel. Even though the surgery on Innocent was successful, we could well be dealing with a sick man. I don't mean to suggest that Innocent is suffering from diminished capacity, but that there may be reason to believe he has been under severe stress."

"I doubt very much Turner will talk to us," Telford rejoined.

"Granted." Laine Compton nodded. "And although there's really nothing we can do to force him to talk to us, who knows? We may get lucky. It could be that Turner is as horrified by what Innocent said as the rest of us are."

"See if you can raise him," Telford said. "But kid gloves only."

The Prime Minister of Israel, Teddy Samulovitch, was the first Sabra ever to hold that office. Of medium height, thin as a rail, appearing perpetually undernourished, he brought a frenetic energy to an office which consumed men all too quickly. Samulovitch ran a hand through his mass of curly brown hair and set his hand on his hips.

"Look at them out there," he said, staring out across the compound that surrounded his house, past the cyclone fence to where an estimated two thousand demonstrators had gathered an hour earlier. More were arriving from the city by the minute. They were holding placards demanding that Israel act to prevent another holocaust and some held aloft banners of Innocent XIV.

"I take it this is happening all around the country," Samulovitch said, turning away and sitting down behind his desk.

"You might." The speaker, whose blue eyes and fair hair had been inherited from his American father, seemed to be daydreaming as he sat in the cane chair in the far corner of the room. He was known only as Morris. "I've been told it's somewhat worse in Haifa and Tel Aviv. As for the *kibbutzim*, well that's another story in itself."

"So what do you have for me?" Samulovitch asked him.

"I think," Morris said delicately, "that in a few hours our religious leaders will demand you acknowledge the Pope's address. The opposition will accuse you of secret deals with the Vatican."

"There were no secret deals!"

"I believe you. They won't. Holocaust has a particular ring for the Jewish ear. Auschwitz has become its own metaphor. Once these words have been uttered, in a living context, as concrete possibilities, they will not be put to rest with anything other than the truth."

"And what is the truth?"

"I don't know."

"In short, the entire country is waiting for me to do something as though it were I who proclaimed this Exodus to the Promised Land."

"Correct. If you do nothing you lose. Some will say that all of Israel has been humiliated since it is, after all, a non-Jew who has proclaimed the dream that lives in the heart of every Jew."

"How dare he do such a thing? What in God's name did he think he was doing?"

Morris regarded him sadly. "Don't talk like that, Teddy,"

he said in reproof. "That's exactly what Caiaphas said two thousand years ago, and the world has never forgiven us since."

"What have you been doing all this time?" Samulovitch asked accusingly.

"Nothing at all," Morris smiled. "My department is an oasis of calm in a desert of irrationality."

Morris was not about to admit to the Prime Minister that the announcement had caught even him off his guard. How could he admit to that when Anna Letelier had a direct line into the Vatican. Surely she must have known.

"So you've done nothing," Samulovitch muttered.

"That is not true," Morris said. "Why, even now a jet is burning precious fuel waiting to fly me to Rome where I shall have a delectable dinner at Savarino's."

"You waste too much money," Samulovitch growled.

"Better than blood," Morris said cheerfully.

"What are you going to bring back?"

"Not a miracle. I bow to others who are better qualified for that sort of thing. But a reprieve perhaps. I will send you a postcard."

"Do better. Send me deliverance."

Morris rose and went slowly to the window to glance at the demonstrators.

"Teddy, what if the tape is genuine?" he asked, not turning around.

"One part of me says I should level Moscow before I allow one Jew to set foot into another camp," Samulovitch said thoughtfully. "Another tells me I would be guaranteeing the destruction of Israel if I did such a thing." The Prime Minister swiveled around in his chair. "Morris, I don't know . . . no man should even have to contemplate such a decision."

"But what *will* you do?"

"I will send you to kill Gorodin."

37

"How did it happen?" Gorodin asked, staring at his own reflection in the partition between the passenger compartment and driver's seat of Suslev's massive car.

"Our jamming devices were not at fault," Suslev whispered hoarsely. "My people have checked the facilities. All our equipment was operating normally. The same is true for East Germany, Hungary, Czechoslovakia, Rumania. It was the damn Poles, I'm certain of it. Sabotage."

"So, Poland," Gorodin said.

"That was where the breach occurred." Suslev waved his hand. "Somehow—I don't have all the details yet—Polish technicians found a way to circumvent the jamming. They relayed the transmission directly."

"The Poles will pay for this, Viktor," Gorodin murmured. "They will pay dearly. What they have done is treason, pure and simple."

"What about Stanislawski? What do you intend to do about him?"

"A denunciation of the mass and Innocent's threat will be issued in an hour," Gorodin said coldly. "I'm also thinking of summoning the American ambassador to make certain that they understand how concerned we are about this. By tomorrow the heads of state of all the people's democracies will issue a joint communiqué. I am going to inundate the Vatican with so much righteous indignation that Innocent will wish he had never uttered a word."

"And our plan?"

"That does not change," Gorodin said. "If we show the slightest weakness, Pavlichenko and Kobalevsky will be able to sway Fadayev and the others. I intend to go before the Central Committee and announce that because of this unconscionable interference in our internal affairs the Presidium requests immediate ratification of my chairmanship. And I will get it. As for the Church in Eastern Europe, I will proceed to make their lives unbearable. Innocent is worrying about the Jews—I will give him something closer to home to worry about!

"What I will need from you, as quickly as possible, is all the material you have on Innocent. I want to destroy this man, Viktor. He caused us enough trouble when he was in Warsaw. Now he has gone just a bit too far." He turned to Suslev. "But Viktor, once I begin the attack on Innocent, I cannot stop. You promised to get me information that would crucify Stanislawski. As of this moment I still haven't seen it."

Suslev tugged back his jacket sleeve and squinted at his watch. "A few more hours," he said. "It is now only a matter of hours."

38

Michael Turner's luck was holding. The Central Holocaust Archives had not yet closed for the day.

"I am looking for Madame Levin."

The crippled woman behind the desk looked up at Turner, rose, and slowly hobbled to the platform behind the counter.

"I am she."

"My name is Michael Turner. I am the personal physician of His Holiness Innocent XIV. I was also a friend of Father Gregory Rowitz's."

"Father Gregory Rowitz?" The woman's voice trailed off. "I'm sorry, I don't know anyone by that name."

From his jacket pocket Turner produced a blue-and-yellow sheet of paper, which he handed to the archivist. "The telegram you sent to Father Rowitz two days ago."

Hannah Levin glanced at the telegram. "May I see your identification, please?"

She examined Turner's Vatican passport carefully, then beckoned him to come around the counter. When they entered her office, he noticed that the television was on but the sound turned off.

"You say that Father Rowitz *was* a friend of yours . . ."

"He was killed in Berlin the other night."

Hannah Levin acknowledged the news with a resigned

nod. She walked over to the television set and adjusted the volume.

"His death was reported on the news," she said. "The Pope is in West Berlin. He made an incredible announcement during a memorial mass. Can what he said be true?"

"It is," Turner told her.

"And you are here . . . ?"

"To finish what Father Rowitz began."

Hannah Levin switched off the television and gathered up her shawl.

"Come," she said.

The neighborhood was primarily residential, the sandstone façades of the apartment buildings freshly scrubbed, the grill-work on the door shining. He followed Hannah Levin into the foyer and stepped into the ornate elevator. The first floor fell away as the lift started up, moving with exquisite slowness, then shuddering to a halt. Turner drew back the grill, allowing her to lead the way. There was a brass knocker on the door fitted through a lion's mouth and a mezzuzah on the doorjamb.

"Please go right into the living room," she called out, then disappeared into what Turner thought must be the kitchen.

Turner hung up his raincoat in the hall and walked into what was really a music room, largely given over to a Bechstein grand piano, a harpsichord, and a music stand. There was a small chaise longue, a small divan, a coffee table in front of the fireplace, and a portable television set hidden away in one corner. Hannah Levin came back with a carafe of mineral water on a tray.

"I'm afraid I'm not allowed any stimulants—neither coffee nor tea." She smiled. "But if you'd like, I can make some for you."

"That won't be necessary."

"I see. Doctor," she said quietly, "perhaps you can tell me how I might be of service to you?"

"You must forgive me, Madame Levin, but my business is with a man by the name of Telemann."

"Yes, I understand that."

"From the papers Father Rowitz left behind I understand that he asked you to undertake a search for this man."

"Yes, he did. May I ask how you came by this information?"

"Father Rowitz took the precaution of leaving the appropriate papers with attorneys in Geneva, the firm of Pallenberg et Fils."

"Yes, Louis and his son were also murdered," Hannah Levin said tonelessly.

For a moment Turner was startled. "Yes. They were. I was in their office when the bomb went off."

"In some ways you are a very fortunate man," Hannah Levin observed. "Yes, Father Rowitz asked me to find a man by the name of Adam Telemann. Unfortunately when he came to me with his request, I could not tell him then that Adam Telemann was never really lost."

"I'm sorry, I don't understand."

"Adam Telemann was my brother. Levin is my married name. Adam died six years ago."

"I'm sorry," Turner said. "I didn't know."

"Does my brother's death in any way affect your reason for coming to Amsterdam?"

"It very well may." He clasped his hands. "Father Rowitz believed that your brother had a ledger, a ledger he had kept with him after the liberation of Auschwitz. There was something in that volume that was, and remains, incredibly important."

"Important to whom, doctor?"

"Since you've already heard the Pope's broadcast, I should think the answer would be obvious."

"My brother was only seventeen when they took him to Auschwitz, Dr. Turner. Our entire family was taken. Adam and I were the only survivors. He saved many lives in that camp. He took incredible risks. After the war Adam worked for a time with organizations that helped displaced persons. He was in Cyprus in '47, and he fought in Palestine the following year. He returned to Holland ten years ago and started a very fine antiquarian bookstore. He devoted his life to it."

"Surely your brother must have left a number of papers

behind him—correspondence, records of his business affairs. Somewhere there may be a reference to a person both he and Gregory Rowitz knew, a woman called Katrina Jaworska, from Warsaw."

"There may well be," Hannah Levin said calmly. "As his only heir, I still have everything he left behind."

"Madame Levin," Turner said slowly, "I must ask you to think carefully about the papers your brother left. Among them can you remember an old leather notebook, a ledger containing the names and identification numbers of a particular group of Auschwitz inmates?"

"There was a substantial amount of material dating back to that period, Dr. Turner. Most of it was in the form of letters and official documents which Adam managed to salvage before the SS could destroy them. This material was later used in several war-crimes trials and then donated to the Central Holocaust Archives." Hannah Levin looked up at Turner. "Why is this so important to you?"

"What is in that ledger could be very important to Innocent XIV," Turner said. "To him and to every Jew in Russia, and everywhere else in the Communist bloc."

Hannah Levin sighed. "I feel now as I did then. How could it be that God would allow such a thing? And how could He allow it to happen a second time?"

"The ledger still exists, doesn't it?" Turner said. "You yourself have read it. You know why Gregory Rowitz came to you and why I am here now."

"Yes, I know about the ledger." Hannah Levin folded her hands. "Adam told me about it before he died. He told me about all the lives that had been changed. About the hundreds that they saved—he told me that they might come back to haunt him."

"And what did he tell you to do when this moment came?"

"Adam had no desire to inflict any further suffering on the people whose records he had changed. He alone bore the responsibility for this. As a result he never actually permitted me to read the ledger. You see, he was being kind, because sometimes there is knowledge that a human being should not have.

He told me that if someone came asking for the ledger, I was to give it to him."

The bookstore was housed in a tall narrow building with a red brick façade. Across the lead-lined plate glass window, in gold leaf, was printed in French *Livres Antiquaires*. The second and third levels were visible from the vestibule. A wooden railing separated the vestibule from Telemann's desk in one corner. A short staircase led to the second level and the gallery, which swung right around the room. Floor-to-ceiling bookcases covered the walls. On the third level was a recessed carrel where clients could examine their prospective purchases on slanted library desks.

Turner closeted himself in the wood-frame carrel, placing the tattered ledger on the slanted desk top that was affixed to one wall. Running along the edge of the pages, his fingers discovered a marker. He opened the ledger to a page marked by a frayed paper strip. Across the top line was a date: June 27, 1944. On the left, in a neat column, were names, written in black ink, the script clear and concise, as though the author had taken great pains to ensure that the names could not be misread. The names meant nothing to Turner. He looked at the second and third columns. Both consisted of five-digit numbers, which Turner knew were concentration camp identification numbers. Tattoos . . . Quickly he scanned the second column. Nothing. Moving his finger along the page he read through the numbers in the third column.

"Oh, my God!"

The number almost leaped up from the page. Turner reread it to make certain it was the Pontiff's now famous serial number. Then he looked across at the numbers in the second column. Then the name—*Abramovich*. Not even a first name, just the family's.

Turner felt the sweat on his brow. Suslev would use this to destroy Stanislawski. Rowitz and the Pallenbergs had died for it. For these few digits, frightened and desperate men had sent killers to hold his son and Jeanne's parents for ransom.

Why didn't you destroy it? he asked Telemann silently.

Why did you feel the need to keep a record like this? Wasn't it enough for you that you had saved them?

Turner called downstairs and asked Hannah Levin to come up.

"I want you to promise me something," he said slowly. "I want you to pledge this on your brother's memory."

"You have my word that I will help you in any way I can," she said. Gently she ran her fingertips over the cover of the ledger. "I trust you, doctor. I realize that somehow what is happening to us now is connected with this book that my brother preserved for all those years. I am obliged to help you."

"I have to go to London on the first flight in the morning," Turner said. "There is something I have to do there. If I don't call you within forty-eight hours, I want you to call this woman in Rome and tell her what has happened." He handed her a slip of paper with Anna's name and private telephone number.

Hannah Levin was silent, then she reached across and touched Turner on the shoulder. "Will the Pope's demands be met?"

"I pray they will, Madame Levin. I pray they will."

"What are you doing with the ledger, doctor?"

"Burning it." Turner watched the fire catch the edges of the pages and begin to consume the binding. He placed it carefully on the grid in the small fireplace and watched until he was satisfied the book had been consumed in its entirety.

39

Across the Moskva River, in his office on Arbatskaya Ploshchad, Sergei Bibnikov took a final drag on his second cigarette of the morning. The auburn-gold spires of the Church of Saint Basil shimmered in the sun. The time was half-past eight. Roy had called a few hours earlier. He was in position. Bibnikov reached down and from the bottom drawer extracted a lightweight multibarrel machine pistol of Czech design and manufacture. Bibnikov checked the breech and the ammunition feed, spread his coat out on the desk, and fitted the pistol between the leather straps sewn into the lining. Bibnikov slipped the coat on, smoothing out the folds. He looked around his office with the thoughtful expression of a man who understands that tomorrow his chair may be occupied by someone else. Except that for Sergei Bibnikov there would be no retirement, no pension, no loving wife with whom to share his twilight years. At any time within the next twelve hours he might be killed. If he failed at what he was setting out to do, no mercy would be shown him. Bibnikov contemplated the thin line between loyalty and treason, and sighed.

"Enough," he said to himself, and set off. His car was waiting.

The streets of Moscow were quiet at this hour. The drive between Arbatskaya Ploshchad and Number 2 Dzerzhinsky

Square took only a few minutes. Bibnikov approached the Lubyanka from the rear, slipping into the underground car park on the strength of his pass. After his name was entered into the day log at the central security desk, Bibnikov proceeded to the archives on the fifth floor. Once again he went through the charade of filling out request forms for dead files. When the girl brought them out, he signed the chit and moved over to a private cubicle. Spreading out the files' contents in a haphazard way, Bibnikov sat back and during the next sixty minutes smoked three more cigarettes. When he saw the librarian disappear into the stacks, he slipped out.

The guard on duty at the entrance to the holding cells was Sergeant Gugarin, whose cooperation had already been secured by Aleksandr Roy. Silently Bibnikov flipped open his pass, watching the man stiffen. The pencil, poised to write down his name, dropped from the sergeant's fingers. As Bibnikov walked past him into the corridor that led to the cells, he unbuttoned his overcoat. He stopped in front of cell 536 and looked back at the sergeant. The door drew back automatically.

In size the cell was no different from any other. That was where the similarity ended. Instead of a hard bunk or straw pallet, there was an ordinary bed, with sheets and blankets. The air was warm and dry, with a hint of jasmine. Instead of the bucket there was a flush toilet. Books and magazines were piled neatly on a small table beside the bed.

"Who are you?"

Dr. Bauer was a short slim man, with a carefully trimmed goatee and pince-nez. Dressed in an elegantly cut three-piece suit, perfect down to the watch fob, he held a fountain pen in one hand, in the other a copy of a British medical journal. The anesthesiologist from Rudin Hospital looked up at his visitor without giving any sign of fear or surprise.

"Who are you?" he repeated.

"I have come from Suslev," Bibnikov said.

"Suslev said he would come for me tomorrow."

"Matters have arranged themselves differently."

"I take it, then, Razminsky has confessed."

"He has confessed, that's correct."

Bauer reached for his overcoat, which was draped carefully over a chair. "In that case I presume I can leave this wretched sty."

"Suslev wants to see you first."

"I should think he might."

Bibnikov drew his coat together so that the physician would not see the gun as he went by him. Following a few steps behind, Bibnikov kept his eyes on the far end of the corridor, watching for that almost imperceptible signal that would reveal a trap. If they were waiting for him, he would die, but not before Bauer.

Bibnikov exchanged glances with the sergeant, who shrank back into the cubicle as though willing himself not to see the two men go by.

In one hundred and thirty seconds Bibnikov had Bauer in his car. A few seconds later the last chance of stopping them had passed. The car cleared the underground ramp and turned into Dzerzhinsky Square.

"Are we going to the Foreign Ministry?" the doctor asked.

"Comrade Suslev felt that a more convivial atmosphere might be in order." Bibnikov forced a smile. "Undoubtedly you've heard of the Mermaid."

"My favorite restaurant," Bauer exclaimed, beaming.

"The director is waiting for you there. It has been opened especially for him and his guest."

"Splendid! I could do with a decent meal, even at this hour. The slop they were feeding me in that place was intolerable."

"You won't ever have to worry about corrupting your palate again," Bibnikov said. "I have been assigned as your personal debriefing officer," he went on. "Undoubtedly you've been told that we will have to go over the exact details of your involvement in this matter."

"Suslev mentioned something to that effect." Bauer lit a cigarette, rolling down the window a fraction. They were heading toward the outskirts of the city.

"I have been involved in this from the beginning," Bibnikov said. "I had hoped I would be able to congratulate you personally. Your technique was flawless."

Dr. Bauer sat back, luxuriating in the strong tobacco and the compliment.

"It was a question of finding the appropriate moment, coupled with the precise means," he said. "Of course the matter was complicated by the fact that the chairman's death *had* to be laid at Razminsky's door. To induce death itself would have been no great problem, you see. The man's age and condition made that part of it rather easy."

"Is that what led you to hit upon your particular solution?" Bibnikov asked.

"As a matter of fact, it was. You see, coating the intravenous Decadron bag was only one of several possibilities. I had considered, among other things, lining the inside of the actual needle that is inserted into the skin. However the problem was one of opportunity, and of finding the correct dosage. Ever since the American performed his surgery on Komarov, the chairman spent less and less time in Moscow. Razminsky was the only one who went up to the Sokolniki Hills to look in on him. I told both Suslev and Gorodin that our only chance would be when Komarov returned to the Rudin, as we knew he must eventually. Once Rudin had been decided upon as the place, the next problem was the method. Since Razminsky had to be implicated beyond any doubt, the treatment had to be initiated by him. Everything he touched, every order he issued, had to be seen as part of a logical progression that would end with Komarov's demise."

"You must have been working very closely with the Foreign Minister and the director," Bibnikov observed.

"At first, yes. However, once they approved my plan, then the rest was left entirely to my discretion."

"Obviously they had a great deal of faith in you."

"It was a very delicate business. However, as you must understand, there was no choice. Komarov was going to die in a few months anyway. I look upon the whole affair as a case of euthanasia."

"As a professional in a related field, I can appreciate the difficulties you must have encountered—the waiting, making sure that suspicion never fell on you. . . ."

"I confess that as the months wore on, it began to be a burden. Yet I knew that eventually Komarov would have to come to Rudin Hospital. That was inevitable. Knowing how Dr. Razminsky worked, I selected certain instruments and materials which could be easily adapted to my purposes. Decadron was my first choice. Komarov needed the drug. There was only one possible way of introducing it into the body, an IV. It had absolutely no effect on the potassium cyanide, even over an extended period of time. It was the perfect means of introducing the substance into his system for it allowed the nitroprusside the time needed to break down into cyanide. There was only one drawback."

"What was that?"

"I had to learn exactly when Komarov was coming in, so that I could remove the other bags and leave only the one that was coated."

"Nurse Mayakovskaya must have been a great help to you on that point."

"She was indeed."

"The way things worked out, Razminsky could not help but be implicated," Bibnikov said. "He ordered the Decadron solution set up. He took the bag—the only one which you had left there—out of the refrigerator, watched as Mayakovskaya prepared the patient to receive it. Then, thinking everything was in order, he went home to his wife."

"The cyanide solution was so diluted that it would not affect Komarov's system for at least two hours."

"Not only that but Kobalevsky came to see Razminsky that evening at the Rudin, as soon as he heard that Komarov had been transferred there. Gorodin got a bonus on the surveillance tape. . . ."

"I really don't know anything about that," Bauer said nervously.

"No. Of course not."

They had cleared the second circumferential highway and

were heading north. Two miles further Bibnikov slowed down and turned off onto the narrower road that led into the forest. He swung the vehicle up onto the shoulder of the road.

"Why are we stopping?" Bauer demanded.

"You probably didn't notice, doctor, but there's been a car behind us since we left Dzerzhinsky Square. One of ours, I assure you. I want them to take the lead."

"You are not expecting any trouble?" Bauer said, looking back nervously.

"Not at all. Standard security precautions. The chairman was quite insistent that you were to receive the very best care."

Bibnikov heard the grating of tires on gravel and got out of the car. In the dirty-brown Volga sedan he saw four men. He nodded to them briefly and came around to the passenger door. With one motion he flung the door open and heaved Bauer out of the car, gripping his lapels so tightly that his fist crunched against Bauer's Adam's apple. He slammed him up against the car while his subordinates ran up, one man sliding behind the wheel, the other two slipping handcuffs on Bauer's wrists.

"Bibnikov, what are you doing?" Bauer shouted hoarsely. The director of Special Investigations cuffed the physician across the face, almost negligently. From the expression of pain that contorted the doctor's features, Bibnikov knew he had achieved the desired effect. With Bauer in the rear seat between two of his agents, Bibnikov gestured for the fourth man to go back to the Volga while he himself slipped in beside the driver.

The two cars drove along the deserted road for another three miles. At a junction the driver took the fork to the left and led the convoy to a clearing at the edge of a marsh. A helicopter was waiting, rotor blades swinging lazily, whipping the reeds and tall grasses.

"Get him inside," Bibnikov said. He reached over and, from a hidden panel in the roof, brought out a tape recorder. He ejected the tape cassette and passed it over to the driver.

"If I don't come back, if something happens to Roy, get this to Marshal Pavlichenko."

"You should let one of us come with you," the driver said.

"You know better than that," Bibnikov admonished him.

"If none of you knows where I've gone, you'll have nothing to tell in case Suslev somehow gets hold of you, and vice versa."

When the two other agents had returned from the helicopter he looked gravely at all of them.

"You may listen to the tape, so that if you're to die, you will at least understand what you're dying for. I commend all of you for your trust in me."

Bibnikov shook hands with each of them. If something went wrong, these men, their relatives and loved ones, would end up in anonymous graves. That they would die as patriots seemed small consolation. Abruptly he turned and ran to the helicopter and got into the pilot's seat.

He kept the machine low, staying well away from the military airfields in the Moscow District, pushing the engines to the limit. Bauer, strapped to the seat beside him, mouth taped shut, represented no danger. The flight took thirty minutes, by which time the Russian capital was the better part of one hundred kilometers to the south.

Bibnikov had discovered this abandoned dacha four years ago, after a Politburo member had casually mentioned that it had once belonged to Beria. A large cottage with an impressive porch, the dacha was completely deserted. As in the other safe houses Bibnikov maintained around the country, the cellar had enough dried food to feed four people for a month. There was a fresh tank of water, two diesel generators for electricity, propane gas canisters for heat and hot water. Past the shattered window frames and peeling walls of the outer rooms was a tiny house within a larger one.

Bibnikov set the machine down near a grove of trees. Pulling Bauer out of the seat, he ripped off the tape covering the physician's mouth and pushed him forward.

"You can't kill me," Bauer rasped, gasping for air. He shook his head violently, from side to side. "I knew Gorodin would try," he chortled suddenly, on the verge of hysteria. "Execute the executioner."

"Why can't I kill you?" Bibnikov asked him delicately as they mounted the porch. He pushed back the lopsided door and stepped into the dead leaves and dirt that covered the floor. He heard the scraping of field mice.

"You think I would have agreed to do what I did without taking precautions?" Bauer sneered. "I have written everything down. Everything. Do you hear? From the first moment when Gorodin approached me. So I will not die on this dungheap. You will call Gorodin. You will tell him that unless the bargain is kept between us, *he* will be the one who kneels to receive the bullet."

Bibnikov looked at Bauer and a slow smile crept over his lips. "But I don't work for Gorodin. I'm still working for Komarov."

Bauer sagged. He staggered back. The terror in his eyes was so rank that it filled Bibnikov with loathing. This man had sold his country.

"So you will tell me about this arrangement of yours, this insurance policy you thought it so prudent to draw up," he said. "You will tell me about that and the exact details of how you murdered Komarov. We have time enough for everything."

The BEA Trident jet touched down at Heathrow Airport a few minutes ahead of schedule, taxiing immediately to an open gate. Michael Turner strode past the harassed stewardess who, smiling bravely, welcomed him to London. He was one of the first to reach the customs desk and offered his passport to the immigration officer, who stamped it routinely.

"Dr. Turner, would you mind stepping this way, sir?" The immigration officer gestured toward a corridor.

For an instant Turner was uncertain that the inspector was addressing him. When he turned around, he saw that two ruggedly built men had fallen in beside him.

"What's wrong?"

"Only a formality, doctor," the immigration official answered. "Would you be good enough to go with these gentlemen, please?"

He did not return Turner's passport but handed it instead to one of the plainclothesmen. Gently Turner was nudged out of the line and fell into step, heading toward the customs office.

"Dr. Turner, I am Chief Inspector Ballantyne, Special Branch."

The man addressing him was tall and heavily built, with an athletic bearing that belied his age. In one hand he held a nauseatingly aromatic cigar. They stopped in front of an unmarked door and knocked. It opened instantly.

"These gentlemen"—Ballantyne gestured at the half-dozen others in the room—"I think you know."

"Good afternoon, doc," Charlie Thompson said, stepping forward.

"Doctor," Aleksandr Roy said.

"I don't understand what's going on." Turner's pulse was racing. "I suggest you have another look at my passport. You have no right to detain a member of the Papal household."

"Doctor. We know why you're here," Thompson said quietly. "We know you're going to your in-laws' house. We know what you expect to find there. We're here to help you deal with it."

Turner shook his head. He had less than forty-five minutes to travel across London to Berkeley Square.

"Unless you have a valid reason for holding me—"

"I have a message from Sergei Bibnikov," Aleksandr Roy said. "You remember him, don't you, doctor?"

"Yes. Yes, I do," Turner said.

"He asked me to tell you that this time you will not be alone. There will be no repetition of what happened to you in New York."

"Her Majesty's government has been informed that your wife's parents and your son are being held as hostages," Ballantyne said. "We have also learned that the men holding them are Russians. The Home Office has permitted Mr. Roy and his associates to enter the country to help rectify this situation. As for Mr. Thompson, it was he who brought the matter to our attention. We are ready to help in any way possible. But given the delicacy of the matter, it is preferable that Mr. Roy handle this affair . . . with your cooperation."

"Did you bring them what they wanted?" Charlie Thompson asked.

"No."

Turner saw the exchange of surprised glances among the three men.

"Then what were you planning to do?" Roy asked him. "Are you carrying a gun?"

"I am not armed," Turner said. "I was going to offer a trade. I was going to tell them that what they want is in London, but before they get it, they would have to release my son and Jeanne's parents. I would take their place as hostage."

"But you just said that you don't have what they want," Thompson said.

"That's right," Turner said. "It doesn't exist. The incriminating information, I mean. The numbers were changed by the tattooist, yes, but the names didn't change. The Germans cared nothing about the names of those they had reduced to such a state. The inmates had no identities for Telemann other than numbers. Do you understand what I'm saying? I have *nothing* to barter with, and they have my son and his grandparents."

"Once they found out that you had lied to them, they would kill you," Roy said.

"Yes. And there is no other way. What they want just doesn't exist." He looked at the three of them, his eyes pleading that they understand. "If you truly want to prevent a recurrence of what happened in New York, then you will let me walk out of here and do what I have to do. If they have the slightest suspicion that I'm being followed or that you're planning some kind of trap, they'll kill my son. Please, gentlemen."

"No, they won't," Roy said. "I want you to listen to me, doctor. You are a brave man, and I will not permit you to throw your life away like this. Besides, I am quite certain they will never release any of you. Listen hard and do exactly as I say."

Even during the London rush hour Berkeley Square remained as sedate and tranquil as he had remembered. Turner stepped out of the taxi on the east side of the square, in front of the Rolls-Royce dealership. Diagonally across was Sloane Street which led up to the Dorchester. He seemed to remember there was a pub there, the Jade Unicorn, a favorite of his father-in-law's. Directly ahead of him was a row of elegant Victorian town houses, each with an ornate gas lamp already lit. Slowly he looked from one yellow light to the next until he saw the gleaming black door with the lion's head knocker. A man walking a Borzoi strode past him. His peripheral vision registered a Daimler limousine gliding silently up toward the hotel. Somewhere in the distance he could hear the soft thunder of city traffic.

Turner began to walk, legs moving stiffly. He crossed the square and came to the wrought-iron gate. Sidney must have oiled the latch, he thought. The last time, he remembered, the latch squeaked. The soles of his boots scraped against the rough stone steps. For a fraction of a second he hesitated, asking his son to forgive him, praying that the people he loved would understand. His finger found the buzzer.

When the door swung back, there was no one to greet him. Turner stepped into the hallway, recognizing the Queen Anne side-table his mother-in-law had given to Jeanne as a wedding present. He heard the door shut.

"Please go in, Dr. Turner," a voice spoke to him. "You know your way."

They were sitting on the sofa in the drawing room, Sidney, Mary, and Christopher, who was sketching on a pad. Turner looked at Jeanne's parents, at Sidney Harrington's defiant expression, then across the room, at the two men who were standing in front of the fireplace, hands at their sides. Quiet, competent-looking men in three-piece suits.

No weapons.

A hand took his elbow. "Please, there is no need to stand on ceremony."

The speaker's inflections gave him away. He was Russian. But then Turner had expected as much.

"Have you brought us what we wanted?"

"Yes."

"Then by all means show it to me."

Turner placed the flight bag on the card table and pulled down the zipper.

"I do not think you are a foolhardy man," the agent told him. "If you have a weapon in there, your mother-in-law will be gone before you get it out of the bag."

"There's no gun." Yet the hair on the back of his neck was standing on end. He couldn't help but turn toward the windows. The curtains were drawn back, leaving only the gauze drapes against the glass. To anyone looking inside it would look like a few friends were having drinks.

"There is no need for delay. We realize this is a distressing situation for you. We know you brought no one here with you and we do not wish to prolong this."

He would have one chance and only one. Turner reached into the bag and brought out a clothbound ledger.

That was when the glass in one of the panes behind him broke with an almost musical tinkle.

Aleksandr Roy had chosen the smallest stun riot grenade in his arsenal. Sixty seconds before it was thrown, one of his team had neutralized the lookout who had been watching Turner's approach to the house. The other three were in place. It wasn't Sidney Harrington who had oiled the latch. Turner had been wrong about that.

Turner saw the grenade rolling on the floor. He leaped for the sofa to cover his son while deafening gunshots rang out. Turner rolled off the couch onto the floor.

Aleksandr Roy shot one of the men by the fireplace through the heart. As he fell back he jogged his partner's gun hand. The stream of bullets that would have torn Roy in half studded the molding over the archway. The Russian who had brought Turner in jerked like a demented puppet as the bullets slammed him back against a china cabinet.

"It's over," Roy said. He nodded to his men, who instantly began dragging the bodies into the corridor. Roy leaned down and brought Turner to his feet, pushing him out of the way as suddenly the house began to fill up with Special Branch detectives. Three men made their way into the living room and immediately turned their attention to the Harringtons and

Christopher Turner. Turner watched as they ministered to his family, their swift, sure movements reassuring. One of the Special Branch physicians turned to him.

"Doctor, they are all all right. They may have some ringing in their ears, but otherwise they're fine. We'll take them to a hospital for observation if they wish."

"There is one last thing you must do," Roy said, taking him by the elbow. "You must call Stanislawski. Only you can convince the Pontiff not to go through with what he has planned. Tell him that we will take care of Gorodin in our own way. Please, you must convince him not to interfere further."

"But how?"

Roy led Turner out of the house to a large unmarked van that was standing at the curb. He rapped on the doors and, when they were drawn back, Turner could see that the rear compartment was filled with electronic equipment.

"The British have arranged a satellite linkage with Berlin," he said. "Call Innocent . . . call him and tell him to call it off."

Turner climbed into the truck and sat down beside one of the technicians, who handed him a receiver. Turner waited for the connection to be established. He looked back at Aleksandr Roy, standing by the open door. But instead of being put through to the Pope he found himself speaking to Auguste Cardinal Mirabeau. Turner broke the connection after their conversation was finished.

"It's too late!" he said, turning to Roy. "Innocent has repeated his demand for the release of Russian and Eastern European Jews. It's more serious than we had feared. Gorodin's pogrom is already under way."

Fifty miles above the surface of the earth a Paladin satellite swept over the rim of the Pacific, on course at fifty-one degrees north latitude, and seventeen degrees east longitude. As it cleared Russia's easternmost port of Vladivostok the onboard computer received a course change which swung it in a gentle arc, away from the Russian missile installations and onto a heading which took it across the deserts of Inner Mongolia, then over Kazakhstan. The seven infrared cameras picked up the exhaust of the Trans-Siberian railroad and caught a locomotive on the spur line which trailed off toward Rozdensk. At fifty-one degrees north and twenty-two degrees east, the command to activate was received.

Seated in the highback chair at the command post of the Situation Room in the White House, President Jonathan Telford watched as the giant circular screen on the lower level displayed the Paladin transmissions in a series of fast-moving snapshots that blended into a slow-moving collage.

"Thirty seconds, Mr. President," Laine Compton said, eyes fixed on the circular television screen. There was nothing on the screen except shapeless masses of white and gray, interspersed with brown smudges.

The President's hand moved forward toward the intercom on the desk, depressing a button.

"Toby, General MacAllister, Paladin is moving into position. Any time now."

"We're ready, Mr. President," MacAllister's voice responded. The Chairman of the Joint Chiefs was watching an identical screen at the Pentagon.

"We count fifteen seconds, Mr. President," the head of the CIA said from his vantage point in the Analysis Room at Langley.

"Are the lines clear, secure?" the Chief Executive asked.

"The Secretary of State of the Vatican and the Prime Minister of Israel are standing by, sir."

"I hope to Christ Charlie Thompson is wrong!" Telford said suddenly. "I hope those coordinates he sent us show Patriarch's Ponds in Moscow, with kids playing in the park."

Laine Compton said nothing. She didn't have to tell the President that the coordinates received from the American Embassy in Moscow forty minutes earlier wouldn't be anywhere near the Russian capital. In fact, after Compton had studied them, she berated herself because neither she nor the National Security Agency had sent the Paladin so far to the northeast.

"The Pope," the President said. "Anything new there?"

"Nothing since he reiterated his demand, sir."

"Damn."

"Transmission coming up on mark." The voice of the course controller floated into the command room. Paladin satellite's onboard computer made an infinitesimal course adjustment. All sensors were now activated. The cameras fixed on predetermined coordinates, swiftly calculating altitude, velocity, cloud cover.

"Mark."

No one spoke as a vast, sprawling industrial complex came into view, the images slowing up as Paladin reduced speed. With great accuracy the cameras swept from east to west, north to south, bringing low-level buildings into focus, tall chimney stacks that might have been part of a heating plant, and endless rows of barracks. Then the barbed wire coils of the wide perimeter came into view . . . and railroad tracks.

"I'm going to be sick," Telford snapped. "God Almighty, that's ten times bigger than Auschwitz." He looked at Compton. "The people. There aren't any people."

"Not yet," the Secretary of State intoned, unable to take her eyes from the screens. "But God help us, there will be—hundreds of thousands."

"Christ, the bastards almost pulled it off . . . they almost made it!" He leaned toward the microphone that connected the two sections. "I want definition," he said, his voice quaking. "I want to read the manufacturer's label on those fucking ovens!"

"Definition is being taped on a separate channel, sir," the technician answered. "Shall I put it on the screen?"

"No, keep giving us the big picture."

"Switching over to second set of coordinates. Five seconds to mark."

The President looked up at his Secretary of State; there were tears streaming down her cheeks.

"That's only the first of them, Laine. There are at least four more."

"Mark."

The pneumatic door behind Compton opened with a sigh

of compressed air. An orderly officer entered and handed the Secretary of State a computer printout.

"Mr. President."

Telford did not respond, transfixed by the enormity of the horror he was observing on the screen. In this sequence there were people, hundreds of them. The heat sensors were showing smoke.

"Innocent was right," Telford said. "He was dead right. God help us, the Russians have gone berserk. The damn fools."

40

Sitting at the center of a long conference table, Foreign Minister Dmitri Gorodin watched the illuminated Mercator projection map on the panel twenty feet away. A red dot was moving slowly across the longitude lines, on a steady, even course toward Moscow. Two blue dots, one above the other, below the red dot of the Vatican 747 showed the position of the Soviet air force interceptors.

"Classic," Viktor Suslev wheezed, leaning forward on his elbows. "The planes are deploying to escort the intruding aircraft. I estimate they are two hours from Moscow."

"And are being tracked by American satellites." Gorodin's voice was tinged with sadness. "Two hours . . ."

The doors to the left of the conference room swung open. Bibnikov came through first, followed by General Borgatov of the Guards Directorate.

"Chairman Gorodin, Director Suslev, I inform you that you are both under arrest for the murder of Semyon Arkadyevich Komarov."

Suslev smiled very slowly. Bibnikov did not reply but simply watched as Suslev slowly rose to his feet.

"You're a bourgeois fool," he said to Kobalevsky as several others entered, all of them white with anxiety.

Kobalevsky looked straight at him. "For the first time in my life, Minister, I was afraid for us—for us, for our sons. We have brought them to the brink of a new era, a different time, and suddenly men like you would have them return to the old days, the violence, the needless terror and coercion. Minister, you do not understand just how disgraced our country is. For more than seventy years you leaders of the Revolution have not been able to trust the very people in whose name it was fought. If the situation is not corrected there will come a second revolt. One day the knives again will come out. No one will report to the factories, no one will tend the farms. The people will simply refuse to submit anymore. And we will lose everything we have paid for in blood." He looked down, his head bowed. "Gentlemen, if there is anyone you wish to call and speak to, do so now, because you will not be leaving this room alive."

Sheremetevo Airport was closed to all traffic. All flights, military and civilian, were diverted to Vnukovo. Along the length of the northwest runway, generator trucks were parked at one-hundred-yard intervals, their lamps bathing the concrete apron. The terminal itself had been cleared out by Guards Directorate detachments under Bibnikov's supervision. Likewise the controllers in the towers had been replaced by military personnel from a base sixty kilometers outside the city. To add a certain piquancy to the situation Bibnikov floated a rumor about a cargo jet that was having landing-gear problems. He thought that would be enough to satisfy the Western press.

The pilot of the 747 brought his ship down. As soon as he switched off reverse thrust a signal jeep darted out in front of the aircraft.

The pilot glanced over his shoulder. "Holiness, what are we to do now?"

Innocent unbuckled his seat belt and leaned forward, his arms resting on the backs of the pilot's and co-pilot's chairs.

"Now we shall meet with those whom we came to meet," he said.

No sooner had the pilot cut his engines than there was a knock on the forward hatch. An attendant swung the safety bar away and opened the hatch. Innocent took a step forward and looked up at the Russian sky, studded with stars; a cordon of armed soldiers was drawn up on the runway. At the foot of the ramp stood a heavyset man in a battered leather coat. Beside him a taller, slimmer man. Innocent took a few tentative steps forward and identified him as Oleg Kobalevsky.

Innocent descended the ramp, looking over the right-hand railing. The man who spoke was reaching out for him.

"I am Ambassador Farraday. As of this moment you are under the protection of the United States government."

Innocent XIV grasped Farraday's hand. "I thank you for your offer, Mr. Ambassador. I'm also gratified to feel that I may not have to take advantage of it."

Oleg Kobalevsky stepped forward. "I'm glad that your journey has been a safe one," he said, looking steadily at the Pontiff. "Nevertheless your presence here is highly irregular."

"I am here to plead with your government," Innocent said, "and to avoid a serious confrontation, if at all possible."

Kobalevsky and Farraday exchanged glances. Then the Russian minister spoke: "Are you truly proposing to bring them out of their countries, just like that, without any explanations, without giving us a chance to see who they are?"

"These are ordinary people, Minister." Innocent waved at him in exasperation. "No scientific or industrial secrets will leave with them. I ask you to accept my word for that. I did not come for the sake of what they know or possess. . . . I came because of what was about to happen to them."

"Perhaps I should inform you that Gorodin is dead," Kobalevsky said.

"I am indeed sorry to hear that," Innocent said. "For all the evil Gorodin intended to do, he was still a human being. But there are hundreds of thousands of your citizens who feel as he did. I doubt very much, Minister, that you could assure me that nothing will happen to the Jews."

"But you can't expect to take several hundred thousand people out through a hole in the Berlin Wall!" Kobalevsky exclaimed.

"There are many more who could fly out," Innocent said. He glanced over at Bibnikov. "It is not only in Moscow that people are waiting but also in Kiev, Odessa, Leningrad . . ."

Kobalevsky looked at Bibnikov. The head of Special Investigations nodded. The Russian minister took Ambassador Farraday by the arm and led him a few steps away from the group.

"He is placing me in an intolerable position," Kobalevsky said. "You know I can't permit such a thing. We are in the middle of a political crisis here. What he says about Gorodin is true: There are many like him who will have to be dealt with. I need calm and order, both in Russia and in Eastern Europe."

"With all respect, Minister, I suggest it is a problem that is not of Innocent's making but your own." Farraday crossed his arms. "Nevertheless I understand how it would look to all of Moscow—really, to all the world—if the Soviet Union were to permit a token emigration of its Jewish citizens."

"You have until tomorrow morning," Innocent said calmly.

The Russians colored.

"If I might make a suggestion," Farraday interrupted.

Bibnikov and General Borgatov came over to Farraday and Kobalevsky.

"I submit, Minister," Farraday said, "if you agree to this gesture and allow these people to leave, it could surely be done. I'm sure we will work out satisfactory arrangements."

Kobalevsky considered this for a moment, then turned to Bibnikov.

"I have your assurance that we will lose nothing?"

"Nothing," Bibnikov said with finality.

"Is this acceptable to you?" Kobalevsky asked Farraday.

"To my government, yes. But I cannot speak for His Holiness."

Kobalevsky stepped over to Innocent and brought him into the group. He explained Borgatov's proposal, adding that the United States would guarantee the safety of the passengers. "The border will be open for twenty-two hours. That's all."

"Agreed," Innocent replied.

Even over the dull beating of the helicopter blades, the rumbling swell of cheering from the earth was clearly audible inside the cabin. Anna Letelier touched Turner on the shoulder, gesturing out the window.

"It is unbelievable!" he said. "A miracle!"

As far as the eye could reach Turner saw nothing but people. Although the helicopter was moving very quickly, its low altitude permitted Turner to glimpse whole families kneeling as the craft thundered overhead, young men and women standing on the roofs of cars, arms outstretched, children solemnly clutching tall poles with banners held aloft. It was an outpouring of faith the likes of which he had never witnessed, not even in St. Peter's Square.

The helicopter swept in low over the central platform, which stood thirty feet above the ground, surrounded by sawhorse barriers. The West Germans had urged that the podium be encircled by a cyclone fence as an added precaution against the more enthusiastic of the faithful, but Innocent would have none of it. The mammoth crowd would not harm him here, any more than they would in a cathedral. And there would be no more fences at the breach in the Wall.

The pilot set his machine down softly on the fenced-in pad behind the platform. Anna Letelier and Dr. Michael Turner disentangled themselves from their seats and stepped out, stooping beneath the blades, then straightening up, the wind catching and snapping at their clothes.

The wreckage was incredible: On either side of the railroad tracks that led through the Zone a strip of land fifty yards wide had been cleared of all mines. Barbed wire had been swept away. A great section of the Wall had been reduced to rubble.

"If someone had told me that I would live to see the day when the Wall had crumbled, I would not have believed them," Anna said.

As Innocent mounted the steps of the platform a mighty roar swelled across the earth. The Vicar of Christ raised his hands in a final blessing, and the response of the multitudes rolled back over him. The sun had risen to the point where he could scarcely see the faces of the people standing in front of him, and the wind was cold and brought tears to his eyes. Around him the smell of broken mortar mingled with that of incense. Behind him, the banners and flags of the Church flapped proudly in the breeze. He looked to one side and saw an altar boy staring up at him.

"Say it now," he murmured. "The moment is at hand!"

"Hallelujah!" the boy cried. "The Lord God has delivered them from bondage!"

Innocent turned toward the altar and crossed himself. Then he faced the multitude and stepped closer to the microphones.

"Brothers! Brothers and sisters!"

His voice rang out across the fields, carried by the wind. It felt strong to him, strong and sure.

"We are in a place of horror, and shame. Each of us, whether Christian or Jew, has to share this burden, for beneath our feet rest our people. We have prayed for them today, prayed that from our words they might derive some comfort, that they might see that they are not forsaken or forgotten.

"But to remember is not enough! Evil cares nothing for memory. It understands that the present is stronger than the past, and the future stronger still. What is with a man now, what he dreams of, aspires to, is more important to him than that which has gone by. Evil preys upon memory, at first distorting, then slowly eroding, until we ask ourselves: Did such a thing actually happen? *Could* it have happened? Or was it all a monstrous nightmare we should forget completely?

"For all of us the world moves too quickly. No tragedy escapes us, no horror, no matter where it might occur, fails to reach our eyes, ears, and eventually our hearts. Yet we grow weary of such news. We are numbed by its repetition, disillusioned because we think ourselves powerless before it. So it is easier to turn away, to pretend not to hear, to busy ourselves with our own affairs. Such is the triumph of evil and with it our shame—surrender.

"But we *know* the price of such abdication. We still bear the scars of such ignominy. And today we have come *here* to pledge to those who are beyond our help, our comfort, and our tears that we will not turn from evil. We will resist it, search it out wherever it might be."

A tremendous roar went up behind him from the thousands of people that flooded the streets surrounding the Wall in West Berlin.

They came out. Huddled together in groups, gazing fearfully about themselves, squinting at the harsh white lights from the floodlamps that covered the Zone, gazing upon the cordon of armed soldiers with incomprehension. Innocent went among them, moving from group to group, family to family, speaking soft reassurances in Russian, German, Polish . . . letting them touch him so that they might believe the moment real. Some broke down and cried, others kept following him, ignoring everything else. Still others fell to their knees, bowed their heads and murmured tearful prayers.

"You did it . . ." Anna Letelier whispered as Innocent embraced her. "You did it!"

"*We* accomplished this," Innocent said. "It is the beginning for us."

The Pontiff began to move among the people once again, urging them to get on the canvas-covered military trucks, telling them over and over again.

Finally Turner and Anna escorted Innocent to the embassy car. The Pope looked back at the blazing lights of the trucks rolling toward the streets lined with throngs of Berliners.

"Nothing will befall them," Turner said. "You have succeeded in what you set out to do."

"I wish I could say I thought that," Innocent said. "With all the might of the Church we have only managed to pry open this tiny crack for twenty-two hours. No, not everyone will manage to leave. And what of the millions who remain on the other side of this stubborn, ignorant barrier?"

The convoy rolled without pause. Ahead of it police and military units blocked off roads and avenues.

"The track has been cleared straight through to West Germany," Farraday said.

"Deliverance!" Innocent whispered. "The Lord has granted some deliverance."

"Yes," Anna said, looking at Michael Turner. "You have been delivered, Holiness, from your enemies."